C000145975

BATTY GREEN

Batty Green

Dennis Brickles

JANUS PUBLISHING COMPANY
London, England

First published in Great Britain 2009
by Janus Publishing Company Ltd,
105–107 Gloucester Place,
London W1U 6BY

www.januspublishing.co.uk

Copyright © Dennis Brickles 2009

British Library Cataloguing-in-Publication Data
A catalogue record for this book is available from the British Library

ISBN 978-1-85756-725-0

All rights reserved. No part of this publication may be reproduced,
stored in a retrieval system or transmitted in any form or by any means,
electric, mechanical, photocopying, recording or otherwise,without the
prior permission of the publisher.

The right of Dennis Brickles to be identified as the author of this work
has been asserted by him in accordance with the Copyright, Designs
and Patents Act 1988.

Cover Design: Warren Kujawski

Printed and bound in Great Britain

Contents

Dedication   vii

Acknowledgements   ix

The Prospect: Spring 1869   1

The Pioneers: Early 1869   7

To and From the Camp: Spring 1870   15

Strangers: Spring 1870   23

Tensions: Spring 1870   31

Men at Work: Spring 1870   43

Temptations: Late Summer 1870   53

Intruder: Autumn 1870   61

Another Family: Winter 1870   67

Suspicions: Spring 1871   77

Batty Green: April 1871   83

Bella and Bane: April 1871   91

Readings and Reactions: April 1871   97

Troubled Minds: April 1871   109

Soirée: April 1871   115

Escape: April 1871   127

George: April 1871   137

Planning and Improvising: April 1871   145

Profit and Loss: April 1871   157

Patience Unrewarded: May 1871   169

Plan and Counter Plan: May 1871   179

Intuition: May 1871   187

Traps: May 1871   191

Bernards: May 1871   199

Realignments: May 1871   209

The Winding Gear: May 1871   217

Bella's Story: Summer 1871   227

Joy and Anxiety: Late Summer 1871   239

Journeys: Late Summer 1871   247

Coming and Going: Autumn 1871   259

Dark Days: Autumn 1871   265

Light and Shade: Winter 1871   279

Gearstones: Winter 1871   287

Oatcakes: Early 1872   293

Water and Wakening: Early 1872   301

Labouring for Love: June 1872   307

George and Hetty: Summer 1872   319

Endings: May 1876   329

For Barbara
for everything

Acknowlegements

I would like to thank Peter Eastman who worked with me on a play that became known as 'The Iron way' and was performed at Settle High School in 1975. My interest in this period of history stems from that enterprise.

I would also like to thank Mary Askew, Chris and Peter Frost and my children, Paul and Anna, for their comments on the text of *Batty Green* and their generous encouragement and support.

The Prospect
Spring 1869

One of her earliest memories was a small fragment. It was grey and grainy, emotionally charged with childish temperament, set in a wintry landscape. She was very little and was at the bottom of their long, narrow garden at Selside. The bare vegetable patch came to an unruly end in dry, hard earth and a straggle of gaunt gooseberries, choked with the bare spikes of thorns and brambles. She could not recall how she had got there, or what had made her upset, but she was tiny, unsteady and alone. She could still feel the rhythmic stamping of her little wooden clogs, the tears running down her face, her pinafore snapping in a shrill wind. She was whimpering and then shouting at the plants, the earth, even the silver birch that splintered its spidery branches against the drystone wall beyond her. She was telling them that it was not fair. They just had to listen.

She would remember the scene throughout her life, hoarding it like a fragmented jewel, and she would refer to it, with a little embarrassment, as her first memory of "talking to the trees". At moments of childhood unhappiness or adolescent rage, her explosions were always outdoors. Stepping out of sight of others, she would slowly suck in air as if she were drowning and then erupt, giving way to her emotions with total indulgence. Time after time she berated fields, lanes and byways, talking out her grief or her doubts, addressing whatever plant looked sympathetic or ready to argue. But, inevitably, with the onset of greater self-consciousness, this all stopped and was put behind her as a thing of the past.

Then, early in 1869, when she was twenty-four and had been a married woman for six years, it began again, albeit in a modified form.

Now though, it was mostly a silent tirade, a monologue of temper or of febrile excitement, projected outwards when she was sure she was quite alone. She would fix on an object, a tree, a stone or an unsuspecting cow and screech at it or sing out her feelings, silently and often with passionate intensity. She recognised this reversion as a disturbing barometer of need and dislocation. What is more, she knew very precisely the turning point within her marriage that brought about the change: it was the coming of the railway to the bleak uplands beyond their farm. It was when the Midland Railway finally brought steam engines and an army of navvies to remote Ribblehead and to a muddy, inauspicious basin, which became known as Batty Green. The turmoil that followed disturbed so much more than the resident grouse and sheep.

Emily Robinson, born and bred in Ribblesdale, had been married at eighteen and had moved a mere 4 miles, at least as the crow flies, from Selside to Elterbeck. She had also moved from poverty and obscurity to security and comfort. She became a farmer's wife and was expected to become a young mother: some jealous tongues whispered that it was the prospect of pregnancy that had hurried the nervous George Wright into a proposal. The gossips were silenced, however, as the years passed and the Wrights settled to quiet, childless, self-supporting domesticity.

Emily Wright seemed well suited to her new role and began to win the respect of the flinty dales' sceptics. Her horizons remained limited and she remained comfortable within them. She sometimes reflected that even if she included her occasional walk over to Kingsdale and her weekly visit to Ingleton, then her known world was probably no more than 40 miles square and she loved every inch of it.

Until the coming of the railway, she had never wanted more. Her quiet community, whilst not large, was supportive, familiar and constant. She and her husband were respected as both farmers and as regular worshippers at the little church in Chapel le Dale. They were viewed as a sensible, serious couple, who could be relied upon to keep their word, help their neighbours and cherish their 100 acres and their growing stock. The only cause for concern amongst the small handful of family and friends that knew them well was that five years of marriage had brought no child to George and Emily Wright. It was common knowledge that they hoped for children.

After all, George was thirty-five when he married Emily Robinson, almost twice her age. He was inclined to be reclusive: a thinker, a solitary, a bit of a puzzle. He was tall, slim and shy, with pale blue eyes. His fair hair was already thinning, his face coarsened by sun and wind and he was showing small, abraded blood vessels and tiny, fan-shaped eruptions at cheek and temple; it was as if he had been roughened by sandpaper or left too near the fire. The red in him showed in his close body hair: "my Red Indian", she called him teasingly at times.

'Nay,' he would reply, 'A'm the Norseman; tha'rt the Celt. Tha'rt dark an' dangerous an' tha needs to be subdued.'

'Come on then,' she would taunt him in the first months of their marriage. 'Thy hot red fire should light up ma dark ways. But tha'll have to catch me first.' And she would slip away from him at the parlour door and scurry off, waiting to be caught.

No one who saw them relaxed together at home could doubt their love. But dressed in their best at church or at a social gathering, you might wonder at the stiff, rather ungainly man, with his air of intensity and earnestness and, at times, a hint of temper. You might speculate that the younger wife, dark and glossy, with a solid compactness about her that was in contrast to his slender height and ranginess, was the earthy, practical one. She bubbled with energy and would focus on a person or a problem as if there was nothing else in the world that mattered and she would stay fixated until she was satisfied. She seemed to quickly adapt to any situation. She had a sweet, easy smile, full dark lips to match her very dark brown eyes and a mass of black hair that was always threatening to escape her control. She was solid and stocky, without being in any way fat.

'If tha wor a horse, tha'd be a Welsh cob,' George once told her.

'An' tha would be a roan stallion, with a quarter Arab,' she had retorted.

He had an air of the strange and unpredictable about him. Yet, he was also resourceful, shrewd in his dealings and careful with his stock.

He conserved much and ventured little. It was the wife who wanted to try things. He listened and indulged her; she encouraged him and made things work, especially with people. 'They will get on, those two,' the locals said.

Yet, as with many couples, their lives could as easily drift apart as closer together. She had the purpose and the drive, but had no clear end in view, other than increase: more security, more land, more stock and a family of her own to drive it all forwards. She was all energy and needed direction. He wanted to please her and to hold fast to her, but also to secure what he had inherited and to feel sheltered in his control of it. He wanted to be able to hold up his head in the company of other farmers and landowners. He did not want to follow in his father's footsteps and he often wanted to rein her in.

His mother had been tall and blonde, from the poorer streets of Kirkby Lonsdale. She had married Harold Wright: a dour, obdurate man, who was older than her and no match for her in spirit or energy, but did happen to be comfortably settled in Elterbeck Farm. It was a marriage that was soon fraught with conflict and he had not the stamina for it. She proved her excess of spirit over him by running away with his life savings, his best mare and an army sergeant when George was six and she had never returned or been heard of since. George's father had struggled on, apparently with stoical acceptance, but had died of pneumonia when George was just thirty, after five difficult years, with increasingly long periods of morose introspection, prolonged by regular drinking at the Hill Inn. This had depressed George as a young man, forcing him to act as nurse and counsellor to his own father while watching the slow, insidious decline. He knew the grim, childhood impotence of being unable to stop an adult who was set on a downwards course. He spent his time reading or at the church: what little respite he had from running the farm.

Then, a year after his father's death, on his way back towards Ribblehead after selling cattle at Hawes, he called at the Gearstones Inn. He was not normally one to frequent inns, but this was a fine autumnal evening, he had got a good price for the cattle and he felt that he wanted to celebrate the moment with someone. Emily served his meal, brought him drink and cleared his plate. They only exchanged a few words, but he left with images of her form, her voice and her hair, which would not leave him. Troubled, he soon returned to the inn, but she was not there. He found out that she lived with her mother in a small cottage at Selside and that she only worked at the Gearstones occasionally. On a blind impulse, he rode down to Selside, found the place and stood, irresolute, in the lane, not at all sure what he was going to do or say, if anything at all.

Luckily, she saw him. She came out, took one look at him and said, 'Did tha enjoy thy supper so much then?' And when he failed to answer, she continued, 'Shall we walk back up the lane awhile an' you can tell me all about it?'

He had never met anyone with such natural charm and he was hopelessly captivated and soon entangled. She told him later how she would spy on him as he drew near the cottage door, approaching it as if the very act of knocking was the hardest thing that a man could accomplish. She observed his uneasy, stooping pose on the doorstep and his hesitant greeting of mother and daughter. No sooner had he greeted Mrs Robinson, with a bow and all the dignity that his nervous frame could muster, than Emily would grab a shawl, take him by the hand and call out laughingly as she went, 'I'll take George a walk along the beck, Mother. We shall be back later for a pot of tea.'

He had allowed himself to be tugged, badgered and teased, until he hardly knew how to behave. She loved his stubborn strength, his stability and the fact that he owned his own farm. She respected his integrity, his knowledge and his position. She knew, almost at once, that she wanted to be his partner and the mother to his children and she knew that he could be won.

He proposed within three months of their first meeting and they were married three months later. It was all neatly arranged by Emily. He bought a small cottage for Mrs Robinson in Ingleton, but she had died quite suddenly in her first winter there. Emily was shocked, but settled with even greater resolve to building a new life. With cheerful determination, she rearranged the farmhouse and worked assiduously to perfect herself in her new role as farmer's wife. She felt that she had arrived where she had always wanted to be, without ever knowing that it had been her dream all along, and so she was more than content with her first five years as Mrs Wright. Only two things threatened her peace and equilibrium. The first was that she had no child or even any hint of the pregnancy that she impatiently craved. The second was that the Midland Railway had been forced to go ahead with the building of a great railway line between Settle and Carlisle. It would cut through their valley and although she did not know it yet, it would shape the rest of their lives.

The Pioneers
Early 1869

In June 1860, when she was fifteen, Emily had travelled in the back of a cart with her mother and father to witness the celebrations in Ingleton that marked the opening of a branch line linking Skipton to the main line to the North and hence to Scotland. It was almost the last time that they had done anything together as a family, as her father had left a few weeks later. On this bright Saturday there had been brass bands, jugglers and sideshows and for once there was family harmony as they had walked nervously across the new viaduct that curved elegantly across the gorge of the Greta, hardly recognisable 80 feet below. She had then become embarrassed when her father had got into an argument with a railway official the other side. Her mother, a portly lady, had needed to sit down, but all the seats were reserved for dignitaries and representatives of the London and North Western Railway. When a seat was refused, he jeered at some of them.

'Is this how you'll treat your passengers then, when they stagger over viaduct carryin' cases an' trunks? What you tryin' to do wi' your two stations in a little two-horse place like Ingleton? Think you're in bloody London, do you?'

She and her mother had tried to pull him away, but he had the attention of a small crowd and there were murmurs of support for some of what he had said. Ingleton, for all of its thirty buildings, now had two stations, built by rival companies, at either end of a sixteen-arch viaduct, and some passengers had to walk across to make connections. The absurdity, and the inconvenience, was not lost on those living in rural Yorkshire.

'Couldn't Lord Muck on yon side get it sorted with Lord Arrogance on this? Is that the sum on it?' he went on.

A policeman began to move towards them down the platform and he allowed himself to be pulled away, back across the river. The father that she never thought of now: the father that was spineless and lazy, but an avid reader and always roused by ideas. The father that always challenged her to look about her and "mek something of thi sen". The father that had plied her with books, as well as guilt.

It had been railway talk that had often stirred her, and had also made her uneasy, in the years that followed. There were always rumours. No market day could pass without some talk of plans, routes and deals.

After her marriage, she found that one of the great pleasures in George's life was to sit, when the work was done and their meal was finished, and read a newspaper and this included reading things out to her, when she was too tired sometimes to do anything other than sit by the stove. He always followed the railway stories, wherever they were, and with enthusiasm. It was almost like a crusade for him. He believed in the railway age.

'The railways,' he said to her, 'they're shaping country now. It's all like a new map with veins an' arteries reachin' out an' penetratin' parts as was like to 'ave bin left behind. In the past, how many folk would have come to Ingleton or Carnforth, eh? Not likely. An' now they pass through, an' some stop, an' goods come an' go. It's never going to go back to like the dark, quiet times as was before. The pity is that it's a bit far from us.'

And then, just three years into their marriage, the news came that brought the bells ringing and the locals arguing. A bill had been passed to allow the powerful Midland Railway Company to build a fast main line right up the Ribble Valley from Settle, then through Ribblehead into Dentdale and on again into the Eden Valley and Carlisle, and thus to Scotland. It was controversial and it was challenging. There were many who said it could not be done and there were many, including powerful landowners, who said it should not be done. George went to meetings, where he declined to sign petitions against the railway, despite pressure from Mr Farrer who owned much of the land in the area. He continued to argue for the railway, even though he did not stand to gain the large sums of compensation that some farmers were likely to receive.

'But it'll be the making of us, ma lass,' he said to her after one meeting. 'They say there will be thousands of men coming reet up 'ere to work an' great machines an' a whole town that will be built for 'em.

An' they'll all need bread an' meat an' eggs an' milk an' cheese. An' we can supply 'em.'

'They can't build a town here, tha daft numbskull. Whir will it be, eh? There's ne'er a bit o' decent flat land an' the road's all broken. An' the trains can't go over Batty Moss or round Blea Moor, even if they get to Ribblehead. An' winter weather will freeze 'em to statues afore they start. You're as bad a dreamer as any on them,' she teased, trying to break down his serious, crusading zeal, which both alarmed and amused her. She liked her life as it was. Yet, there was a part of her that was also excited. It seemed that fate might be about to deliver a bizarre opportunity into her lap and she was ready for it.

But the speculation changed again and all the talk was of delay, argument and frustration. Farmers had better things to do. In the dales of the Ribble, the Swale and the Dent, there was a present reality that had always to be grappled with: developing your stock, gathering hay, salving sheep, draining and ditching, building walls, raising children as best you could and acting always as your fathers had done, securing your future beneath the long shadow of the past. And so it dragged on for a further three years, until the late summer of 1868, when the Midland Company moved to abandon the line, but the bill was defeated and the Midland were suddenly forced to go ahead. There was a sense of shock in the community. It had always seemed so distant, but now the slow shuffle of change was just around the bend and the first tremors could be felt.

Their very first railway visitor came in late January of 1869, just as the sun was setting over the hard crust of their frozen fields. He was a tall and heavily built young man and he knocked on the door at Elterbeck Farm and asked if he could talk to them. He was a Tasmanian surveyor, wind-burnt and energetic. He wanted permission to walk the hillside behind Elterbeck the next day and to take some levellings. What is more, he wanted George's views on the rock strata and watercourses on the near slopes of Whernside and up towards Blea Moor. They knew who he was almost before he announced himself. The stories had been circulating for weeks of the young surveyor from "down under": Mr Sharland, who had been trapped at the Gearstones Inn for six days by heavy snow and had been forced to dig his way out just to get across the yard to the netty. They asked him in and gave him ale, cheese and cold pie. To Emily, he was like a creature from a different race and time. His bustle, his accent, his easy familiarity and the talk of change, of plans and of distances that he brought to their familiar kitchen table: it was as if a small window had opened and a hand had reached through and reshaped the landscape of her thoughts, bringing the premonition of a new shape to her life in quite a personal way. She felt it move through her like a ripple though water.

'Hospitality is wonderful round here,' he was saying. 'It's a fine sight better than down in some other parts where I've worked ... Do you know,' he went on between mouthfuls of pie and not waiting for comment, 'when I was stuck at the Gearstones in that blizzard, me and three lads, we had to melt the snow to make a brew of tea; after all, you can't drink beer all the time, can you! And then Mrs Thomas heard about us, she lives about 2 miles away, and she made a huge suet pudding and she made her old man bring it over. He fell into a 6 foot snowdrift, but held the pudding over his head, so that it didn't get ruined or wet. We couldn't believe it. Hell of a good pudding, too.' He laughed so loudly that Emily jumped.

Later, she sent the two men outside to smoke, while she cleared their plates and tried to calm herself. Her heart was racing and her pulse seemed excitable. It was as if the air was charged with new particles. She washed her hands and face, gulping in cold air and water. Then she pulled the settle and a couple of old armchairs round the range and called them back in.

'Will you take a glass of whisky, Mr Sharland?' she asked as they struggled out of their heavy coats in the porch.

'I've never been known to refuse the local hospitality, mam,' he replied with a wide smile as he settled himself close to the fire without further ado.

'Do you know, lass, Mr Sharland says as we should prepare ourselves for some changes fairly soon,' said George, slightly slurred in his speech and oddly expansive in his gestures. He showed no sign of resenting the easy way that their visitor had taken the best chair; indeed, he seemed eager to defer to him, pleased to be a part of the railway mania. 'I'm right glad that we 'ave made your acquaintance, sir, an' I would be glad to help thee tomorrow, up on t'hill there. Not many know their way around these fells as well as a do an' I could show thee a thing or two, perhaps.'

'Be glad to have you with me,' said Sharland, taking the large glass of whisky that Emily brought him and looking around with an amused glance as if this were the best of times. 'You'll perhaps be taking in a lodger or two when the men start arriving, will you, Mrs Wright? They get good wages these lads and are always on the lookout for somewhere homely to lay their heads and have themselves some good tucker. Mind you, not that all of them are quite used to sleeping in a regular bed in a regular kind of home like this.' He laughed loudly. 'Some of them are half wild, I can tell you. You'll have to lock up your chickens and watch that they don't milk your cow for you when your back is turned.' He laughed again at their bemused expressions. They just did not know what to believe. 'What is more, Mr Wright, if they find that Mrs Wright is the prettiest woman for 10 miles, and I have a feeling that she may be just that, then you will have to stand guard round here day and night. 'You will have a couple of thousand hungry navvies and all the hangers-on that come with them, just camping out on your doorstep, like an army of hairy Israelites looking for a way home.' He swallowed with a gulp and raised his glass to them. 'Here's to health and prosperity and the days of the railways.'

'I'll drink to that,' said George, raising his glass. 'But surely you exaggerate the … behaviour and the numbers an' that?' He stumbled to a halt as if uncertain whether or not the visitor was just making fun. He was shaken by his easy reference to Emily and the fact that other men might look at her in that way.

'No. Not much doubt in my mind, Mr Wright. I've been working up some rough ideas for a great viaduct at Batty Moss and a tunnel right through Blea Moor. There's a meeting coming up with Mr Crossley himself, he's the Chief Engineer, and we hope to confirm the plans. I've walked the whole route, ten days it took me, and soon he sets out to do the same. I'll bet he takes a fair bit longer than I did, you know. We are to meet next week at the Gearstones Inn. Soon as that's done, then hey, look out, all hell comes to the Ribble Valley and the invasion begins. Come the spring, you'll have more visitors than daffodils.'

The men settled to discussion of a map that Sharland had produced and for a while it became a blur to Emily. She smiled whenever Sharland roared with laughter, she refilled their glasses with whisky and she took a small glass herself, but she made no attempt to fasten her attention on the detail of the talk with George and the arrangements that were being made. She stepped outside and watched the dark mass of Ingleborough as moonlight illuminated the cloud base. She felt that they were talking about objects, while to her the landscape was more than an engineer's plan or a surveyor's map and what is more, her own body and spirit were being challenged and changed with this sudden shift of energy into her own backyard. She had a strange vision of a haphazard jumble of animals, men and machines – arms, thighs, eyes, hands, shovels, steam engines, hooves and sinews – all driving into, all straining to change and adapt her earth. On the fringes would be the women and the children. He was right. It was like an invasion. She brooded on it.

'What will the people be like?' she asked later, taking the men by surprise.

'Hell, mam,' said Sharland, 'there's good and bad in every crowd, I'm sure, but mostly they are hard in their work and in their play. I've seen great courage in some of the men and in some of their women, too, but there are some as I wouldn't want you to meet too often. And when they are in their drink, I'll tell you, there are some that none of us wants to meet. They scarcely get along together, either. There's a fair amount of fighting and falling out all the time. What the Midland is reckoning is that now that the Liverpool Docks are finished, a lot of the men, perhaps 1,000, will move from there straight on up here to work on this line. They're the Liverpool Irish most of 'em and they seem to fight with everyone, but are especially aggressive with all the Scots, the English, the Welsh and any foreigners. In fact, they fight with everyone except their own kind and if there's no one left, I hear they are not averse to a backhander to their own family.' He roared at the memories. Emily was even more confused.

Sharland returned to his map and his talk with George and soon he left. George came to bed smelling of whisky and entered her quickly and passionately. She clung to him and was soothed for a while.

The next week there was more talk. Apparently, a strange hut, set off the ground on four iron wheels, had been brought from London on a train. It had been unloaded at Ingleton and it had taken six horses to pull it up the hill to Storrs Common and along to Batty Moss. Her neighbour was eager to bring the news to Emily, who had been on a visit to a friend in Kingsdale when it had all happened.

'They say as it's whir t'engineers an' surveyors are to live, like, until they get properly set up. An' there's tents, too, for some o' them navvies, but they'll die o' the wet before the cold kills 'em, I reckon, don't you? Cos you know yourself what it's like up thir. You'll sink past yer knees an' no bother; one or two 'as bin lost in them parts.'

She and George went to look after church on the next Sunday. It was a fine but cold February day, with a keen, light wind. They walked directly up from Chapel le Dale Church and found a small group of neighbours similarly curious, but not standing for long to look, either on account of the cold or not wanting to be seen to be nosy: it was not usually a place to invite the casual observer.

Batty Moss was a large, flat saucer of bog and mire, covered by patches of peat and heather, backed by the solid wall of Whernside and the bleak mass of Blea Moor. There was scarcely a barren swelling upland in the North of England that lived up to its name as well as Blea Moor. It frowned over the head of the valley. It was squat rather than imposing, heavy with massive bulk, like the side of an old sow. Its solid mass stood between Ribblehead and Dentdale. Whernside, Batty Moss and Blea Moor together proved a massive obstacle to the planned railway as it swept upwards, following the Ribble, to suddenly be faced with a wall of rock, a dreary headwater and a blunt mass of hills.

The low, treeless basin of Batty Moss displayed rough, tussocky grass, patches of heather and peaty ridges. These were interspersed with gashes of dark, boggy subsidence, draining into the cave locally known as Batty Wife Hole. Some of the local men, in their private, smutty moments, compared the cave entrance, as it sank darkly away in fronds of moss and bracken, to the ways that they had known into various local women and they said that the cave 'wor reet well named'. Certainly, the land had its secret dark entrances and exits. Local folklore told of murder hereabouts and of bodies dropped into fissures, linked with tales of marital conflict and unrelenting strife. There was little to brighten the scene and the constant background was the wind whipping through the gap, the croaking of grouse and the cry of curlew. The few bright outcrops of limestone round the edges of this rough bowl seemed only to make the centre the more forlorn.

Yet, now there was new interest. Just off the road, on a patch of land, scarred and disordered by boots, wagons and animals, stood the odd hut with its four large iron wheels keeping it some feet off the ground. Around it were heaps of stone, sacks, rubbish, stacks of timber and a rough shelter for a few bedraggled horses. There was a ramp up to the door of the hut and a sign, crudely lettered, said "Contractors' Hotel" on the side. Smoke came from a chimney, angling through the wooden roof.

'They'll need a good fire,' said one local farmer, nodding to the Wrights in greeting. 'I wouldna' leave ma beasts to live out 'ere in such a spot. Today's a fair mild one, but still fair nithering. They won't know what's hit 'em when storms, hailstones and sleet are whipping through 'ere. There's not a tree can survive it. The sheep have snow on their backs for months and yet they reckon as hundreds of men, women and bairns'll come 'ere and live. I can't see it meself.'

George replied with some fervour, 'I wor talkin' to one o' the engineers an' he says that they've started test borings out at t'other side.' He raised himself up and pointed north-west towards the moor where, indeed, they could make out a series of muddy craters and debris. George was cheered by it all. He always had to be on the side of the railwaymen. 'They had to go down 25 foot to find solid rock. They was on the point o' giving it up in some parts, where they couldn't reach rock bottom at all. But now they've hit rock for twenty great pillars to hold up a viaduct from one side to t'other.' The other farmers nodded in sceptical and dour amazement.

As they walked home, braced against the chill of the wind, Emily came to a decision that had been coming clearer to her over the last few weeks.

'They must eat,' she suddenly said. George smiled at her statement of the obvious, but seemed lost in his own deliberations. 'George,' she stopped him and turned towards him. 'We must tek on an extra farmhand, no … two, an' a proper maid. We must build alongside the house an' take lodgers. We must have more hens, another dozen milking cows, a proper dairy an' some more pigs an' geese. We should buy in some more horses. We'll tek supplies each day an' a must have at very least a new horse an' wagon to tek t'Batty Moss. Tha'll have to go down to Settle an' speak t'bank. We have to take advantage of this, cos a don't agree with them pessimists an' moaners an' them as wouldn't shift off their arses if Christ himself was coming up on a wagon from Helwith Bridge. I think this is going to 'appen an' we must be ready.'

So they talked and planned with eagerness and around them change worked its slow fingers through their dreams and their landscape. No one knew where, when or why, but somewhere in this process the low, focal point of Batty Moss began to be known as Batty Green. Emily turned her thoughts that way more and more and with restless impatience. But what she waited for, she could not tell.

To and From the Camp
Spring 1870

With the slow warming of a late spring, the movement of men, animals and machines suddenly and noticeably accelerated. Large wooden huts were quickly constructed on Batty Green and on the slopes around.

From the distance, they looked like discarded boxes, left in chance patterns, white against the dark earth, or like tokens in some strange board game, waiting for a giant hand to move them. By steady stages, a community evolved; it was spreading and changing in shape and emphasis every week, so that there were always new elements and surprises. Emily and George were busy expanding their farm business and had little time for reflection. Yet, at any time, to raise your head at Elterbeck was to hear distant cries of men, the dull thud of an explosion, the sharp blast and rattle of a steam engine or the clatter of iron on stone. Change was volubly beating ever closer to their doors. The cry of a curlew or the shrill whine of the wind was often and surprisingly obliterated. They were not used to it.

Navvies would pass wearing moleskin breeks, canvas shirts and long velveteen coats, with incongruous hobnailed boots beneath. Often, there was a hint of the extravagant and eccentric in them that went even beyond this motley. Some wore battered top hats, silk scarves or bright kerchiefs tied round the neck or round their brows. They were the working elite, the city slickers, earning more than any other workingmen in the British Empire and then spending most of it in extravagant and wild indulgence. They were wealthy for a while, but mostly took no heed for the future and what they earned they spent.

Moving into Ribblehead, they carried their few belongings wrapped in a sheet and hanging down their backs or bundled at the end of a stave that they balanced on their shoulders. They came singly, in groups and sometimes by the dozen, with a couple of donkeys and other animals between them, and they would sing and bicker and pass round flagons of beer. Seeing Emily at work round the farm or standing at her farmhouse door, they would shout or whistle a greeting, but never with any disrespect. Sometimes, one or more would call at the farm asking for water or milk or to buy eggs, but Emily sensed with some, as they stood close to the house and breathed deeply, that it was also for the comfort of knowing that there were real homes still, even if they could not enter. Like all other local farmers, George and Emily had so many requests for lodging that they were compelled to put up a sign saying that they had no more vacancies. The truth was that the Midland Company had booked two lodgings with them and with a new maid to find room for and various farm workers coming and going, they were full. They also had less time for each other.

Then, one morning in March, Emily walked with her new maid Hetty towards Ingleton on the toll road. Hetty was from Cold Cotes on the other flank of Ingleborough. She had been one of a farming family of ten, barely making enough of a living to adequately feed and clothe half that number; two children had already died at an early age. For a year, Hetty had been maid to an old couple in Clapham, until the old lady had died and she had had to leave when the house was sold. She was dutiful and grateful for the chance that had suddenly presented itself when she had heard that Elterbeck wanted a maid.

It was market day and Emily had promised Hetty a new dress, if one could be found at the right price. The girl was fourteen and she was already a few inches taller than Emily, sparse and gangling, brown hair tied back sharply, giving her a pinched look, but one that evaporated quickly when she smiled. It was a smile that changed and lifted her face, bringing her brown eyes into dramatic focus. Emily guessed that as she filled out and became more confident she would be quite a stunner. For now, she was quiet and rather shy still, but they passed a few comments to each other as they met strangers on the way, nodding a greeting to most of them, but taking care to keep their distance.

Hetty then ran rather skittishly ahead when they came to a quiet stretch, glad of the brief respite that the morning promised. Emily smiled to see her playing a kind of hopscotch in the road, jumping from foot to foot in her wooden clogs and then scampering clumsily ahead in her gawky way. But then she reached a field gateway and abruptly clattered to a halt. She was some way ahead, but Emily could make out voices, questions and appeals, but no details. She saw Hetty pause, standing hesitantly, and then turn back with an anxious look. Emily quickened her pace. She caught up with her maid where the drystone wall gave way to a poor wooden gate. Sitting on the ground against the gatepost was a woman, with a child in her arms and two toddlers sitting beside her, clinging to her skirts in confusion. The woman said nothing, but tears ran down her cheeks and she sobbed almost in silence; a dry, rasping catch in the throat was all they caught. She was crying to herself. She was waxen, drawn and lined, her clothes threadbare and dirty.

Emily bent to comfort her. 'Now then, what ails thee, Mother? Can tha tell me?' The children recoiled and the little girl began to cry, whilst the other, a sturdy little boy of about three, pulled himself to his feet and scowled fiercely. The mother stared blankly upwards at her for a few seconds as if she could not focus, but continued to cry and said nothing. 'Come, let us help you,' said Emily softly, trying to make some contact. There was still no response. She turned to Hetty. 'What did she say?'

'She just said something like "what will a do?"' whimpered the tender-hearted Hetty, beginning to cry herself. 'An' when a said, "what do you mean, missis?", she just burst out crying and grabbed the children to her.' She flinched as the woman suddenly waved her free arm as if to drive away Emily and Hetty.

'You're not to come near,' she hissed, snuffling through her tears as she pulled the baby tight to her chest and tried to hold onto the toddlers at the same time.

'A don't want to tek the bairns,' said Emily as calmly as she could. 'A just want to help thee along the road to some shelter for thi' sen an' little ones. Where art thou headed?'

'To t'camp, I reckon.' The woman suddenly seemed to become calmer, as if she remembered where she was. 'My man, he goes by t'name of Black Jack an' he sent me money for the train an' that. He said to bring the littl'uns an' he would meet me today an' how all was ready for us. An' a haven't seen him since last summer an' he doesn't know as how I have had another, like. But he wasn't there at t'station an' so we walked. An' ...' She stuttered to a halt and the tears and sobs came again.

17

Emily crouched beside her and took her free hand. For a moment, there was nothing but the fading sobs, the sounds of a skylark and a whistle of light wind through the bars of the gate.

'Come,' said Emily, 'let us get tha up on t'feet now an' we'll help thee on t'camp to find your Black Jack. It's not so far, tha knows. Tha can't sit out here. The bairns must be taken somewhere.' She tried to ease the woman to her feet, but the resistance was sullen and then she suddenly turned spiteful as Emily applied pressure.

'Get your bloody hands off me,' shouted the woman. 'I don't need your help.' She made to swing at Emily, who pulled back, and the little boy suddenly launched himself at Emily and Hetty, spitting and trying to kick them, but without saying a word, just snarling like a little terrier.

They backed off and tried to fend him away. The mother yelled at him to stop and began to struggle to her feet. But in making a lurching upward movement, the baby somehow slipped from under her arm and seemed to twist and dive towards the floor, the grey linen bands unrolling rapidly, until the tiny form lay almost naked on the ground; stiff, blue-grey and obviously lifeless. There was silence, save for the wind and the birds. They held their breath. Emily recoiled and clutched her hand to her mouth. Hetty gave half a scream and turned her head away and the two children began to cry. There was a long moment's inertia as they all felt the horror of the instant and then the woman quickly scooped up the little one and wrapped it hurriedly into a bundle. She struggled to her full height and stared straight at Emily, who was lost in a fog of thoughts, fears and hesitation.

'She just died on the train, I think. She always was a sickly little bairn an' had yella fever an' all. It was very peaceful, her end, like. I tried to waken her for a feed an' found that she'd gone. I didn't know what to do,' the woman almost pleaded with Emily. 'I'm not a bad woman, but I didn't want to frighten the children or the people on the train. I thought they might make me get off or call a constable or something an' I had no money for another ticket. I've to get to the camp,' she said, straightening herself with more determination. Rousing herself, she turned to hush her children and to pick up her bundles, but she swayed and looked unsteady. Emily resolved to act, too; to be firm but friendly.

'Come with me,' she said. 'Ma farm is just a little ways up yonder. Come, Hetty,' she called the girl over. 'Tek the children an' some of the bundles. We'll help them up to Elterbeck an' then send a messenger to t'camp. It's the least we can do. Or we can get the horse a'd cart an' tek them there from the farm. Come on, Hetty; look lively, lass. Happen tha'll still have time to get to Ingleton before the market closes.' But Hetty, half in sulks and half in fear, was reluctant to get too close, until the little boy settled it by setting off himself, taking his little sister by the hand, leaving the adults with no choice but to trail after, following their little leader and the patterns of their own thoughts.

Emily hastened the mother as best she could and turned the little party in at Chapel le Dale. As they passed the church, she drew the mother into the lychgate, where there was a seat, and told her to rest for a moment while she fetched more help. Emily was relieved to find that all the fight seemed to have gone out of the woman and she meekly complied with the request, but kept tight hold of the dead child all the while and watched her two little ones with sharp eyes. "Thus close and no closer" seemed to be her message. Hetty felt it and stood some way off, looking unhappy and confused.

Emily returned with the vicar and his wife and after some cajoling, they persuaded the woman and her children to come over to the rectory, where they were given tea and bread. The vicar left the children playing quietly on the kitchen rug while the woman dozed. Nothing had been said directly to her, but it was as if she had begun to accept that once there was official knowledge of the dead infant, then others would take over. She waited and rested, knowing that there were other trials ahead.

After about an hour, the vicar returned with the constable from Ingleton and they woke the woman and spoke to her. She gave her name as Ethel Newman, of no fixed address. She was asked for the name of the dead child and for the first time, a look of real fear and dread seemed to pass over her face, leaving her skin grey, and her eyes shrunk to dark points of light.

'Black Jack always named the children,' she said as if some deep dread had swelled up in her. 'He'll tek it sore amiss if I do it. An' he's a man that has to have his way on some things, as I can tell you, an' he'll be worrying about us not arriving as I promised. He don't like to be kept waiting or out of it. He'll be workin' up to some steam an' nonsense, I'll be bound. But he'll be pleased to see the other babes, as he's terrible fond o' them an' 'e wrote to say as he was missin' us all, not that he writes much, but I think I know that much of him by now. Course, he won't miss what he's not seen, like, will he? Unless ... you're not to tell him, are you?' she asked them as if a new possibility occurred to her. 'Nay, an' happen he'll understand,' she said more cheerfully, 'under the circumstances an' him not being by or havin' seen the bairn ...' She stumbled to a halt and smiled at them as if a solution had been agreed.

'A name?' asked the constable after a pause. He was a blunt man, with limited sympathy for the navvies and their ways.

Ethel gazed around and looked at them each in turn. Then a nervous smile seemed to illuminate her face.

'Hetty,' she said. All the adults drew back fractionally and hesitation stole over them. There was a low wail as if from a cat trapped in a door and it came from the girl herself. Ethel drew herself up and offered the bundle to the girl. 'Hetty she shall be and Hetty shall take her for me.'

The vicar and his wife both began to speak. There was the beginning of a protest from Emily, who knew how her maid had suffered much after the death of an infant sister just a year ago; she spoke shyly of her now and then, of how she missed her. 'This is not fair on Hetty,' she began to say, not sure how to save the girl from this distress.

But Hetty herself stepped forwards and held out her hands, with a dignity that belied her age and maturity. 'Give her to me,' she said. 'I will see to it that things are done right.'

A tear rolled down Emily's face as she saw the courage and the trembling in her little maid. Within minutes, they seemed to have concluded the business and the vicar had sent for his pony and trap.

Hetty sat quietly with the dead child cradled loosely in her arms, deliberately not looking down, struggling to stay calm. The constable had made his way out, saying that the magistrate would have to be informed and that he would be back to speak to Ethel at the camp. Without further ado and acknowledging that the family must be moved on to be housed and cared for, the practical realities exerted their grip.

They were about to move out of the kitchen and had got Ethel and her children to their feet, when amidst the scurry of straightening of clothes and of persuading the children away from the warm rug, they heard boots clattering in the courtyard and the heavy breathing of one or more men who had been running. This disturbance was quickly followed by a knocking at the door. The mother seemed to sense that it was on her account and she raised herself up and swept a hand over her face and hair. She had more colour now and drawing herself together with dignity, she faced the door. Emily admired her, wonderingly. The children sensed the moment also and quickened themselves to her side, almost magnetically. Their eyes grew wider and they listened cautiously.

It was a man's voice that they all heard in the almost silent room as a maid answered the door.

''Scuse me, missis. Ma name's Black Jack, or at least that's what I pass for in these parts. I believe you have Ethel with you and ma bairns. She was seen along the road aways an' a'm told she's here. I'd like to see her, if you please, mam.'

'Is this what you want?' the vicar asked kindly. Ethel nodded.

The vicar went out into the hall and they could hear quiet words spoken; the soft, southern timbre of the vicar's voice, restrained and murmuring, contrasting with the sharper Scottish burr, deeper, too, and more staccato. They soon returned, the vicar leading the way, followed by a squat, angular and powerful man with a ruddy complexion, a black beard and a shock of black hair escaping from a felt hat. He wore moleskin breeches above thick brown leggings smeared with mud and boots that were scuffed and dirty, showing glints of metal cladding through the grime. He had on a thick grey shirt that looked greasy and a waistcoat that was quilted and showed some padding where it had been ripped. He was breathing heavily and he looked around with energy, as if expecting an ambush or a threat. But for all his rather alarming exterior and the instinctive momentary recoil that they had all experienced, as he took in the scene before him he changed and there was no doubting his joy to see Ethel and the children again.

'Why, Ethel, ma lass. It was next Thursday as a was expectin' ye, not today. But you're welcome now for sure.' And with almost a demure modesty he stepped over and kissed her cheek. 'An' where's ma wee laddie then, eh, where's Georgie?' He teasingly pretended not to recognise his son, who beamed and wriggled on the spot. 'Cos this bairn here can't be him, cos he's too grown up an' tall an' ...'

But he could get no further, as Georgie threw himself at his father's waist and swung there crying out, 'It's me, Pa, it's me, Papa.'

The little girl, silent all the while, stared at her father, who suddenly swooped to pick her up and nestle her against his chest. 'An' we mustn't forget the little Laura lass, must we.'

She spoke at last, with a lisp, 'Daddy, carry Lawa,' as she entwined her fingers in his long black hair.

The vicar stepped forwards, smiling but cautious about the next move, yet knowing it fell to him to speak. 'Mr Jack,' he almost simpered, 'I need to have a word with you about something, if you wouldn't mind just stepping into the parlour. Could you?'

He indicated the door through to the hall and beyond and Black Jack, still holding both children, looked around as if for help. Ethel said nothing, standing head bowed, holding her breath.

Emily stepped forwards. 'A'll come, too, if you don't mind. A've a bit of a story to tell you, sir, if you please.'

So they led him across into the chilly front parlour, where Emily gave him the outline of their story, stressing the distress of Ethel at her loss and at having to name the child without him.

He seemed to have difficulty taking it in at first and he asked questions more in sorrow than anger. Then he thanked them and turned, still holding the two silent children, one now on each hip, and returned soberly to the kitchen. 'A want to see the bairn,' he stated.

Ethel began to cry and the children snivelled, hiding their faces, feeling the tension in him that rippled through the silent room.

Emily stepped forwards again and took the little ones from his side. 'Let's take the children into the yard, Ethel, shall we?'

There was a murmur of support for this idea and it was achieved without further distress, leaving Black Jack standing, now almost downcast, in the centre of the room. Hetty came forwards and handed him the bundle that she had nursed. He pulled open the cloths and gave a gasp to see the little wizened face, with its pursed mouth and pale, bruised skin. Tears fell from his eyes. He struggled to breathe as he bent to kiss the small brow and to hold her to his lips; the red of those lips and the black hair of his beard in stark contrast to the dull grey of the child's skin.

'She's called Hetty,' the girl spoke softly. 'I've promised to see to her, sir, an' mek sure that she is treated right, an' I will, I promise you.'

'Thank you, lass.' He spoke with a low grumble of pain in his voice. 'A want her properly buried an' a want to be there. Be sure to see that it's proper, mind. I'll pay what it takes.' And so saying he passed his dead child back to Hetty and with his family he went soberly and silently on his way.

Strangers
Spring 1870

New workers and lodgers were soon settled at Elterbeck and their arrival brought further change to the dynamics of the little farming community. Emily found herself with three men to attend to and sometimes four or five if any of the farmhands were in for a meal. What is more, she was quickly aware that her new residents were particularly attentive to her. She was grateful for Hetty's presence and the girlish chat that they sometimes had about the men

James Taylor was a puzzle to them. He was a young man from another of the Yorkshire Dales, from the little known town of Pateley Bridge in Nidderdale. He was 26 years old. 'But he don't look that age, does he, miss?' said Hetty. 'I mean, he's like got softer face an' hands an' he hardly ever shaves, you know, miss. An' he's that quiet sometimes, when he's sittin' in the parlour reading or looking at his maps an' plans an' things. T'other day, I went in to light the fire an' a didn't know he were there, like, an' a were grumbling a bit at state o' coal bucket an' that an' he spoke to me. I nearly fell in the fire for fright.' They laughed and yet they were none the wiser about James for quite a while.

Not that he set himself up to be enigmatic. His family had originally been labourers and had known poverty and privation. Over two generations, they had worked their way up to become respected as stonemasons and builders, with their own yard and carts. But children came plentifully to the Taylor line and there seemed always to be babies to feed and more men than there was work. Certainly, Nidderdale could not support them all. James had been working at Skipton for over five years, lodging in the town, working for a large building contractor there. He had worked his way up: starting with estimating, then preparing drawings, refining his draughtsmanship by copying for local architects,

23

and then moving into supervisory work and advising customers. He lived a steady and private life, returning home most weekends to his family, whose abundant energy seemed more than enough for him.

Yet, as weeks of this routine turned into months and then years turned past him, he began to feel restless. From the office window in Skipton he would watch barges moving with silent and stolid ease on the canal; but he could also hear the noisy, gasping bouts of steam from the trains that now pulled up on the edge of the town. He did not see his future as his father and grandfather had seen theirs; rooted to the yard, the town, the district or the local girl. He liked to think his horizons were broader and he wanted to push outwards, to test his limits. He wanted to be a part of the age, not content with a shady corner. The national mood was for building and expanding, and it was felt even in the quieter dales of the North. James Taylor felt it tug him forwards.

By a stroke of good fortune he had an uncle who worked as an engineer for the Midland Railway and when the time came for James to leave the layered web of his family and locality, this uncle was able to put in a good word for him. So now he worked as an assistant to Mr Ferguson, the resident engineer, and he was specifically assigned to the team working on and near to the Ribblehead Viaduct. His journey had certainly begun. His ambition was to build railways across America or Canada.

As Hetty had remarked, he was fresh-faced and youthful looking, quiet and settled in his ways, but with an air of competence and control about him, so that he was treated seriously, even by the most hardened of the navvies. They took his composure as a sign that he knew what he was doing. Moreover, he had an instinctive feel for the ways of working with both timber and stone and he was painstakingly pedantic over safety. He would be the first to order the men down from the scaffolding when the wind began to rise and chafe at the workings that were just going into position; he had a healthy respect for a force that could quickly make the wooden spars and cross-beams shudder, groan and twist as if in pain. He was proud of the fact that there had been no injuries so far on the sections that he was supervising and he was determined to keep it so.

He was of medium height and of a slim, wiry build, clean-shaven and with thin, wavy hair, black with hints of grey showing already at the sides. He had a neat, open face, made striking by heavy eyebrows that shaded his blue-grey eyes. He was always moving round the works, leaving his paperwork for the evenings, so that he was a familiar figure to all the men, often clambering around the scaffolding himself or riding out on the edge of the nearby embankment as it began to rise on the edge of Batty Moss. He was always greeted cordially and the men had learned that he was not likely to respond to the occasional bantering that was stock in trade with many of the gangs. His self-control and sobriety were well known, so there was little for others to fasten their jokes or satire upon, even if they had wished to. He did not preach to others or censure the men, except when their work was shoddy. He was a Methodist and occasionally attended chapel in Ingleton, but it seemed to be a matter of routine and familiarity, rather than a spiritual necessity for him.

Yet, for all this regularity and openness, there was a subtle air of uncertainty about James that some were quicker to sense than others. It was with women that his composure seemed to be at its most fragile. He was shy and nervous with Hetty, as if he did not know quite what to say to her, and he was almost silent with Emily. Her warmth and energy seemed to freeze him; yet, he watched her and so she giggled with Hetty about his hooded and mournful eyes following her around the room.

Even George noticed and spoke to her with some concern. She laughed it off and promised him that she would not break the young master's heart, but would try to find him a partner amongst the local girls, to divert his attentions. But whenever she invited an eligible young lady round to take tea, James would excuse himself and retire to his room or make his apologies and say that he had to return to the viaduct to check on the work there. Nevertheless, Emily felt that she had the measure of James Taylor. She was less sure about his room-mate.

Robert Macintosh had just turned forty-five: at least that was what he said. But it was always wise, Emily said behind his back, to be a little cautious in how much you believed of what Robert told you. He was loud, where James was quiet. He was muscular and brawny, where James was slender and neatly composed. He was not very tall, but he had presence, and he was not conventionally handsome, but was quite striking in a weathered and greying kind of way. He was almost bald, with just a few tufts of springy peppered hair, which he made the most of. He was a self-made man of no formal education, but great experience, as everyone was regularly reminded.

He spoke with a South Yorkshire accent, having been brought up as an orphan in Sheffield. But he had lived and worked in Scotland, in London and in the Midlands, so that there were traces of all these dialects and expressions in his speech. He brought colour and challenge to their table. He was wary with George, possessive with Emily and mildly provocative and often patronising with James.

Whenever they ate together at the farm, which was not every day on account of their different work patterns, it seemed that Robert inevitably gave James advice. However, it was a matter of debate as to how much of this wisdom James regarded as beneficial. One of his early offerings provided insights to many at the table.

'Thou's to remember, Mr Taylor, that the average navvy is like to turn up to work drunk from time to time. A've seen it many a time. Fact is, a've done it meself more than once. An' it's not just a matter of a glass or two with breakfast, as does happen, but you can waken up in t'mornin, after a steady few pints night afore, an' you're just still in the grip o' the drink. You're still drunk is what a'm sayin'. You need twelve or eighteen hours mebbe, to rid yourself o' a belly full of ale. But what workin' man 'as that, eh? Thou'st be a bit green, laddie, to assume that your men are all sober at first light. Always assume the worst an' plan accordingly.' James seemed to find it distasteful to reply.

'Nay, surely you're exaggerating, Mr Macintosh,' said Emily, who almost always got in before James was faced with any serious embarrassment and did so now with a smile, whilst handing round potatoes and cabbage. 'As tha knows, a go up t'camp once a week, sometimes twice; always in good daylight hours, admittedly, seein' as how Mr Wright insists that a'm back 'ere before nightfall. A truly think he believes that the whole of Batty Green becomes a den of vice at the exact same second as the sun goes down.' She laughed and the warm light of her lustrous brown eyes and the energetic toss of her head were watched with warm appreciation by at least two of the men present. Her husband looked down at his plate, a nervous smile crossing his face, but before he could protest, she went on. 'A've never seen a drunken navvy at all in any of my visits. In fact, a'm beginning to think all this talk of wild goings-on is a bit of a story. It's just men talking an' blowing up a few exploits into a grand parade of unruly a don't know what, so that they can all appear to be part of this clan of hard-drinking, tough men that no one can control. Dost tha agree,

Hetty?' She turned to Hetty, who was just struggling through the door with a dish of lamb cutlets.

'What's that, Mrs Wright?' she asked, keeping her eyes fixed hard on the dish.

'A've a theory,' Emily giggled almost girlishly, 'that all t'men at Batty Green, including the navvies, are actually well behaved an' quite like proper gentlemen. And that, well, it suits them all to put out all kinds o' stories of drunken fights an' so forth, cos they all get a bit of the glory, somehow. D'you know what a mean?'

The men smiled, humouring her. Hetty paused to place the dish safely on the table and then stood, shifting hesitantly, as if her feet were burning as hot as her face. 'A know as some of the men folk that a've met have been really well mannered an' that ...' She glanced up briefly in the direction of James. 'But a've heard of some strange goin's-on last Sunday, mam.' With all eyes now on her, she had to continue and did so bravely, lifting her head. 'A heard as how there was a fight on the moor. But not just a personal kind of, you know, an argument or summat, but a crowd an' a proper space for the fighting; one man near got killed an' the blood's still on the ground up there. At least, that's as a heard it.'

In the brief silence that followed, Robert took over. 'Aye, that's true; it was t'establish who's cock o' the camp.' He eagerly grasped at the chance to develop his role as the expert witness. 'Fightin's a special tradition, almost, of the navvies, for at least the last thirty years an' more. An' ivery major workings has its own champion, its cock, just like your farmyard, least so a'm told, as how one cock usually rules the roost. Isn't that so, Mr Wright?'

George, apparently absorbed in his own thoughts, was startled at this sudden invitation to offer an opinion. He stammered a brief response and his embarrassment brought a temporary halt to talk of fighting. But he then surprised them by revealing what was really on his mind. 'I reckon thir's a price to pay for all this change an' upheaval,' he said. 'Think of Hetty's generation. Hetty's known nowt but rural sorts of folks all her life an' now she's meetin' men an' women such as her mother an' father would never expect to see or hear of. And what kind o' example are some o' 'em? What happens when our young folk mixes with some o' these navvies an' their women? They say as some o' the women up at t'camp, some as have had children by their men there, well, they're not married at all. Not in the proper Christian sense, but they just jump o'er a broomstick an' say a few funny words. Am a right, Mr Macintosh?'

Robert looked uncomfortable for a moment but nodded. 'Aye, there's a few odd ways o' goin' on, to be sure. A navvy camp kind of exists like nothing else. I mean, thir's no vicar, churchwarden or constable as lives with the men and contractors tek care to live some ways off, I can tell you. So rules emerge, kind of, and traditions kind o' grow and develop and are sometimes particular to one place. And a group o' men will go off an' start thir own ways o' doin' things. Like here at Batty Green, there's already a start made at creatin' new huts further up on t'moor. There's Jericho and Sebastopol already named and pegged out. In time, they will have their own ways an' loyalties an' certain characters will dominate in some, rivalries will grow and sometimes a fight or two will break out. There was even a cricket tournament one summer where a was workin'. I recall one camp just called The Cockpit, famous for its fightin' arena in t'middle, and one was named Billy's Gaff, after one navvy called Billy, as he was practically the lord and a master of it; he ruled it mainly by brute force an' had a kind of throne in's hut.' He picked up his knife and fork again.

There were smiles and comments and a return to the business of the table, until Hetty suddenly spoke up. 'I heard as you was married over a broomstick once, Mr Macintosh, is that right?' She went pale as they all looked up and Emily gasped and tutted.

'Hetty, tha should not ask such things.' She was shocked at the rapid changes that were to be seen in Hetty. 'Please ignore the girl, Mr Macintosh, a don't know what's got into her.'

'Nay, she does right to ask,' said Robert, looking a little abashed. 'Stories always go round in any community and a've no right to expect particular favours, not wi' ma past history. So, Hetty, yes, a' took a woman down in Cheshire, as lived wi' me for two year an' more. And there certainly wor no ceremony, except some dancin' an' singin'. She jumped a broomstick as t'other women held and she promised herself to me as I did to her. I wor a young man, just turned twenty, an' you could say as I didn't know better. But in t'end, she wanted to go back to Walsall whir she'd come from an' a was wantin' another contract, cos a was savin' for the right to run a contract o' me own. So we parted on good terms and no 'ard feelings.'

'And there were no … children?' Emily hesitated in her question, biting at her lip, well aware that it was now her turn to intrude, but driven to know. It was George who this time drew audible breath as if to protest, glancing sharply at her and half rising from his seat; but Robert raised a hand and smiled at him.

'Nay, don't concern yourself, Mr Wright. It's a natural question and perhaps it's there in most of you. Well, Mrs Wright, a had a little boy, but he died after a few days, poor little mite, an' his ma nearly went at same time. A can tell you, a'd have ended it meself an' all if she had gone. But she pulled round, did the lass, but doctor said as there would be no more children. So, as a say, in t'end she wanted to go back to her family and we parted. But t'were as good as a marriage to me an' she were a fine lass.'

There was a pause and no one spoke as Robert collected himself, which he soon did. He looked up and sought the gaze first of Emily and then of Hetty, as if no others were present. 'So, ladies, now you know. No marriages for me since then, o' broomstick type or the reg'lar church, though one or two ladies have featured in my life since. But she were the best an' a've never forgotten her.'

'But … Why didn't you go with her?' Hetty almost whispered, hoping for a happy ending and saddened by the tale.

'It wor just the worst o' times,' Robert continued as Hetty and Emily began to move dishes, but still carefully tuned to his every word. 'A wor an ordinary navvy, dragged up in various orphanages an' knowing nowt about owt, if you know what a mean. But a could always handle meself and a'd worked hard since a wor fourteen, labouring on canals an' the like, in t'Pennines mostly. So a got to see how things wor done an' a reckoned after a while as how a'd be better fixed working wi' me head as well as me 'ands and so a started planning. And a' wanted to save fifty pounds to buy a few horses an' some carts an' set to and work for meself, wi' a couple o' men, perhaps, and tek on a little bit o' subcontracting. And a' wor getting close to this dream, as a'd been working for, for nearly a year, when she said as she wor goin'. So I had a choice and perhaps a' made the wrong 'un, but a wouldn't be here now if a'd gone to Birmingham wi' her.' It was a sober statement and no one followed it up.

Emily and Hetty were subdued and were inclined to like Robert more. James was jealously disappointed to be eclipsed in this way. George was uneasy.

Tensions
Spring 1870

A week or so after this discussion, Emily and Hetty were making their way towards Batty Green with their horse Milly and their bright new cart, which they had painted as vibrant a yellow as they could find, to make it stand out amongst the many tradesmen now descending on the area. Emily had been right to sense the opportunities that the railway works would bring. But so, too, had others. The streets of Ingleton reverberated to the clatter of carts, wagons and horses, bringing provisions, animals, people, steam engines, metals and coal up to Ribblehead. As well as all that the contractors ordered, there was the human tide and its army of suppliers: hawkers, merchants, tinkers, brewers, bakers, tailors, farmers and fundamentalists. People of all sorts and every persuasion had heard that there was money to be made and there were souls to be saved and so they converged on the growing township, ready to answer the needs of the men and their families. Where money is more prevalent than judgement, the market place always thrives.

The traffic of people, wagons and animals along the turnpike road was almost constant, so much so that the parish council was already petitioning for the road to be relaid and widened. Yet, despite the competition, the Elterbeck Farm Cart, its name proudly emblazoned in black across the yellow tailgate, was well patronised. Emily and Hetty had begun to make a steady business selling fresh produce: mostly eggs, chickens, milk, cheese and sometimes joints of lamb or pork, or some sausages, black pudding, vegetables or home baking. Sometimes, they brought a few bales of hay, as many of the navvies had animals of their own with them, or they brought logs or whatever else they could supply easily from their own resources or those of their immediate neighbours.

They went often at midweek, but always on a Saturday, and had begun to develop regular customers, but there were always new faces.

They now stayed on the side of the turnpike road, not venturing down into the shanty camps, where the going was very difficult. They had tried it just once, on a misty, damp morning, and had found that thick, oozing mud soon sucked at Milly's hooves and their cart had slid and jolted against hidden boulders and then settled into the squelching mud base up to its axles. Men carrying lanterns had appeared from nowhere, sliding in the mud up to their thighs to help pull them out, shouting almost unintelligibly, offering to lift the women clear with gruff and genial humour. Emily had shivered appreciatively at the thought, but declined for the sake of her nervous maid, and they were soon pulled free.

The whole area had become a new and fascinating landscape to them, with rapid growth and flux and many surprises. By their own reckoning, there were now over forty huts concentrated around Batty Green and they tried to count them each week, but there were more scattered further up the line, with some that they had not yet seen right on Blea Moor itself, to serve the tunnel workings that were just starting there.

On this particular Saturday they were looking forward with some interest to seeing if the planned "market train" would make its first run from the tunnel huts on Blea Moor down to Batty Green. The contractors had built a tramway to carry men and materials to and from Blea Moor and to serve the workings between. It was a narrow gauge single-track line, roughly laid over the open moor and clinging audaciously to the contours as it circled upwards. It was a precarious journey at times, with heavily laden wagons sometimes swaying and then toppling on the sharper curves, once pulling the whole train, engine and all, over into the long grass that sprang from the boggy watercourses seeping down from the moor. On that day a dozen men and horses had to be assembled to haul it all back onto the line.

The sparky little steam engine always seemed to have a life and spirit of its own as it rattled and grumbled its way up, clattering loosely and angrily downwards, often threatening to gather enough momentum to jump the rails completely. Today, it was a feature of added excitement. The women of the various huts above Batty Green had been promised a special train of their own at two o'clock each Saturday to take them down to Batty Green and then back two hours later. An impromptu market was therefore set up and a sense of excitement and holiday was brightening the day for the two young women with their yellow cart.

They found a scene of almost frantic activity. There were brewers' drays and bakers' carts blocking the road; there were hawkers with baskets over their arms shouting their wares for all the world as if it was Billingsgate Market. There were fish carts with oysters and herrings piled up and butchers' stalls dripping blood in the pale spring sunshine. There were pie shops, beer stands selling flagons, a few flamboyant whores standing in a group and even some entertainers singing ballads and bewildering the children with tricks and novelties. Many of the men were still at work, but there were navvies with clay pipes standing watching, laughing at the scene or swigging beer, the younger men scuffling or jeering. There were women and children, dogs, geese, chickens, horses and a couple of donkeys that seemed to be wandering at will. And all the time the perpetual backdrop of engines shuffling, men calling, and hammers braying into metal spikes or chipping at masonry as the work went on around, above and beyond them.

Emily and Hetty excitedly squeezed their cart into a space, uncoupled the horse and quickly set themselves up, with their baskets and purses ready and the produce laid out on trays. They had barely set up, when they heard the snort of steam and the brave whistle of the little train. Looking across the broad basin of Batty Green, filled with huts and the shifting mass of people and animals, they glimpsed the engine and wagons as it turned down from Jericho and then swung north to one of the further groups of dwellings. This settlement the navvies had wryly named Belgravia, on account of the fact that it was rather elegantly placed looking down on the heaving township and the accumulation of workings that was spreading beneath.

Soon, the train was swinging back the other way and cutting across close to where the middle piers of the viaduct would be, but for now there were just muddy holes and piles of lumber for all to negotiate. The train blustered towards them and shuddered to a halt not far from the road. A little round of applause broke out. Emily and Hetty watched as best they could, but were puzzled that while they could hear voices calling and laughing, they could see no passengers. As the sides of the wagons were lowered the reason became clear: the women and children had been told not to stand but to sit in the bottom of the wagons and most had brought an old rug or piece of cloth to protect their clothes.

As the wagons were opened, they were trying to right themselves amidst much pushing and laughing and some shrieking, as many had fallen against each other or had got squashed at one side as the wagons turned and tilted on the way down. They brushed themselves down as they gathered in small groups and it was clear that most had put on their best bonnets for their spring market. To Hetty, for whom Ingleton Market was a bit overwhelming, this gave the finishing touch to the sense of an exotic carnival.

After an hour, they had sold all that they had brought. Hetty was looking longingly across at a cart that was selling scarves, gloves and trinkets. Emily smiled at her and told her to have a look around for ten minutes, but not to wander too far. The girl skipped off clutching her purse, with a whole shilling to spend, but a mixture of nerves and excitement making her shiver. What might she buy, or should she save it? She was hoping to visit her home at Cold Cotes soon and wanted to take presents for them all: how far would her money stretch? So she rather stumbled in haste from one point to another, getting anxious about the time that was passing and whether Emily would be cross with her, but still deciding on nothing.

She found herself near one of the huts, facing a gaunt-looking man in a black cap and a threadbare black suit. He had a large tray of sweets strung round his neck and a knot of unkempt children were staring with blank attentiveness at the treasures that were so alluring to them, but so inaccessible. Hetty noticed that one child was barefoot and one had raw blisters and scabs all up his dirty legs. But their rapturous gaze reminded her of her own brothers and sisters, who looked no better, and it came to her that if she could get a large bag of humbugs it could be subdivided into little parcels, so that they could all have a few. The man smiled at her request, showing a few blackened teeth, and she bought what she wanted for a shilling. The man grinned at her, licking his cracked lips and looking her up and down.

'What about a present for you, my lovely, or for your mother, eh? I'm sure I could find you something special? Eh? Just round here, I've got some special things for a pretty girl …' He motioned with his head to a space behind one of the huts. Hetty was confused and hesitated, moving half a step forwards, until he reached over and took her wrist in a hard, calloused hand and started to pull her away from the pathway.

She pulled back in confusion and pleaded with him to let go. He whined, like a cur that had been trodden on, and urged her, 'Just show a little kindness, lady.' He pulled her hard again towards a narrow gap between huts, at which she panicked and shouted at him to let go, kicking out at him and knocking his tray up upwards. He recoiled, shuffling his feet to gain his balance, like a tired marionette. He seemed deflated suddenly, dropping her wrist, looking around as if fearful of being seen and hastily tidying his sweets. Hetty turned hurriedly away and almost ran into James Taylor, who was moving towards her with a look of cold resolve on his face. She realised, at once, that he must have seen at least some of the incident. Perhaps he had been there for a while.

'Are you alright, Hetty?' he asked, flushing and then taking her by the elbow and moving her away from passers-by. She nodded and smiled gratefully. 'What a horrible man,' said James. 'Wait here.'

He stepped back to where the sweet seller was still standing, watching Hetty, with a foolish, nervous grin stretching his lined face. Hetty saw James go close to the man and speak quietly but firmly to him. The man seemed to shrink into himself. James looked round, spoke again to the man and then something was passed over from the sweet seller, with obvious bad grace. James stepped back and indicated that the man should move on. He then turned and gave sweets to the little assemblage of shabby children and then came back to Hetty's side, wiping sugar from his hands, a shy smile on his face, pleased with himself.

'He did not fancy a conversation with the constable,' said James. 'So he agreed to a few free sweets. Shall I walk back with you to the cart?'

Hetty was beaming and tremulous at his chivalrous behaviour and she took his proffered arm, blushing at this unexpected signal of adult intimacy, but holding her head up brightly as they threaded their way through what was still quite a crowd as they headed up to the turnpike.

They had to pass a brewer's dray, where a crowd of customers were leaning against a bar made of straw bales. The atmosphere was cheerfully suffused with the smell of beer and tobacco, men were quietly drinking and one had fallen asleep with his head on the bar. There were also women, who appeared to be equally at home. Hetty quickly glanced at them as they stood together drinking beer or gin and some smoking pipes. One of them, a tall, florid woman with no bonnet, but with hair that was dingy grey and dishevelled, stepped back clumsily to allow a customer to the bar and stood on James' foot as he tried to marshal Hetty through the crowd. 'Watch your step!' he exclaimed.

'I could say the same to you,' she replied in a deep, brusque voice, looking down on him and breathing brandy and tobacco fumes into his face. A large grey dog, standing as high as her waist, growled threateningly.

'I'm sorry, but you did step on me first,' said James in a more placatory tone, not wanting a scene with Hetty alongside him.

The woman frowned, but then broke into a smile and said, 'No harm done, young man.' The voice was deep and the accent unusual. James was a little startled, but moved on gratefully. The matter was quickly over and the woman had turned away, when a rather flushed young man at the other side of the bar saw it was Hetty and called her name.

He pushed his way towards her, mumbling, 'Hetty, Hetty,' and almost tripped over as he reached her. Then, he steadied himself by leaning at a sharp angle against the straw bales and twisted his head uncomfortably to focus on her. He smelt of beer and sweat. 'It's Hetty Brownlove, isn't it? From Cold Cotes? Don't you remember me? Daniel Petty? I used to live at Ridge Farm, just outside Cold Cotes. Moved away three years since.' He tried to stand up straight, swaying slightly. 'We went to school together one time, at Clapham, when we were littl'uns. Do you recall?'

Hetty did remember him and they exchanged a few words, Hetty nervously aware that she was the object of attention from several sides, including James and the tall woman with the dog, who seemed to have drifted into her own world of thoughts and had not moved except to reach for her glass. Hetty then told Daniel that she now lived at Elterbeck and at this the woman seemed to focus more closely, but said nothing. After a few minutes, and with Daniel enthusiastically promising to call at Elterbeck and see Hetty again, she and James moved on towards an anxious-looking Emily, the blushes now crowding into Hetty's face so fast that she wanted to hide. As Emily got the story from them, they were not in the least aware that they were being watched very closely.

But as is the way sometimes, the repercussions from this encounter quickly became more significant than the incident itself. It started later, when sharp words were exchanged between Emily and her husband. George came in late, just as the evening meal was finishing, tired and hungry after a difficult lambing. Hurrying after her market day and talking excitedly of Hetty's adventures, Emily had miscalculated the meal. There was little left for his dinner and what there was had long since chilled. He grunted his displeasure. Then, when George had listened again to what had happened, he blamed Emily for letting Hetty wander off. She retorted that the girl was not a child and she could not have eyes everywhere. He accused her of being more interested in the gossip and the tittle-tattle of the camp than in the safety of her maid or the needs of her husband or the farm, adding that going there was changing her and Hetty, and for the worst. She reminded him of his enthusiasm for the railway venture and his liking for the extra money that was coming in. He retorted that she was the greedy and selfish one, with no time for anything other than her own schemes and certainly no time for him.

The words threatened to grow more bitter, but Emily cut them short by shedding a tear and then walking out of the kitchen and across towards the barn, before he could react. This left George shaken and annoyed, still feeling self-righteous, but baffled at why this was happening and confused by the suspicion that he might be losing touch with his wife's feelings. They rarely argued and never like this, with a raw gulf threatening to separate them. They had both been striking in vulnerable areas as tensions surfaced, but it was not over, he felt guiltily sure.

So he sat, unwashed, and ate bread and dripping at the kitchen table, while Hetty nervously worked round him. He did not know how much had been heard by Hetty, or Robert or James, and neither did he really care. But he was concerned about Emily. As he grew calmer, he felt her absence more painfully and at last he looked up wearily and spoke to Hetty, who had settled to her sewing by the fireside. 'Will you please find Emily for me, Hetty, and ask her to come back t'kitchen?' Hetty smiled tentatively at him and nodded.

The light was beginning to fade and a chill wind was rattling the timbers of the barn and flinging dust into the air as she crossed the yard. But before she had scurried more than a dozen paces with her head down, a figure emerged from near the gate and hailed her. 'Hetty, can I speak wi' thee?'

She paused and squinted. She could see a young man in his working clothes, swaying slightly, and after a brief hesitation she identified him as Daniel Petty, the young man who had spoken to her at Batty Green.

'What art tha doin' 'ere, Daniel?' she hissed, not wanting further trouble. 'You mun go away, please.'

'A've come to see thee, ma lass.' He giggled as he spoke and moved towards her, but stumbled. She could see that he was drunk. 'A was 'oping for a goodnight kiss.'

'Go away, you fool,' she hissed again and ran for the door of the shippon, yanking it open and crashing it shut behind her, half afraid that he was following. She had brought no lantern and she could see little inside. 'Mrs Wright? Are you there, mam?' It was more of a timid cry for help than a question, but there was no answer. Hetty heard a shuffling of footsteps coming closer to the door that was still shaking from when she had slammed it. She hurried across the shed in the gloom, backing away into one of the stalls, the sharp smell of cow's urine rising from the straw that she kicked over as she crouched nervously behind a manger. She was shaking and she did not want to get into trouble. They might think she had encouraged him. She certainly did not want Daniel Petty. And where was Emily? Emily would understand. She began to cry a few salty and confused tears.

After a minute or two, she thought she heard movement. She braced herself for the door opening, but then she heard more voices and the sound of running feet, followed by a scuffling and a cry, perhaps from Daniel. More heavy footsteps were heard and she was surprised to hear Robert's deeper voice. Then it sounded as if James shouted something, but it was all faint and unclear to her. She swayed back against the greasy wood of the stall and tried to calm herself down by counting slowly to fifty. Her heart was pounding, so that she could scarcely count and certainly could not hear or understand what was happening. After a few moments, once all noise had died away, she crept out and opened the door a fraction. She peered out cautiously and was surprised to see James and Robert, face-to-face in the yard, as if they, too, were arguing.

'All I'm saying,' said James, breathing heavily, 'is that you had no need to fetch the lad a heavy clout like that. He wor goin', weren't he? Now, after you've laid into him, who knows; he may not even make it home. He might be lying in some ditch all night.'

'He needed teachin' a lesson, Mr Taylor, an' then the little bugger will think twice before comin' 'ere again, with his belly full o' beer an' his few brains lost in's trousers. A' know these men and how they should be tret. You've a few things to learn, as a' keep tellin' you.'

Robert turned away, content with the last word, but it was at that moment that Hetty, nervously agitated by what she had heard, shifted her weight slightly on the door that she was holding and it creaked and swung open. Both men jumped and swung round to face her.

'Are you alright, lass?' Robert asked kindly, coming towards her, assuming that she had not heard what they had said.

'Have you hurt him?' she asked shakily.

'Not so's anyone would notice,' said Robert with a smile.

'But a didn't want him to come to any harm.' Hetty felt close to tears again as she shifted uneasily from one foot to the other and chewed at her lip. 'He's just a daft lad, always as been. I'm sure –' Robert cut across her and took her arm, leading her back to the farmhouse. James was left standing, watching them go, simmering with resentment and more than a dash of reawakened jealousy. He listened sourly to Robert's deep voice, with just that special coating of protective concern for a young woman that James hated. 'You just don't know, m'lass. A've seen the likes of this 'un many a time, as gets himself a skinful o' beer and then pesters local women, cos he thinks they are just cravin' attention. If we don't mek it clear to his sort, then you'll be proper bothered.'

James was turning away, when his attention was caught by the sound of footsteps approaching the yard gate – heavy, oddly dragging steps – and the groan of heavy breathing, broken by gasps of air from someone struggling for breath. He hurried over and found Emily, half pulling a lifeless Daniel, his face badged with blood and mud, which was also richly coated all down one side of him; one eye was closed by swelling and his head swung as if loosened from his neck. James said nothing, but quickly opened the gate and stepped up to help, pulling Daniel onto his shoulder, so as to take the weight from Emily, his arm half circling round her in the process. As she shifted her position, his hand trailed down to rest in the small of her back, where he could feel the heat of her. She seemed unaware, but he was not.

'Oh, thank God it's you, Mr Taylor. A was walking back up the lane, when a found this one clinging to the wall. A think he's fallen. He's bleedin' an' he fair stinks of ale an' muck.'

'Aye, he was here a while back,' James grunted as they moved towards the house. 'He wor tryin' to get to Hetty and Robert and I drove him off. I'm not sure …' he hesitated and then carefully added, with only half a smile, 'I think … Robert persuaded him not to come back and may have clipped him rather hard –' Their conversation was suddenly halted with a gurgle from Daniel that rose to a guttural retch as he stood straight for a moment and then, as if being thoughtful, he turned neatly away from Emily and was sick, throwing blood and vomit down the front of James instead. George came quickly from the house, alerted by the strange confusion of noises, and he took the weight of the boy. James excused himself and went to change his clothes. As he changed he could hear more raised voices, three or four of them, but had no stomach for more argument, so he retired to the room he shared with Robert. He threw his clothes outside. It was half an hour later that Robert entered, clearly displeased, with coiled tension in his every movement. James pretended to be asleep and almost despite himself he soon drifted off.

At breakfast, James found himself alone with Emily. She sat opposite him as they ate porridge, while thick bacon sizzled in a frying pan. It was intimate and tense. Nerves were stretched and tender. She had greeted him, but had said nothing else, and he felt awkward, unsure of her mood or his own feelings and not knowing how to ask about the events of the night before without upsetting her, so he resorted to silence. But that was not Emily's way. She reached across and placed her hand on his forearm. He looked up and found his pulse racing as he looked into her dark eyes that were wet with incipient tears. She seemed to be breathing in a shallow, restless pattern. Her springy black hair was clinging damply to each side of her face and the contrast between this dark border, her pale skin and her red lips made her look more vulnerable and exciting than ever to James.

'A thank thee for thy help last night, Mr Taylor,' she said, her hand grasping his arm a little tighter as if he might pull away. 'We got Daniel home an' a don't think there was any real harm done to him. Pity about your clothes though, eh? We'll have to see how they come out in t'wash.' James swallowed hard, but was not sure that he could trust his voice. His arm seemed to burn from her touch and he felt his face beginning to glow. She smiled wistfully and wiped away a tear with her other hand. 'A've told Mr Wright and Mr Macintosh how they must behave better. A do know how you an' Hetty were nowt to do wi' the ill feeling an' that last night. A do hope as tha'll not think ill of us.'

'What … happened?' he managed to croak nervously.

She let go of him and stood to turn the bacon. With her back to him she answered falteringly, feeling her way with the words. 'Oh, we cleaned the lad up and Mr Macintosh tried to make out as how Daniel wor lucky not to have had it worse. An' that fair made me blood boil an' a told him that a'd no desire to run a house where violence was the normal way o' dealin' wi' things an' if he wanted to behave like that then he'd better find new lodgings at the camp. P'rhaps he will. But then my husband said summat to me as he shouldn't a done an' that led to more words an' he went off. A think he must 'a slep in the shepherd's hut, cos a've seen neither hide nor hair o' him since an' Hetty is abed sayin' she's poorly, but she's frightened that she'll get the blame, so a reckon she's just keepin' out o' sight. Oh, an' Mr Macintosh went off early wi'out breakfast. So …' she paused to catch her breath and then let a racking sigh pass through her with a shudder, 'it's just two o' us.'

She turned and managed a smile that brightened her eyes through her wet lashes as her bosom heaved and her hand trembled.

James felt his whole being melting and he stood clumsily and moved in front of her, just wanting to be close and to touch her. He reached out and took her by the elbow and she let the tears flow and stepped up close to him.

'I think that you're in the right, you know,' he stuttered as his arms lightly folded round her and she rested her cheek on his coat front, tremors rippling unevenly through her. 'I'm sure it will all come out alright in the end,' he said, despising himself for his trite comments, just wanting to soothe her.

Whether his words had that effect he was destined never to know, because just at that moment the door opened and George entered, scowling. They stepped quickly apart, but George took in the scene at a glance and strode immediately out again. The moment became etched on Emily's memory, suffused with embarrassment and guilt, and it set the tone for some difficult times ahead.

Men at Work

Spring 1870

Mr Crossley was the chief engineer for the Settle to Carlisle line: he had postponed his retirement to see this project through, fearing both the best and the worst from it. Mr Edgar Ferguson was the resident engineer for Blea Moor and Ribblehead; a man "as likes a challenge", he was heard to say regularly in a broad Yorkshire accent. Mr Charles Hirst and Mr Walter Hirst, two canny Scots brothers, were the men responsible for the Ribblehead Viaduct. James Taylor was one of several young assistant engineers, working mainly under the careful eye of Walter Hirst and acting as the company's eyes and ears at the southern end of the viaduct, particularly on the slowly developing embankment there. He was also assigned to monitor the first of the southern piers of the viaduct itself. But, as yet, these were just unlined holes in the ground, trial sinkings, unconfirmed. Mr Crossley had not finally decided how many piers there would be, so work had only started in earnest at the northern end of the viaduct. For a little while, James was able, at times, just to watch and learn from a distance.

One cool day in March, as part of his training, he was taken by Walter Hirst to view the first few northern piers as they began to rise from their foundations, 20 feet or more below ground. At every muddy opening, a noisy, stuttering steam engine powered a simple hoist, taking men and materials up and down the shaft, its close timbered sides like a vertical doorway through the rock or a long deep coffin stood on its end. Leaning over a crude low fence, more designed to keep the cattle out than anything else, James could make out a group of shadowy men working with candles to supplement the weak spring sunshine. They were hauling a masonry block off the hoist, carefully drawing it towards the thick mortar bed that was ready prepared. James was pleased to observe that there was order and purpose in their work below ground and they eased the massive block forwards as if it were made of glass.

On the surface, however, he noted that there was every familiar appearance of bustle and confusion. A small, urgent train was approaching, clattering and shuddering along the tramway; machinery was grinding and screeching from all quarters, turning and fussing; coal was being dumped from a cart, masonry blocks were chiselled rhythmically and baulks of timber were being split and stripped in preparation for scaffolding. Men shouted and whistled, gangers cursed, horses snorted, dogs barked at each other and at nothing, curlews wailed overhead as if bored of it all and engines, pumps and steam travellers whined and occasionally coughed out sharp gouts of steam, clearing their tubes. In the midst, James caught a glimpse of a mother trailing two little children, moving aimlessly from group to group, her shawl wrapped tight around her, a look of desperation on her face. Just audible amongst it all, a group of men were singing as they worked in a neighbouring pier shaft. A light wind whimpered over the scene, ferreting at coat tails and breathing under tarpaulins.

Walter and James strode further down to where a new pier was being started. This would be the sixth pier and Mr Crossley's plan showed that every sixth pier had to be a king pier of double thickness, so that even if the first five fell, the damage could be limited. They had reached solid rock at just over 25 feet here and were preparing wooden shuttering to take the 6 feet of concrete that they would build up from. Walter Hirst, a jovial, well-meaning, middle-aged man, raised a quizzical eyebrow at James and nodded towards the dark shaft. 'Fancy a look, laddie? You could check it out for me. Mek sure they're prepared, that they've got the full double width we need. And check that the bedrock's not splintered or too wet. It'll be reet, a'm sure; they're a good team this one: mostly nonconformists and the like. Morris will tek you down. He's a good man, though I don't like to admit it, cos he's Welsh and has a face like a plate of liver; but don't tell him I said so.' He handed James the plans without waiting for a reply, tipped his hat and began to walk back, shouting over his shoulder to the foreman, 'Morris, you Celtic madman. My assistant Mr Taylor is going down. Don't drop him now; it will just slow up the work and upset his mam.'

Morris was short and dark haired, with blotchy skin, livid with purple scars in places. James guessed that he had been a coal miner before this.

A ghost of a smile flitted across Morris' face as he explained kindly, in his lilting Welsh voice, 'The bucket will be up in a minute. We may need more pumping down there. Tell me what you think, Mr Taylor. Here's a candle now: but look you don't light it till you get down there. It will only blow out as you go down. And pull yer 'at on tight. The ganger down there knows his trade: he's the wee red-headed one. But he'll soon find you, o' that I'm sure. I would go with you, but I need to watch these lads here.' He gestured across to where five men were laying a new tramway to this sixth pier, to bring more masonry, timber, concrete and mortar. 'They don't seem able to grasp how important it is to keep the tramway level and on firm ground. This is their third go at laying it. I've made them tek it up twice. If they had a brain between them it would help. If they had a brain each, they would be dangerous.'

At that point, a bell rang and the steam engine began to turn up the wheel, bringing up the rope and then the bucket. It clattered to a halt at the top and James grabbed the rope and lowered himself into a dirty, wet metal bucket, capable of holding two or three men or perhaps fifty bricks. Morris nodded and the operator sent James quickly out of sight with a shrill blast on a steam whistle. James felt himself drop briefly downwards, his stomach rising uneasily as the damp, moist air surged past him and the bucket bounced off the sides of the shaft. In a matter of seconds, he felt the descent slow and he bumped heavily into a bed of sand, the bucket tipping to one side, and he half fell, half scrambled out, his head ringing and his vision blurred in the gloom that met him. He hardly felt that he had made a dignified entrance.

A Scottish voice assailed him, breathy with smoking or shouting, and he felt an arm guide him to his feet with a welcome gentleness. 'A visitor no less. And who might you be, ma bonnie lad?'

James squinted in the gloom, finding himself staring into the face of a shrewish-looking man, with wisps of dirty red hair escaping from all round a woollen cap and an empty clay pipe clamped between his teeth.

James hastily drew himself up and put on his top hat, brushing mud from his knees. Other men stood, shadowy in the background.

'I'm Mr Taylor,' he smiled. 'Assistant to Mr Walter Hirst, who has asked me to have a look at the work down here.' He gave a tentative half bow, conscious that he was the raw novice down here, and so he just smiled, a little apologetically, and offered his candle stub for lighting.

He looked round as the ganger lit it for him. They stood on bare rock, coated with sticky mud and wet sand in places; all was damp and almost black in the poor light. The rock glistened and shimmered with a metallic haze. Water dripped from above and James could feel that the wooden shuttering around them was swelling, heavy with damp. It was seeping towards them as if it wanted to reclaim the space so rudely carved out of the dark earth. A pale liquid sky was caught in a jagged picture frame above them, wires and lines crossing it, and distant clouds skipped across, intent on escape. It was cold and James shivered and pulled his long coat around him. 'Can you show me around?' he enquired politely.

The ganger smiled roguishly, showing broken teeth held firm against the stem of the pipe. 'It'll be a quick tour, laddie, but you're welcome.'

James felt that this familiar deference, almost invariably displayed to the Midland's engineers, was bred out of genuine respect and he was grateful for it. He wanted to sound authoritative and began to ask questions, learning all the time.

Robert Macintosh was in a very different situation, in almost every sense, though he, too, was learning powerful lessons. At this precise moment, he was 2 miles away from James and he was a worried man. He had real autonomy and, in fact, was often threatened by eddies of anxiety, quickly stifled when he reflected that he held most matters very much in his own hands even if future prosperity and success depended on the outcome. The Midland Railway did not employ him at all; he was a subcontractor to Mr Ashwell, who in turn held the contract for the whole of the first section of the line. Robert had his own team of men and had won the contract to lay the permanent way from the northern end of the viaduct almost all the way to Blea Moor Tunnel, to construct the necessary bridges, also the culverts and drainage channels needed to keep the main line clear of water, and finally to build the sidings near the tunnel mouth.

It was the biggest contract he had ever managed and he had already engaged over seventy of his own men to work for him, divided into three gangs, and he had also laid out money on animals, materials and equipment. He had more anxieties than he would ever care to admit to.

For one thing, he had not won the contract for the whole section and so he had to cope with an uneasy division. A different subcontractor was building the embankment and abutments at this northern end of the viaduct and another was managing the works around the tunnel. Although the three men needed to work closely together, it was not always proving easy. They were already facing potential trouble.

Like a number of the subcontractors, they had underestimated the costs, the difficulty of the work, the huge problems of labour recruitment and the high turnover. Moreover, they still had a full Pennine winter to experience. There was sparring, spite and hostility between them at times and the Midland Railway Company watched this with concern, while watching its rising costs with alarm. The two Hirsts were keeping a close eye on Robert and the progress of the works under his control.

They could not have asked for more in effort and drive. Robert Macintosh pushed himself hard and expected the same from the men that he was paying. Most days, he left Elterbeck more than an hour before sunrise and he rode at a steady pace to the sprawl of huts known as Jericho and then on to Jerusalem. He was often rousing his men before seven in the morning and he had them at work soon afterwards.

They trudged forwards, many of them heavy with unfinished sleep and a night's drinking and gambling. They cursed him, they cursed the weather and they cursed the place. "The devil's arsehole", they called Blea Moor Tunnel, the dark gash gouged out of the swelling mass of hillside that loured down on them as they worked. There was a chaotic jumble of mud, timber and stone. There were spoil-heaps of dark boulder clay soured with grey peaty water. Wagons and carts were everywhere and horses were tethered to lines and stakes, their heads abjectly low as they stared out at the cold winds thrashing the sparse grasses in impatient, turbulent patterns. Robert glanced at the horses as he passed, some of them his own, and he felt their mood and knew that he was beginning to share it. He had put in a low tender for his contract and was paying his men top rates in a gamble to get well on with the work while the better weather held. But he would have to reduce their pay eventually or face the fact that he would be ruined. And when he tried to do that, most of them would leave. Already, they had started to drift away. Every pay day saw another group pack their few belongings and head for easier work in softer country.

Meanwhile, the terrain was throwing up big problems. In particular, Littledale and its various watercourses were proving a nightmare for

Robert, so much so that he always referred to it as Little Hell. After much prospecting, the engineers had agreed that the best source of local black limestone to build the viaduct was the broad bed of a tributary stream, which the navvies had jokingly nicknamed the Maiden's Tinkle when it was quiet and Pisspot Torrent when it was full. It ran directly into Little Dale Beck. This stream, tinkle and torrent, would have to be diverted and carried over the line on an aqueduct. Robert negotiated for more funds with the Midland and a price was agreed. The work was in hand, but he was under pressure to complete it, because the limestone was now needed and most of it was still underwater. And this was how it went up and down the line: the Midland's costs were rising, problems continued to block progress and siren voices persistently questioned the wisdom of the whole tough exercise.

Robert Macintosh had also presented them with another difficulty. He had to confess that Little Dale Beck itself, the main watercourse, was causing him far greater headaches than its modest tributary, for the beck would swell after heavy rain. It was usually a steady, malleable stream, falling gently, almost benignly in its upper courses and then bubbling and surging over rocks and gravel beds, before sinking almost without trace in sedgy channels, only to seep back to the surface, to broaden out again into boggy basins that could be dangerous to the unsuspecting traveller. However, in flood, it had been known to uproot trees and move boulders; heavy rain was commonplace on Blea Moor. The beck had already washed away a week's work on the aqueduct after a thunderstorm. Robert watched it with trepidation and some disgust.

The beck's natural course was south and west, a major threat to the mainline that Robert was responsible for building. The beck simply had to disappear or be re-routed. The contract price agreed with Robert had contained an allowance for this work and the plans drawn up by the Midland's engineers showed a large culvert, stone lined, taking the beck 12 foot under the track. But after three weeks of digging in various places and at various depths, Robert had been forced to call in the Midland's engineers and explain that it just would not work. He could not afford to go on exploring and getting nowhere, wasting precious time and money.

He put it to them bluntly. 'There's a solid bedrock of black limestone in some places that splinters to the pickaxe, that's when pickaxe in't bouncing off and likely to tek someone's eye out on t'way past. And then everywhere else there's layers of boulder clay as is like cement when it's dry and like lumpy soup when it's wet. Slides like shit off t'shovel or sticks like glue. To be honest, whole area's a bit o' nightmare and in winter a should think we'll freeze to death or drown. Gentlemen, I could not be sure of any footings at all whir bleedin' culvert's supposed to go. And a've seen this beck in flood and it'll need a drain big enough to take a wagon and horses just to be sure of getting water away.' Robert had a graphic way with words that others were likely to remember, even whilst they smiled at him.

Mr Crossley, the chief engineer, reluctantly agreed with the analysis, if not the language, and asked what Robert suggested as a better alternative. They went further up the flank of the moor and stood on a low crag. Robert pointed out below them, where the beck emerged from a murky defile that was shrouded in bracken and a few stunted alders.

They could make out its course as it swung south and east, directly alongside and then under the wooden tramway that marked the line's eventual course, where even now they could see horses patiently pulling wagons of timber up towards the tunnel mouth. Robert then pointed south and west. 'Take a direct line down there. Blast a gap in that knoll an' line a broad culvert in the soft shale below the line. Put a proper stone bridge across, supported in the middle on two 6-foot piers.'

Broadly speaking, the plan was a good one and boldly conceived. It had been accepted and yet more funds were allocated to Robert for the new work. So that now, two months later, he was urging his men up the cold side of Blea Moor, where they were about to blast a wide gap to take the beck through the knoll that for thousands of years had forced it sideways in a wide arc. 'The bastard's got to go,' Robert told his men. They drilled and plugged with dynamite in four places, each at an angle to the others, and then primed the charges with powder fuses. For most of his men, working with dynamite was still new and somewhat untested. Robert supervised fussily, nervously, and he knew that this gamble might make or break him.

He had spent two days deciding where the charges would be laid and with how much explosive. His ganger was a foul-mouthed Lancastrian, who answered to the name of Tar Brush. He was tall and craggy, with a long black beard and black hair tied back in a knot at the nape of his neck. His normal style was to sit chewing tobacco and shouting instructions and obscenities at his men, but even he seemed on edge, or was reflecting the tension in Robert. Eventually, four holes were finally drilled and packed and fuses laid. Tar Brush ordered everyone to the other side of the knoll and he kept a lad with him to light the fuses.

The lad was Marty, just fourteen and a nephew that Tar Brush was looking after. Robert had refused to have him on the pay roll, as he was skinny, malnourished and looked uncoordinated. 'A'm not paying that piece of piss,' he had declared when Tar Brush had first brought him along. 'He's as weak as watter.' But Marty always had a smile, although it was a little twisted and leering for one so young, and he was always willing to run for beer or bread and he never complained, so the men had got used to him and even Robert found himself looking out for the lad. Now, it was the nimble Marty that scampered quickly from fuse to fuse and then scrambled down behind the rock face, where the men all stretched out and waited, affecting an indifference that only a few of them felt.

The ripple of explosions seemed to swell out of the earth, shaking the ground thunderously, and then it rolled away with charged menace deep though the strata and, after a pause, was thrown back from Ingleborough and Whernside. Soil and rock fragments were cast high into the air and began to fall in staccato patterns on their heads and shoulders as they hunched over. Dust swirled and eddied and then it began to sift more softly downwards. After a few moments, they all began to look up and some edged towards the crag to raise themselves, to see what had been achieved.

'Three bangs or four?' Tar Brush asked. 'A'm not sure.'

'Must o' been four,' answered a young navvy they usually called Poker Man, because he was always riddling the fire in the hut. 'They was all fused the same way and had the same length and they made a hell of a bang.'

Robert was anxious to see the effects of the explosion and he quickly poked his head over the rim of the rock face, but could not make out much in the dust that was still obscuring the sun. 'Bloody hell,' he said wryly, trying to raise a laugh, 'I think half of Yorkshire's been flattened.' He chewed tensely at his inner lip.

'A'm right glad a was 'ere for this 'un,' said Marty, his grin sliding into a lopsided grimace as it often did. He turned to his uncle. 'Shall a see how 't is?'

'No, you stay thir,' grunted Tar Brush. 'Give it a few more minutes.'

'Well, a'm off,' Robert exclaimed. 'Can't wait forever. Come with me, lad, if you want.'

Marty was on his feet and scampering up the side of the knoll before Tar Brush or Robert could even react. He had gone just 10 yards, when the fourth blast tore part of the hillside away in front of him, knocking him backwards, flipping him over like a disjointed rag doll and rolling him almost back to their feet. When they could get him turned over, he was whining softly like a dog and choking away the blood that was seeping from an ugly wound in his head and running down his face in a gory trickle; one leg was badly twisted and possibly broken. There was a flurry of activity as they sent for help, roughly bandaged his head and then laid him on some wooden spars covered with bracken and several coats, Tar Brush all the time solicitously holding the boy's hand and snapping out brisk commands around him. They all made to move off together when Robert, looking grim and agitated, called a halt.

'It don't need all of us,' he barked. 'There's still work to do 'ere. A'm not paying you to nursemaid a bloody kid.'

Tar Brush roared as if in pain himself, turned and stood, glaring at Robert, drawing himself up to his full height. 'There will be no more bloody work here today, Mr Macintosh, out o' respect for Marty.' He almost spat the words out with slow deliberation, his fists clenched and his brow red amongst his black hair. 'Ma nephew would still be in one piece if you had had a bit more patience. A'll hold you responsible for this an' you'll pay for it if he's badly hurt.' He looked around. 'Any buggering scum as works today will answer to me, in person, and a'll mek sure that they never work again, here or anywhere.'

There was muttering amongst the men, nods and glances, mainly of support for Tar Brush. They avoided looking at Robert, until he turned away and strode up the hillside on his own, cursing and slashing at the grass with his stick. He could sense them break out into muttering and complaints as he moved away.

It was an hour later that he reappeared, briskly seeking out Mr Ferguson's office to report that the blast had been successful and that the beck would soon be diverted. He made enquiries about Marty and learned that the doctor was still with him in one of the Jericho huts, but the bleeding had been halted. Tar Brush was sitting smoking on the steps of the hut when he got there. Men were passing by towards the tramway, talking quietly, glancing over at the silent figure outside the hut: news of an accident always travelled fast. There was the faint sound of sobbing and a low murmur of voices from within. Robert asked after the lad and offered to pay the doctor's bill. Tar Brush just grunted, staring off into the distance, glaring.

'A need to know that a've got all the men working tomorrow, without fail,' Robert blustered, not feeling as authoritative as he would have liked, but driven by a growing sense of urgency. He stepped towards Tar Brush and the ganger slowly rose to his feet. 'A'm the boss an' a pay you to keep the men working,' Robert continued, unsure where this line of assertion was heading. He sensed that some of the men moving past had come to a halt and were probably watching, but could not turn to look. He fixed his eyes on Tar Brush's dark pupils and set his face into a defiant stare.

'If Marty's right, then a'll be there and so will the men,' growled Tar Brush in a guttural snarl. 'If he's not, then you and a have things to sort out.'

Suddenly, Robert felt the energy drop from him as he briefly pictured the broken boy twisting on the hurdles they had used to make a stretcher. He sagged almost perceptibly and stepped back, his eyes still fixed on Tar Brush, his voice softer.

'A'm sorry for the lad,' he said. 'A hope as he pulls through. Got quite fond o' him, actually. A think we all did. If you don't mind, a'll step by later and see how 'e is.'

'Fair enough,' Tar Brush replied and turned away, resuming his solitary vigil.

Robert felt soiled, deflated by pressure and anxiety on a number of fronts, but not humbled. Feeling grey and isolated, he looked up to find James Taylor looking on with concern. Getting sympathy or concern from that quarter was more than Robert could cope with, so he scowled and hurried off.

Temptations
Late Summer 1870

Accidents were commonplace on any railway working. The traditional buck-navvy had a seeming disregard for personal or collective safety. To match the swagger in their dress – which resulted in holiday displays of top hats and dress coats, with velvet waistcoats sporting pearl buttons, set off by brightly patterned cravats – there went an almost reckless flourish of abandonment in their actions. They tore into hillsides in a flurry of pick and shovel, they ran wheelbarrows at wild angles down the faces of embankments and they drilled holes in rock alongside other drillings that might still contain gunpowder charges. They jumped into moving cages and off moving trains. Even in relaxation, they ran fell races and organised dogfights and badger hunts, but above all, they loved a good bare-knuckle fight and often wagered a week's wages on a local hero. Many of them gambled through the night, drank intemperately and fell asleep on the job. It was the norm, among many, to drink a gallon of beer a day and to eat 2 pounds of beef. They courted disaster as if she were "the sonsiest wench in the land" and they spat out contempt for any cautious, dithering approach in work, play or drinking.

Not all accidents, however, were acts of fate. There were times when one or more of the hands of men helped to shape events. The day before Marty was hurt, the little train had been coming late up to the tunnel huts, bringing food and provisions from the stores of Burgoyne and Cox, respectable Settle grocers who had moved with speed and determination to supply the growing camps with all that they needed. The train had carried a side of beef, several fat lambs, flour, sugar, butter, dried fruits and sacks of potatoes, as well as several barrels of beer and some flagons of spirits. The engine had laboured up the tramway's weaving inclines and had then rolled and bounced recklessly down towards Little Beck, until it had hit a sudden and unexpected dip.

It had then twisted off the rails, clattering heavily earthwards, the driver flinging himself acrobatically onto some well-placed piles of bracken and turf, clear of the churning engine with its burning coals and blasts of steam that shot with menace high into the air. He had rolled away and then raised himself cautiously to see a dozen men suddenly appear from behind a stone wall and silently set about clearing the train. They had a horse and cart at the ready. He watched and waited. They wore scarves around their faces and pulled their hats down low. He had stood up slowly and then gave them a wave to signal that he was safe, before setting off to walk back and report the accident that he claimed must have been caused by a sudden subsidence in the ground and a broken rail. By the time others returned with him, there was not a scrap of food anywhere, even the animal carcasses had simply disappeared. Burgoyne and Cox learned a hard lesson, whilst at many huts they ate and drank their fill, the train driver toasted at many a turn as their hero of the hour.

This prevailing mood of celebration perhaps helped many to quickly forget about the accident to Marty. In any case, as accidents went, and by their standards, the blow to Marty was a modest event. He soon recovered and was seen around the huts with a grey bandage round his head and a tooth missing in his permanent grin, giving him even more of a ghoulish, leering look. As it turned out, the leg was twisted and sore but not broken and he limped gamely for a good while. He bore no grievance towards Robert, but his uncle, the foreman-ganger, continued a surly and studied hostility: he now sat back when the men grumbled about their lot and took no action to stop their whining or to support their boss. Discipline was in danger of becoming lax and Robert struggled to exert his authority. Tar Brush and he only exchanged the minimum of words necessary to arrange the work in the northern section. The weather was poor and local men, tempted in the spring by the high wages, began to drift back to the farms and the smallholdings to help with the harvest. Few returned. Robert saw what was left of Tar Brush's hardened navvies. They looked at him sourly, as if he were decayed. He felt drained, his anxiety a clinging layer, like a damp blanket across his shoulders. He became a more sullen and introspective figure.

Even from a distance, Emily saw and heard most of what was going on. She and Hetty had developed a modest network of connections, mainly through their women customers at the camps. At times, they now received visitors at the farm, where gossip and news were the colourful currency of many an exchange. The young farmer's wife and her maid listened, wide-eyed and fascinated. They spoke sometimes of how dull life would be when the building work stopped and the valley emptied. They smelled danger and it was alive and novel for them. They sensed a community loosely held together in fear, greed and bravado. Hetty was shy of it; Emily was greedy and wanted to be amongst it.

The source of the news that they eagerly sought was certainly not that of James Taylor, who continued to keep his counsel around the farm and was wary of Robert's dark looks and brooding manner. Nevertheless, James had begun to come out of himself. He had a more knowing look and manner these days, almost a swagger at times, and Emily wondered if James had perhaps been with one of the looser women at Batty Green. It was well known that there were some there that provided personal service to the navvies and to any others that would pay. James had taken to engaging in regular teasing of Hetty, whilst treating Emily more and more like an elevated but homely goddess: it seemed to be his way of handling the emotional climate that the two women of the farm had wrapped about him since he had arrived. Having separated the two women into such distinct positions, he seemed to relish manipulating both of them. But he did not get it all his own way.

With Hetty, he regularly invented young men that he claimed were waiting at the gate or were asking him questions about her at the works or at the Hill Inn, where he sometimes played cards or dominoes in the evenings. She coloured and pretended not to hear or believe, but her pillow was sometimes wet with tears and her mood could become acrid and flighty. One day, she dropped soup down his front and Emily, finding Hetty in excitable tears that soon turned to laughter, suspected that it was premeditated. Emily spoke to James and told him not to break the girl's heart. He listened seriously and said, with a colder look in his blue-grey eyes that was in contrast to his trembling smile, 'It's alright for others to break hearts, I believe.' He promised to behave, but within days it was Hetty that was angling for attention and the sparring began again. George laughed and said nothing meaningful, Robert scowled in irritation and Emily dithered.

And all this time, whilst stoking the fever of Hetty's adolescent obsession, James was moving himself closer to Emily and to a declaration of love. She knew this, for he was already bringing discrete gifts for her, being careful to leave them when neither George nor Hetty was around. Once, it was a small pot of primroses that she found on the kitchen table. Then a new cushion appeared on the seat of her pony cart. In her accounts book, pressed flowers would appear and under her pillow one day there was a slim volume of poetry. He brushed against her sometimes in doorways, with fractionally too much weight, so that her breast or her hips touched him.

And then one evening, as night shut out the valley, whilst undressing alone in the lamplight, she thought she heard a faint sound from outside, the lightest scrape of boot on stone and the movement of a gorse bush snagging on something. She paused and stared at the window. She had pulled the curtains herself, over an hour before. Yet, now she saw that there was the slimmest gap in them. Outside, at the rear of the house, the ground rose quickly. An observer who carefully positioned himself would be almost on the same level as her. The occasional sheep had been known to peer myopically in at her, but now she suddenly felt sure that she had a new audience.

She thought about it and decided it must be James. He had left the meal table first; had he sneaked up here to part the curtains slightly himself, to provide this chance to watch her prepare for bed? George had gone to the Hill Inn and Hetty was in the kitchen minding the bread; Emily could hear her singing. She was sure that she was being watched and glared outwards. Why was she sure? Had he moved deliberately to let her know that he was there? Was it a challenge, a tease, a provocation? The whole business enraged her, but it inflamed her, too. Well, if he wanted a show, then she would give him one: this was her bedroom and she was free to act as she wished. But she trembled at the thought. She unpinned her black hair and shook it free slowly and deliberately, washing the waves of air over her shoulders, steeling herself. She then placed herself carefully, opposite the gap in the curtains, turned her back to the window and slowly removed each item of clothing, down to her shift, throwing each one carelessly onto the bed beside her as if glad to be free of it.

As she peeled off each clumsy layer she felt more and more wanton, adventurous and exhilarated; stroking her limbs, flexing her arms, lifting each foot onto a chair and rolling down her stockings with slow, lascivious care. She warmed to her performance, brightening, flushing, moistening. At last, she stood in her thin shift, the material clinging to her as she took deep breaths and swayed her hips from side to side. She was quite relaxed and was feeling more in control now that most of her clothes were off. She knew her own body, it had always pleased her, and she knew that it was still desirable, especially in the softening glow of a bedroom lamp. The cool evening air soothed her skin and she savoured the moment, bringing her hands up to slowly stroke her breasts; then running her fingers over her stomach and entangling them in her wiry pubic hair. But still she did not turn. He would have to guess where her hands went. She wanted to provoke him, but she also wanted to startle him and to make it clear who was in control of this showpiece.

Finally, she turned and reached down for the hem of her shift as if to lift it over her head, but instead she stepped briskly forwards towards the lamp and in one quick movement she snuffed the wick, dropped onto all fours and scurried to the window, yanking back the curtains, keeping her own body beneath the level of the sill. She banged on the glass several times and shouted to him to go away. In the dim evening light she saw a figure stumble clumsily and flounder ineptly around the corner of the field. She recognised James and slumped down breathlessly and giggled. But she slept badly, whilst George snored fitfully beside her.

At breakfast he looked crushed, but he managed a smile. He would not make eye contact after that and he ate little and spoke less. Her triumph was short-lived and it piqued her. As she saw him leave her mood sank even further and a tear threatened her cheek, but she knew that she now had to stop this before it got any further out of hand. As she worked around the farm that day she prepared a speech and waited for him at the gate that evening, but he did not come. She returned thoughtfully to her supper, cross with herself, cross with James, cross with everything. Why had she allowed this to develop? What was it in her that she should seem to need the attentions of this young man? Was she leading him on? Yet, he seemed to be in control now as much as her.

She felt misplaced. She was a married woman, but was allowing him to construct romantic, fervent dreams of her and it could only end in tears or tragedy. But she did enjoy a lot of it. Some of its sweetness and innocence charmed her; it flattered her and the hint of lust made her feel desirable. It was hard to put that behind her. When and where would it come again? She felt it would not come from George. He no longer chased her around the farm in skittish high spirits, pinning her to a wall or roughly taking her in the barn, as he had more than once in their early-married days.

Her heart felt burdened. She was childless still and every month she felt ashamed and inadequate. She saw the first bloody smears as a judgement on her, a failing. Her youth and vigour should have brought a child out of passion; at least, that was what she had believed would happen when she was first married. She had believed that if she gave herself fully to George and loved him passionately, then the seeds would be sown and the children would come. Now, the repeated failure brought an ashy emptiness: colours had faded, tastes had palled, gravity now pulled at her and she sometimes felt a chill of loneliness that was threatening. A child would change all that. But where was it to come from?

Perhaps she was jealous of Hetty? But what exactly did she want? When she was faced with the question she panicked. And beneath it all, hardly acknowledged, was the fear that she would now be forever barren and therefore isolated and alone. James was just the shadow of a dream that she still clung to, a dream of her future. Otherwise, what was it all for? Yet, she could not disentangle these strands. To get a child, did she need another man? Or was it much simpler? Was she just a whore at heart and was this all just self-delusion?

She was not good at introspection: she preferred to ride life's currents with an easy bridle and until recently, until the railway came, she thought she knew where she was going and what she wanted. But now she had seen new ways of moving life on, new patterns that others shaped their lives into, different choices made or chances seized, and her limited boundaries seemed fragile and restrictive. She could not be just as her mother had been or like the women on the neighbouring farms, whom she sometimes admired and sometimes despised.

She had to make herself face these thoughts and drag them out, step by step. As she walked the fields, checking the sheep, she would stop to stare at the drystone walls as if the answer was there, if she just looked hard enough. Or when slowly plodding up to Ribblehead with her horse and cart she would silently address the back of Milly's head. It was more of that old "talking to the trees". Restless uncertainty was clouding her thoughts, dragging her down. She struggled to clear herself, like trying to throw off thistle burrs. She argued with herself. Why am I like this? Why can't I work out what I really want? Why can't I be content? She had more than most women could ever dream of. But even as she said it she wanted to shout out loud: But it's not enough! Not for me. And I don't care a jot how I do it, but I will have my day. And soon, before I lose the will and the strength and just give up. I am not ready for the rocking chair. I won't yield. I won't fold. No, that time is not yet. I want what I want. All I want is what most women want and most women get. Why shouldn't I? Who would dare to stop me?

All the time she knew that when the railway was built she would be drawn back to older, more regulated rhythms and expectations. Just now, the tumult of shifting energy unsettled her, as if the very disturbances of the raw earth set free a force that could undermine life's familiar forms. But, in time, in the rural north, that force would be caged again. And in this repeating pattern, winding round daily, the unanswered questions fluttered on, like the light gossamer that the wind sometimes flicked and filtered through the afternoon air, strewing it over the fields. Then an incident occurred that complicated her thinking still further.

Intruder
Autumn 1870

Late one afternoon, Emily returned alone from Batty Green in heavy rain. Hetty had stayed behind with a friend and would come on later. Emily was wrapped in an old gaberdine and she had placed an oilcloth over her head and shoulders. She sat, hunched and disconsolate, the rain chafing her hands and beginning to gather in her hair and creep callously down her neck. The wind was unfriendly, from the north, sharply tattooing exposed skin and giving an insistent early portent of winter. She was grumpy and tired and as she turned off the road, down the track that ran for a mile across the valley floor, the wind came round onto her right side, so she turned her head away, staring down towards Twistleton Scar, its rugged limestone outcrops now bleary grey in the rain.

In the foreground of her view, out on the edge of Four Stones Rigg and at the top of a slowly rising field, they had an out-barn for winter stock. A dozen cattle would be penned there through the darkest days of the year, fed and watered twice a day. George and one of the men had recently begun to prepare it by filling it with hay and squinting through the rain it looked to her as if one of the barn doors had been left partly open. Staring harder to be sure of her facts, she was surprised to see a small child run out from inside and appear to jump in a puddle and run back in again. She reined in the horse and sat still to watch for a moment. Shortly afterwards, she saw the child do the same again, this time staying out to stamp, bare-legged, in a few puddles in the muddy entrance, until a young man came out and roughly pulled the child inside, closing the door behind him. Emily was annoyed.

For time immemorial, barns like this had been used as temporary shelters, but since the coming of the railway local farmers had been forced to lock and bolt them, as many of the navvies were only too willing to sleep out, especially in the summer, to save themselves a week's rent. And they liked to smoke and look about for a chicken or a few bits from the kitchen garden to eke out their meal. Now, Emily could see that someone had quickly taken advantage of the unlocked door and, moreover, they had a child with them. She moved on to the gate, tethered the horse and walked slowly up the field to tell them they must leave in the morning. She was in no mood for more problems.

The door was again half open when she got there and she pulled it back to let the grey, watery light into the old building. The barn was roughly built on two levels, with the hay stored above and the ground floor open and dirty underfoot, where the animals could be sheltered in the worst weather. But here, George had built a simple shippon along one side for milking or isolating stock. At a glance, Emily could see that the hayloft was more than half full. Hayricks, fragrant and full, were stacked high to the back wall and motes of dust swam crazily in the light that shot through the door. What Emily also noticed at once was that the first pen in the shippon had been made comfortable with a thick layer of fresh hay. Stepping closer, she found herself looking down on the little boy, who was sitting disconsolately on the floor. He was dressed very shabbily and he looked dirty, tired and badly nourished.

'Hello,' she said.

There was no response, just a dull stare from cold blue eyes and a mouth sagging open. The boy twitched. Emily was about to turn away, when there was the scrape of boot against floor and from the second pen a man suddenly arose and stared over the partition at her. He was an old man, quite tall and severe, with white hair sticking up, a narrow, sickly face and a straggly grey beard that had a few wisps of hay stuck to it. He was wearing a dirty collarless shirt that might have been white once. Oddest of all, he had no teeth, so that when he suddenly broke into a broad and sunny smile, as if greeting a long-lost friend, it shocked her to see his wide red mouth and bare gums and she almost stepped backwards.

'You can't stay here, mister,' Emily began. 'This is our barn and we need to use it.'

Her words brought no response: they sounded weak and she felt herself not only unkind, but also powerless. Still no one spoke, but the strange pair watched her and she began to feel uneasy. She hesitated and then she registered a noise and movement behind her and swung round to find a sturdy, dark-faced man of more than middle age just coming through the doorway, a large knife in one hand and lengths of wire and some pegs in the other. Clearly, he had been setting snares for rabbits. He was wet through, mud was splattered over his heavy grey shirt and dark trousers and water dripped from his low black hat, running down his bare arms. The light was behind him, but she could see enough of his face to feel concerned: he was grim and sullen-looking, his features fixed in a scowl that found its darkest concentration in the blue-black of his eyes and narrowed his brow into lines that might have been scored into his flesh. He waved the knife at her, but did not speak. With a glance around and with slow, deliberate movements, he moved back to place himself within the doorway, his feet wide apart. It was a calculated, threatening move. Emily began to panic. She felt very alone.

A few seconds of ominous silence stretched painfully outwards and it was now that she realised how tired and overwhelmed she felt. The light was poorer because of the dark form in the doorway, but her eyes were adjusting and with a desperate breathlessness she scanned the barn for another way out or means of defence, but could see nothing.

Once more, there was movement behind her. She glanced round to see that the child had stood up and moved forwards, as if to watch: the old man was still grinning absurdly over the top of the stall. The space around her seemed to be contracting. Still she faced the man with the knife, but the rustling behind her was alarming. She knew she had to exert some control and so raised her voice, speaking slowly as if they were deaf or mindless.

'We own this land and we own this barn. My husband is George Wright and he'll not let you stay here.' There was a low giggle from behind her. She whipped her head round and found her attention transfixed by the sight of the old toothless man now laughing in a strange, bubbling manner and pointing at her, or was it behind her?

She switched her gaze rapidly back to the door and found to her astonishment that the menacing man with the knife had stepped aside and a younger man now stood there. He was dressed in a neat rusty-black coat, buttoned up to the chin. He had a rather square, weather-beaten face, with the most piercing blue eyes and a dark beard: yet, the face was trim and neat, illuminated by a boyishly sweet smile that showed fine white teeth and a mobile pink tongue that he ran over his lips as if he were tasting the air. His tall black hat dripped onto his shoulders and he lifted it gracefully and shook his long dark hair, before bowing very formally to her. When he spoke she was astonished to hear a soft, musical voice, with a lilting Irish accent.

'Mrs Wright, please allow me to introduce myself. My name is Dermot O'Reardon. And will you please excuse the lack of greeting from t'other members o' my family. I know dat they are maybe after looking a little wild, but I can assure you that they mean no harm. The truth is dat the old man there don't speak the English so well, neither does the wee lad, and my older brother here, well, he looks alarming, but he wouldn't hurt a beautiful lady like yourself. If you would be so kind as to step this way, I will explain what we are about here and when we will be away from your property, which I assure you, Mrs Wright, we will not damage in any way at all.'

Relief flooded through Emily with rough energy and seemed to melt her from the inside. She felt the blood pour back, beating in waves into her face and neck. The young man's handsome features, his soft manner and warm smile touched her heart and left her gasping and bewildered at the sudden change in her fortune. He held out a hand and she rested tremulous fingers lightly on his. He smiled all the while and talked soothingly as he gently led her out through the door, though her legs felt like liquid. Then, without breaking contact, he dipped his shoulder in a quick movement that shook her afresh and reached behind the door to retrieve an old umbrella, which he opened and raised above her, as if she were a duchess. With slow, dreamlike steps, they walked across the field, keeping close to avoid the rain that still thrashed across the valley in spurts. All the time he continued to talk in a warm, musical flow that washed around her and she held his wrist, moving slowly and pensively.

Afterwards, she could not recall the exact words that he had used, but her flesh tingled at the thought and sound, as if these were moving still inside her. He told her something about a family crisis and having to come to rescue the family, as his brother's wife had died in childbirth in Dentdale. And how his brother, in his grief, had got into a fight and they had been forced to run. And how they would only stay the one night, if she could find it in her heart to let them. He also told her that the child was hungry and could she spare any small things for them? He would be so grateful and said that he would watch for her and wait for her, all night if necessary. And would she, he asked, walk up later and let him know how things stood? She did not say no and he helped her into the cart and stood, radiant in his smile, and watched her leave.

As she meandered the last half-mile in a warm daze she felt confused and fragile with excitement. She resolved not to tell George about these visitors and without further analysis she decided that yes, she would stroll up the lane later, with a loaf of bread and some milk for the child. But it was not the face and voice of the child that was imprinted upon her inner self; it was Dermot O'Reardon's form, his touch and the caressing sway of his voice. She felt as if she had been subtly and spicily licked.

She focused on making and serving their meal, though she ate little herself, but to her great annoyance the rain got dramatically heavier as the evening drew on and the wind picked up strongly. She was thwarted. She could think of no excuse to go out on such a night. It was impossible. She tried to work this message through to the restless demons that had lodged low in her spine and pelvis, but she was driven to pace and fidget nevertheless.

Then, late in the evening, in the rain-filled squally dark, George heard barking outside. Stepping into the rain, he swung a lantern around and glimpsed a squat, dark-haired stranger in the yard, shouted at him to be off and then snatched up a pitchfork and ran at him. The stranger shifted rapidly away, keeping to the shadows. George pursued him up the yard, shouting all the while, trying to drive at him with the fork, his dogs snapping at the man's heels. But just as George was gaining on the intruder, another figure jumped out from behind a wall and shouted something. George swerved and swung the fork, but he slithered on the greasy cobbles and this second younger and slighter man was able to knock him off balance. In an instant, the first man had turned and grabbed the stem of the fork and had twisted George sideways, so that he slid and then fell awkwardly backwards, shouting out in pain as he hit the corner of the barn, jarring against the rough, wet stone. He crumpled. The man then kicked him several times, until the younger man called him off. The accents were Irish.

The intruders were never caught, but Emily was convinced that it had been Dermot and his brother. She was relieved that it was no worse and was shocked at how close she might have come to some sort of disaster. Nevertheless, with a selfish perversity that she could see but not control, she nursed a private and bitter disappointment. She brooded on what might have been and what might have become of her: Dermot, coming to her, wet from the dark, slim and vibrant, caressing and intriguing her, like a dark and subtle snake. She could not let go of the hypnotic thought of him.

George had injured his back in the fall and he had to be carried back to the farmhouse. She tended her husband in a confusion of anguish and remorse, mingled with self-contempt. Her distress, guilt and uncertainty left her miserable, as if her wayward thoughts and desires had conjured this injury. Yet, she also felt a faint subdued anger at George for coming off worse, though she knew this was unjust. He would recover, the doctor said, and he would regain most of his mobility. But how long would it take, wondered Emily. And could she remain patient? She felt shackled once more.

Another Family
Winter 1870

That winter brought hardship and trouble for many at Batty Green and the huts beyond. A wet autumn passed suddenly into a cold, hard early winter of sleet, snow and biting cold winds, leaving casualties in its wake.

Robert Macintosh was forced to abandon his subcontract, admitting almost with relief that he could not bring in the work on time at the agreed price. The whole of Contract No 1 was proving difficult to manage and the main contractor Mr Ashwell was also considering quitting, handing the work back to the Midland, who would manage it themselves. Mr Ashwell was generous to Robert and they let him leave with a little cash and they also found him a supervisory job at the brickworks at Batty Green. Robert left the farm and moved into one of the huts, saying little, nursing the remnants of his pride. On his last visit to the farm he had taken Emily aside when George was resting and had spoken to her with such a gentle, wry, almost defeated tone that she had cried when he left.

'You've been a kind of inspiration to me this last year and a don't like leaving you, lass. When a came here a thought this was a real chance for me to make some money, move up a bit an' start to behave a bit properly. A've bin wild an' not known much o' livin' wi' decent folks afore this. A know as a'm not right easy to tek at times, but you an' Mr Wright have not teken offence or always believed a was serious, which is just as well. And a've tried to act as a thought you would want me to, here and up at the works.' He paused as if unsure whether to go on or how to compose his thoughts and feelings. He seemed older, hesitant, a slight tremble in his scarred workman's hands, a moist touch to his deep-set eyes. She waited, a little anxious as to what might be coming. Then he reached over and took her hand.

'A've thought o' you as a kind of daughter or perhaps the kind o daughter a would have bin proud to 'ave. There's bin many a time a've bin about to shout or curse at someone, or throw a spade at 'em, an' a've thought, no: Mrs Wright – Emily, o' course, I think o' you by that name – would be put out to see me like this and so a've tried to be more patient. Not that it's done me a power o' good, like, cos I came in wi' nearly 200 pounds in me pocket, saved over a few years that were, an' now a'm back to labouring an' startin' all over again. But a'll do it, lass, an' when a'm on ma feet again an' can see me way clear to a more settled life, a'll call here again, if a may, an' pass time o' day with you an' Mr Wright.' He suddenly stopped and, pulling himself away, he managed a nod and a wry smile and left.

With Robert gone, Emily and George paused to consider what to do with the room that Robert had shared with James. They had built it in something of a hurry, alongside their parlour, a good size but with no separate entrance and only on the ground floor, so it was inconvenient as a long-term addition. They now discussed building a room above and putting in a staircase and lobby, with a little scullery and outhouse at the far end to give it privacy. Then they could take in a family in the future, when James left. As if by unspoken agreement, they now avoided talk of how to adapt their house for children. James was consulted and he agreed that the idea made sense, even offering to draw up the plans for them. He was willing to move for a while to a little cottage just up the lane, which George had bought as a derelict shell and had now made snug and habitable. James would still come to them for his meals. Stonemasons were quickly on site and George was able to supervise, now walking a little and bored with the farm kitchen.

Emily found herself busier than ever, running the farm, preparing her market cart, which now went twice a week to Batty Green, and supervising the farmhands, as well as Hetty and now Mary, another girl whom they had brought in to help. She also nursed George and prayed with fervour for his full recovery as winter gripped the valley and Christmas approached.

Amongst the regulars who bought from her yellow cart was Ethel, the partner to Black Jack. A bond had been forged in those early days following the death of the infant Hetty, and Ethel, who was with child again, usually stopped to chat, the children invariably looking for a treat of some kind. Georgie was still a stern and independent youngster, with dark eyes and a quick resentment if he thought he was missing out on something. Laura was clinging and almost silent, usually sucking her thumb and sniffling away a cold. As a bleak December began, Emily and Hetty were surprised one week to find that Ethel and the children had missed the normal Saturday market. It was getting dark and they were just harnessing the horse to leave, when a young navvy, not known to them, hurried through the crowd and called for them to wait. He explained that Black Jack had been injured in a fall of rock at a cutting that morning and that Ethel had rushed off to collect him and send for the doctor. Apparently, he may have broken an arm and he had certainly crushed his foot, but they did not know the full extent of the injury. He was refusing to go to hospital, but was back in his hut, where the doctor was treating him. Ethel was begging for Emily to call and see her; the young navvy emphasised how anxious she was. Emily looked at the rapidly darkening sky and sent back the message that she would call at noon on the following day and then left with Hetty. It would be her first visit to one of the huts.

It rained through the night and the next day the mud was thickly glutinous, the ways across Batty Moss mired with foul water and the air thick with a swirling mist that swept the odours of human and animal waste into a miasma, wreathed with coal and wood smoke. The two women picked their way across the Moss, lifting their skirts as best they could above the worst of the filth, and forced to kick away at dogs that splashed around them. On a little piece of rising ground, they found the hut that they were looking for. It was known as the Garden Room, the words ornately painted on a flowery name board that showed roses and lilies floating in grey soil. Georgie was sitting in a crude porch, outside a central doorway, waiting for them: a lurcher pup in his lap. He ran in screaming, 'Ma! Ma! They're here, Ma.'

Ethel stepped briskly to the door, as if she had been waiting just inside, and she urged them in with words of kindness, gratitude and distress. They tried to calm her.

The hut, which was home to two families and several lodgers, was roughly divided in half. It was fashioned to provide a living space at either end, each with a stove, table and some benches and chairs. In the middle were a series of crudely partitioned areas, some with beds and some with mattresses on the floor; one was subdivided by an improvised curtain made of old blankets roughly stitched together. On one mattress, they glimpsed two men asleep in their working clothes, one still with his boots on. It was Sunday. Ethel whispered that the men had been drinking through most of Saturday, but they were mostly well behaved. The air was sticky and fetid, fusty with body and animal odour and fumes of stale beer and beef stew.

At Ethel's end of the hut there was evidence that she had tried to make it homely. There were pictures on the walls, cut from magazines. Some dried flowers were in a vase: a Bible, a child's slate and a rag doll were on the small table near the stove. A kettle swung over the fire and a large pot was bubbling groggily. Emily and Hetty were invited to sit and Ethel bustled around offering them tea, which they were pleased to accept. They soon grasped the reasons for Ethel's anxiety.

Black Jack was apparently asleep: Ethel gestured to the first of the partitioned spaces. Emily registered that the whole family must sleep there. The two lodgers that they had seen on the mattress were in the next room, if you could call it that, separated only by a thin pine panel. Ethel explained that she cooked, cleaned and washed for them all and the lodgers paid her each week. 'Not but they're greedy and mean sorts,' she said. 'Forever moaning about gettin' their money's worth. If it wasn't that they're afeared o' Black Jack, I'm sure they'd try to take advantage o' me.' It was not a boast, but a weary and bitter reflection, revealing her fears. 'Look what a've to do to keep peace,' she said. She showed her visitors how the pieces of beef, stewing slowly in the pot, were attached by string to a peg above the stove. 'Each has their own peg. We have the big one, Birmingham Joe has the small peg and Adam has the metal one. That way they can have a cut of their own meat and no arguments.'

She told them of her life there and her worries now that Black Jack had several injuries, including a broken arm. The child was due in a few weeks and Black Jack would not be able to work for several months. They had a few savings, the Sick Club would pay them something and the other navvies would help with a few shillings, she had no doubt of that.

'But there's the rent and the food. Black Jack's a good man, but he's a devil when he's not well. So I worry for the bairns, for Georgie and Laura, poor mites.' She looked up imploringly. 'Would you take them for me, when the child comes, just for a few weeks, till I get mesel back on ma feet? I know as how you always seem keen to have the little ones at the farm when I bring them and I thought you might want to …' She came to a clumsy halt. Emily was suddenly aware that Ethel must have picked up on her childlessness and the tensions that it evoked. She was startled and a silence developed that she felt was centred on her. She almost panicked.

In the end, Emily gave no definite answer, but promised to talk to George and return in a day or so. Ethel seemed pleased and they relaxed with chat and tea, whilst Hetty played quietly with Georgie and the puppy and Laura slept in an old rocking chair. Emily savoured the calm domestic harmony. She realised that she liked Ethel, who had a warm heart, even if her judgement might be questioned at times. The smoky hut seemed to settle into a quiet hum, almost hypnotic or somnambulistic, moving to the rising and falling rhythms of the breathing of the sleeping men and the quiet talk of the women, backed by the hiss of the simmering pots and the low crackle of the firewood. Outside, the rain fell.

The tranquillity was broken by the return of the two women who kept the other half of the hut. They were mother and daughter: Mavis and Agnes. The mother was a large, brassy woman with no teeth, her mouth a mobile pink hole in the sagging mass of her face: she gaped and wheezed heavily, before slumping beside her cold stove. She wore a greasy black gown with a red shawl, had a bottle in one hand and clutched a small boy in the other. The younger woman was Agnes. She was slim by comparison, but had a snub nose and similar coppery burnish to her skin and hair. She affected a certain sophistication, sometimes sang romantic ballads at the Railway Inn or the Glee Club and was keen to point out that she had been married to "her Arthur" in a church in Bradford and that he was an "ostler". Other navvies, particularly Black Jack, sneered at her pretensions.

'He's got a couple of old 'osses and a rickety cart. He'll fetch and carry owt, but mostly it's old furniture, sacks of tatties and jars o' stuff as he teks to many a hut round here and over to Dent. If the polis catch 'im trading anything what he shouldn't, well, she'll soon forget the ostler nonsense and find some other fool to keep her in her fancy ways.'

The two women were not popular: one a drunkard and the other who felt herself wasted where she was and who dreamt of a life more in keeping with the themes of her sentimental songs. She felt she deserved altogether a more gracious treatment. Clearly, Ethel was uncomfortable with them. She thought Mavis capable of lying and stirring trouble; she had once suggested that Black Jack was watching the women whilst they washed. It had taken some persuasion to get Black Jack not to throw them bodily out of the hut. She thought Agnes a neglectful mother, very often leaving her little boy in the haphazard care of her hard-drinking mother.

Emily felt the pressure of the place and the difficulty of raising children in such a home. Registering that the rain had stopped, but still preoccupied with what she should do, she prepared to take her leave and asked Hetty to take Georgie out to play hide-and-seek between the huts, whilst the older women woke Laura and began their farewells. The increased noise and movement had also woken the sleepers. There was cursing and growling from behind the thin walls and the sound of boots clattering to the ground. Birmingham Joe stumbled out and made for the door, his brain still fuddled with beery sleep, his bladder blazing with pressure. He stopped just a few feet from the hut and urinated noisily and copiously onto the muddy earth, just as Hetty skittered round the corner and slid to an ungainly halt, urine splashing the edge of her gown. She shrieked, more in anger than distress. The navvy made no move to cover himself or to stop the torrent, but he raised his hat nonchalantly, belched and made an ungainly bow. Hetty turned with a flounce and called over her shoulder, 'A true gentleman would have introduced himself properly.' The women laughed over the story all the way home.

George looked sternly at Emily when she explained Ethel's situation and request. It was late in the evening and they were alone in the farm kitchen, with an icy rain beating against their door. He was silent for a few minutes and stood to gather his thoughts, moving away from her and then turning his face aside. 'We have no children of our own,' he began as if addressing the wall and rather formally. 'We have the space here and it would be a Christian and charitable act.' Then he turned and her heart was contracted in sorrow as she saw the struggle in him. 'But I want us to be a family, with you as the heart of it, as you deserve. If it can't be our child, perhaps we could take another, even if just for a while ...' he paused and gave a rather bitter snigger, 'but I don't know if that is real charity or just us playing at the happy family we can never be.'

She felt her eyes swimming and her voice grainy with emotion. 'Don't say that, George.' She came up to him, but he turned again. Uncertain how to cope, she wound her arms round him from behind, pulling herself close, breathing in the musty odour of his damp fustian jacket. 'A've not given up hope of us own child an' nor should tha. With some couples it takes years, tha knows that. If tha keeps loving me, we'll be alright. And now that your back's on t'mend, you know ... we should get back to tryin'. That's what a want.' She felt a shudder go through him. Still he did not relent, but she felt the tremors of tension pass through him and he half turned his head towards her. She went on as positively as she could. 'And this is not us playing at anything. A like this family. They are decent folk trying to do what's right an' we can help them, and maybe they can help us.' She brightened as an idea came to her and she tugged him round to face her.

'Tha knows a don't think much to this new girl Mary. She'll never be much use to us. Has to be told simplest things a dozen times and eats more than she's worth. When Ethel has had t'baby, perhaps she could take on Mary's work. Maybe Black Jack can do some things around the farm? It will be a help while you are still not fully fit to work. Why don't we offer them that little cottage where James is? After their hut it will be like a little palace. And when Black Jack is better he can go back to the works and we can decide then if the family stays here or ...'

'Not so fast,' George interrupted with a smile, turning fully towards her, his eyes also clammy with tears. 'Th'art like one o' them little steam engines when tha gets hold of an idea or two. Teks some energy just to keep up with thee an' sometimes it looks like tha could come right off rails.' He leaned forwards and kissed her passionately on the mouth, bearing down on her, demanding.

She felt the full force of his need and was willing to answer it, but broke off to mutter, 'A take it that was a yes, then?'

'Tha knows just how to get thy own way.' He laughed. 'Now, let's go to bed. And tha mek damn sure tha don't bugger my back again with thy, what did tha call it? Trying?'

Over the next two weeks it was all put in place and with surprising ease. James asked to stay at the cottage and it suited Emily to put some distance between them, reducing the uncomfortable tension, which neither had the will to dissipate. Black Jack and his family were able to move into the new rooms attached to the farmhouse, which were just finished. The only sticking point was Black Jack himself, whose pride was founded on self-belief as the provider for his family. He took some time to come round to the idea, but could see how it would be better for all of them. He resolved his thoughts, with Ethel's help, and rehearsed a little speech that he made when he came to see the farm and the rooms that might be theirs. He coughed and hesitated, and then spoke with a stiff dignity, as if addressing a large gathering.

'A'll not tek charity,' he declared. 'A'll work as best a can to cover the rent, but we'll manage for us own food. A don't know as a understand much o' farming, like, but I'll work where I can, if you'll give me chance, an' so will Ethel. An' when a can get meself back to navvyin', I'll pay me way here an' not be a burden to ya. So, if you'll agree wi' me working round here, and Ethel and Georgie can do a bit an' all, then we'll take your offer kindly and a'm sure you'll not regret it at all.' They all smiled and Emily clapped with pleasure. 'Oh, an' another thing,' he went on with some embarrassment. 'Just call me Jack while a'm 'ere, if you don't mind. Black Jack's all very well when a'm swinging a pick, but it's Jack down 'ere.'

The baby came a few days before Christmas and Jack proudly announced that she would be called Angel. When the child thrived she was like a Christmas gift that lifted all their hearts. Emily often took the child and tended to her with some wonder. Her joy was tinged with brief flashes of bitterness. She now felt less of a woman than Ethel, less human, almost fraudulent. Neither could she escape the persistent thought that it was her fault. Others had children, but she did not, and it galled her. Yet, self-pity was not a powerful frailty with her as it is with some who are the focal point of their own universe, and for the most part she accepted her role as a blessing and a pathway to understanding. Despite her rural background, she had never lived in a house with infants.

And so began a brief period that they would all look back on later as rich in memories of harmony and union. Jack was a squat, powerful man and a look of intense concentration often settled on his brows, only to elide into a spontaneous smile as understanding came to him or as he saw a job through. Even with one arm strapped up, he was able to lift weights that two men normally handled. He could lift a gate off its hinges with one hand and once used the same one-handed technique to wrestle a frisky bullock to a halt by twisting its horns. He and George became a unique and sometimes comical partnership that brought the farmer out of George as he marshalled and instructed the navvy; a man whose great energy was not always matched with discretion. One had a stiff back and could not bend; the other hobbled and had one usable arm. They sometimes had to call out Arthur, their morose farmhand, or one of the women, just to help them harness a lively horse. They tripped over each other, laughed at their ordeals and shifted as best they could. And where they went little Georgie often followed.

Sometimes, when George needed to rest, he sat on a stone bench outside the shippon and Georgie came and sat beside him and chattered on, in which they would seriously discuss where worms came from or why cows gave milk. With his father, Georgie would work in almost silent imitation and great intensity, matching the serious commitment that his father showed, knowing that this was the perfect model of adult behaviour.

The women, too, found solace and companionship in a relationship that was built in the farm kitchen and spread outwards in increasing circles, as if following ripples of water. Ethel loved to cook, but that was not enough for her and when the sulky Mary was sent back to Ingleton, Ethel soon took over the dairy as well, learning avidly from Emily as if time was running out. A day never passed without her expressing gratitude for what the Wrights had done for the family and her devotion to Emily seemed limitless.

Hetty cleaned the house, fed the smaller animals and helped with the milking and the lambs. She also watched the children. She began to teach Georgie a few letters and she taught Laura to collect the eggs, which she did with squeamish eagerness, shouting at the hens and then scurrying among them with her childish lisp: 'Shoo, shoo nasty beaky beaks ... Lauwa tekin' eggs for Hemily and Gawge.' When the lambs came then it was often Emily and Hetty that tended to any that were orphaned or rejected by the ewe. When they all gathered in the kitchen, as sometimes happened in the middle of the day, there was scarcely room to move and the crying of the child was sometimes answered by the bleating of a pet lamb from under the kitchen table.

Emily was busy to the point that she was sometimes so tired that her bones ached. She went to market and rode or walked out to the farther fields to check on the stock and their walls and fences. She arranged cooking, shopping, bottling and brewing, as well as the butter and cheese making. She also checked on Arthur, the farmhand, and helped the others when she could with the milking and the rounding up of sheep. Arthur knew his work, but was surly and uncommunicative and he seemed to resent Jack's position. Emily began to hope that Jack might learn from him and eventually take his place. But much fell on her shoulders, with little respite.

In the evenings, when jobs were done, Jack and Ethel withdrew to their rooms. James Taylor still came along for his evening meal, which they ate in the parlour, and now Hetty joined them also. It was Emily's suggestion after Robert had left and the two couples were comfortable in the quiet domesticity of these moments together. Occasionally, Jack hobbled up to the Hill Inn, where some of the navvies gathered. On a few occasions, Jack and George drank at the kitchen table and played cards. The children grew and put on weight, the adults were suffused with the rigours of the day and so the bonds grew stronger as the winter dragged towards a fretful end, reluctant to concede to spring.

Suspicions
Spring 1871

On one such chilly evening, with a northerly March wind scraping and sculpting the bones in her face, Emily stood at her back door, wrapped a long scarf round the back of her head and tucked it into her bodice. Then she pulled on her old, cracked brown boots and set off across the farmyard to the stone barn, to check the ewes that were ready to lamb. She felt tired and frumpish. The wind whined through a broken lintel on the side of the barn and the sheep bleated complainingly. Muffled as she was, just as she was about to open the barn door she thought that she heard the merest echo of distant laughter. It jarred with her mood. She now stepped inside out of the wind and released the scarf. Standing with the door ajar, she listened and now clearly caught what she recognised as the distant sounds of an exchange between James and Hetty, followed by a giggling and scurrying of feet. It came from a little way up the lane towards the little cottage that James lived in now. Emily was surprised, then irritated, then amused. She had thought that Hetty had gone next door to read a bedtime story to Georgie. Hadn't she said that was what she was doing? Or was that last night? Perhaps this was happening every night? If so, what else was happening? Had Hetty made a move? Or had James? And why did she not know?

She hesitated and then withdrew into the barn and began to examine the twenty ewes that were kept there until their lambs came; one was agitated, dragging herself anxiously around in small circles, unable to settle. Emily stood back to watch, knowing the likely pattern that was to be enacted. Her thoughts shifted to Hetty, whilst her eyes followed the anxious ewe. She was fond of the girl and knew that James would be a good catch for her. Clearly, there had been some feeling between them for some time. She should let it take its course. Besides, could she be really certain of her own motives in anything to do with James? A part of her still savoured the thought of his feelings for her as a woman and she thought back to the evening when she had undressed for him and then tried to shock him into … into what: leaving her alone or really declaring himself? Whatever she had wanted, he certainly seemed to have received the message that enough was enough. The gifts and the subtle physical insinuations had stopped. So, was he now again focused on Hetty and was this kind of switching and changing a sign of someone to be trusted? Or was it just the normal male tendency to try it on with anyone who was moderately attractive and possibly available. He remained a bit of a mystery and that made him intriguing. He had not come home once or twice in the last few weeks and would not be drawn on where he had been: 'Staying up at the camp,' was all he would say. What exactly was he up to? Emily thought that perhaps she would ask around. It would be a kindness to Hetty, she thought. She ruefully added that it would also be quite interesting for her.

She watched the ewe give comfortable birth to twins and once the lambs had staggered dizzily to their feet and had found their mother's milk, she left the barn and walked thoughtfully up the lane towards the cottage. She met Hetty coming back alone, a little flushed and breathless. Emily made no reference to events at all, simply observing that she was surprised to see Hetty coming down the lane. The girl stammered and then smiled broadly, her excuse at the ready. 'I took Mr Taylor some milk for his breakfast. He's away early in the morning.' They walked back together: talking of other things.

The next day, Emily took Ethel into her confidence regarding her concerns over James. It was only a lightly edited version of events and Ethel was cautious in her response. She said that James, like all the engineers, was well known at Batty Green. Hesitantly, she added that there were vague rumours about James and one of the women up there, but she did not know who the woman was. She had kept quiet about it because she did not want Emily to think her a casual gossip or troublemaker and they were only rumours. But if he was now showing an interest in Hetty, then they should do their best to protect the girl, if that was necessary, shouldn't they?

As it happened, Hetty was going home for a few days' holiday at the end of the week. Emily arranged for Ethel to come with her on the Saturday market run to Batty Green. They took Angel and Laura, leaving

Jack and George in charge of the farm with Georgie. They had agreed that when the majority of their customers had called, Ethel would "have a walk around" and talk to some of her former friends and neighbours. She would then slip the name of James Taylor into conversations.

The simple plan worked well enough and brisk business tailed off, as expected, by mid afternoon, when Ethel moved off to seek news. Whilst she was waiting, Emily tidied the cart and hearing a cough behind her, she turned to find Robert smiling at her. With him there was an odd-looking young man with a lopsided grin and a number of teeth missing. He shifted nervously from leg to leg and watched Emily closely.

Her face lit up roguishly. 'Mr Macintosh. It's fair grand to si' thee,' she said, dropping automatically into a broader dialect as she always did with him. She truly was pleased and realised that she had missed him. 'How art? Is the brickworks very trying work?'

'Nay, lass. It's not so bad an' a reckon on getting the hang of it in a year or two without burning meself reg'lar.' With a rueful grin, he held up his right arm, which seemed to be twice its normal thickness and wreathed in a dark cloth. 'It's not quite so bad as 't looks,' he said. 'But I'm learning the 'ard way that kilns get 'ot and bugger me, they stay 'ot.' He laughed and she did, too, whilst his companion stretched his grin a little further. Robert saw her eyes flick over them both. 'This is Marty,' said Robert. 'He used to be in one o' my teams an' a'm sorry to admit that my impatience caused him some injury a while back. 'Appen you heard 'bout it.' She nodded. Marty appeared unconcerned. 'Well, since then, a sometimes treat him if a see him 'bout an' we was off t'pie man, when a saw this vision of beauty an' a said to Marty, let's just have a word wi' my favourite farmer's wife.'

She swelled at the compliment and they went on to chat about the farm, Jack and Ethel. Robert gave Marty money for pies and sent him off to buy them, leaving the two of them alone. Emily deliberately mentioned James, adding that whilst he still lived with them, she saw less of him now. Robert was unabashed and direct.

'A see him around the camp an' fact is that he comes to check the brickworks. A'm Assistant Manager now, you know, movin' up in the world again.' She beamed her approval and gave her congratulations. 'Mr Taylor checks production levels and quality sometimes, so he's almost my boss, in an indirect kind o' way. We stick to business, you might say, an' we don't speak o' owt else really. An' a see him around the camp at times, 'ere an' there, an' a know as he's been seen in one hut in partickler, or so a've 'eard. Maybe that's the one that you've heard about, too.'

He looked her in the eye as if willing her to ask or even inviting her. She smiled. He always was quick on the uptake where she was concerned and he seemed to anticipate some of her thoughts. Perhaps she had introduced his name clumsily, or was he just good at guesswork?

'Oh,' she pretended a kind of innocence that she did not feel, 'what hut would that be?'

'Well, a' don't want to mek mischief for the lad. We never exactly got along, as you know, but a don't wish 'im any ill. All a'll say is that it's well known as a colourful hut, got a blue light outside at times, an' them as lives there are not your reg'lar churchgoers.'

Emily's mouth must have sagged open or her eyes widened, because he roared with laughter at her. 'Nay, lass, if you're going to go probing about a young man's behaviour, you'll 'opefully be a little more subtle next time.' They both laughed and then a difficult pause developed, edgy with embarrassment. Robert shuffled a little and dropped his voice. 'Is the lad in trouble?' he asked cautiously.

'Nay, it's not that, it's just that a have a few worries about … something,' Emily muttered, dragging to a halt.

'Is it on his account that you worry, or because of your own feelings?' he asked, more like his old, direct approach coming through now that they had located the area of concern. She didn't answer; caught in the web of her own mendacity and sharply aware that Robert would be quick to detect any ambiguity in her.

He went on, 'A've no wish to pry an' too much respect for thee, lass, to ask any more, but a was aware, as we all were, that the lad had a strong feeling for you at one time. Fact is, a tried to tell 'im to worship more discreetly and from afar, like the rest of us, but he didn't tek kindly to such words from me. Told me it wor just because a wor jealous, which may 'ave bin true.' She blushed and held her breath excitedly. 'But a would not like to see you get hurt or upset over our Mr Taylor, so that's why a mention that he's not so innocent as he's kitten-like at times. Tek care in that quarter.'

He waited and although she looked into his eyes and he registered their appeal, she said nothing and he acknowledged that with a slight bow of the head. 'An' you know, if there's owt that a can do for thee, then just send word to brickworks or to Aidan's Hut.' So saying, he stepped away, waved farewell and sauntered off, leaving her moved and a little baffled.

She called after him, 'Thank you, Mr Macintosh. Come and see me again … soon.'

Shortly after this Ethel returned and from the shake of her head, Emily could tell that she had little news. 'Let's talk on the way back about our mystery man,' she said and they busied themselves with wrapping up the children and harnessing the mare as they prepared to leave.

'The mystery is in this camp somewhere', Emily thought to herself as she turned the cart and looked out over the darkening scene, illuminated by flashes of fire and fractured by the sound of a man yelling somewhere nearby. 'A shall bottom it soon.'

Batty Green
April 1871

"The navvy camp in and around Batty Green", as it was referred to in the local press, now held over 1,000 inhabitants and almost as many animals. It was a small town built out of next to nothing, where the raw and seedy elements of Victoria's kingdom found work and money. Some found solace, while others found pain. Nothing comparable could be found within many hundreds of square miles, perhaps in the whole country. It bustled, it breathed, it smelled and it was frequently racked with conflict, rumour and raw human emotion. Pay day was looked forward to eagerly by most of the inhabitants, but dreaded by some, for many of the men would go on a "randy" and would be drunk for days, blind and literally fighting drunk, until the money was gone and they crawled back to work to earn or borrow more. Life was often brutal and dangerous. Murder was committed; theft and larceny were rife; promiscuity, drunkenness and violence were commonplace. The courts were busy, the doctors harassed and the churchyard at Chapel le Dale was filling up.

However, it was not without its countervailing influences: a school had opened, a constable was on permanent duty, reforming bodies made well-organised forays and a preacher was allocated to bring the word of God to primitive hearts and minds. Some of the locals were horrified and condemned the whole enterprise, but astute traders became rich and some hearts and minds remained willing to see, condone and even forgive where they could. There were many acts of compassion and charity at Batty Green; decent families and individuals kept themselves intact and were respected; concerts, penny readings, book rooms and collections were organised and curious visitors and journalists took tours of the camp or were winched down the air shafts to inspect the working faces deep within Blea Moor Tunnel. It was, to its various observers and commentators, a novelty, a magnet, an excrescence, a blight or an abomination. It provided an outlet for philanthropy and an opportunity for pious outrage or for easy gain. The fact that it was temporary and seemed to suck in life and then spit it out again merely added to its fascination.

Emily found herself drawn back to the camp more and more. As the weather warmed, they expanded again, moving to a daily milk run, collecting milk, butter and cheese from neighbouring farms and employing a cheerful fat lad called Joshua to take supplies on their familiar yellow cart further up the line, selling at Sebastopol, Belgravia, Jericho and Jerusalem each morning. Now that both George and Jack were getting more mobile round the farm and extra help had been brought in for their larger herd, it meant that often she went with Joshua to help with the sales, handle the money and take orders for eggs or chickens or whatever was plentiful and in season. Joshua was from the neighbouring farm and had just turned thirteen. He liked to chat and sing as he worked and customers loved him. She and Joshua were like children at times, laughing and joking, "laykin' around", they would call it, as they went on their way. Twice a week, Ethel went as well, leaving the younger children with Hetty and taking Georgie for a half-day at the school. In the autumn he would go to school every day.

These ventures took the women to the heart of Batty Green and in the interests of drumming up orders, they had licence to make forays through its muddled patchwork of dirt and disorder, calling at hut after hut. There was little that surprised Ethel, but much to intrigue Emily, as each hut brought something new. Huts had one family with lodgers or two families snugly established. Huts had twenty men on crude bunks, with a blanket apiece and a few settles round one stove: often, an old harridan was glimpsed, boiling their beef and hoarding their drink.

Huts were wallpapered, with prints on the walls, rugs on the floor and an air of domesticity and calm. Huts were filthy, rat-infested and noisome: dogs and cats fighting over scraps and the inmates scarcely better. The human tide had washed up some broken and beaten driftwood at Batty Green, as well as a selection of nobler spirits.

They were always alert for a sight of James or news of his activities, but they could turn up little that satisfied them. Robert had dropped the hint about the hut with the blue light. Ethel had picked up hints that James would call at another hut quite often, where a mother and daughter lived, but it was always daytime and the women were thought to be very respectable; rather stand-offish, in fact. But there were also rumours of him spending some evenings elsewhere, somewhere that had a less favourable reputation. He was not known as a drinker or a fighter; in fact, he seemed to avoid male companionship. But there was nothing substantial in the stories. Either he was very careful or very innocent. Meanwhile, Emily had cautioned Hetty to be careful and had been assured by the girl that she could handle James. Emily backed off, a little confused by such a retort.

They soon found Aidan's Hut that Robert lived in and Emily was pleased to see that it was one of the better ones. A childless young couple ran it: they were Scottish Presbyterians, serious and restrained. He had left a wife in Scotland, who had shocked him by taking to drink. His younger partner was refused permission to marry him and they had finally abandoned the kirk, left their hometown together and now lived at Batty Green, rather unhappily and saving assiduously, until they had enough to emigrate to Canada and to set up home and business there. Robert was one of four lodgers, all from the brickworks that were now building up towards full production; it was planned for ten ovens turning out 20,000 bricks a day.

Robert was beginning to prosper in his new job and he seemed to have more of his old bright energy. He mentioned that he had started to save again and that he was hoping one day to become manager at the works. 'A love it,' he said. 'A've finally found a job where a can be warm an' dry all day long, without 'avin' to wear a frock coat an' a top 'at.' He gave them tea and made them welcome. They settled quickly to talk over all the comings and goings of the camp and the farm. As they left, Ethel went ahead to see her old hut-mates and Emily asked Robert, tentatively, why she had seen no sign of the hut with the blue light and why Ethel had never heard of it.

'Ah, lassie,' he said, with a teasing twinkle. ''Ave you not properly considered that lamps is meant to be lit. You really only see lamps at night now, o' that a'm quite certain, so that's one o' yer problems. This lamp stays inside durin' the day, because there's no trade then at this partickler hut. And this lamp is not lit ivery night, neither. What's more, yor in Batty Green an' you'd do better to look in Jericho! 'An' as for

Ethel, well, happen she's never heard of it, but a bet Black Jack has, it bein' more in a way o' man's knowing.'

They laughed together, she wasn't sure why, except that she liked the boyish excitement that he seemed unable to restrain. Then he slipped an arm round her waist and squeezed her. She did not resist. He leaned closer, 'If you come back one evening a should be honoured to escort you on a little stroll around the Jericho huts.' She raised an eyebrow at his offer, but did not say no. She liked his touch and his easy warmth sent her nerves tingling.

Moreover, his offer coincided with another thought that had passed through her that day. Ethel had said that she should like to go to one of the penny readings and she had invited Emily to join her. There was one most Friday nights at Batty Green and quite often Agnes sang a song or two. Ethel had never been and had promised Agnes that she would get there one day. Emily seized the moment. Shrewdly linking the two ideas, knowing the curiosity that was gnawing at her, but also her need for a chaperone, she recognised that if they went to the reading with Robert, perhaps they could walk back via Jericho and down the top lane back to Elterbeck. She did not ponder long. Feeling more alive than she had for a while, she quickly arranged with Robert that he should meet them at the mission room at six o'clock on the following Friday. He agreed to be their escort and to walk them home afterwards through Jericho. Emily felt pleased at this contrivance and restless with simmering tension for the week to pass. She hurried home and hurried George to bed, feeling the need for another "try" coming on.

The next day, Emily took Ethel completely into her confidence about everything that had happened with James and about her own fears of infertility, her longing for a child and the intermittent nature of her physical relationship with George. She also hinted at her confused and occasional desire for other men. She explained her frustration, her selfish restlessness and how she felt more and more infected by the life of the camp, whether for good or ill. They skimmed the milk, they churned cream, they moulded butter, they made a rabbit stew enriched with smoked bacon, turnip and potato, and all the while they talked.

Emily felt some relief. The talking helped her to pull the threads of her own story into a shape that she could recognise, with familiar peaks and troughs, but also a new perspective. Looking back over her marriage, she saw herself as too often the passenger recently, rarely the driver. That was not how she operated before she was wed. Why shouldn't that change? She thought back to how her own mother had become passive, silent and downtrodden: Ethel had some of the same characteristics.

Emily would not be so pliable and oppressed. She tried to explain this to Ethel, but was not sure that Ethel understood. They sat in the kitchen that evening, Ethel with the baby at her breast, nodding and singing quietly. Emily sat a little apart, staring into the flames that rolled around the ash logs in the grate.

To Emily came the thought that perhaps she really was different to most other women. Either she saw more than they did or she was more wicked than they were, or perhaps she had inherited some of her father's feckless attitude to responsibility and had a self-seeking desire to please herself. Was it simply that she was one of those shifting souls that cannot settle: someone that must have the next stimulus, the next challenge? Whatever the explanation, she felt again that things could not stay as they were. If only Dermot O'Reardon had been different. As she dozed by the open grate of the range, her calves singeing in the heat, how she wanted the warm glow of a dark Irishman to whisk her away and a mellifluous voice to stroke her through and through.

Ethel had listened carefully to her friend, watching the bubbles of energy and uncertainty pulse and fall as words surged and faltered. She thought her a fool to risk the comfortable life and prospects that she had on some wild dream that could barely bear the weight of words that were wrapped around it, so casually did it slip away. All that Ethel could see was that Emily would become difficult to manage at Elterbeck, without the children that she craved or some other challenge to shape herself to. She admired Emily, loved her, indeed, and saw her embarking on a journey that could well prove dangerous or disastrous. She finally and carefully offered her advice.

'A can't tell thee how to get with child, if its not to be your husband as is the father, which is what you seem to have at the back of yor mind, my dear. A've only iver bin wi' one man an' Jack seemed to 'ave the knack of givin' babies almost without tryin': A'm just grateful that livin' 'ere, and perhaps gettin' less drink in 'im, he seems to be less interested. A don't fancy any more, to be honest. But a do know as how a woman in your position has a deal to lose an' once lost it cannot be brought back. So, tek care that you don't follow this thing in your 'ead and lose some o' good things that you have around you now.' She paused, seeing Emily looking crestfallen for a moment. 'A don't say as a've understood all that you've told me, so don't judge me harsh. But just give it a little time, you're still young and George is still capable ...' She stumbled to a halt, distrustful of words.

She then stood and gathered herself, as if a decision had been made, and began again. 'What a will say is this: there's a woman at the camp going by the name of Bella as gives out a few remedies an' things to women as needs them, usually to bring a babe away, sad to say, not to bring one on. But those as knows her say she has a knack o' findin' what's needed and she don't charge much, not that that will matter to you, but it might be worth seeing her and I could help you wi' that. An' I will if you think it will 'elp yer in these difficulties and t'will be just between us two. You can trust me, you know.' The two women folded their arms around each other and cried a little, almost crushing the baby, not knowing why the tears were those of sorrow.

The next day James Taylor called at the brickworks to check how the new ovens were working and to see how soon they would be up to full capacity. Bricks were needed now for lining Blea Moor Tunnel and for bridges, walls, culverts and aqueducts and they would be needed later for turning the arches of the viaduct itself. The brickworks was thick with dust, ash and coal grime and they were smeared with clay, but the warm ovens and flashes of fire being stoked seemed to give the whole proceedings a homely air; the ground resonated with energy. James listened to the report from Robert and he expressed his appreciation of the progress being made and the clarity of the report. The two men stood quietly for a moment, watching coal being unloaded into a compound that had timber sides and a large gate that was dragged across at night.

'I walked round this way last night,' said James, 'and chased off a fellow that was climbing the gate with a sack over his shoulder. He dropped the coal and ran. I didn't catch who it was, but I thought you had a night shift here and a watchman for thieving.'

'Aye, we do,' said Robert. 'But sometimes they turn a blind eye to a mate or for a couple of pence worth o' coal mebbe they don't challenge someone as they know will return wi' a pick handle and metal boots. A'll look into it an' see as it don't get out o' hand. But it's hard to stop wi' so much goin' on an' gangs needin' access to coal at all hours. But ...

any road, you should be down at farm o' nights, not up 'ere. Bit o' courtin' goin' on wi' young Hetty as I hear, eh?' He watched closely to see how James reacted to this tentative thrust. In the past, James would have been quick to shut down any such inroads. Now, he smiled, ran his hands over his neat, wiry black hair and turned to Robert, apparently quite relaxed.

'Well, word does travel fast, don't it.' He paused. 'Fact is that I have been friendlier wi' Hetty these last few weeks. Felt it best to step back from Emily, you know, as you once told me. It was gettin' a bit strong and I didn't want any trouble for her, you know. And I've found other friends and interests, some o' them up here as it happens.'

They parted soon afterwards. Robert ruefully reflected that the lad was almost smug, almost bragging. He would really enjoy bringing him down a peg or two one day.

Bella and Bane
April 1871

The huts had developed into communities: leaders and personalities emerged as focal points and then through wider but unspoken negotiation, each had somehow acquired a name. A mile to the south of Batty Green was a group of huts known as Salt Lake City. Jericho, on the other hand, was almost a mile up the fell from Batty Green, going north towards Blea Moor. Almost at the tunnel mouth was Jerusalem and right up on the moor, over 2 miles from the turnpike road, were the tunnel huts themselves; almost too grim to attract any softening sobriquet. Batty Green remained the largest concentration of buildings, with Belgravia on elevated ground nearby, and almost under the line of the viaduct itself was a small grouping known as Sebastopol. All were woven around the storage huts, the brickworks, the blacksmiths, the animal shelters, the offices and the engine sheds of the Midland Railway and their contractors. It was amongst this complex that Emily and Ethel went to look for Bella's hut on a chilly Wednesday afternoon, with rain threatening from the north.

Emily was dressed in her working clothes, with a shawl wrapped round her shoulders and swept up over the back of her head. She carried a basket of eggs to sell: the pretext for her excursion. They had agreed that Ethel would do the introductions and make sure that the meeting would be confidential. She knew Bella by sight and reputation; she had once got some syrup from her when Georgie had a cough, buying from her as she had passed through Batty Green with a deep basket over her arm. She was a striking woman, made all the more distinctive by some wayward dressing and the fact that she was usually accompanied by an Irish wolfhound that she called Bane. Sometimes, one or two other women followed her around. Her hut was easily found and Emily sat on a bench outside when Ethel went in. She soon reappeared, smiling encouragement.

'She'll see you an' she's on 'er own, so it's quite safe. A'll tek a walk down to have a pan o' tea wi' Mavis an' Agnes, if they're in. Or a've some other folk as happen a can call on. Shall a come back in about an hour?' They agreed plans and Ethel left, whilst Emily gathered her thoughts before pushing at the door of the hut.

Inside was warm and quiet. She found herself in a small lobby, with doors leading off left and right. Most huts had crude partitions or blankets hanging from nails in the rafters, which served to subdivide the space and give the flimsiest degree of privacy; but here all was more substantial. The door to the left bore the names "Bella and Bane", painted in a flowing copperplate done in red ink on a piece of damask cloth stretched on a frame. Emily was intrigued and knocked briskly. Footsteps approached and the door swung open.

A tall woman of about sixty, in a flowing red skirt and plain white bodice, invited her in with a sweeping and rather theatrical gesture. She had a florid look, as if heated by drink or argument, a beaked nose, a wide mouth that she breathed though heavily and piercing blue eyes. She had grey-blonde hair that she wore long and unevenly, as if part of it had been cut, but not all. There was a little black bonnet rather precariously perched on the back of her head, with its strings hanging loose as if forgotten. The voice was deep and suggested a northern background, but there was a strange transatlantic drawl as well, as if she had lived in America for some time.

'Please come in, Emily Wright, you're sure welcome. Come an' sit awhile and I'll mek tea. Or I've a jug o' porter if you care for it? Or would you like a nip o' something stronger?'

Emily opted for tea and while a billycan was filled and brewed, she looked round her in some amazement. Bella and Bane had half the hut to themselves, as far as Emily could tell. Their large room was set out as a kind of parlour on one side, with a stove and three substantial chairs ranging round it. A large table near the door was covered in plants and vegetables, with small dishes and phials of coloured liquid in racks. A naphtha lamp was hanging from the ceiling on a chain, swaying slightly, casting gentle moving shadows. There was a large bed and a few sturdy wooden chests against the farther wall and even a bookcase, which looked to be well stocked. It was dry and stuffy with heat from the generous stove that seemed to be penetrated by a strong, earthy smell of tobacco from a long clay pipe that Bella had obviously just put down. And to that was added what Emily recognised as the fumes of brandy and the musty odour of a large dog that was stretched across the floor in front of the stove, snuffling in his sleep. There were small rugs scattered around, some of them coloured with red and blue Chinese patterns, others crudely woven of hemp and sisal. On one wall there was a dark portrait of a man on horseback cradling a shotgun in his arm.

On another wall was a seascape with ships preparing to do battle; it was hanging next to some large bunches of dried herbs and beneath it was an aspidistra standing in what looked like an old brass coal scuttle. Emily smiled at the thought that it was somewhere between a gypsy caravan and a fashionable but rather faded and eccentric drawing room. To find it in a navvy camp called Sebastopol intrigued her.

The women settled to their tea without much conversation. Emily felt soothed and she appreciated the relaxed approach. As she sipped her tea, she noted that Bella drank from two chipped cups: one held tea, the other brandy. She picked up her pipe, cut a small wedge from a plug of tobacco that she pulled from the pocket of her skirt, lit up and then looked thoughtfully at Emily.

'I make a livin' out of helping others. I sell some elixirs and a few pills that I get from reliable sources or mek meself. I brew a few drinks that I sell and I provide some of what you might call personal services to those in need. Mostly, I choose to help women and children, but some men come to me an' all. I pull some teeth, deliver some bairns and help women as have just given birth or are finding things hard. I try to mek meself useful. I charge what I think folks can pay and dependin' on how desperate they are. In your case, I'll ask a shillin' this time. It might be more if you come back. Nothing that you tell me will ever be passed on to others; that I can promise you. You can trust me. I'm no doctor, but I worked in a hospital for many years and I know a thing or two that I've picked up here and there. Now, pass me your money and then we can settle to talk for a while. If you don't like the sound of it, then you can leave and I'll gi' you your brass back.'

Emily passed over the coins, all the while struggling to place the voice and the oddly mixed expressions, because something seemed familiar. Bella, too, seemed a little less in control now that they had begun, perhaps aware of the scrutiny she was coming under, and she shuffled her chair a little backwards, so that her face was in shadow.

'Now then, tek your time and tell me what troubles you and what it is that you want from me.'

After an uneasy start, the talk flowed and Emily once again, as with Ethel, found herself describing her dilemma, her restless urges and her longing for a child. She hinted at her toying with the idea of relations with other men, without mentioning names. She described herself as almost giving up hope of her own family, settling for a share of the children of others, like Ethel. She said, half jokingly, that she had found herself thinking about either buying or stealing a child. 'But then,' she added, 'a'm greedy and selfish. A can't help it. A want to bear my own child, not snatch a babe from some desperate woman in a slum.'

Bella turned their talk to physical matters and details, including sexual acts with George, Emily's part in those and her appetite for them. She was a good listener: her voice was soothing and deep, prompting and guiding and never arbitrating or trite. She did not take sides or offer platitudes, but seemed to embrace and recognise Emily's dilemma as if it were a familiar and everyday discussion. Emily began to believe that she might not be uniquely wicked or perverse.

She told Bella of the incident with Dermot and how it still haunted her. The details had slipped into the past, she said. 'But a wake up at times an' think to meself that today he might come back. It teks breath out of me sometimes an' a get as so a can 'ardly breathe. And a followed a young man one day as looked like Dermot. A soon found as a was mistaken and almost cried. 'E's like to some kind o' demon that 'as begun to share my own story in ma sleep an' ma waking. Dost tha think a woman can be possessed by devil like this?'

Bella just smiled. 'I need to think about all that you've told me,' she said gently. She had heard enough and for her the talk had taken them as far as she wanted. She refilled her brandy cup and her pipe, pulled off her boots and stretched out her feet towards the fire, resting them on the flank of her dog, who stirred and then settled down again. A few moments of peace ensued: the woman's lips puffed and pulled, the dog stirred and grumbled deep in his chest, Emily sank into herself a little, hardly aware of any thoughts, except a subdued expectancy.

The moment changed almost before it developed. Bella spoke briskly and Emily was surprised to detect a new austerity in the voice and manner. 'I can gi' thee somethin' to tek. Try it afore yor 'usband is likely to come to you. It may help with conceivin'. Some women as 'ave teken it, well, they say it did the trick. There's no danger in it any road.

'If that fails in the next few months then you've a deal o' thinkin' to do about the alternatives. You've been tryin' for t'child for a good few years. Who's to say why you've not fallen lucky. Fault may be wi' you or yor 'usband. If it is yor 'usband that can't provide the child, well, there's other ways and means o' changin' yer situation, as you can think of fer yourself and already have. I'll not help wi' that. Or it may be that this just ain't meant to happen, for you or for him, an' you'll maybe reconcile yourself to that in good time.' So saying, she moved briskly to one of the chests and brought out a small bottle that she gave to Emily.

A little chastened and taken aback by her subtle change of mood, Emily rose to leave. Bella stood beside the door and the two women faced each other; one young, dark and compacted; the other ageing, grey and rangy. Bella put her hands on Emily's shoulders and looked down at her sorrowfully.

'I wish you well, truly I do. But I don't wish to see you here again.' Emily stared, puzzled and shaken. Could she have offended in some way? Then Bella frowned and turned her shoulder away and Emily became conscious of a ghostly parallel vision, which just slid into her mind. It brought an idea, which she at first rejected, but then could not shake off.

The door was opened and later Emily could not recall how she left, how she found Ethel or how she got home. She scarcely spoke. She was now truly shocked. A piece of dramatic and unlikely understanding had penetrated her, like a thin dagger of ice, and she could scarcely breathe. She stored it away.

Readings and Reactions
April 1871

Emily brooded about Bella, uncertain whether to trust her intuition. The world was unsteady for a few hours: the furniture had shifted almost imperceptibly and she needed time to learn the new layout. She was abstracted throughout the next day, in a way that suggested to Ethel that Bella had probably been discouraging. Despite the silence it was some relief to Ethel, who knew that for her part she would baulk at involvement in any unseemly vice or deception, but she was sad that she could not see what else she could do to help Emily. Yet, on Friday, the mood changed again and Emily seemed to be her old self, excitedly looking forward to the penny reading that evening and to their escorted walk back through Jericho. In truth, Emily was glad for action and escape.

The mission room was the only public space at Batty Green that was large enough to support the penny reading. The missionary, Mr Tiplady, was pleased to see it used. He was an engaging, eager little man from Bradford. He had no airs or graces and he did his best to make a difference, offering his zeal but also his sympathy and understanding. He threw himself into providing both entertainment and solace and did so with as much energy as the little engine that worked up and down the tramway. He always took a part in the readings; piety leavened with a little humour went down well and he was always careful to avoid being patronising or hectoring. He worked on a human level and was the more effective for it.

The two women, in their best bonnets and shawls, met Robert as arranged and they warmly admired his waistcoat of cobalt blue and the crimson scarf tied loosely round his muscular throat. The mission was filling up with an excited crowd, eager to see and hear the three performers that had come all the way from Lancaster. Mr Tiplady welcomed everyone in person, asking for penny donations, which were to go to Leeds Infirmary. Robert insisted on paying a shilling and then he escorted Emily and Ethel in a proprietorial manner to the benches near the front. These were plain deal but had simple backs to them and Mr Tiplady promptly gave cushions to the ladies. Ethel seemed a little overcome by it all, nervously excited to the point where she could scarcely speak.

Emily felt uncomfortably exposed and was conscious that without George, and with Robert fussing noisily around them, her presence was likely to be noticed. She was aware of a few of her farming neighbours near her, but also navvy families and groups behind her, not least a group of men standing near the door that Robert had scowled at when they had arrived. She was also surprised to find that her own vicar from Chapel le Dale, Mr Harper, was going to preside and introduce the items. He came down from the platform and greeted her warmly, congratulating her on taking an interest in events at the camp. She introduced her companions. Robert explained that he was "a lodger at the farm and a good friend" of Emily's. She did not know what to say and could only smile, feeling uncomfortable, as if the vicar could see through her.

All was soon forgotten, however, in the novelty and excitement generated by the performers and their eager audience. Readings were interspersed with songs and monologues, all receiving enthusiastic acclaim that Mr Harper cleverly manipulated by his warm praise and the light banter that he enjoyed with the crowd. Mr Carr read *The Deceitful Lover* first and Emily felt herself a little flushed by this tale of lies and evasions, made worse by Robert leaning towards her at the end and with a broad wink asking her if she had ever heard of such a thing. Then Miss Ellis sang *The Ladder Stile* with such a sweet grace that the audience were captivated, falling into a glowing silence and then erupting rapturously in their applause. Mr Carr returned to read a long, amusing piece about a cow that would not give milk that Emily lost track of. Then, Mr Wildman sang two serious pieces and Mr Tiplady gave a short address. Mr Carr returned with a monologue in broad Yorkshire dialect; one of the navvies shouted that they could not understand a word of that language and could they "larn proper Hinglish?" This was thought to be greatly entertaining.

Then Agnes was introduced, to great cheers, as "the Nightingale of Batty Moss". She was dressed in a pale blue gown and a large bonnet stuck with paper flowers. With a basket over her arm, she sang a song about a sad shepherdess that was received in almost reverential silence. She had a thin, wavering voice that Emily found rather grating, but the cheers and applause at the end fairly thundered round the hut and Agnes retired with huge smiles. Mr Wildman then sang some comic pieces that had them all laughing heartily and Miss Ellis returned with a rousing *Barney O'Shea* and got the audience singing along to the chorus of *Tapping at the Garden Gate,* whilst she and Agnes took alternate verses. Applause and a stamping of feet shook the simple wooden building and echoed round the hills. There were demands for encores from all the performers, who duly obliged, and the evening finally closed after nine o'clock in an atmosphere of animation and jovial spirits: faces glowed in the heat and there was much good-natured chafing and commentary as they filed out.

As Emily and Ethel emerged with Robert into the cool evening air, they gave their thanks to Mr Tiplady, who waited at the door, and turned away towards their path across the green. Groups were still standing near the mission, talking over the performances, unwilling to leave, savouring the cool air on their faces and arms. Robert led them past such knots of people and round one group of men, who were less vocal than the rest and who seemed aware of Robert's party. The men did not automatically step aside for him and Robert chose to step off the path into the muddier margins, but as the women came through the men moved apart to make a passageway for them. Emily was aware that one of the men in particular looked directly at her, not dropping his gaze when she glanced at him, with the hint of a sneer at the corners of a downturned mouth. He was a tall, weather-beaten navvy, with black beard and black hair tied at the back, under a dark, shapeless hat. At his elbow she recognised the odd youth with the grin that had been with Robert at the cart recently.

She moved on quickly, unsure how to read the mood of this group and anxious to move to somewhere less public. Robert led them on, stepping in behind them on another muddy pathway, a scowl on his face now, which turned to a look of thunder when he heard some comment from behind him; the words "toff" and "whores" particularly emphasised by the tall navvy at the centre of the group. Robert swung around and with quick, sharp strides he was back and amongst the men in seconds. They recoiled and most stood aside intuitively, leaving the black haired navvy facing Robert in the centre of a small ring. There was no pause in Robert's movement and in one sweep he was up to the man and had shot out his right hand to grip the other round the throat. Tar Brush, for it was his old ganger that had baited him, was taken by surprise and he slipped backwards on the damp grass, gasping and flaying his arms. Robert continued the forward movement skilfully, flinging the man down on the ground, and then dropped quickly to plant one knee in the man's chest and pin his arms down. He leaned over until he was inches from the man's face and in a voice convulsive with distaste he growled, 'Don' you ever refer to those women again in my hearin', you evil, uncircumcised piece o' shit, or a'll rip off your balls and bake them in the centre of one o' ma bricks and then sell it to the highest bidder. Do a mek meself clear enough for your weak, befuddled brain?' Tar Brush nodded slowly but stared back at Robert, implacable as iron. Robert stood and looked round the rest of the group, focusing especially on Marty, who shuffled, trying to control his grin. He returned briskly to Emily and Ethel, who were only just becoming aware that something had happened. 'Nowt to worry about,' said Robert, bristling with purpose as he strode back to them.

A Lancastrian voice called from behind them, 'Thou'll be hearin' from me, Macintosh.'

But despite this, or perhaps on account of it, Robert seemed powerfully energised now, offering his arm first to one woman and then the other. They walked from Batty Green as the evening darkened, following the tramway, indeed sometimes walking along it with others, heading up towards the moor, looking ahead for the lights of Jericho and Jerusalem. While they walked, Robert talked and joked. He seemed determined to maintain a cheerful front. He told them that Jericho was a bit wild. It was a small community of ten huts, he explained, but it was dominated by two or three large huts of working men, who were more often than not fighting with each other. Of these huts, one was known to hold over twenty bedsteads, crammed round the edges of one large room, with a large stove and table at one end. A few benches were all that the men had to sit on, some round the stove and the rest down the centre of the hut, and these were often smashed in fights. Some men rented blankets from the gaffer of the hut and just slept on the floor for sixpence a night. The gaffer was an older man. He called himself the Iron Duke and he kept order with a pickaxe handle. He sold beer from barrels that he kept to one side of the stove and food and clothes from old chests on the other side. He made money at every turn, which he guarded with jealous passion. He was respected only for his brutality, Robert explained.

'It's one way o' mekin' a name for yourself an' a fair livin'. An' he needs to keep things tight in that pertickler hut, because one of the men there, name of Policeman Jack, killed a man on his last job with his bare hands. Not the sort to pick a fight with,' Robert laughed.

Ethel surprised them by suddenly adding, 'A know the man as you refer to. He used to work alongside my Jack and they were butties together for a while. Could fill a wagon wi' muck in no time, the two o' them. Once filled twenty wagons without a break, one shovel after the other; even horses couldn't keep up with 'em. Made plenty o' money, too. And niver a cross word if you left 'im to 'is own ways. Always made a fuss o' the bairns an' all; gave them sixpence ivery time he saw them. So, there's good even in the worst o' them, that's ma view.' She looked over to Robert as if daring him to disagree.

But Robert was cut short from any reply, because they were now entering the Jericho camp and could suddenly hear shouting from ahead, in the very midst of the huts, where a patch of dirty ground often served as a meeting point for one thing or another. Robert paused and listened. He knew at once that two men were scrapping up ahead and a gang of men and women, some of them drunk, was urging on the fighters. He had seen it so many times and he could picture the crowd circling, pushing at the men, betting, arguing, screaming insults and banter, baying for blood. In such a crowd, Ethel would pass for a navvy's woman, but he was worried that Emily's cloak, bonnet and better boots would mark her out as an outsider. If there was trouble ahead he had better take a wider route around it.

He suggested that they skirt the centre of the camp and head for their main objective, the Blue Lamp, which was just a little way above the other huts. The women agreed and after some delay, they found themselves passing between two huts and looking up a muddy slope to a hut with a distinctive blue lamp, clearly visible in the gathering gloom. Compared to what Emily could imagine as the riotous scenes that she could hear behind her, this seemed to be a silent, decorous location.

She could make out voices and some gentle laughter from within, nothing to what her imagination had been creating. She looked first at Ethel and then at Robert in confusion. 'A was expectin' … well, a don't know what … but this is almost like a vicar's parlour.'

It was Ethel that answered. 'A couldn't get much out o' ma Jack about this place, but a reckon it's a long way from bein' a vicar's parlour. Sorry, Emily; perhaps a should've satisfied yor curiosity earlier.' She shook her head almost in sorrow.

Emily could scarcely bear it. Her blood was beating impatiently through her veins and her heartbeat was painful in her ears. 'Will someone tell me what's goin' on here?'

Ethel did not want to hear the explanation that Robert would offer. It stood some chance of being more graphic than the few hints that Jack had given her. Again, she took the initiative. She shook her head, now smiling at them both. 'A'll leave her to you awhiles, Robert. A'll tek a step down towards the fisticuffs an' just watch from a safe distance. A'll be back soon; time's getting on, tha knows.'

As she moved out of sight, Robert took a step back towards the deep shadow of one of the huts, grasped Emily's hand and pulled her close to him. 'A'll explain as best a can,' he said. 'But let's just agree the fee.'

'What?' she giggled, her blood surging to her temples with a fierce flush.

'A kiss now,' he said, drawing his other hand up to the side of her face. 'And another later. That's the deal.'

'Thou art nowt but a devious blackguard,' she hissed at him, but her low, warm tone told him all that he needed to know. He leaned his face towards her, his eyes settling on the dark line of her mouth. She felt him move his head downwards and the first brush of his lips on hers. Then she jerked her head back and pulled free. 'That's the first and it's all tha art getting if tha're not careful. Now, tell me what James Taylor is up to in that hut,' she demanded.

Robert reflected ruefully, licking his lips as if to savour the taste, but he knew that he needed to offer her something in return. 'First, a've no proof that James has been up to anything in that there hut,' he said. 'A know what happened the night a went and a've heard from others, but men are inclined to boast about some things, as a'm sure you know, an' this place makes them act oddly.'

'Well?' she almost hissed at him.

'The hut's run by a man as was injured in some kind o' explosion a few years back an' he can scarcely walk. He hobbles with two sticks now; one's a crutch; t'other, always in his right hand, is a silver cane. But some say as most o' the injury was to 'is 'ead. Apparently, he's a changed man from what he wor. He's called Mr Bernard. He was no navvy. He's an educated man, travelled all over, includin' the Crimea. Speaks a few languages an' all. He was an engineer with the Midland an' was well known; high-up, like. But, apparently, the accident changed him in a number of ways. He is real sour, aggressive if he's crossed, an' he sees no good at all in anyone or in't whole damn world. When he's sober he's mean. When he's drunk he acts the charmer, but you'd better watch your step that he don't lose his temper wi' you. See, after his accident, there were nothing for 'im ... nowt, cos they claimed it was his mistake. Maybe it was; who knows. But they took his job away from 'im and 'e got real bitter and vowed to get 'is own back on t'Midland, so he 'as a go at any o' their employees an' is prepared to use any means to hurt 'em.

'Meanwhile, he has to make whatev'r livin' 'e can. An' he follows the Midland around from one site to another. He's not liked; for 'imself, that is. Reason he's tolerated is 'e supplies a special moonshine liquor as can fair tek your head off, but it's a canny drop, nowt like it round here. Nobody knows exactly where it's brewed, like. Certainly, it's not in the hut or nearby. An' 'e must 'ave some kind o' partner somewhere, perhaps in a deserted barn or summat, like, who does the brewin' to 'is specifications an' so on. But it's a secret, right enough, and there's always a supply at the Blue Lamp. Durin' the day he'll sell it to a few that 'e trusts, but not many, cos he fears t'excise and polis gettin' onto 'im.'

Robert paused, gathered his thoughts and then continued, more slowly. 'Then there's one or two special nights each week, usually a Friday and perhaps a Sunday, where he'll be on his best behaviour, wi'out a doubt. See, he'll invite a few friends in to drink with 'im and 'is missis and their four handsome daughters. An' they are handsome, a can tell you, leastways the eldest two are. Nowt like 'em round here. There's a few hands o' cards and some chatting and 'appen a bit o' music if the girls is asked to sing, cos they've a piano an' all in there. 'E calls them 'is soirées, or some such thing, an' you 'ave to go an' kind of ask to be invited, in a roundabout kind o' manner. Some 'e turns down.

Always prefers the engineers and their like, not your common navvy. You can't just barge in, either. There's some as 'ave tried that, in their drink an' all, but they don't get far. See, he has that silver stick thing to 'elp him, but inside the stick is a long, thin sword, sharp as 'ell. The first man 'ere that thought 'e would join the fun uninvited had 'is cheek sliced open an' nearly lost an eye. Bernard's vicious when he's crossed and few that know 'im like to do any crossing. And that includes 'is family, who 'e treats like slaves an' worse. Keeps them very much under 'is control an' direction, day an' night. Fair belts them around, so a hear.'

Emily shuddered and sighed, but was still confused. 'So why, apart from the moonshine and the social occasion, should men bother to go there?'

'Well,' said Robert, taking another deep breath and looking ill at ease as he struggled to find the words. 'There's only four or five men invited each time. You've to hand over a guinea when you arrive. You drink for free for that and play the cards and whatever for an hour or so. Then the wife and girls withdraw an' he asks you if there's owt else you want.'

Robert looked abashed. 'You can leave at that point, if you've a mind, though few do. Then, basically, 'e teks bids for any o' the girls or the wife, if that's your fancy. Or you can take two o' them, if that's what you want, for a couple o' extra bob. You can stay all night an' some do an' Bernard meks sure that you've no brass left when you leave.' He paused and waited. His brow furrowed as he looked her calmly in the eye. 'Sad thing is, the youngest child is ten and the next one is no more than 12 year old,' he said. 'As a've heard it, but it's only tittle-tattle, mind. Our James 'as shown an interest in the 10-year-old, t'youngest one.'

There was nothing more to see at the Blue Lamp Hut and nothing more was said. Emily felt as if a poison had swept through her. She stood in lumpen stillness, overwrought, unable to function. When Ethel returned a few moments later, they set off across the line workings to turn east down the valley back towards Elterbeck. She walked mechanically and was silent. Robert had put a couple of lamps in a hut nearby and he lit these to help them make their way. The night was cooler now and the atmosphere was subdued. Emily felt as if her nerves were being stretched tight, to the point of breaking. She was distressed at what she had heard, sick at heart for the girls, the mother, the whole situation and barely able to comprehend it. She did not know if she could ever speak to James again. Crossing fields to gain the lane she began to check the story with Ethel, who had heard roughly the same, without the addition of James' preferences. Ethel advised her to say nothing.

'You've no proof. The lad may not have been with the girl or anything serious ...' It was a lame suggestion and they both knew that it was unlikely, but it was also a well-intentioned caution and Emily nodded her agreement. She actually knew very little, but she would watch and she resolved to speak again to Hetty.

'Why do the Midland let this Bernard get away wi' it?' she asked Robert, her anger flaring brusquely.

'Well, the huts is the contractor's business, is one reason. If the Midland wanted to clean up huts, they'd 'ave a job to know where to start and end. And men wouldn't stand for it anyway. What's more, our Mr Bernard is careful to slip reg'lar bottles of moonshine to the engineers an' contractors an' they say that some o' them, quite high up ones, even directors an' such, 'as been known to attend 'is soirées. Useful that, ain't it? Mr Bernard has a handy way of gettin' what 'e wants from the railway and then in return he tries to destroy some of their men, one way or another; one took his own life last year, others move away, after Bernard gets his claws into them. He seems to get away with it, except 'e 'asn't got his job back, not yet anyway, an' that's the real purpose, so far as a can tell. In some ways, the arrangements suit the customers and Mr Bernard. Perhaps it suits 'is family. A've known worse,' he added, but without conviction.

They reached a silent Elterbeck as the moon sailed out from behind the clouds, bathing the valley in light, picking out the familiar humpbacked outline of Ingleborough gazing over at them, having seen it all and worse. Ethel quickly slipped indoors and Emily walked round to the farmyard gate with Robert, who had said that he might just try to reach the Hill Inn whilst there was still a chance of a drink. They leaned on the gate together for a moment, looking at the moonlit valley. He blew out the lamps and turned towards her, leaning his elbow on the gate and looking at her profile.

'The moonlight's making your eyelashes sparkle,' he said.

She looked at him. It was such a typical Robert comment. He made her feel noticed, perused, attended to. He had the ability to lift her spirits with comedy, but he always showed sensitivity to her as a woman.

His look penetrated her. She did like him and she was grateful for his open, direct purpose. She felt her anxieties lift and a warming flush of vigour pooled through her veins. She would no longer bite her feelings off, or fasten them down or always put herself second.

'A owe you a kiss,' she said, walking away and glancing over her shoulder to make sure he followed.

She walked steadily over to the barn, where the high doors were recessed and where in the dark shadows was a space unseen by the house. She slipped into a corner and waited. He was close behind her and he groped towards her in the dark. She slipped into his arms and their lips met in a long, deep kiss that seemed to weave dark patterns in her belly and send warm waves through her limbs. She pulled her mouth away and gave him a quick push backwards. 'That is definitely thy last. Now be off with you, before the beer runs out.' He understood her and was content, for now. He smiled, waved and moved off jauntily, with a silly skip in his step. She laughed at his clowning and then went inside. 'Just like a daft kid,' she muttered, but did not identify exactly whom she was talking about.

It was well after midnight when Robert completed the circle of his long, eventful walk and found himself back where he started, crossing the works at Batty Green. He was whistling cheerfully to himself, a quart of beer warming his stomach and the kiss still a focal point in his recollections. He did not know what he would do about Emily, but at that moment the present pleasure was enough; he did not care to plan.

Musing and whistling, he approached the brickworks in a darkness that was woven from shapes and shadows. He was half conscious that a man had crossed the path from the other side and then was suddenly startled into looking up when the man stepped in front of him. He was aware briefly of a tall figure in a black coat and hat, pulled right down, the head bent forwards, with just a glimpse of dark eyes in a face that wore a kind of leering scowl, as if amused, a little excited; there were furrows in the knitted brow.

Suddenly, with a snarl, the man swung at him, his right fist striking across and upwards, with almost no back lift, a half swing, a half jab, catching Robert in the throat and knocking him backwards. He staggered and gasped, in shock as much as pain. Then the man stepped forwards and hit him again on the side of the head this time, with a wooden club that he held in his left hand. It was swung with fierce speed and precision, sending Robert staggering against a pile of stones.

At almost the same moment, two others ran up from behind, grabbed him by both arms and yanked him back into a narrow alley that divided two storage huts. It smelt of urine. Robert fought only for breath. His throat felt as if it were swelling, as if a hard lump had been thrust into it and the air was trapped. His head seemed crushed and sounds were splintered. He could taste blood and saliva. He was confused and couldn't seem to grasp who or what this was all about or why it was happening. He began to struggle. The men behind him pulled his shoulders back sharply and he felt something crack. Pain shot through his shoulder and down his spine.

In the darkness, he could just make out the first man coming at him again, so he lashed out with his right leg. The man dodged easily, stepped forwards smartly and smashed his fist down into Robert's nose and mouth. Then he brought his knee up sharply between Robert's legs. Robert curled and spat. He wanted to cry out, but there was something wrong with his throat. He went limp and he was dumped sideways to the ground, his head banging against a wall, his face sliding in the mud and filthy waste. He curled again, foetus-like. He was aware of hands pulling him round, his cravat being ripped off and thrust into his mouth. He couldn't breathe through his swollen nose. He gagged, fighting only to keep the panic, the pain, the sickness and the shame at bay. His trousers were heavy. Had he wet himself?

A hand grabbed his collar and pulled him up to his knees. A voice grated, 'Enjoy your whores, did ye?' Again, he was flung backwards, his shoulder hitting the wall. There was blood seeping down the side of his face and into his eye. He tried to turn his head to clear it. 'Keep bloody quiet about this, unless you want your farming whore to get a taste o' this, too.' The man then kicked him in the back and he fell heavily forwards again, pain arcing through his face as his broken nose hit the ground.

Then all went quiet, apart from the rasping of his lungs and the pounding of blood in his head. He heard footsteps scuffling away, a few mumbled words and some low laughter from the men as they left. He tried to lift himself, but his head felt crushed and nausea welled up. He dragged the cravat out of his mouth. He could taste beer and blood. Then, out of the darkness, a familiar voice said, 'A said you'll be seeing me again, boss.' It was followed by a weak giggle that he also recognised: Tar-brush and Marty were certainly two of the three.

Then it was confusing for a while. Robert struggled to a sitting position. What he wanted above all else was to clear his mouth and throat. There were shards of teeth and wads of flesh there. He could feel the front of his face glowing and swelling and blood was oozing from his nose. His right ear was wet, too. His lower stomach and testicles pulsated with a sickening throb. His shoulder seemed braced at the wrong angle. He shut his eyes, trying to think, to conserve and to centre himself. He gasped and his stomach heaved; he focused on trying not to vomit, not wanting more pain, more dirt; simply looking to survive. His head fell forwards and he seemed to lapse out of consciousness.

Troubled Minds
April 1871

Emily brooded on the connection between James and a 10-year-old girl, who might have been his daughter. She also brooded on the connection between herself and a man in his late forties, who might have been her father. She went out into the meadow and stood still, like a falconer in a whirl of movement, her thoughts spinning wildly. She was again unsettled and was not easy company on commonplace matters.

It was late in the day before she heard that Robert had been injured. She had been to the Saturday market, but driving rain had limited customers and had shortened conversations to the essentials of trade and so she had left early. Late the same evening, Ethel came in to tell her that Jack had heard talk at the Hill Inn that Robert had taken a beating very late on Friday evening. According to Jack, the word was that Robert's old ganger Tar Brush was behind it, having been heard threatening to get his own back on Robert.

When Emily looked confused, Ethel explained that when Robert had lost his subcontract he had given a bad opinion of Tar Brush, said he was a lazy ganger and unable to keep his men up to the work. So when Robert had lost his position, Tar Brush lost his in turn.

Emily remembered the incident outside the mission room and the piercing, unflinching looks she had received from a tall, black-haired navvy and the comments made, just loud enough for her to hear. So was she partly to blame? How could she be? She was stirred with impatient anxiety for Robert and she was desperate to see him: to soothe and to comfort him and to learn more. She thought that she could take the milk with Joshua the next morning and then slip away to Sebastopol, catching up with Joshua later. She could probably manage an hour. She paused, realising with brief embarrassment that she had no intention of telling George any of this or enlisting his help. She immediately began to plan a visit in secret: a secret she would keep from Ethel, too, if possible. What was she becoming?

It was a question that kept her awake for several hours, George snuffling and restless in his sleep beside her. She did not condemn herself outright, but neither she did want to examine her motives and feelings too closely. I've done no wrong, she kept repeating in her mind. But another voice came back with the teasing question: what will you do next though?

She could not just draw her head back into its shell and retreat into the cabined confines of a life with George and a group of farmhands. I'm not made for self-denial, she asserted. What was the alternative?

The night was long. She fell at last into a nervous doze, irritable with tension, conflicted and disappointed. Then, this nexus of unease slowly contorted itself into a serious and punishing headache, as if it had a malignant life of its own. Being beyond her control, it could pull her back from sleep, with its tiny iron bars squeezing her skull. She was awake before the spring dawn could finally dispel the demons of darkness, but she could no longer move her head without a pulse of pain surging from one temple to another. She lay very still and fragile, her eyes closed as she tried to see the pain and get it to stay still. Physical pressures were multiplying and now nausea was souring her stomach, stirring malevolently.

With some difficulty, she shook George awake and got him to understand that she was not well. He roused himself and then was so tender and solicitous in his nursing that she almost shed tears of guilt and loss for her old self and for simple comforts. She stayed in bed and dozed.

She was rarely ill, so Hetty and Ethel also visited with anxiety, offering palliatives and advice. Emily tried to be the patient focal point of all this good will, but at last could only wave them away with the request that she be allowed to rest. She did not want kindness. She slept eventually and woke mid afternoon, feeling weak but no longer crushed and confused by the pain, which had certainly receded. She pulled herself up in bed and listened to the sounds of the farm and the fields around her, focusing on each in turn and picturing the source of each separate strand. She told herself that she should be grateful to be loved, to be secure in such a place, to be at the heart of such activity and such compassion.

I am grateful, she said to herself tremulously, and I'm glad I kept away from Robert today. She smiled, though, at her weak attempt at self-deception. Do you mean that you wouldn't have gone if you had felt well? she asked herself. She declined to answer. As she moved gingerly to get out of bed, thus avoiding any further introspection, she felt a familiar drag pulling downwards and a weak discharge between her legs. A knotted tension gripped her hard. Her bleeding had started. It was a week early. She fell clumsily backwards and cursed her fate and that of all women.

But she was certainly not the only resident of Elterbeck with an uneasy mind that weekend. James Taylor felt paralysed by an unusual indecision and turmoil. His fate seemed to be in suspension. It was not so much in a balance – for as an engineer, he could have weighed those scales and set himself to logically respect the outcome – but it seemed to him that he was at the mercy of an elaborate interplay of forces and personalities. For him it involved feelings of pride, anger and shame, as well as a physical desire and a yearning to be loved. On the part of others, there were three young women offering themselves to him in one way or another. There were also some older, more ghostly demons to confront or set aside; notably Emily herself and an evil force that went by the name of Bernard.

James' life so far had been mercifully free of major complications. Yet, he now found himself pinned beneath a net, weighted by temptations, needs, hopes, lusts and expectations; not all of them his own. He was sorely tempted to do nothing. It was usually his way in such matters; withdraw into isolation, so he would not get wounded or compromised.

His personality was partly epicurean. He dwelt, with refined intensity, on the notion of love and loving; yet, it was mostly innocent, shading into the passionately romantic. In his fervid imagination, he would distil any pleasure to its subtlest and most appealing parts. However, he had lived a life of passionate, imaginary gratification, unsullied by daily realities, for too long now and he was increasingly aware that this extreme idealisation might finally leave him without any real partner or friend. He had put so little to the test. In fact, so far, he had never even wanted to engage totally with anyone that he had met for fear that he would be cruelly disappointed. Emily had been an erotic fantasy of maturity, passion and self-possession. He could yield to that fantasy completely, if she just took him as her reclusive slave, subject to her every whim. But it was more Arabian Nights than Yorkshire Dales and he could not see an everyday relationship being fulfilled with her. She was perverse at times and moody. She patronised him and could be coarse to the point of vulgarity. She exuded too much packed flesh and energy and there was a powerful need in her at times, which alarmed him. Also, he ruefully added, she was married.

Of the younger women, Hetty was the simplest case. Dear Hetty, she was so besotted and so vulnerable that he despaired of her. Almost any other young man would have made the most of the opportunity that Hetty presented. He knew that. It was Hetty who had urged him to take the little cottage. It was Hetty who had somehow obtained her own key and who now sneaked in and out with little gifts or weak excuses. And he loved her for her sweet, childish devotion. She was sisterly and giggly and she fussed over his food, his linen and his coal. He kissed her cheek tenderly when she left, it was a ritual that she expected as of right, but she turned her mouth fractionally away and almost flinched as they touched, such a minimal hesitation, but he noticed it keenly. Hetty's love was nervously reverential and domestic: he guessed it would stop at the bedroom door. Just once, had James tried to rouse her to anything like a physical act of love, drawing her into an embrace, searching for her mouth, pulling himself close to her. She had wriggled defiantly and then fought free, distressed and confused, fearing that her inadequacy would drive him away.

'I'm not that kind of girl,' she had spluttered and run off in tears.

'I fear you are right there,' James had answered silently.

He knew that he could get her into his bed, almost at any time, just by threatening to leave or turn elsewhere. She would yield to the right sort of emotional blackmail. But did he want a callow, squirming village girl? He had had one several years before and had regretted it. Yet, he must not hurt her.

He knew that the safe option was a solid and sensible young lady called Ann Hargreaves. Each week, he went to tea with a Mrs. Smith, recently made a widow for the second time, and her very pleasant, very available daughter Ann. She was quite a cultured young lady. Mr Hargreaves had been a man of modest means, which meant that as far as he was concerned, he did not need to work at anything seriously, so he had dabbled in astronomy and as a sideline, he had imported tea from a cousin, who happened to own a plantation in India. It turned out to be a lucrative business, but its easy profitability had tempted Mr Hargreaves into further speculation in coffee, molasses, zinc and South American railways and he had finally lost everything, including his house. As a further inconvenience to his family, he had then died of a heart attack and Mrs. Hargreaves, having no family of her own, had faced debtors and destitution. It was at this point, and completely out of the blue, that a Mr Smith had stepped up and made her an offer. He was a contractor on a local railway and had admired her from afar at church and at social gatherings. She and her daughter, facing ruin and homelessness, had therefore exchanged a small manor house in Sussex for three rooms of an isolated farmhouse on the road to Hawes. Scarcely had the change of name been properly secured in her memory than Mr Smith had contracted a fever and died. He had fallen into the icy waters of Little Beck in the early days of surveying that area and had never recovered.

The ladies now tried to maintain standards in a hut in Belgravia, doing some washing and sewing, and they had two respectable lodgers. Ann Hargreaves was twenty; she could speak some French and she could sing and play with some musicality. She could knit and embroider and she did some work at the little school, bringing in a meagre income. She was solid and cheerful, deep bosomed and short waisted, with a sweet smile and dimples in her cheeks. James felt insubstantial beside her. But she spoke and behaved very sensibly and did not fawn.

He liked her smile and her love of books and music, which she by no means forced on others. She would be faithful and interesting, indeed, quite practical, and Mrs Smith had hinted that she had kept back a "few hundred" for a wedding and home making. He could do worse. Why then was he so loathe to do more than drink tea?

A large part of the answer was that for the last few weeks his thoughts had increasingly become focused on a 10-year-old girl named Grace Bernard. Over the last weekend, he had been able to think of little else.

She had haunted his sleep and her image stepped beside him during the day: fragile, demure and winsome. He told himself that he could resolve nothing else until the question of Grace was settled. He was unhappily aware, and it chilled him with dismay, that his interest in her looked likely to cost him dear in a number of ways.

On the very night that Emily wrestled with temptations, guilt and pain, James Taylor gave up the attempt to sleep and sat staring at his meagre fire, heavy with indecision. So close, and yet so divided, they both felt that their futures could be shaped by the coming days or weeks.

Soirée
April 1871

The link between James Taylor and the Bernard family was Walter Hirst. Walter and Charles Hirst, Scottish engineers of some experience, were well respected by their fellow engineers, by their subcontractors and by the Midland Railway Company. They had worked now on a number of major undertakings and had always proved their worth. They had good banter with the men, exacting standards and pride in their work. They also liked a drink. Walter Hirst was not married and he lived with his brother and family in a cottage near Colt Park. It was the bachelor Walter that became a target for Mr Bernard, supplying the best liquor to him and plying him with regular invitations to join one of his celebrated soirées. Walter went along sceptically and with every intention of leaving early, but his fall from grace was as rapid as it was predictable, once he had tasted the charms of the elegant and shapely Nancy Bernard.

For several weeks he was a regular at the Blue Lamp, concealing from his brother the level of infatuation that he had rapidly succumbed to. But then his invitations, his rights as he saw it, were withdrawn suddenly, nastily and without warning and the threats began. Some were for money; others were requests that he write to the Midland demanding the reinstatement of that eminent engineer Mr Oliver Bernard. If he wanted to see Nancy again ... if he wanted to keep his reputation ... if he did not want his brother and sister-in-law to know what had been happening ...

Among the engineers and officials closest to him, it was obvious that Walter had changed, had hardened and become edgy, that he was under pressure, and word soon spread that he was Bernard's latest victim. He was not the first that had placed himself in this dilemma.

James heard this and although he was not aware of all that had happened, he could sense that a scandal and possible disgrace hung over his mentor. It grieved him. Out of respect for Walter he was upset, but he also knew only too well of the powerful temptation that the Blue Lamp offered. He had been to a soirée himself a month earlier. A little naively, he had been persuaded to attend by another engineer, who enjoyed teasing young James and who wanted to ruffle his composure. This young man, Abel Lomax, had stressed that the soirées were genteel affairs, musical gatherings with the company of accomplished young women. There was strong drink, but you did not need to partake, and you only went by invitation, so the clientele were select.

Had James been more inclined to drink and gossip with the men, he would have heard enough to be pre-warned. As it was, he was confused by the whole atmosphere, which seemed to be both cordial and exciting and yet, at the same time, threatening. He was excited by the apparent geniality, the relaxed ease of the occasion, and he was aroused by the warm approaches of the girls. But the responses of the other men troubled him, with two of them quickly becoming very drunk and openly licentious with the older daughters. A couple of others like him appeared uncertain of how to proceed. Then, Bernard took the others off to another part of the hut, along with Nancy, Marie and Olive, and James was left for a good while sitting almost silently opposite the youngest girl, who seemed at one moment to be trying to shrink out of sight, but then in an instant would suddenly engage in chatter, giggle at anything he said and simper falsely but with a suggestive leer that he found alarming. Her lips were painted and her cheeks rouged. He refused to drink, which caused a stir, and he left quite early, before any more compromising behaviour could be initiated. Yet, he called himself a coward later. He had felt the pull of unlicensed action and wished he had been more courageous. He had lived a sheltered life and had encountered few opportunities to let himself go and, it might have been easy: such a possibility was very alluring to men working in harsh and isolated conditions, with little access to the exotic. But he had turned away, adopting his usual bystander stance.

Apparently, Walter Hirst had fallen into the trap that James had glimpsed. He sympathised. James was capable of great loyalty and compassion, where he had been treated with kindness and respect, and now he wanted to repay the good faith shown by Walter and to try to lessen the difficulties of his situation. But Oliver Bernard rarely left his hut and for two weeks, James had tried to intercept him or to find a way to plead for Walter's release. At last, not sure where this was leading, uneasy about the wisdom of the move or of the full nature of his own motives, he had got himself invited to another soirée. It was the very same evening that Emily, Ethel and Robert had stood as observers just outside the Blue Lamp, equally unsure what James was up to.

Once again, there were five guests present: two looked at ease and James thought he had seen them working down the line at Horton; one little man in a sober, dark suit seemed out of place. The fourth, again, was also a stranger. He was a middle-aged, slightly stooping man, with a self-deprecating cringing air about him, as if he were used to being subservient. He wore a long coat, rather greasy with wear, and a grey cravat tied sharply at his scrawny neck. He was sallow, but the drink or his nervousness had brought an unconvincing flush to his cheeks and he kept licking his lips nervously. To James, he somehow looked more like an undertaker or a shopkeeper than an employee of the railway or in any way connected to it.

James had been careful to take a modest drink and he now sipped it, cool and neat in his best coat, and placed himself in a corner seat. He needed to observe and to look for some kind of opportunity; his planning amounted to no more than that. So he was careful to try to appear at his ease and appreciative of the charms on display around him. Despite himself though, he began to relax. He had to admit that it was not difficult to feel privileged: the occasion was uniquely engaging, in a way, and he was soon in danger of forgetting his altruistic purpose in being there. He could see that Mr Bernard knew just how to manage the event. He kept himself well back, so that the focus was always on the ladies. He was a massive, jowly man with a greying beard, cut quite short, and very formal dress. As far as James could observe, he drank steadily yet orchestrated the evening vigilantly, with subtle nods, flicks of his silver cane and occasional instructions to family or guests, in a high-pitched, insinuating, almost effeminate voice. 'Nancy, my dearest, Mr Taylor needs another drink, I do believe. And Jane, my love, would you sit with Mr Grantley awhile. Come, Marie, a little music if you will.'

James was aware that it would not be easy to confront him and he had no evidence to present or leverage to use. He was wary now and confused, unused to powerful liquor or the blandishments of five women, now taking turns to win his favour. Nancy was certainly stunning. She was tall, with thick black hair, vibrant and shining, arranged in ringlets, drawn back over her ears but leaving tendrils to fall free to frame her clear, regular features, soft blue eyes and dark lips.

Her elegant gown, drawn tight at the waist, emphasised the swelling white porcelain of her breasts that were thrust together in a thin cotton blouse, buttoned carefully to reveal their fullness, tempting to the impatient eye. She wore heavy pearl earrings and a choker of black ribbon, supporting a large sapphire that nestled at the curve of her cleavage. On his last visit, the two drunken men had jealously monopolised Nancy; now, James felt the full force of her attractions and his bones melted, whilst his head spun.

Marie, the second daughter, was shorter and sparkier, pert and earthy, ready for any suggestive remark, pushing herself close, seeking contact. She was obviously a drinker. Her appetites dismayed James, but at the same time it roused him uncomfortably. He was almost frightened of her and he hoped to keep her at bay.

The mother was a surprisingly delicate and timid woman, overdressed and yet timid. She simpered at the guests and flinched at the sound of her husband's voice, whatever he said. James pitied her but silently condemned her compliance and he found it difficult to manage polite niceties with her.

However, James was again moved, almost to tears, by the two youngest as they worked, with a kind of desperation, to win him over. Mr Bernard seemed to be watching this with particular attention. Had he instructed them to target him? Olive was a sultry, ill-tempered 12-year-old, dressed and decorated to look five years older. She resembled Marie in looks, with the spasmodic appearance of a similar touch of vitality and vulgarity, which was quickly withdrawn beneath a protective veneer of boredom and spite, especially at the expense of her sisters. James guessed that this sour image was her way of keeping the men at bay on evenings such as this and he wondered what punishment the father considered such betrayal might deserve. He thought he could detect bruising around her neck, when her high dress collar, too big for her child's neck, revealed too much. Her courage and spirit made her almost admirable, but the need for it made him angry. She smiled at him with ghastly insincerity and he told her a story about the ponies at the works.

The youngest, Grace, was like the mother, cowed and compliant, pale-skinned with mousey-brown hair, always glancing towards the father, desperate to please. She was restless and pressed James hard, moving in role from the coquette, like Nancy, to the willing whore, like Marie, and succeeding in the process in creating an ugly pastiche of both that James could not handle. He was dismayed to find that she had been dressed, on this occasion, in an almost doll-like fashion, with a simple shift dress, dark stockings and little ankle boots. Her cheeks had red circles of rouge. It was almost an hour into the evening and the atmosphere was mellowing around card tables, when James was suddenly horrified to realise that one of the other guests, the sallow and nervous Mr Grantley, had eyes only for Grace and had placed himself so close to her at one of the tables that he must be able to feel her against him. James felt sick and panicky.

When the merry-go-round stopped and the ladies withdrew, James had not advanced his cause at all and now could think only of Grace at the mercy of the sickly, salivating Mr Grantley. His heart was making irregular patterns against his ribs and his mouth was dry and papery. He gulped at his drink. Mr Bernard made a halting round with a jug of liquor and James allowed his glass to be refilled. As this was happening, he summoned the courage to say to Mr Bernard, 'I would welcome a private word with you, sir.' He had meant to sound imposing; but he realised that he sounded as if he were nervously pleading.

'Oh, Mr Taylor,' the voice was dropped lower and Bernard leaned over him, so that James felt the weight and force of the man. 'Many of my guests start to try to make private arrangements with me, but you must know that at this very interesting stage of the evening I only operate in full view of all my guests. So, come along ...' And with this he leant on his stick, swept round and called the others to attention, before James could reply. 'Pull your chairs to the fire, gentlemen, or at least up to the stove!' This being done, he then proceeded, with as much calm as if he were solving a simple engineering problem, to point out to them that he had five guests and he would be happy to match them to any of the five interesting ladies that they had met, 'For further pleasure or entertainment.' He reminded them, with a mock attempt at sobriety and in a quietly sneering voice, that if they wished, they could, 'Retire now to their own beds, wherever they may be.'

One man left without a word, ignored by them all. Bernard then smoothly switched into a bartering mode and with ease he was able to find customers for Nancy and Marie, taking the money and escorting the working men from Horton to small partitioned rooms at the other side of the hut. James was left sitting alongside Mr Grantley. He could smell the sweat of the man, mingled with the sour odour of unwashed clothes and something else, was it flour or yeast? He was obviously not a navvy and James could not connect him to Batty Green at all. He glanced at the man's face. He was breathing fast, almost panting, eyes protruding, a poor skin with dark blotches, uneven and pointed teeth.

The idea of that man touching Grace was convulsing James. Yet, he knew he was falling into Bernard's trap and he could hear the dragging footsteps returning across the hut as if they dragged the child's doll-like body with them. James again gulped at his rough whisky and then was on his feet instantly. Before another word was spoken, he offered a guinea for Grace, thrusting the coin aggressively at Bernard. At his side, Grantley gasped and shot to his feet, pushing James aside and facing Bernard belligerently, beginning to demand his rights.

Time seemed suddenly to slow down for James, the room swayed around him and the immediacy of his surroundings paled, slid away, withdrew as if a gauze curtain had silently descended. He felt shaky and he tried to take in what was happening, but it seemed to involve someone other than him. He knew that he was standing, the heat from the stove like a wall in front of him, the men to one side arguing – one voice high and penetrating, the other low and grumbling. He saw Bernard raise his cane, for all the world as if he were about to conduct an orchestra, but then James realised that Mr Grantley was being pointed towards the door and Bernard was threatening to write to his wife and children. It occurred to James that he ought to feel pleased, but he was not sure why. Then Bernard was at his side, gently ushering him down to the other end of the hut and into a side room, which was cooler and darker. James found a chair, sat down and closed his eyes.

After a short while, he felt the tension begin to seep away from him and he was able to focus on the room. Grace was on the bed. She posed, perhaps as her sisters had taught her. She sat with one leg curled beneath her, the other trailing over the edge of the bed. Boots and stockings had gone. She wore a plain linen smock, hitched up above her knee and loose at the front. A single candle on a wall-mounting threw wavering patterns of light across her pale skin and the dark eyes that were fixed on him were passively attentive. She neither moved nor spoke, but waited with the patience of a monument. With utter dismay, he realised that he had bought her, this child. She was his for an hour or two to deal with as he desired. His deepest wish was to be away from here, dissolved into atoms, washed away from the trial that he knew he was about to go through, which would test him cruelly. I am not fit for this, he thought. He had a vision of himself as a much older man, like Mr Grantley, wanting to touch this young flesh and to take joy in besmirching it. He shuddered. Another silent moment passed. He forced himself to bear his better part.

James looked at her, fragile and yet quite calm now that it had come to this point. It had all happened so fast and what could he do? He needed time to think and he had so little. He had to deal with Grace first, that much was clear. He turned to her. 'Get into bed, Grace.' He spoke bluntly and coldly, hoping for simple compliance. She glared at him, startled, and then began to reach behind to lift the smock over her head. 'No,' he ordered. 'Keep that on and get beneath the bedcover.'

He turned away, listening for her movements, but also trying to focus on other sounds in the hut. There were voices, male and female. There was a burst of laughter that he thought sounded like Marie, a bed shifting with weight, a door banging somewhere and footsteps. He couldn't make it all out. There was some shouting outside, but some way off. It was probably not connected. He could not tell where Bernard was, but he felt the venom of his presence, permeating the very air they breathed. He had to get out.

He turned back to Grace. She lay quietly waiting, her eyes almost black in the gloom, the bed clothes loosely pulled over her. He smiled at her and without a word he began to tuck her in, as if she were one of his younger sisters. It was almost a reflex action. He was taken aback when she shot upright, a look first of panic and then of terror contorting her features.

'Aren't you … getting in?' She whispered urgently, unable for a second to disguise her sudden fear of failing to please him. 'Oh, please, sir … please. I will be good, you can see, I will do whatever you say, anything …' She was almost fighting him now, pulling the bedclothes loose whenever he tried to fasten her in.

'Grace!' he ordered, trying to keep his voice down. He did not know what to do. Despite having paid his guinea, he had the irrational fear that one of the parents might come to the door to check what was happening. Again, the tone of voice seemed to organise Grace into automatic compliance. She became still. 'Lie down and listen to me.'

Tears of hopelessness and grief spilled from her eyes, but she settled uneasily. 'I am not annoyed with you. I will tell your father ...' Again, he got no further. She was striving to be up and reaching for him, pleading in her desperate murmur.

'No, don't speak to him; don't say ... he'll know anyway. He always knows what's gone on ... he'll look in ... oh, please, just lie down with me ... please.' She flung herself free and thrust her arms around his neck, dry sobs barely stifled in her breast.

He held her ... and held her ... and waited. He had to try some other tactic. He sensed that too much sympathy might make her too clinging and perhaps that was one way that she dealt with a certain type of man that came to her.

'Would you rather I called Mr Grantley in?' he asked in apparent seriousness.

She shook herself free and wiped her eyes. 'He's horrible,' she said petulantly, now throwing herself back onto the bed, careless of how her clothes fell, glancing to see if he would follow. James kept his eyes fixed on hers, showing real determination, covered her and began to tuck her in again, hoping that the worst was past. 'He smells funny and he wants me to sit on his knee and he touches me under the table.'

James stopped her. 'Enough,' he snapped. She was quiet again and she looked at him sulkily. He sat on the bed and smiled at her. 'Why does he smell funny?' he asked.

She shrugged. 'Don't know. I think it's biscuits or flour or animals or something. But it's always stale and a bit sickly. I hate him. He's always got his googly eyes on me or his sweaty hands.'

'You're a sweet girl, Grace, and I would like to help you, but I don't know how.' He paused and sighed; unhappy, friendless and faced with things beyond his experience. A phrase came into his head: take this cup away from me. He could just walk out. No one would stop him.

Almost in despair, he opted for honesty, hoping with blind intuition that she might help him. 'I came tonight because your father is threatening a friend of mine,' he explained. 'Then I saw the Biscuit

Man looking at you and I … didn't want him to … win, if you know what I mean.' His halting speech petered out. He knew he was hopeless and should leave. He was helping no one and was harming himself: the fate of many a well-intentioned innocent, who goes unprepared into dangerous waters. He slumped and another silence began to grow as if spreading slowly across the floor, like a pool of oil, soundlessly dispersing. Somewhere, he could hear "goodnights" being shouted, dogs barking and a dull, rhythmic thumping.

'I'm glad you beat the Biscuit Man,' came a rather drowsy reply at last, 'whatever Father says or does. What was your friend's name?'

'Walter. Walter Hirst.'

'Oh, I liked him,' she chirped. 'He told me funny stories about Scotland and little men that lived on whisky and tatties.'

'That's him,' James nodded. He could picture Walter entertaining Grace and whisky and tatties were a common theme for him. 'He is a good man, but I think he loved your Nancy too much. And now he's in trouble with your father … and … and I would like to help him.' He stopped, not knowing exactly what hold Bernard had over Walter. 'What can I do, Grace?'

She shrugged and settled herself back into her pillow, yawning. She was fighting sleep and it gladdened him to see her comfortable. An eye opened and with a slightly sharper tone, she said, 'The only one that can handle Father is Nancy. He don't dare hurt her or spoil her good looks. Tell Nancy. She liked your friend, I know. She told me. Nancy has plans, Nancy has.' her eyes closed.

James smiled at his sleepy friend, bent over and kissed her cheek. 'Sleep well, Grace,' was his simple benediction.

With an upsurge of hope in his heart, he left the room quietly and strode down the hut. Mr and Mrs Bernard were seated near the door and as luck would have it, Nancy was sitting nearby. He guessed that her customer had lost his nerve or passed out. She looked bored, but managed a curious glance and a half-smile at James as he approached.

Mr Bernard, too, must have sensed something in the way that James approached, because he stood up, braced himself and tapped his shin with his silver cane.

'Ah, Mr Taylor, I trust your evening has been … how shall I say … satisfactory?' The high, curdling voice did not intimidate James, who had decided not to hold back.

'I didn't touch your daughter, Mr Bernard, other than to stop her tears. Usually a father's duty that, don't you think?' James was surprised by the vehemence of the anger that he had stifled too long. 'Or even a mother's duty,' he almost snarled at Mrs Bernard, who kept her head down.

'They often say that they've not touched her,' came Bernard's softly insinuating reply, high in pitch and wheedling. 'I'll be the judge o' that when I see what she has to say,' he continued, tapping the cane against his leg and fixing James with a stony stare.

'And I'll let the constable and the magistrate be the judge, too,' countered James, his blood thumping through his veins in mighty drumbeats, his only card played early and straight. How he longed to be out of the door.

'Well,' came the measured reply, 'they are both customers, so I think I know their answer, young man. Now, run along and don't threaten me, cos I know you have a little sweetheart: Hetty, ain't it? Or shall we speak to Miss Ann? I'm not sure which you prefer, but I'm sure that they would both be surprised to hear that you like to pay a guinea a time for much younger material. Or, perhaps, a letter home? I know someone who would be happy to tell me exactly where you live.' James felt the blood seep from his face and his tongue swelled thickly. 'Get the young man's coat and hat, Nancy, would you, dear, our young friend is leaving us.' Mr Bernard lumbered heavily away.

James was floored, defeated and humiliated. How did this man know so much? What would he do to Grace? He had got it so wrong and had merely spread the filth of Mr Bernard, not stemmed it. He fumed, absent from time and space for a few seconds. Then he became aware that Nancy was standing before him, impassive, as beautiful as marble.

He sought her eyes, whilst dropping his hands, refusing to take his coat and hat. She stared back and raised a quizzical eyebrow.

'I work with Walter Hirst,' he said very quietly. 'Your father is blackmailing him and destroying his life. Is that what you want, Nancy?'

A light flickered across her eyes. It was an almost imperceptible change in her demeanour, but the only one. James was defeated. She was the same height as him, but he now felt insubstantial beside her.

'I will see you to the door,' she said, with an icy deliberation that James now had to obey.

He took his coat and hat wearily and followed her. She opened the door, said thank you to him quite formally and allowed him to pass; then she stepped through it behind him, closing it firmly. He jumped, his nerves jangling afresh. What now? She raised a finger to her lips and then pointed to the deserted pathway between two storage huts just below them, the very spot where Robert had tried to win a kiss from Emily an hour earlier. They moved in silence.

'Enough,' she said, when they were between the huts, but still had a view of the Blue Lamp. They faced each other, but she had control. Her pale blue eyes, the rapid rise and fall of her breasts, her ringlets and jewels, her full lips roused by fire or passion: she leaned closer to James and he almost buckled. 'Don't fall down, Mr Taylor, after your brave stand against my father. Stay the hero for a little while longer, if you please.' She steadied his arm with her hand and drew him in. 'Just come close, in case my father is watching,' she whispered. Her lips brushed his ear, her breasts pressing into his coat. 'Make it look as if I'm making a convert of you,' she sighed. 'Put your arms around me, please.' He had barely strength to obey. He held her close. Her moist mouth was pressed to his ear.

'I have plans to escape,' she whispered to him. 'I will take Grace, perhaps Olive, too, if she will come. I have a friend to go to, a man that will treat us well, I know this, so you needn't worry. We will be gone and Walter will be safe then, because without me my father is nothing. He is a pig, a bully, nothing more. But I need some help. I need a pony and trap at the Hill Inn, at six in the morning next Wednesday. Can you do this, James? It will take me to the early train from Ingleton, which is all I want. I will manage the rest. But I need someone I can rely on. Can it be you?'

He had no time to reply. Suddenly, a wheedling, sinister voice cut through the air and they both jumped, especially James. 'Is that you there, Nancy?' It was as if the man had just materialised. A footstep was dragged across the top step. Luckily, cloud was obscuring the moon and the area was complex with shadows.

She pushed James hard back against the storage hut, lifted her skirts in one deft movement and pushed herself hard against him, pulling open her blouse and twisting her mouth hard against his. She then began to grind her pelvis against him and pulled her mouth away to call out, breathlessly, 'Just a moment, Father. Mr Taylor's getting his money's worth, after all.' A sickly, curdling laugh followed and a door closed. Nancy slowed her tempo and glanced around. They were both breathing rapidly. 'He's gone,' she said, moving away a few inches. James stared at her heaving breasts and the firm flesh of her thighs.

'I'm almost sorry that he didn't stay a little longer,' he said. They both laughed and she dropped her skirts, but left her breasts half exposed, knowing how they would assist her bargaining.

'So, can I rely on you?' she asked.

'I have two conditions,' James replied.

She gave him a mocking side-glance and swept back her hair, lifting her breasts to the night air. She spoke with affection, not contempt.

'Well, Mr Taylor, you are not so very different to all the others, are you? You are not a selfless hero, after all. What's your price?'

'First, you must bring Grace. You arrive without her and I will leave; whatever excuses you make.'

Nancy nodded and stood, hands now on hips, awaiting the rest, a smile half breaking across her face.

'I think you have already guessed what my second condition is,' James mumbled. 'You have only yourself to blame. You put the idea into my head.' He grimaced and she bent forwards and kissed him gently.

'We have a deal, my friend.' She lifted her skirts again. 'Now, open your breeches, Mr Taylor. A vicar that I once went with was lifting his surplice like this and he told me that there are many gateways to heaven, and some are in surprising places. Come into my heavenly places, Mr Taylor, but mind that you don't step on my new gown in the process.'

They both laughed and the sound was one that James never forgot.

Escape
April 1871

The next morning at breakfast, James asked for the loan of the pony and trap early on Wednesday. George simply nodded his approval, but there was something in the way that James had asked, a fractional hesitation or rise in tone, that alerted Emily. She looked over at him, but he avoided eye contact and busied himself buttering bread, as if the buttering were a mission with far-reaching consequences. He looked pale; indeed, slightly yellowish around the mouth and drawn around the eyes. She asked what he wanted it for. He glanced up, hesitated again and then said that he was meeting an important visiting engineer at the early train, but the blot of colour in his cheeks made her curious and his blue-grey eyes were shifty and mobile. Again, she sensed that there was more to James than she knew.

'A shall be up early meself on Wednesday for the milk run, cos a've given Joshua the day off to visit his sister, who's not well, so a can help, if you like.' He stammered a brief thanks and then shot her one of his broad, boyish smiles.

A mystery and a challenge: quite like old times, she reflected as he left. But she did not entirely believe the story about the visitor. She no longer trusted him and was determined to watch his movements where she could.

Other thoughts and preoccupations soon crowded in and left her little time for reflection. She wanted to see how Robert was, Georgie was going to school for a full day for the first time and George had to see the doctor in Ingleton about his spine, so there was a flurry of activity in setting off in various groups and different directions. Jack waved them off, looking a little disconsolate at losing Georgie and with Laura clinging to one of his legs. Hetty stood alongside him, rocking Angel in her arms, framed by the farm doorway in the pale sunshine: it created a picture of harmony that would have graced the pages of any sketchbook or journal, of that time or since. Emily and Ethel carried the image with them as they made their way up the lane, walking beside the cart for the first half-mile, as was their way, and for each of them the image meant something different, but they both felt that it was fragile.

Emily had a ready excuse for going to the camp, as the school, now growing in numbers, wanted a milk delivery, but she gratefully reflected, as she jogged along later on her yellow cart, that no one even asked her where she was going any more. She always had business at the camp and she was now earning enough to take on another worker and perhaps expand further. But this morning's business was different: it brought a sparkle to her blood and a glow to her cheeks. She sat up straight and savoured the soft spring air, threw off her bonnet and opened her blouse, until she felt cooled and invigorated at the same time. How would Robert receive her? What were his needs? Was he disfigured? He would be a terrible patient, but she was sure that she could handle him, soothe him and bring him round. She pictured herself attending to him, laughing with him, being herself and also free of the farm and her anxieties there.

They split up when they got to Ribblehead, tethering the mare near the reading room. Georgie was being difficult: sullen and silent as he got closer to full time "schooling". Ethel coaxed and then bullied him along and Emily slipped away, basket on her arm, saying that they would meet in an hour. But Robert was not at his lodgings. She was told that he had gone back to work. She found a lad playing fivestones on the path and paid him tuppence to take a note to the brickworks, asking Robert to meet her at the reading rooms within the hour. She waited restlessly and a note was brought back by the same lad, saying that Mr McIntosh could not get away and that he could not see Mrs Wright at the moment. She felt cheated and aggrieved by the formality of the note.

She went over to the little school and tried to speak to the teacher about the milk order, but again was politely turned away and told to speak to Mr Tiplady or "someone on the board". She tried to find Mr Tiplady, but he was out. Then Ethel was late and so Emily's mood was acid and resentful as they made their way back to Elterbeck. George did not return until nearly four o'clock, smelling of drink and unwilling to discuss the doctor's comments, other than to say that he was making tolerable progress and could not expect a full recovery; at least, not yet, anyway. To cap it all, Jack had gone to meet Georgie as he walked home and had come across some former butties from the works. They were short-handed and had offered him work at the tunnel, labouring for the stonemasons, who were lining the roof. It was well-paid work, with a cheap bunk at one of the tunnel huts. Jack and Ethel came straight to tell her and it was clear that the idea was being taken seriously. He was talking it through with Ethel now, but Emily could see that the man was alert and eager at the thought of a return to his navvy life. Emily wanted to talk all this through herself, with George, but her husband was heady with beer and brandy and was dozing by the fire.

Emily took a chair outside into the plain front garden. She looked across the valley as the sun set; it was a view that always settled her. She could sit watching like this for an hour at a time, passively preoccupied, observing the changing shape and texture of the clouds on that far hillside as they clung with unseen tentacles to the top, or trailed slowly northwards or swept towards her with menace. She felt the clamour of her own thoughts and needs begin to diminish, fading like an ashy fire, subsiding and falling inwards.

The prospect from all her front rooms and her garden was dominated by this sky, hill and cloudscape, a frame for the emphatic sweep of Ingleborough's steep northern face, just over 2 miles away. From its summit, the hill curved unremittingly to the north and east, falling away with elegant precision to Park Fell. When she was first married, she had made a point of walking these clean limestone uplands several times each year. Perhaps she should go again.

The farm at Elterbeck had its back wedged close to the opposite valley side. It was always mossy and damp there, where the shoulder of the hill dropped with a craggy flourish to the wells and yards of the squat white house. But at the front, the bright, open face of the farm looked south-east across an open, featureless valley bottom; one that had been bludgeoned and scarred by slow-moving ice many millennia ago. Then, the opposite valley side curved ever more sharply upwards, a severe grey wall rising to the long blister of bare crag that dominated the distant skyline.

She imagined herself up there now, looking down at this cluster of buildings, little specks of white and grey, and if she had eagle vision, perhaps she would make out the little dark-haired figure, sitting on a kitchen chair just outside the door: a tiny fragment in the huge landscape that had persisted for thousands of years, relatively unchanged. Why should the miserable thoughts of that small speck of humanity matter to anyone, other than the speck herself? Who was there to care? She had no parents or any close family. She had turned away her husband, or so it seemed. She had also turned away from James in disgust and Robert seemed to be avoiding her. And now it was possible that Ethel, Jack and the children could leave. She walked down the path and looked at the trees. 'I'm not finished yet,' she said, with as much defiance as she could muster. She shivered with cold and went indoors.

But her negative mood persisted. Ethel and Jack said that they would make a decision by the end of the week and Ethel would not be drawn, so Emily feared the worst. George continued to be morose and remote, refusing to become involved. So that it was with some relief that she rose early on Wednesday to help James prepare the pony and trap and to urge Arthur and Ethel to hurry up with the milking. James was very quiet and he was quite tense and pale as they worked together. There was no banter or flirting. Again, she sensed that there was something of real consequence in prospect and her interest was piqued. James scarcely spoke, but seemed hesitant to leave.

'A'll walk up the lane aways with you, James,' she offered, when the trap was prepared. 'Then a'll come back for the milk.' He nodded and they set off in the dull grey of a misty morning, a cool wind occasionally cutting through the mist to skim over them and then disappear, as if searching for someone more fitting to investigate. Their lane crossed the flat valley bottom and then dipped down to an old, flat stone bridge, before climbing up to the toll road near the Hill Inn. She led the horse, with James walking, head-bowed, on the other side, clearly trying to avoid contact or discussion. She resolved to walk to the bridge and then let him get on with whatever it was he was doing. Once again, she felt rejected and was annoyed by it all.

She knew every rut and stone on this track and in the fields around; they were almost an extension of herself, so that when a more vigorous gust of wind cleared the mist a little she looked up instinctively, mapping their progress. About 100 yards ahead, and at the other side of the bridge she instantly picked out two female figures, wrapped in cloaks; one, tall, with a protective arm around the other, who was much shorter.

Their heads were close together and they were not looking down the lane at all. They were sheltering in the lee of a blackthorn bush and something about their hunched posture, their lack of interest in their surroundings, the long fall of weary shoulders and necks, suggested to Emily that they had been there for some time. The mist closed and Emily glanced over to James, but he still had his head down and his hat pulled hard down over his brows. She gently brought the horse to a halt and James suddenly became alert and looked over at her with anxiety.

'There are two women sheltering up ahead,' she said. He stared, as if staring would bore a hole in the mist, and then looked back at her, a look of appeal and confusion crowding his features. 'Are you goin' to tell me what's goin' on here or shall a just keep on and ask 'em meself?' She waited.

'I may need your help,' he said. 'Oh, thank God they are there.' He seemed to sink down into himself and then resurfaced. He turned to her now. 'They are waiting for me, cos I've agreed to help them to get the early train, because ... they're runnin' away and I wanted to help them, because they deserve a chance ...' He was agitated and almost pleading, his manner and his words infused with a hesitant, nervous emotion that quite startled Emily. 'You would agree with me, Emily, I know that you would, if you knew what I know, but I can't explain it all now, not at all. Their lives are like a kind of ... horrible slavery to men and to their father in particular, who's a bully and who hurts them and ... makes them do things. But we don't have much time and one of them's just a little girl, at least I hope that one of them is. But if their father catches us, I don't know what might happen, to them, I mean, but also to me.' She had never seen him so troubled: by turns, there was an air of purpose and then he was uneasily overcome. He was shaky. She needed no more information. The reference to the "little girl" sent her heart crashing against her ribs. Was he trying to abduct someone?

'Are these the girls from the Blue Lamp?' she asked. He nodded. 'Are you running away with them?' she blurted, this new thought seizing her dramatically and with a sense of sudden loss and anger.

'No, there's nothing in this for me, except a deal of trouble. I will come back, that is if you'll have me. Now, I must get on to them,' he said. 'Every moment counts now. Please, just trust me and help or leave me and I'll take my own chances with all this. I can't go back and if you want to go, just go, please.'

'A'm not sure. A'll help, if they need help, a suppose,' she said. Beset with doubts as she was, she also relished his need of her and a part of her heart went out to him in his boyish fear and uncertainty. And part of her wanted to trust him and to find out what this was all about. 'But, if a think or a find that tha's not been behaving rightly with this little one, then a'll probably kill you meself, so thou had better be sure that there's nothing to be ashamed of here.'

He shook his head and there were tears in his eyes. 'She's like my little sister and it fair breaks my heart,' he said. 'I've never touched her, I swear. I just want to get her away from … all this …'

Emily nodded and braced herself, but a part of her was charged with energy and curiosity. This was better! Here was hope! Here was challenge! Without more words, they moved on briskly, James jumping up onto the driving board and pulling Emily up beside him. The horse was jolted into a trot and they soon clattered onto the bridge. A tall figure loomed up out of the tree-lined mist, bonnet tightly drawn and a dark cloak, streaked with mud, wrapped close about her. The face was hidden.

'Nancy, is that you?' he called, pulling the horse to a halt. She half stumbled forwards and steadied herself against the wheel of the trap.

'Oh, James. Thank God you are here, I had almost …' Then she stopped as she looked beyond him and realised that there was someone else present.

'It's alright, Nancy, this is Emily. She's a friend and will help us. But where is Grace?' he demanded.

'She's here,' Nancy quickly reassured him, her hand reaching up to grasp his leg as if he might suddenly ride off. 'But we almost got caught. My father was very suspicious, I don't know why. He put extra locks on the door last night and I had to …' She faltered, catching her breath in a sob.

'What? Oh God, what did you do? Nancy, tell me.'

But Nancy's lip began to tremble and she hesitated. Then, almost silently, through the mist, a small figure appeared at her side, damp wisps of hair snatched from her bonnet by the wind as she lowered her hood and looked up at James. There were smears across her pale face. Emily could swear that there was a yellowish tinge to her. But her voice was calm and clear.

'She hit him with a bottle, cos he was laughing at us and saying that he made all the decisions in our family,' said Grace with simple

132

clarity. 'And then he went down on his knees and she hit him again with another bottle. He was bleeding and she tied him up real tight and stuffed something in his mouth. And Marie took his stick thing away and hid it and so I got the keys and we got out. Olive took his money from his box and threw it out of the window to us and then she and Marie were going to lock all the doors again and throw the keys in the fire. And Mother said nothing, but just cried. But he's not dead, more's the pity, cos he was beginning to moan and groan as we left. So we had to hide and we were afraid that he would send someone after us, so we slept under a hut, with the rats and that, and then came here.' She ended with the simple statement, as if the events were quite commonplace.

Nancy had recovered herself and she smiled through her tears at her little sister's account, drawing her close. 'I think someone is out looking for us,' she said. 'There was a lot of noise and voices at one point, but we lay very still and then came along through the fields and hid under some trees for a while; got wet and everything. And we're tired and hungry. Please help us, cos I can't go back. I'd rather kill myself.' She raised her beautiful dark eyes and sobbed a little.

Emily, thoughts and impressions spiralling through her, still had time to reflect that it was quite a performance and she knew that she was dealing with an expert. James turned to her, uncertain, looking for a sign. Emily quickly assessed the options.

'A shall go up to the road an' check if there is anyone there looking for you,' she said. 'Wait here.'

She climbed down and hurried off up the lane, the mist quickly opening and closing round her as she made her ghostly passage through a curtain of fine, damp lace.

At the road, she could see nothing and so she went up to the Hill Inn, which was just 20 yards away, where a brazier was burning, with several figures huddled around it at the roadside. She approached and they turned to look at her as if she was an unwelcome addition to their watch. She pretended to be waiting for her husband, who was on his way from Hawes. They said they had seen no one. Then they asked her if she had seen 'Two young ladies, wanted by the constable on suspicion of theft of money and property from a hut at Jericho last night'. She shook her head and quietly turned away, doing her best to appear casual and uninterested. She had no plan and returned to the bridge thoughtfully.

The little group there was disconsolate and holding onto each other: the horse steamed and shook his bridle, a living statue in a dreary scene.

She spoke to James. 'They're watching the road here, so a think they will probably be doing the same at Ingleton, though a don't know,' she reported. An idea was beginning to assume a shape inside her head.

'Even if tha gets thir, tha art too conspicuous in them clothes. Thou mun tek 'em to your cottage, James. Try to avoid talking to anyone at the farm. Give 'em some food an' a'll be there as soon as a can.'

She turned to Nancy and Grace and spoke more formally. 'A don't know as to what or who you are, but a will help you, because James has asked me to. But a shall only go so far with this an' no further. A did not choose this business. If the constable comes for you, a shall hand you over.' She was thinking aloud, her brain trying to marshal the possibilities, the strategies, the risks. She was also beginning to feel resentful at being thrust into leading their mission, while James held hands with the girls and comforted them. Then she saw how it might work and put them to the test also.

'James!' She demanded that he take note of her. He turned and stepped close again. 'We still have the old cart in the barn. We need to get it out and harness the old grey cob; he's quiet but strong. Throw a pile o' old sheepskins and other stuff in t'back and a pile o' hurdles and some old tar buckets an' stuff. Mek it look dirty. We'll dress these two to look as scruffy an' as dirty as we can; get all that fine hair out o' sight and get old scarves round their faces and dirt on their legs. You, too, mun mek yourself as rough looking as possible. Then tha'll have to put them in t'cart as gypsies who have begged a ride. Cover 'em wi' the old sheepskins and some sacks and stuff. Try to hide the littl'un. They'll be watching for two girls on their own, not a lad an' a lass. Tek 'em to Ingleton. If the station's being watched, you'll have to go past, over the moors to Bentham or even Lancaster, or whichever way you can. Say you're looking for work or something. Just mek up a story. Hurry now. Get them to the cottage, mek 'em stay there an' then come back an' 'elp me. I'll have to borrow from Ethel.'

Nancy stepped forwards. She had obviously been listening. 'It's a good plan, thank you, Emily. I know you don't know me and you probably wouldn't approve if you did, but if we get away, you will have helped to save our lives and possibly our father's. Because if I had stayed any longer, I'm sure I would have killed him. God bless you for your kindness.' A single tear ran down one cheek and she bit her lip. 'Whatever happens, Grace and me will never forget this.' Almost as if it was a rehearsed gesture, a tearful Grace appeared from behind her sister and wrapped her arms round Emily, who held the little girl to her and smiled uncertainly. Was she truly saving souls from tragedy or was she just being taken in? She did not know, but her heart was full and she wanted to believe.

Within the hour, the plan was put into effect and the rough old cart, with its equally rough old horse, was moving away, with the fugitives under fleeces and old tarpaulins in the back. James was driving, looking like a vagrant himself, wearing several old coats of various workers and also the old shepherd, one over the other, and an old straw hat tied down right over his face. Luckily, although the mist had cleared, a low dirty drizzle was now falling, restricting visibility and probably disheartening anyone watching for the fugitives.

Emily had decided to walk with them for the first mile: she needed time to think and she knew that she could always slip away if they met an officer or other pursuer. They went down through Chapel le Dale without meeting anyone and then cut up to the Ingleton Road. It was quiet. She told James to pause and there she parted from them, wishing them luck and again receiving their heartfelt gratitude. Both Grace and Nancy were tearful beneath the dirt that had been smeared on their faces.

'Good luck with George,' James ruefully called as she turned her back. So far, George had proved to be their only significant problem.

George
April 1871

At Elterbeck, Emily had bustled Ethel and Hetty into action and she had got them pulling out old clothes and bonnets. She had then sent them off on the milk run to the camp, safely out of the way. They had been curious and confused, but Emily had abruptly halted all questioning and luckily, they had caught neither sight nor sound of the two girls. Once they had gone off, Arthur was ordered out to a distant meadow to check the sheep and Jack was told to stay in the house with the children. All was almost complete as they put the horse to the cart, when George had ridden down the lane. He had left earlier to go down to Twistleton's Farm to look at some cattle, but had turned back, as the weather worsened and the horse seemed to be going lame in one foot.

He rode up just as Emily and James were helping the girls across the yard towards the cart. There was a difficult moment, when they had all looked at each other: alarm in the faces of the girls, who had backed against the wall of the farmhouse and huddled together, grim determination reflected in James and Emily, who had stood their ground, a look of bewilderment in the face of George, who had remained on his horse and had circled them in astonishment.

At first, he had laughed at James in his beggar's disguise, but getting no response and sensing the panic, the agitation and a welter of emotion that was imbuing the air, his manner had changed and he had stopped beside Emily.

'Are you goin' to tell me what the deuce is happening in my yard, wi' mi old horse an' cart?' He raised his voice, a rare surge of temper funnelling through him. For some while, he had had the sense that he was cut out of something that others were a part of, particularly James and Emily. The constant talk of the camp, its intrigues and its characters; the exchange of meaningful glances or the occasional private smile or word signifying a special understanding; these had all made him feel insignificant. Hetty, too, seemed sometimes to be communicating with James and Emily whilst bypassing him, as if he were an object, a mere piece of old furniture. And now this dressing up, as if James were going into hiding, and two strange beggars in his yard, his wife in the thick of all this, when his back was turned and when she should be on the milk run. He was being made a fool of behind his back and he had had enough! He leaned over, closer to her, his face meaner than she had ever seen it.

'Well? Cat got your bloody tongue?'

Emily did not answer him, feeling lost for words and desperately trying to think how she could explain this situation. Her silence itself surprised him. Then, a brief, unaccustomed look of panic crossed her face, which told him better than any other communication that there was something important at stake here. James began to speak and he moved round to face him.

'This is all my doing, George. Emily has just been trying to help me get out of a ... well, a kind of a problem that I caused, and ...' He stopped as George suddenly wheeled the horse round and clattered over the cobbles to the two girls. Nancy swept Grace behind her and stood up straight to meet him as both Emily and James tried to intervene, but George ignored them, a brash new energy exuding from him, his spirit ablaze.

'My God, who'd a thought it!' he exclaimed urging the horse up close to the girls. 'A reckon a know who you are, in a manner o' speakin'.' He dismounted, threw down the reins and pushed roughly past James to come face-to-face with Nancy. He almost sneered as he spoke. 'I met Tom Borston on the road, the shepherd, and he told me o' some right goings-on last night at one o' them huts. A couple of whores that nearly killed their father, stole his brass an' then ran for it – and half the county out looking for them – one that is said to be tall an' remarkably 'andsome. Why, you're no beggar or tramp. a reckon on you're one o' them murderin' whores and who's t'other 'un behind you, eh?'

He made as if to push Nancy aside, but she screeched and grabbed his hand, whilst James grabbed the other arm and Emily shouted at him to stop. There was a moment's baffled hiatus, almost a stalemate. Of all of them, it was Nancy that was quickest to regain her self-composure.

She released his hand almost contemptuously, tossed back her hood, pulled off the filthy bonnet and shook out her hair, lustrously black and rich, bizarrely contrasting with her dirty face and piercing eyes. She brought Grace round beside her, whey-faced and snivelling, and then addressed George.

'You're right,' she stated simply, with a half-smile. 'We are not beggars and whore may be a harsh word, but there are many who would call us that, though we really only did what our father made us do from a young age, and that includes Grace, and we got not a penny for it.'

She now took a step forwards herself, forcing them all to edge backwards clumsily. She pushed herself close to George, the passion rising in her voice and the colour in her cheeks and lips peering through the dirt.

'Yes, we are on the run and you can turn us in if you choose. Prison would be better than living as we had to live. I won't go back to that hut though, I'd rather die here than face that again, and I won't let Grace become what I have become, just to satisfy the blind hatred that has made my own father into a twisted monster. So the decision is yours, Mister ... whatever your name is. But don't fool yourself into thinking that you will be separating right from wrong or setting the world to rights to put us in the hands of the magistrate, because my father deserved far worse than I gave him. Mr Taylor will tell you more, but he does not know the half of what we have had to endure, so listen to him and then multiply the worst of it several times over. And if you want the proof, Grace will tell you and she will show you the bruises, the cuts and the burn marks. And I can show you a 6-inch scar, if you've a mind to look. And don't blame James or Emily. James could recognise something thoroughly bad when he saw it and he had the courage to try to help us, though it may cost him dear. Many another man has just taken what they can get from us, including from Grace, and some of your farming friends from round here have been among them, and they have all been happy to walk on and turn their backs.'

She paused for breath, her chest heaving and the tears sparkling in her eyes as they blazed at him. Grace simply added, 'Please, mister, give us a chance.'

George looked from the older girl to the younger and the blood drained from his face as he absorbed the pith of what they had said. He felt with disgust that he was somehow implicated, just through being a man. He felt the anger and spite start to seep away, confusion taking over, and he turned to Emily as an easier target.

'What in the name o' God are you doing bringing all this to my door: whores and … children, too?' He stopped and then went on as he remembered other details. 'And there's money stolen an, a man with his 'ead splintered an' all, so they say. Why, for bloody hell's sake, do you have to be involved? I can't grasp what's got into you at all. Perhaps you'd best be goin' wi' them, eh? Is this the life you choose, when you could have a decent, honest life and …' He almost broke down, but pulled himself up with a final snarl at James.

'And you,' he turned to the younger man with his almost comic appearance. 'Don't come back 'ere, cos you're not welcome.' He looked at them all, raising himself and pointing. 'Now, get off my land sharpish, the whole bloody pack o' you.' He strode off in anger, self-pity and bewilderment, his horse following, and they watched him go.

It was Emily who again moved them on, ordering them back to the cart and telling James to go just a little way down the lane and then wait for her. She went after George, her mind clear only on a few points that she needed him to grasp. She found him, forlorn, sitting on a bale of hay, his head in his hands, the horse still patiently standing at his side. She knelt and placed one hand over each of his, but he would not move or look at her.

'George, a'm sorry, a really am. A should ha' thought more about what a was getting into an' a was wrong to bring 'em 'ere. Please forgive me.' He looked at her; his eyes seemed to have shrunk and there was still that sharp look of meanness about him. He made a strange snarling, spitting noise, but guttural, from deep within him, and he turned away, throwing her hands off with a violent, sweeping gesture.

'A'm not 'aving it,' he barked. He had become like a defiant, blind animal, refusing to listen or connect, staring at the wall.

'Just give 'em a chance,' she begged. 'A don't know all that James knows, but a trust him in this. He's not an evil chap. An' that little girl, George, she must 'a been treated real bad.'

But George said nothing; stony and ashen. He held his ground in flinty obduracy and distrust and would not turn. Emily said bleakly that she would be back within the hour and left.

The farmhouse was really just one large room, with a porch at the front and a small parlour tacked on at the end, where they now fed their guests. The kitchen was the main room of the farmhouse. It was stone flagged, with a scattering of clipped rugs. It had whitewashed walls that offset the dark beams and the black of the old iron range that filled most of the end wall. The range had an open fire held in a grate, raised from the floor level, and this was their only source of heat. It heated a water boiler on one side and two ovens on the other. On either side of the range were old leather armchairs and there was an overflowing bookcase in one corner, with a stack of old newspapers, various sacks and a pile of boots, clogs and pattens surrounding it. A large dresser dominated the other end of the room and near it, a selection of ill-matched chairs were clustered near the large, plain table.

On the back wall was a sofa and a high-backed oak settle and these were often dragged in front of the range, making an inner room, where the dogs liked to stretch out on the rough matting. To ease his back pain George would often lie on the floor there himself, basking in front of the stove, one or more of the dogs beside him. This was where she found him when she returned from Chapel le Dale, his eyes closed and his face reddened by the heat.

She bustled about making tea, stirring up the porridge that had been keeping warm at the back of the range and then frying up some bacon, but he did not stir. Even when she called him and asked him if he wanted to join her for some breakfast, he managed no more than a disdainful groan. The rain splattered their windows in an untidy flurry. She heard the baby crying next door and then the distant sound of Jack crooning a lullaby: she could imagine the black-browed, powerful man bending cautiously over the cradle, rocking the child with delicate care, as if she were made of porcelain. Meanwhile, she began to eat mechanically, watching George, wondering mournfully if he would ever get the chance to tend a child like that.

She felt dismayed at the gap that was now growing between them. He seemed like a different person, older, more unapproachable, intransigent and showing signs of harshness that she had never expected to see. Perhaps I seem different to him, she pondered. She had come back meek; she had come back prepared for retribution and ill feeling; she had expected grumpiness and dissatisfaction. But what she was frightened of was the indifference, because that meant that he did not care sufficiently to strive against her, that he no longer cared to save the person that he once said he loved. And part of her needed George; needed him to be the constant thread, spun through her life, but just one thread out of many. It was getting late. Hetty and Ethel would be back soon. She wanted to know what to tell them. She wanted it settled, in her way.

For his part, George was well aware of her movements and her needs and he was damned if he would help her. He thought about the many times in the past that she had won him over with one thing or another, going about to justify what she had already decided to do or had already done, twisting him around with words or kisses, or both, though not so many kisses these days, he reflected. He realised, though it must have been obvious to others, that right from the first moment of their courtship and all through their marriage she had been the active one, the persuader, using her wily charms. He had usually given in.

He recalled, and saw clearly now as if for the first time, how she had led him on in those early days. He remembered vividly the impact she had made on him from their first meeting. He must have been putty in her hands, because the courtship had quickly established an intimacy that was both delicious to him and compulsive. She threw herself into it, with such bursts of enthusiasm that he could scarce believe existed.

She appeared to be delighted with the serious formality with which he played the role of suitor: the flowers, the small gifts, the best clothes and the polished boots. He knew she felt flattered and elevated and she had let him know with girlish abandon that swept him away.

He had loved her vitality and the dangerous challenge that she presented as she drew him forwards. As their courtship quickly developed, their kisses became more passionate and searching. He was startled and enthralled to find her yielding and yet insinuating herself against him, pressing back, so that he felt her body shape becoming burned into his imagination, whilst her hands explored the furrows and ridges of his back, sliding beneath his shirt. He wondered whether other young men had been with her, but did not know how to ask the question and feared the answer. He had wanted her so much and would not take the risk of losing her.

The memories held him warm, lulled him for a while, and he began to drift, until a stab of pain jarred through his back and set him gasping. Then, just as suddenly, he felt tired, weary of reflection. The memories confused him, as if other people were involved, and the spasms in his spine blotted out too much: they seemed to send daggers into his neck and ice into the bones of his skull.

Why couldn't he come home to a quiet fireside, savouring the glow that comes through discharging your duties to the best of your ability, knowing that your wife would be there to share that time and rejoice in it? Jack came home to Ethel, placid and homely Ethel, a good mother to her children. Part of him envied Jack. He hated Emily's restless reaching out for some new corridor of experience, real or imagined. And he knew that partly he hated it, because it took her away from him. He was no longer the new experience that she craved. She was young, he regularly told himself, closer in age to Hetty than to him, and the young looked for danger and challenge and they wanted to share it. He tried to make allowances, to leave her room to be a young woman still. But she owed a duty to him and he believed in duty. He clung to these words: he had his rights and she had her responsibilities and if he did not start to change things now, then who could tell where they would end.

His thoughts were not as linear and coherent as this, more of an untidy spiral in fact, as he lay drowsily on the floor, aware of the sounds both within and outside the kitchen, but his resolution was unwavering and his displeasure quite focused. He heard her swallow her tea and place the cup down. Then she moved quietly across the room and he sensed, through creaking boards and a change in the light patterns, that she was standing over him. Then, she was kneeling beside him, pushing the dog aside, which grumbled deep in his throat and then went back to his dreams. George kept his eyes shut. A hand gently moved some stray hairs from his brow and her cool touch was soft, but he steeled himself and resolved to act.

'Help me up,' he said coldly, opening his eyes and raising an arm for her to help him. She did so and with stiff, ungainly movements he levered himself across the room and took his place at the table. Without a word, she poured him tea as he liked it. She knew him well enough not to hurry him when he was in this mood. Emotion should be controlled, that was George's belief, and he put his all into the struggle; it brought out the mulish aspect of him, just as it brought out his accent. He would say what he wanted to say in the manner and time of his choosing. She waited, all the time listening, attentive to the sounds in the yard, where the rain still splattered down into the mud and where soon the yellow cart would return, sliding over the cobbles, slopping through the puddles. How is it that my thoughts are always bending outwards, to things beyond the farm? she wondered. His voice startled her when it came, because it was low and unkindly.

'A've nowt more to say about this morning's carry on, 'cept to say that if it happens again, then either you or I will leave here. You must sort out the consequences of today as you see fit. A shall say, if asked, that I wor suspicious, but that a took 'em to be beggar women, an' James were off on some private trip an' you lent him the use o' horse an' cart. A'll not lie about it.' He paused and looked up, scratched his two days of reddish beard with impatience and then placed his words, quite coldly and deliberately, before her.

'On how we are to go on, like ... a mean, me an' you, lass, a want less o' you tekin' off without a word an' a want more o' just the two of us 'ere, as we used to be back awhile. And we'll go back to church more reg'lar on a Sunday, a think a've missed that. An' if it's to be just the two o' us, well, happen that's disappointing, but we mun mek the best o this as we 'ave to do about other things in life.'

A sharp hailstorm strummed and skittered across the windows and they both looked up. Emily thought of the exposed cart and its frightened occupants and wondered where they were. She thought of Hetty and Ethel, too, who were probably out in this, and then of Robert in his warm brickworks, toasting himself; how he would relish the situation! She smiled at a strange image of him that came to her: Robert as a jolly baker with a floury apron, turning bricks as if they were loaves of bread, and she forgot George for a moment, slipping into reverie.

When she turned back to him he was scowling. 'Did tha listen to a word a said!' he demanded. She realised that her careless slip would be difficult to retrieve and began to appeal to him.

'Of course a did. Oh, George, gimme a chance. A'm sorry, a'll do whatever you say, truly ...' and she reached for his hand across the table, but he swept away the contact and stood briskly. He now spoke with venom.

'Thou needs to pay heed or else we'll be moving' further apart than iver. A'm not 'aving it, summat's got tae change,' he shouted as he backed heavily towards the door. She slumped and he stepped out into the cold spring sunshine that glimmered on the ivory fragments of hailstones that littered the yard.

Planning and Improvising
April 1871

As Emily had imagined, Robert was warm in his brickworks that day as the hailstorm stung the eyes and withered the hides of men and animals that were exposed to it. All work on the viaduct came briefly to a halt. But Robert was in no mood to savour his comparative good fortune. His ribs still ached from the kicking he had received and his face was still puffed and sore; the cuts were healing, but the bruising was darkening daily and his nose was swollen, blocked and ugly. He was not the sort to bear the pain or the expressions of sympathy with fortitude; every cringe and grimace drove iron nails hard into his consciousness and he knew that there would be no solace until Tar Brush had suffered a similar torment, or worse.

He gnawed at this bitter bone, plotting, weaving fantasies of punishments and retribution that were the only relief he could get from the shame and the anger that consumed him. But he would not hurry it. He would heal and live again and he would let Tar Brush think that he had triumphed. Then, some time later, he would take him down, one on one, like the gladiators, in some private glade or shed, and beat him till the flesh was pulp and bones splintered and broke beneath his heel. Until then, Robert told himself, he needed to repair his injuries, rebuild his mental and physical strength and prepare the ways and means to avenge this insult. All else was peripheral. So he had sent back Emily's note. The thought of what might have been with her made his humiliation worse. He couldn't stomach the idea of witnessing her reaction to his injuries: her pity or even her sensible compassion. He couldn't bear for her to see him as he now was, a man incapable of looking after himself. How could he pretend to look after her or anyone else? He would see her in a few weeks, but she was second best

145

in his thoughts now, almost an embarrassment. The kiss they had shared seemed to be part of the history of another man, an unbeaten man, a man who could cope, and that other man was not him and, indeed, may never be him again.

He had found out that Tar Brush was now working inside Blea Moor Tunnel and that he was living in one of the tunnel huts, high up on the moor. He would rarely come down to Batty Green. No one knew where Marty was and Robert preferred to keep him out of this; he had hurt Marty before and he wanted no more guilt on that account. Robert had been to the tunnel workings a few times in their early days, to check on the use and quality of the bricks they were to supply there to line and arch the tunnel, and also to talk to the engineers about supply and delivery as the work moved on. But the pace of work was increasing significantly now and he had plenty of reason to return and check on the arrangements that had been made.

All was frantic purpose on Blea Moor. Fixed steam engines at each end of the tunnel were now winching up materials daily on a wire rope. Previously, they had used donkeys, horses or mechanical crabs to move coal, bricks, mortar and other materials, often topped out with bags of flour and sacks of bread or vegetables for the huts. Each of the three shafts that had been sunk from the top of the moor down to the foundation level had now been lined out and each had its own engine for pumping and for winding up the shattered rock and for taking down the bricks and mortar, the men, the candles and the explosives.

Robert considered that he should ask not just to walk into the northern heading, which was where he had gone before, but to actually go down one of the shafts to look at the works from inside the tunnel. That way, he stood more chance of finding out where Tar Brush was working and living. He would give it a week and then start his moves. It pleased him to think that he had at least a primitive plan.

That Wednesday found James Taylor in a very different setting, but similarly preoccupied with the need to plan several moves ahead. The slow, deliberate pace of the old horse and the creaks and rumbling of the old cart became hypnotic as they made their way on the quieter back lanes and these sounds calmed James as he pondered over how the girls might best make good their escape. He also tried to focus on his own future. He had kept his passengers well hidden as they made their way cautiously along the toll road and down the hill from Storrs Common. Luckily, the steely drizzle and occasional gusts of blustering wind were keeping most heads down and the traffic light. They passed a few wagons and solitary horsemen, but no one paid them any attention.

Nevertheless, he had decided that he would not risk Ingleton at all and he breathed more easily when he had turned off just before the town and made his way south towards Clapham. The rain was patchier now, with odd bursts of sunlight amid scuttling clouds. Again, he turned off before Clapham Village and took a green lane across to the Bentham road and soon the moist, verdant pastures gave way to rolling commons, with young bracken showing its tender shoots amid the dark, wiry fronds of heather. Curlew lifted and swung away from them and sheep scuttled, stiff-legged, off the quiet roadway as they lumbered up.

He would need to rest and feed the horse somewhere near Bentham and he called to the girls to sit up and get some air while they had the chance. Nancy's head emerged, bleary eyed and tousled. She had slipped into a doze, despite the jolting, the itching and the acrid smells of old fleece and sheep fat, tar and damp canvas. She made a dumb show of a sleeping Grace and held her fingers to her lips. He nodded to show understanding and whispered, 'Come up here awhiles. I think we're safe for five minutes. It's open country for a few miles. Most o' the time we can see t'road ahead and you can jump down again if someone comes.' She extricated herself carefully and clambered round to sit beside him, slipping her arm through his at once, pulling herself close and kissing his cheek. His heart lifted. 'You'll get dirty kissing that face,' he said jovially.

'James, I have so much dirt plastered on me I don't see how a peck more will possibly make any difference. I think there are fleas or ticks or something scratchy in that pile of old stuff we've been lying on. Something has been biting at me. There may even be a couple of mice or rats in there, too. Something ran across my leg at one point. Ugh.' She shivered and placed her head on his shoulder. 'Hold me, James, my Sir Galahad.'

He laughed and slipped his arm round her shoulder, wondering at her courage and how the brief, sweet pleasure of such a moment could be carved out of their desperate situation. Neither of them spoke for some while as the horse took his slow, weary way and the rain held off. He began to talk through his plans with her.

'Have you got any money?' he asked.

She pulled open her cloak and began to unbutton the old blouse that Emily had given her. She leaned forwards and slipped her hand inside the blouse, feeling between and beneath her breasts. 'Stop peeping,' she giggled as he glanced over.

'I've seen it all before,' he smirked, feeling roused by the memory and the tone of her voice as much as what he could see. She produced a pouch containing a thick sheaf of notes of various values. He was shocked. There must be several hundred pounds there. 'My God, Nancy. You'll get prison for sure if you get caught with that lot.'

She smiled. 'First, they'll have to catch me. Then, they'll have to find it. Third, they'll have to be quick to stop me using this.' And she leant forwards, the wad of notes firmly in one hand, whilst she used the other to pull a slim leather pouch from the lining of her boot. She held the pouch in her teeth and slowly withdrew a slender 6-inch knife, slightly curved, with a bone handle. The narrow blade was honed to a stiletto point and it glinted as if polished. Her sunny smile seemed to freeze over and slide into an icy grimace. She became instantly serious, older than her years and dangerous. She spat out the pouch.

'I'll get away with this and set myself up, with Grace, in comfort. No one will stop me, James.'

He swallowed nervously, alarmed but excited by this glimpse of her wilful determination; he was also reminded of her father's swordstick.

The image of her there, on the cart on the open moor, with money in one hand, the knife in the other, her blouse hanging open and her breasts on show, was to stay with him for many years. He had never dreamed that anything like this would happen to him. She laughed and changed back again, replacing the blade, and he shook himself as if to throw off the image of her sliding that knife between the ribs of an unsuspecting assailant.

'A girl needs to know a few tricks to survive, you know, James. At least, a girl like me does.' He was speechless and captivated.

He took some cash from her and explained that he wanted to put more onto the cart at Bentham, to make it look more convincing, adding that he would buy food for them and for the horse. If they could get clear of Bentham safely, then they could rest up for an hour and then hopefully make it to Lancaster before nightfall. Then they could get a train of their choosing. With typical directness, Nancy came straight out with the question, 'Are you coming with us, James?'

'I doubt it,' was his rather evasive answer. 'You told me that you had a man waiting for you, who would help you,' he reminded her.

She smiled and took his hand gently. 'But that doesn't mean that I wouldn't prefer you,' she said.

'It's a big decision and I need to think it through.'

'Of course,' she answered. 'But you will spend the night with me, won't you, James?'

'I don't think I have the strength to resist that offer,' he admitted. 'Anyway, I guess you might force me at knifepoint if I don't give in willingly.'

'You're right there,' she said. She leaned over and kissed him passionately. After several more kisses the wind shifted, as if in warning, and a hailstorm swept suddenly down on them.

They reached the outskirts of Bentham a little better prepared in several respects. Approaching the town, James stopped at a small, dilapidated farmstead and bought several sacks of potatoes and turnips to throw into the cart; also, some bread, cheese and milk; and a couple of bales of hay and some old blankets that he had seen airing on the clothes line. The grizzled, taciturn farmer was more than content to sell when James showed him a large note and no unnecessary questions were asked. He loaded up the cart and James went on his way down the hill towards the village, working the brake carefully, checking that the girls were well covered and comfortably wrapped in the blankets. The showers were now of light rain on the same cool breeze that would funnel up through the higher valley to chill the flesh at Ribblehead. He was surprised to find a number of people walking towards Bentham.

As a particularly sharp shower passed, leaving him wet and chafed, James heard the sound of sheep and cattle carried on the breeze, suggesting not one or two animals but many, and with the bleating and jingle of bells came a distant babble of voices and the cries of hawkers. Descending the hill carefully, he turned a corner in the road and glimpsed the high street ahead, stretching out below him, and he realised to his horror that there was a cattle and sheep fair in progress and that the whole road was blocked. Temporary pens were in place, crammed with animals; farmers and townsfolk thronged walkways, stalls and booths; wood smoke rose from braziers and mingled with animal and cooking smells to flavour the wind. James hesitated and stopped the cart.

A quarter of a mile ahead, where the road narrowed, there was a barrier across, just before a junction, and a couple of figures stood beside it; one had the distinctive cape and helmet of a police officer. At present, they were turned away, watching something down the street, but James could not back up a steep hill or risk trying to turn without attracting attention. He looked behind him and could see a pony and cart gaining on him. He was trapped. Was his involvement in the escape now known and had it been passed from Batty Green to Bentham? He had read about the new telegraph system and how the police were using it. He could imagine that Mr Bernard would not take long to get information from his wife and remaining daughters and he was quite sure that Mr Bernard would pressurise the police. James had to assume that he was now a wanted man. And if he were to be taken, then they would search the cart and find the girls. They could all be imprisoned or hanged. He felt sick at heart and deflated.

He was telling himself that he might get lucky and that he just had to brazen it out as best he could, when halting footsteps on the other side of the cart made him look round. An old woman, fat and ungainly, was stepping slowly past. She nodded and stopped to get her breath, leaning on a stick. She wore a round felt hat, pulled down over her ears, and she had a red bloated face, pustular and coarse. She sniffed loudly and then hawked deep in her chest, coughed heavily, turned her head and spat thickly into the hedge. Then she stood and looked down at the fair, just as he did, her huge chest still labouring under a ragged, greasy gaberdine. He noticed the neck of a bottle sticking out of one pocket and, glancing down, he saw that her boots had holes in the toes and one ankle was crudely bandaged and huge with swelling.

'A'm down on luck; nither bread nor watter this two day an' not long for mi grave, bart a doubt,' she called loudly to him, as if he had already asked after her welfare. The accent was thick and the speech slurred.'Are't 'eading for Wennington, by chance? Mi old sister lives by thir; it's a way wurst than a can manage on ma two legs, a can tell thee, an't would be an act of reet Christian charity to 'elp a body along thir.'

He looked at her. There was calculation in her eye, not desperation. He decided to risk using her. Just ahead, the officer was still facing the other way and he was talking now to a couple of children. If he was watching the road he would be looking for two young women, smartly dressed, not a couple of dirty vagrants, with an old cart full of tatties.

He stepped down and went round to the old woman and spoke bluntly to her.

'Can you manage the horse?' he asked.

'Aye,' she said. 'Born an' bred on farms.'

'Right then.' He glanced behind him: the cart was only 100 yards away, but moving slowly. He thought quickly and spoke roughly to her.

'I'll take thee to Wennington and what's more, there's a shilling in it for thee, if you'll do as a say.' Her face brightened and she nodded vigorously, showing toothless gums in a broad grin. He could smell the alcohol on her breath and the close, dank sweat of her clothes.

'I want to avoid notice in town ahead. My wife's father may be there and he's looking for me an' I owe him money.' The old woman's grin broadened further and the nodding continued. 'You drive, I'll walk. If you're questioned, tell them I'm your son and I don't speak, can't speak, on account of a horse kicking me in the head when I were young. Got it?' She nodded, but then held up a crooked finger and licked her lips.

'A shillin', tha says?'

'Aye.'

'Need be 'alf a crown for tellin' lies.' He had been right about her!

'What's your name?' he demanded.

'Sarah Jane,' she reluctantly answered.

'Well, Sarah Jane, listen carefully. I'll gi' thee half a crown if you manage it well,' he said as a fresh shower swept over them, dreading all the time that the policeman should turn and see them talking like this.

'But if tha thinks thir's any more in this for thee, tha's making a mistake and tha try anything funny, well … I'll kick thee into nearest ditch and drown thee.'

'I s'll see thee reet, young man, ne'er fear,' she countered, adding knowingly, 'A'm no lover o' polis meself.' She must have seen his anxious glances towards the back of the policeman. 'Now, 'elp me up.'

He had no time for more debate and so he walked round behind her as she grabbed the side panel of the cart and tried to haul herself upwards. He had no choice but to put his shoulder to her sagging buttocks and bend his knees low to heave her groaning bulk onto the driving board. The cart sagged as she floundered into place and she started to cough again, a barking, bruising cough, followed by a struggle for breath as if her lungs were protesting at this much exertion. James heard the faintest giggle from beneath the tarpaulin in the back. Nancy!

'Keep out o' sight till I tell you,' he hissed. 'Trouble ahead.' Sarah Jane was too busy striving for breath to notice what he said.

They moved very slowly down the hill. As the road levelled a little, Sarah Jane dropped the reins loosely into her lap, pulled out the bottle, took a liberal swig and wedged it between her feet. Then she took a plug of black tobacco from her pocket and began to work at it with her toothless gums, until she had gnawed off a corner, which she proceeded to chew noisily. Then she spat it out and began to sing, or at least hum and croon, a simple, repetitive tune, finally putting to it odd words and phrases, like "half a crown goes round and round" and "kicked in the 'ead and his name was Fred".

James was getting more and more tense, uncertain what she would do or say next. He had wanted to slip through unnoticed; now, with a drunken old crone in charge, the only thing that he could be sure of was that they were bound to attract attention. 'Shut up your noise,' he hissed.

'Tha's lost the power of speech, ne'er forget, an' tha's med me maister o' this ship, so tha can shut up thee own noise, eh?' she cackled, hugely amused at this and chuckling, so that the whole cart began to tremble.

Again, there was a stifled giggle from beneath the layers in the back, like a friendly echo. Luckily, Sarah was once again too busy trying to manage her wheezy, rolling chest to hear anything. James wanted to scream at them all, but he had to bite his tongue and concentrate on his role as the damaged son to this woman of wandering wits. His mouth was dry and his heart was beating a fierce rhythm as he saw the officer turn to watch their approach.

He remembered a boy that he had known in his childhood, who was mentally damaged: everyone called him Mad Morris. He tried to remember the boy and tried to look a little cross-eyed and uncoordinated in his movements, just as Morris had been, letting his tongue drool a little from the side of his mouth. He looked ahead.

There were two other men with the officer and a few more sitting on the wall just beyond, watching the world go by. He could now see that the barricade was just made of a few sheep hurdles and that beyond it there was a junction and a lane to the right, which probably led around the fair, which was still bustling with life.

Sarah Jane brought the cart to a halt within 6 feet of the hurdles, still crooning her odd bits of verses, and with leisurely confidence she pulled a little knife from her pocket and cut a chunk from her plug of baccy, dropping it into a long clay pipe that she withdrew from within her coat.

In a loud voice, she called over to the group of men in front of her. 'A'd count it as reet mannerly if tha'd find me a leet for ma bit o' baccy.'

No one moved, but the men all looked at each other as if there was an answer to be found in someone else's face. She called again and now some other heads were turning and a few children were drifting towards them. 'Is we to be stopped sae near to t'village an' not to be allowed in, eh, does ta think? Cos a could fair do wi' a drop of drink. A'm fair thrapped wi' thirst, tha knows. Mi throat's like bottom o' Saharee Desert.' There were smiles and some laughter from the men.

Then, to James' horror, the policeman crossed over the road, putting himself now on the same side as James. Then he nodded to the two men and began to move the hurdles apart.

'Just pull up here, please,' he said calmly. She flicked the reins and the old horse pulled forwards, James leaning into the wheel and trying to shrink as much as possible, his pretence of fear no longer any kind of challenge: he was shaking. They stopped again, with the officer within touching distance. James cowered and hoped for a miracle. 'Where are't going, mistress?' the man asked.

'Weelll ...' Sarah Jane lengthened out the word as if a lot hung on it. 'A've been fair wearied wi' tryin' tae pass away time i' a queer ole place called Skipton, whir thir's niver a day gone by these past three years when a've not said tae meself, an' me laddie Frederick ... that's 'im thir, about to be engaged to be married to that wheel, on account o' the fact that he's weak in t'head, poor little fellow. An' no woman in 'er reet mind would cast a glance at the poor, twisted critter. And a've said, to Frederick,' she continued, 'hir must be somewhir wi' a bit more life than this, tha knows, so let's up an' find it. An' a'm told as thir's a fine old town nearby here, which they say is full o' genteel folk, like what a mean to become, an' it's called ... Wennington.' There was a chortle of laughter from the small crowd, as Wennington was a tiny, run-down hamlet, just down the valley. Sarah warmed to her audience.

'A'm a simple enuff kind o' body. I see nowt to be grand wi'; all as a possess in t'world is in this cart. But in Wennington, they's all used tae all t'luxuries as money can buy, but a reckon as a can learn an' when a've me new teeth a'll look abowt for a husband. Unless tha can recimend someone who'll tek on me an' Fred, if a can get 'im away

153

from that ther wheel.' Again, some in the crowd laughed and someone shouted. She grinned her toothless grin, lifted the bottle and drank.

James thought the performance would never end.

He could think of no way to stop her. She was singing now, some kind of rambling ballad about "deeds of yore", banging her good foot hard down on the driving platform to keep time. He squinted through the hands that he had wrapped over his face and watched the policeman. He was an older man, with grey whiskers and sideburns, so that he looked very officious. However, he was smiling broadly, enjoying the performance and the banter. But whatever his good humour, if he was on the watch for runaways, he would surely search the cart and want to check on James, wouldn't he? James was not confident about any close examination of his disguise, but it was too late, far too late. He had rashly thrown in his lot with this old woman and so would have to live with it and let things take their course.

He remembered that Morris had sometimes banged his head against trees and he and other lads in the village had taunted him, probably cruelly as James now realised, and Morris would sometimes be seen with bloody gashes across his face and brow that he had inflicted on himself. Would it hide him further? Keep away prying eyes?

James clung tight to the cart and edged a little backwards, pressing his face against the damp wood of the side boards, feeling with his face and his fingers. He soon found a nail head that protruded and a splintered board in the old cart's side. He began to beat his head against the board, in time to her stamping foot, and he rocked backwards and forwards, moaning. The nail cut into his flesh and the pain almost made him cry out as he pulled his head away, dragging pieces of skin with it. Then he banged it down again. But he kept going, until he could feel blood oozing down his face. He would stop when she stopped and mercifully, she ran out of words or inspiration quite quickly. James stayed where he was, holding himself stiffly.

'Tha's a rare musical talent,' a voice shouted. 'Bowt as musical as mi cats, when they sing t'moon! That kind o' noise should be aginst law in a public place, doesn't tha think, Sergeant Clapham?'

But the officer did not wish to be drawn in and when Sarah Jane, goggle-eyed and gasping, in a pretence of being stung by the remarks, began to open her mouth to make some sort of reply, he cut across the whole thing and made a bid for control, raising his voice.

'So, missis, you're from Skipton and going to Wennington. Right?' She nodded. 'Seen anyone on the road? Couple of young ladies, for instance; might be looking a bit well dressed to be wanderin' dales?' She shook her head and looked as if she was about to start again, when he stopped her sharply. 'No more from you now, you hear me, you've brightened up our day, but enough's enough now. There's others coming this way soon and we need to move you along. Now, who's this fellow?' James sensed eyes turning towards him and he cowered further down.

'It's Frederick, mi son,' she said. 'Tha'll get nither words nor sense out o' him, on account o' him being kicked in the 'ead when he were nobbut a little thing. An' he's niver spoke since. He can 'ear you, though.' She raised her voice sharply. 'Turn thee sen round, lad, and show respect to polisman.'

James edged his face round and dropped his hands, keeping his eyes closed, and there were gasps from some of the crowd who could see him and then murmurs of protest and concern. He heard a footstep and felt the proximity of what he now knew to be a police sergeant. A firm hand reached for his shoulder and, squinting up through blood-coated lids, he saw the sergeant peering closely at him, with concern and interest.

He tried to pull back and whimpered and then he began to struggle more doggedly. Some in the crowd called for the sergeant to let him be, but he clung on and called for Frederick to 'Calm down now'. James held on tight to the side of the cart. After what seemed an age, and with panic rising in him, he almost sobbed, when Sarah Jane finally intervened.

'Don't touch him, constable, tha's no idea what 'e might do next. 'E's a strange 'un an' that's for sure. Near killed one old person who tried to 'elp 'im once.'

James felt the officer relax his grip a little and he quickly yanked himself free, sidestepping away round the back of the cart to the other side. 'Come up 'ere, Frederick, an' sit up wi' thee old ma and a'll tek care o' thee. Now don't be alarmed by blood now, iveryone, cos 'e's played this trick before a time or two an' it's n'er so bad as it looks.'

A sizeable crowd was now beginning to gather round them, out of concern and curiosity. There was a troubled tutting from some of them and some hostility to this drunken mother, while the sergeant was now ignored and seemed unsure what to do. James clambered up onto the driving board and huddled, foetus-like, his head in the wide, greasy lap of the old woman. Then, with a surge, there was more noise ahead of them: a small flock of sheep had been released from a pen and it now came streaming towards them, two dogs flanking the animals and an old shepherd hobbling after as quickly as he could, whistling and calling amid the noise. A little blond lad of no more than six was running on the other side with a stick. Chaos would be inevitable unless something was done.

Sergeant Clapham seemed almost relieved. He briskly ordered the crowd back, got the barrier open and told Sarah Jane to move on and clear the road. And so they got onto the side lane before the sheep scuttled upon them and they were soon edging round Bentham and into the open country again.

The sergeant did not pause long to reflect. He had sensed that Frederick had finer features than he expected and softer hands. He seemed generally too well nourished under his dirt and blood. But it was getting late and, after all, it was two girls he was looking for. There would be neither credit nor glory in subduing and trying to arrest a blood-spattered idiot; there would be the crowd and mad "mother" to contend with, as well as a flock of sheep. Moreover, Mrs Gittings had promised him a pint o' stout and a plate o' mutton chops in her back parlour after the fair and who could tell what that might lead to?

Profit and Loss
April 1871

At Elterbeck the following day things were strained and fragile. The day came in damp and cold again. George was maintaining a pained and bitter silence, but then he erupted in a snarl and went out early, without speaking further. Hetty was bereft and Ethel full of curiosity; both were confused by the absence of James, but they saw the warning signs in Emily's grim mouth, sharp instructions and tense movements, so they asked nothing and got on with making butter and minding children.

Jack was the only one who appeared untroubled. He was digging a drainage ditch across one of the meadows, filling it with gravel and pebbles from the beck, and Georgie, who rarely managed more than an occasional day at school, was helping him and building dams in between. Emily could not settle. She went along to the cottage and stayed there awhile, wondering about James, who was now into his second day away. She went up to the little bedroom under the slates and opened the small casement, leaning out to watch Georgie running back and forth across the meadow below. She watched Jack digging, his broad back rippling as he cut and heaved in easy movements. She noted that he seemed fully fit now and she guessed that he might leave soon, back to the railways workings, where there was six or seven shillings a day to be earned for bending his back like this.

George appeared in the meadow and went across to talk to Jack. They made an odd couple: one was tall and slender, auburn going grey; the other short, broad and very dark in hair and skin tone. They found something to laugh about and Emily indignantly noted the ease with which they conversed and compared it to the sour distance between George and herself the previous night and again this morning.

She felt no inclination for further apologies and begging. He would have to come to her this time. As the afternoon dragged on, she went back to help with the milking and there was more cause for discontent when Ethel asked that she and Jack might be excused on the morrow, so that they could go and look at the tunnel huts to check out the accommodation. It was obvious that the move was imminent and Emily could see only that she would be left with Hetty and George.

She was in a blacker mood than ever. Their little community had splintered. When she and George sat down for their supper dish the mood was restrained and icy. George was simply grunting monosyllabic answers. Hetty was obviously very anxious about the continuing absence of James and Emily handled it badly by snapping at her that he would be back when he came back. When Emily explained that Ethel and Jack would be away the next day, where they were going and why, the colour ebbed from George's face and Hetty looked close to tears.

After a silence, Hetty sighed, 'A shall miss the little ones, to be sure a will, cos babies mek it nice round a house, don't they?' She then realised that what she said may have been clumsy and insensitive, because she tried to cover herself by further explaining that a house without babies was also very nice, but struggled and gave up, with a look of pained embarrassment. She was troubled and confused and was wary of looking up. 'An' if James does not come back, a don't know how it can ever be the same as 'twas, don't you think?' But she could not wait for a reply, for tears overcame her and she scuttled out of the room, plunging into the night air.

Another long silence ensued. 'Tha's the cause o' much o' this,' George suddenly blurted, with an ugly downturn of his mouth, as if speaking to her furred his tongue.

'What's tha blatherin' about na?' She always slipped into her broadest accent when he spoke to her like this.

'A say that tha's the cause o' a lot of un'appiness hereabouts.' He stuck to his point, grim-faced and resentful.

'How can a be the cause of Jack goin' back to bein' a navvy?' she demanded, ready to take up the argument and bludgeon him with it if she could. She wanted to hurt him now.

'Oh, tha's got a ready way wi' you o' stirring iverybody up, till we're all as discontented as you, not seein' the blessings that we have in front of us noses. You love it, scrattin' round for news and excitement and foriver gannin' off t'Batty Green and seein' this and that person, plannin' and wheedlin', till some on us don't know whether we're comin' or goin'.' He was warming to his theme. Emily had forgotten this side of him and was taken aback. He took her pause as proof that he was on the right lines and ploughed on, not caring any longer if he hurt her.

'Tha properly confused young James Taylor and took advantage of his innocence, till he saw sense an' moved 'imself away a bit, but now he's properly off t'rails and lord knows how he'll end up. Does tha really think he would 'a' bin consortin' wi' whores and the like if you hadn't stirred 'im up and put ideas in's 'ead? An' where's that leave young Hetty, eh? She's getting' 'urt meantimes an' things between her an' James might 'a' gone well enough for 'em to be wed.'

She was going cold with rage and unease; a guilty conscience is a troublesome guest, even when provoked by half-truths, but she would not let the half-truths pass as gospel. She stood and glared at him. 'A've never given James Taylor any kind o' encouragement, but a've told 'im more than once to stay away and give attention where it's wanted. A can't 'elp it if 'e followed me around like some daft moonstruck calf, can a? A don't recall you doin' anything to put the lad right; you just left it to me, as is your way when it's owt personal or tricky. An' a was the one that helped the lad when 'e wor in trouble, through 'is own wantin' to 'elp a young lass that 'erself were in a far worse mess than tha's ever encountered. A' seem to recall as all a got from you was a fair lot o' hostile words an' moods, when a bit o' understanding might have bin expected.'

'A didn't know what was gannin' on!' he snarled back at her.

'No, and tha won't know what's happening in the lives o' the folk around you if tha lives in t'barn or fields most o' day or in the pew o' the church. An' then tha can 'ardly be bothered to speak a word when tha finally returns from wandering alone in t'wilderness, like a prophet out o' Bible, except tha's not gittin' inspiration out thir anywhere, or even Christian charity, just bloody ill temper.'

'Somebody's got to run t'farm.'

She almost screamed her reply. 'When tha wor laid out wi' bad back a did it, and the milk run, and a managed to keep house and home together. Or has tha forget? Oh, an' at t'same time mekin' everyone unhappy, accordin' to you. Actually, a think we were the happiest we've iver been, about then.' She paused, slowing rapidly, unsure what exactly she was drawing attention to. The fight seemed to be going out of both of them.

He tried to speak calmly and to put into words the thoughts that had been shaping themselves within him. 'Th'art restless and not content. Tha's travelled from Elterbeck to Batty Green an' tha's changed along the way. Tha's got a kind o' shifting disease that spreads to others an' a don't know what it is that will settle you down.'

'First off, a want a baby,' she said, with more of a tremble in her voice than she expected. 'Actually, a want three or four.'

'A'm no longer sure that a'm the man that can help you,' he said. 'But a pray to God that I am, else we're heading for some serious trouble.' He rose, as if the issue could not be brought into daylight by mere words, and left the room, banging the door hard against the wall, setting plates jangling percussively.

She felt, not for the first time, dissatisfied with what she had said and what he had said. Words had again proved to be a poor medium for real communication, having a tendency to obscure as much as they revealed, putting simple labels to complex issues, which are then taken away and examined, believing them to be accurate and clear signals, when they are mostly very approximate tokens, hastily exchanged. They offered spurious security for someone like Emily. At heart, she distrusted words and yet she was conscious of their power. She almost envied George his simple faith in the words of the Church. She did not feel that she could turn to God for wisdom or for anything other than forbearance just now. For everything else, she had to rely on her own resources and judgement.

The next day saw Jack and Ethel set off early, getting a ride up with the cheerful young milkman Joshua on the yellow cart, and breakfast was barely finished at the farm, when two messages arrived in quick succession. A stranger rode into their yard, asked for Emily and handed over a letter. He politely refused refreshment and left at once. Emily had just started to read, when a lad from the works arrived with another letter, this time addressed to George. The two messengers passed as they went through the farm gate. The letters were read and then exchanged. Emily's was not signed or dated. It was written in an untidy scrawl, like rough notes, in a child's hand:

Mrs Wright,

I hope to return on Sunday. Resting and recovering now.
My parcels went off today and I don't know where. Will not
be returning horse and cart, but will pay. Will call at farm,
but willing to move out if necessary.

Please send message to Walter Hirst that I was called away on
urgent personal business. Will be at work Monday. Messenger
has not met me and does not know where I am, so do not
question. Grateful for all your help.

The letter to George was from Walter Hirst, expressing concern at
the absence of James for several days and asking George if he could
throw any light on it.

George grunted, made a dismissive gesture and left. Emily wrote a
short note to Walter Hirst, stating when James was expected to return
to work, and sent it back with the lad. She then found Hetty and told
her that James had sent a note saying that he would return on Sunday,
but that it was not certain that he would remain at the farm. Emily felt
her heart pinched and twisted as she saw the pain and confusion that
was so apparent in Hetty, but she knew that the best course was to leave
James to give his version of events to her in person and told her this.

Hetty cried for a while, but eventually accepted that she would have
to wait. And so must Emily. She busied herself with the lambs and
feeding the young calves and pigs that they were fattening in far greater
numbers this year, aiming to drive them to the camp, where there was
now a slaughterhouse as well as a large bakery. She worked busily,
gathered eggs, fed the horses and helped Hetty with the cleaning and
cooking, but all the time it was as if parts of her consciousness were
scattered, attending on the absent players in her real life: George,
James, Robert, Ethel and Jack all seemed to dominate her thoughts as
she did her best to analyse their needs and her need for them.

Sitting on a bale of hay in the barn, she closed her eyes for a few
moments to try to clear her mind, but her brooding still continued. She
realised, with a touch of amusement, that at times she thought of them
in colour tones. Once, when she was about ten, going to Ingleton on a
fine summer's day, she had seen a man painting in oils, capturing a
scene near the river. He had set up his easel and was working

assiduously, adding colours to a palette and mixing them in different combinations. She was no artist herself, but she had been attracted by the slick, oily paints that he was melding and drawing into each other and she had sat and watched awhile. Now, she daydreamed about the people and places in her life, seeing them as coloured strands that crossed and recrossed each other: grey and green was Elterbeck, with Batty Green as a large mass of orange and ochre; George was a dull bronze, sometimes catching the light and sometimes absorbing it, while Robert was a deep red, almost purple, and James was a pale blue, like an evening sky, but shot with pink; Ethel was a deep creamy pink with white flashes and Jack had to remain black, but it was a black with warmth and energy, like coal newly split. The children were flakes of black and silver, the baby was gold. Hetty was turquoise. And she was the palette and the knife. To lose a colour would be to lose part of her landscape. Then, she understood that if the colours went from the farm, they had not gone from the district or from her mind – she still retained Robert's purple hue, for example – so that she should think of the canvas as bigger than just Elterbeck; she could still locate the strands and feel their patterning and blending. The thought comforted her.

When the news came from Ethel and Jack that they would leave the farm after one more week it was easier for Emily than it might have been with these colours in mind. George took it with good grace, but was still sullen and hostile with Emily, whom he was still inclined to blame for every change that affected him for the worse. Hetty was disappointed, but the imminent return of James was far more critical to her happiness, so she rallied her spirits. Ethel and Jack had found lodgings in a hut with another family at Jerusalem, not on the bleak heights of the tunnel huts. Jack would be working twelve-hour shifts inside the south heading of the tunnel, carting away the rock that the miners shifted, loading wagons that were taken for tipping on one of the developing embankments. They would still visit the farm when they could, which they were sad to leave. And typically of Ethel and Jack, they had thought through what they might do and were anxious not to leave the Wrights with a difficulty. Ethel offered to meet the milk cart each day and to help with business at the camp. She had also found someone who might help at the farm; an older woman, who had worked in dairies in the past and whose husband was now getting too old to manage the rigours of regular railway work, where he was a stonemason. They could come and meet George and Emily next week, if it would help, and the offer was gratefully accepted.

On other days of the week the milk run went early to Batty Green and returned before midday. But Saturday was still market day, with the market train running from the tunnel huts and more popular than ever, and so the cart went later and this particular week it was heavily laden. Emily, Hetty and Ethel took charge of the Saturday sales and would hear of no one else being involved. On this particular Saturday, they set off in better spirits, laden with milk, eggs, butter, cheese, live chickens and ducks, a roll of bacon and sundry cakes and pies that they had made.

Georgie and Laura rode in the back, as Ethel was taking them up to look at their new lodgings during the afternoon. With bright, clear skies and some warm sunshine to enjoy, the mood was more positive than it had been all week. The three women were well aware that it was the big monthly pay day at Batty Green, so there would be a large crowd of locals and strangers from miles around, creating more atmosphere, incident and gossip than usual and hugely increasing the flow of ready cash to be spent.

What is more, it so happened that this particular pay day was followed by a "knock-off Sunday" for some of the outlying contracts: when most of the men would not be at work, so the holiday mood would be lifting the spirits even higher. The contractors had recently moved to this monthly pay day, despite objections from Church members, who felt it encouraged excessive drinking. Furthermore, they were now paying out at Batty Green for contracts from Horton right over to Dent, so there were navvies on the tramp from all sides, all converging on the pay huts at what many of them still liked to call "Batty Wife Hole", with more than a twist of lascivious pleasure. Many came expecting to get drunk.

Wages were rising along the line as contractors struggled with difficult terrain, lack of good accommodation and shortage of labour. A common labourer could earn more than five shillings a day, collected in cash at the end of the month. Much of it he might have to pay back straight away, if he had borrowed to buy food or drink or if he owed for lodgings. Nevertheless, on a day like this, with over 500 men working locally, 2,000 pounds was paid out at Batty Green and that cash would flow liberally for a while in all directions. Of one direction, you could be sure: there was always a substantial portion that turned into drink, with beer at a penny a pint or whisky at two shillings a bottle. At Batty Green, the Railway Inn was a well established and official hostelry with its own brewery; one of the huts was officially registered as licensed premises, with Mrs Mathers presiding over the Welcome Home Inn. But there were many unlicensed huts and itinerant sellers from the backs of drays or even just carrying small barrels on their backs, plying their trade wherever there was a crowd. Others also arrived to try the market: hucksters, packmen, cheapjacks and charlatans looked for custom; as did likeness-takers, tailors, piemen, book sellers and quack doctors. Emily and her team had never witnessed such scenes in their lives. But what particularly surprised and intrigued Emily was the presence of the whores.

She had heard talk of them on previous pay days, but this time there seemed to be more of them and they openly toured the market in the spring sunshine; one even holding a light parasol over her head, laughing at every turn; others standing out on account of their more fashionable dress coats and bonnets, or their hair crimped into tight ringlets, with rouged cheeks looking even more artificial as the sun lit up their sallow skin. A couple of them came to the cart, probably sisters judging by their similarity in looks. They asked for cake and a hunk of cheese. Emily noted that, closer to, the clothes were rather tattered at the edges and that with skin blemishes covered in paste, they perhaps looked better by candlelight; but then, don't we all, she thought. She served them, commenting, ''Aven't seen youse two round here before, a believe.'

'Just up for t'day, ma love,' the older one answered with a smile. 'Kind o' samplin' t'scenery and enjoying t'local wildlife, tha knows.'

They left with laughter rippling back from them and Emily envied the apparent ease with life that they displayed. She wondered when and where they would ply their trade and she noticed many of the navvies following their movements, with nods and gestures and even one or two bawdy comments. The girls moved on, either oblivious or subtly registering the attention by pointedly not responding to it, Emily could not make out which. Heads turned and tongues did not just wag, they clacked, and some of the locals stepped theatrically aside to avoid contact. But the six or seven women took strength from their group and laughed at the sneers, but were wise enough not to provoke any trouble. As the market began to thin, in the early afternoon, they seemed to suddenly disappear.

Emily herself was aware that the atmosphere changed somewhere around that time, too, and she looked around to try to work out why. The sun was now masked by thin cloud and the temperature had dropped a little. The men who were with their families were beginning to lead them away, a number of carriages and wagons were filling up prior to their journeys down the valley, or back to Ingleton or over to Dentdale or Hawes, and some of the women were making their way back to the huts, laden with heavy baskets, going to prepare meals for those men that would finish work at six. The market train would leave just before four and some were grouping themselves, ready to board when it came. All this changed the mood, but the noise level did not drop, it just changed. There were also more men around, she realised. Indeed, it was the presence of so many men that changed the mood. The men were less excitable, but the tone of the day was becoming darker and beginning to feel a little threatening, mainly because so many of them were in drink. Trouble was certainly lurking, circling the area, attracted to excitable males; one or two fights broke out, short-lived affairs mostly, and there was a distant and belligerent shouting from time to time that she could not place.

Emily found herself on her own. Ethel had gone off to the Jerusalem huts almost as soon as they had arrived, taking the children to see where they soon would live. She had promised to be back at four, but Emily was not confident that she would manage it; Ethel's sense of the passage of time had more to do with the movement of the sun than the turning of the hours. Hetty had asked if she could walk back to Elterbeck with two friends that she had met, local girls who sometimes called to see Hetty, and Emily was pleased to encourage Hetty to develop friendships, just in case James did not return or in case he returned a different man, with a different taste in women. She had been gone for half an hour and Emily was packing up the few remaining items on the cart, watching the human traffic around her and remembering that Robert had once turned up at about this time to talk to her. She had watched for him all afternoon, but seen no sign, and still there was none. Her spirits fell a little.

She decided to have a stroll and so she pulled on her bonnet and gloves, took her purse and her shawl and, leaving the cart under the watchful gaze of the butcher, who was parked alongside her, she quickly made her way up the road. She walked up the hill, dodging the passing carts and meandering pedestrians to pause near the Railway Inn. She had to step aside almost immediately as three men almost fell out of the front door, giggling and holding on to each other. They were young navvies, but smartly dressed, with flowers in their button holes, and each wore a bowler hat perched at a rakish angle, so that to her they had a comic appearance that made her smile. One of them noticed her, pulled himself up to attention and saluted, almost falling over in the process. His broad Scottish accent was slurred to the point of incomprehensibility. 'A's hoping as wa didna scare you, mam, an' a must apoligise fer ma two buckos, who wouldna recognise a lady if she slapped him one. Na, good day to ya, ma bonny lass.' Here, he paused to sway sideways and back in a failed attempt to raise his hat and then put it back again. Then he turned to his companions, who had collapsed onto a bench, clumsily propped against each other, nodding sagely as if there was still live intelligence within them. 'Na, ma bonny lads, heave up to yar feet there an' we'll find some other ladies to put us to rights, a little less public. A know where, come on.'

More words proved elusive, so he contented himself with trying to drag his companions upright and then head them off behind the inn, towards a network of alleys, sheds and walls that marked the brewery yard and some of the storage huts of the railway company.

Emily smiled a farewell and was watching them stagger away, when she saw one of the whores appear from just behind one of the walls and approach them. There was some talk and then they all followed the girl down an alley. Without thinking about it, Emily followed at a distance, just in time to see the four figures disappearing between some buildings, the three men blundering into walls and scarcely able to stand. She followed tentatively, clutching her shawl tight about her, telling herself she was doing no wrong, rehearsing a little speech that she was looking for a friend if anyone approached her. She passed nervously between the buildings, to be faced with a muddy yard, with the only exit being on the other side into some gloomy, open sheds.

There was a large packing case upturned in the middle of the yard and a small, skinny old woman was sitting on it, smoking a clay pipe and counting money on a bag on her lap. So it was here, Emily now saw, in the old stables, that the whores were working.

The old woman looked at Emily but said nothing. It was not unknown for women to find their way to places like this or to the doors of brothels or the stairwells of rooms that were cheap to rent and quickly abandoned. Sometimes, they were down on their luck and wanted to work; sometimes, they came to pray or to preach, or to look for their husbands or their sons; but some were just curiously driven to want to see and understand. She guessed that this one was in the latter category and not likely to cause trouble. She continued counting.

Emily was about to speak, when one of the girls came out from one of the stable doors, brushing herself down, soon followed by an older navvy, bareheaded with silvery hair and an old coat over his arm. For an instant, Emily thought it was Robert, but then realised she was wrong. She was agitated and confused, but seemed unable to move. She felt rooted to the spot, bereft of will, a stranger to herself. The man tossed some coins to the old woman, smiled at Emily in a knowing way and then jammed his hat on his head and strolled out, whistling cheerfully. The girl said something quietly to the old woman, who nodded, and then the girl walked past Emily back up towards the inn.

The old woman looked at Emily and spoke gently, 'If tha wants to work, I'sll need to talk to you, me dear. If tha wants to watch, a charge a shilling to the likes o' thee. Whativer it is tha wants, tha canna stand thir; tha'll frighten away the customers and upset ma girls.'

Not knowing why and afraid to move forwards or back, it was with an impulse of blind thoughtlessness that Emily handed over a shilling and was directed into the shadows near the stable doors. She stayed there for twenty minutes and then quickly left, pushing her way through a group of women near the Railway Inn to make her way soberly home. She was startled, horrified and attracted. It was as if she had watched herself back there: as if she was not one person but two and she had not known the division until now. And melding them together again was painful.

Patience Unrewarded
May 1871

It was early afternoon of the next day when James rode into the yard at Elterbeck on a stout black cob. He was smartly dressed, but pale and tired, with a raw and jagged wound across his brow that he could only partly cover by pulling his black wiry hair and hard hat forwards. George and Emily had been to church and George was still dressed in his suit and shirtsleeves and was reading beside the fire in the parlour. Hetty had slipped out, saying she was going for a walk. Emily guessed that she would be waiting at the cottage. Emily had been making bread, stemming her impatience and her nagging disquiet with ordinary domestic activity, trying to block the memories of the day before and the urgent coupling in the hay. She would try to be the satisfied, passive wife that she knew George was looking for and had once known and loved. What else she might become she shuddered to think.

This would be her true self; that simpler soul she had been when first married: though it took willpower to confirm it today, when another self seemed to argue. Her prime motive had to be to please George. But subjugation of her own impulses was no easier for her than for most of us. She knew that today she needed a calm and collected atmosphere, so that George might learn to love this true self again. He would also need space to be persuaded to listen to James and to be tolerant of what had happened.

In that spirit, Emily stayed back in the kitchen doorway when she saw James ride in. She called for George and stepped back to allow him to get past her into the yard, where he held the horse's bridle, while James dismounted and unhooked a bag. James did not appear to be abashed or nervous: he smiled and handed the reins to George. As always with them he spoke quite formally. 'Mr Wright, the horse is for you,' he said.

'The old grey picked up an injury and I had to leave her, but she is well cared for.' He reached into an inside pocket and passed several notes to George. 'And this is for the cart and the bits and pieces I took and for the trouble I caused.' George was silent, but took the notes and looked at them as if uncertain what to do or say. Then he seemed to falter and look tense. 'If you will agree, I would like to go to the cottage and tidy me sen up a bit and then I will come and tell you what I can. Then you can tell me what tha wants me to do.'

George nodded and James picked up his bag and walked rather stiffly away. James had had time to prepare his thoughts and words and to examine his feelings closely. He thought he knew what he would do and say. Nevertheless, finding Hetty sitting in the old armchair beside the fire at the cottage, seeing her rise excitedly and the beautiful smile break spontaneously across her face, followed by a gasp and a frown when she saw his scars, was more of a delicious shock than he expected. And when she stepped up to him and threw herself into his arms, he could do nothing other than hold her and try to stem his own tears. However, he did remember what he planned to say and, managing to lever her off his chest, kissing her gently on the forehead, he spoke to her tenderly and with some difficulty in keeping to his script.

'Hetty, I owe you and t'others a deal o' explaining. Some of it I can tell thee, some I can't. I want you to come down t'farm and be there when a go through it. After you've heard the story, you may not want to speak to me again and I will understand. It may be that I've to leave the farm and perhaps the area. It's goin' to be some time afore all this settles down. Don't judge me too harshly and bear in mind that I never wanted to upset you or anyone at Elterbeck.'

With tears in her eyes, Hetty began to question and protest and to cling to him. He calmly extricated himself, sent her off to the farm whilst he got a wash and then followed her briskly down the lane. But she was lingering outside the cottage, waiting for him, so he offered her his arm and they walked down together, without speaking, both trembling a little, aware that the talk of the next hour might shape the rest of their lives, in one way or another.

He told them the story, rather formally, in the front parlour, with the smell of damp furnishings in the air and an old grandfather clock staring down at them, turning the minutes with a steady, rhythmic pulse. He skirted round the start of his interest in the Blue Lamp and the extent of his involvement there, stressing instead his desire to help his friend Walter and how this led on to concern for Grace and what he described as a hurried conversation with Nancy and her appeal for help. He hinted at what the girls had been involved in and how their father had treated them. He described how they escaped, how he and Emily had arranged the disguises and how they had just scraped through Bentham, with him pretending to be a halfwit, and how he had banged his head on the nail. It had not been the end of his troubles.

Once clear of Bentham, he had sat up and using his fingers, he had tried to assess the damage to his face. It felt like a bloody mess of tissue to him, with some ugly flaps of skin and trails of dried blood that must make him appear a grim and garish spectacle. At a roadside pool, he had jumped down and tried to wash himself as well as he could. His head ached and he was very tired. Sarah Jane was muttering to herself, but at least she was subdued and somnolent now, and he took the reins and moved them on as briskly as he dared, with the horse visibly tiring and rain showers moving towards them again from the west. He knew that he had to part with the old woman as soon as possible and then rest up for a while.

They had reached the first cottages of Wennington as the rain reached them and jumping down, James had ordered the old woman off the cart, walking round to position himself to help her down. She looked at him with sullen resistance and demanded her money. James found some coins, gave her two shillings and promised her a third when she was off the cart. 'Price just went up,' she grunted. 'A reckon as how the polis would like to know whir tha's bin an' whir tha's goin' an' so on. Mighty keen not to be questioned, wasn't tha!'

He had had enough of this fat creature, with her gross appetites and her nose for exploitation, and so he took a quick step towards her greasy bulk, grabbed the front of her coat and pulled her pitted, sweating face towards him. She had gasped and struggled, hissing like a cornered cat, bubbles of saliva spraying from the corners of her mouth as she tried to find the breath to protest, spit or curse. He had then pulled harder and braced himself to try to haul her away from the seat, when he became aware of movement in the back of the cart. Nancy suddenly shot her head and shoulder through the wet tarpaulin, blinking against the sudden light, and then with surprising speed, she had pulled the knife from her boot, unsheathed it and wedged it between her teeth, whereupon she had leaned over to grab the woman round the throat from behind, using both hands to squeeze as much of the blubbery mass as she could. All this time, her eyes were on James and he felt his spirits rouse and stir. The old woman, pulled face-to-face with him, was stunned by this unseen, additional force and she had glared at him, goggle-eyed with terror, unable to turn her head or to take in what was happening. With the old woman struggling for breath, James had smiled at her discomfort and he spoke venomously to her.

'A'm not alone, see! An' ma friend behind you 'as a liking for tekin' slices off fat old shavers like you.' He had freed one hand and had reached up and taken the knife carefully from Nancy's mouth, then waved it in front of Sarah Jane's eyes, the light glinting off the cold metal. He brought it to rest under her chin and exerted a gentle upward pressure to the folds of sagging flesh there. She had gulped in terror and her eyes rolled upwards. James glanced round quickly and saw what was needed. He spat the words at her.

'You will get off this cart, walk with me a little way back down the road and then sit down on a stone back there, facing away. If tha as much as turns thy 'ead or makes a sound, I will hack thy tongue owt soon as look at you. Then my friend will cut though your nose and perhaps 'ave a go at slicing a few inches off them fat jowls. And if you move inside the next hour, or ever mention us to a soul, we will come back, 'ave no fear, and finish you off. Understand?' She had nodded fractionally. Then he had put the knife in his teeth, indicated to Nancy that she should cover up and yanked the old woman forwards, until she was as near double as someone her shape ever could be.

'Now shift,' he had ordered, letting her go sufficiently enough for her to shuffle across, all the while whimpering and making a show of being upset, turning clumsily to descend. Nancy had pulled bonnet and hood right down forwards to cover her head. She now stood, tall, domineering and silent in the middle of the cart, black against the rain that was beginning to beat against her, and the old woman cowered before this strange, ghostly figure.

So they had left Wennington and had pulled into a meadow beside the river to rest and eat. Grace had emerged and she ran in the puddles, laughing one minute, silent the next. Nancy had fussed her hero with passionate zeal, dressing his wounds as best she could, tearing cloth from her petticoat to clean him, and they ate heartily of bread and cheese, sheltering under an old tarpaulin, happy despite the rain. But the poor horse could really go no further. They decided to walk beside the cart and look for some other means of transport and had finally bartered the horse, the cart and its contents, giving them to a kindly farmer, who was happy to take them to Lancaster in his pony and trap in return.

James said little of the three days he spent with Grace and Nancy: how they bought clothes, cleaned themselves up in the river and then took rooms in a hotel. He said little, but the memories were emblazoned on his heart and vivid to his every waking thought. Neither did he say that it was Nancy that had insisted they part and that he come back to Ribblehead to pick up his work and complete it. She had dictated the letter to Emily and had pledged him to agreement. So, at last he had left them in the quiet of a spring dawn, while they were still asleep, and truly did not know where they had gone from there. They could not be traced through him.

When he finished his narrative there was an awkward pause. George looked stern, Emily was proud of James and wanted to hug him and Hetty was white with nervous apprehension. They all looked to George for some kind of judgement or decision. There was a chill silence. At last, George nodded a couple of times and cleared his throat noisily.

Emily knew that he was stalling; that he could not decide what to do. Eventually, he delivered his verdict with an almost portly flourish that made Emily want to laugh. The voice was slow and heavy. She stared at the floor to control herself.

'T'vicar last week used a phrase as he said comes from Shakespeare or summat and 'e said that there's some folk as is "more sinned against than sinning". From what a've heard, and not just from you now, cos a've heard it from others, too, it's happen what these lasses 'ave suffered and in ways as don't bear thinking about. A'm not the person to judge them an' never will be. An' a'm not to judge you, Mr Taylor. Strikes me as you 'ave put yourself out an' teken some big risks to be of 'elp to these young women. No doubt you've your own reasons for that ...'

He paused and Emily looked up and noticed that tears were running silently down Hetty's face as it became clearer to Hetty why James might take such risks. She reached over and took Hetty's hand as George resumed.

'You're a tenant here and 'ave been a good one, ne'er a bit o' trouble until this. An' a'm thinkin' that it weren't you that brought t'lasses to t'farm, that were Emily's doin'. So a've got nothing really to complain about wi' you an' as far as a'm concerned, you can stay on, if you've still a mind to.' There were smiles from the other three, even Hetty grinned rather weakly through her tears.

'But ...' George raised himself up a little before continuing, and Emily had a brief insight that her husband was actually a little smug and quite enjoying this role, as a magistrate might when handing down judgements on certain local offenders. 'As a think a said before, a will not lie. If asked about these young women, a shall say where an' when a saw them and who with. But on t'other 'and, a will not go blagging about it here, there and everywhere. But if more trouble comes, cos a've got a feeling we've not 'eard the last o' this, an' if it affects me or Emily or Hetty or our reputation here, then thou must leave at once.' George stood and extended his hand to James, who took it with some affection and relief. 'You must tek care, James Taylor. A've bin asking around an' a hear that this Bernard is a nasty bit o' work an' he may be wanting revenge.' Hetty began to snivel again, James made a clumsy bow and swiftly left without another word and Emily decided that on this particular occasion, George had done rather well and she was proud of him, too.

In the times that followed she said to herself that for those few weeks following the return of James, she really did try to be patient, quiet and self-effacing. How else, for one thing, could she explain her agreeing to the arrival of Morgan and Ruth to replace Jack and Ethel? They were introduced by Ethel and they came to look around and see what was needed and whether they would fit in. Emily disliked them at once, but George was enthusiastic, seeing them as potential allies. 'Sensible bodies, regular in their habits and in their churchgoing, just the sort to bring a bit o' peace an' stability round 'ere.'

They were childless, in their forties, little, wiry and sallow. Ruth was neat and prim and she kept her arms folded across her meagre chest most of the time, nodding her head frequently, as if that part of her was in reality run by clockwork. Morgan was broad in the shoulders, tapering down through bandy legs to surprisingly little feet, so that he looked a bit unsteady at times. He had a knobbly head and a swarthy skin, covered in a fine downy hair, and a face that was dominated by a wall eye that was milky and pale. He was mostly very quiet, but watchful: Emily felt that he was always looking for evidence, which he could use to lay a damning judgement on her. He didn't laugh much and he was sometimes given to pronouncing that there was virtue in doing without things, in maintaining self-discipline and restraint, as if self-induced misery necessarily cleansed the soul. He had biblical quotations to offer on most occasions, which he seemed to prefer to any views of his own.

Emily felt that he had a dour outlook on life, which she thought could be explained by his spending so much time underground as a miner, with his time above ground being spent at the chapel. "E'd stand more chance o' being completely human if he spent a day or two in the sun now and again,' she stated with a frown.

They were both Welsh and proud of it and they took their religion like medicine, with regularity and with a grimace, knowing that it would do them good. Ruth had been brought up on a farm and she could certainly take over the dairy and milking duties at once and tend the smaller animals. She had met Morgan through the chapel and had married him when she was over thirty and when he was made a widower.

He knew nothing of farming, but the work in Blea Moor Tunnel was getting too much for him and he had fallen out with some of the navvies, whose lifestyle was anything but self-denying. He claimed that he could build, manage horses, fetch and carry and round up sheep or cattle. Emily was wary of them both, but George was positive that they would be good workers and he quickly struck a deal with them. Emily wanted to be compliant and so she let George take control, but cautiously urged that it should be until Christmas in the first place and this was what was agreed. And so the exchange was made. With heavy hearts, farewells were made to Ethel, Jack and the children; Morgan and Ruth moved in quietly, but were never invited to take a place in the farmhouse kitchen at Elterbeck. Emily and Hetty soon nicknamed them the Mole and the Mouse, but only out of the hearing of George.

James was nervous about returning to work, but found that he was warmly welcomed back and no difficult questions were asked about his absence or his injury: something was known of his actions, enough to guarantee him support and even a certain kind of prestige. He asked for an early and confidential meeting with Walter Hirst and this took place as they observed the tipping run on the embankment that was being built up on the south side of the viaduct.

The contractor there was following the standard practice of the time: horse-drawn wagons were brought up in a line and filled with "muck", as the navvies called it; just debris of earth and rock from the cuttings being dug further down the line. A temporary tramway was laid to the end of the growing embankment and a stout timber buffer was fastened across the broad end point. Horsemen would walk alongside the horse at first and then get the horse moving steadily, finally urging the creature to more speed as they approached the end. Then, uncoupling the horse with a deft twist of the harness, both turned sharply aside at the last minute, so that the wagon ran on alone, to hit the buffer and tip forwards, spilling the contents over the edge. It was skilfully done most of the time, with the men and horses knowing what to expect and how to handle it, but accidents did happen. Sometimes, the timing went wrong and the wagon did not tip or if it did, the contents were too sticky or too heavy to spill; or the whole thing crashed through the buffers and was thrown over completely: a few wagons were left to be buried in the base of most embankments.

Sometimes, at the point of turning, a man slipped and the horse was thrown down with the wagon, but the day before, in a squally shower, a man had got tangled in a loose rein and had slithered in the mud and man, horse and wagon had been thrown over the edge of the embankment: the man had been injured, the horse had to be destroyed. Walter and James had come to check that the contractor was not risking life and limb simply to push the work on faster and also to estimate the time and materials needed to complete the necessary work.

But whilst they watched and made notes in their field books and then set to work with chains and cross-staves, their talk was of Nancy and Bernard. A pannikin of hot tea was brought to them after an hour and they sheltered in the lee of a rock face, sitting on some wooden hurdles, and James once again told as much of the story as he thought his listener should hear. Walter was quick to recognise that in part, James had become involved to assist him and was grateful.

'A've every reason to thank 'ee, laddie. The man Bernard was like to put me into a very difficult sitiation an' now it's stopped. Cos without the lasses he's nay proof o' anything, it's just ma word against his now. 'But he's a threat to you, James. He's bound to know who helped the lassies get away an' he's nay likely to let it pass, even if he's now no longer able to run the Blue Lamp in quite the same way, havin' lost its star attraction. There are many men hereabouts that he can put pressure on in one way or another an' 'e will still be sellin' his liquor, so he'll buy whatever help 'e needs to track you down. Watch out for every stranger. Keep with those you trust. Lock your doors at night.' James looked at him quizzically. Walter was stern. 'Never underestimate this man Bernard. He's been in trouble afore now and he's come back from setbacks and built himself up again … an' he's strong on bearing grudges. Don't forget that his whole life is now fixed on reversin' what 'e saw as an injustice done by the Midland Railway. Ma guess is that 'is grudge agin you will be fierce an' personal.'

Walter observed the pallid cheeks of his young engineer and the livid scar on his forehead, which he had not explained. He moved to reassure him. 'But you're not alone in this. A'll bear ma part an' so will ma brother. A've told him o' ma troubles over this man an' if you agree, a'll tell him about your actions. An' there's others that have crossed swords wi' this man or bin threatened by him; we must gather them round us and do what we can. One good thing is that the constable is not making any real effort to trace the lasses or to find out how they escaped. A've a feelin' that there's more than us and the Midland as would be glad to see Mr Bernard pack up an' leave Batty Green.'

'I hate the man,' James muttered. 'I'd happily take a pick handle to him.'

Walter nodded. 'A'd help you. But you rarely see him out o' the hut an' we canna just set light to it for fear o' harming the women an' bairns. An' don't forget that there's many that like their supply o' cheap moonshine; it's a fine tipple, so it is, as a can state personally, and others appreciate it and thir's some as depend on it. If they thought we were about to put an end to it, then we might have a wee problem wi' them as well. You know the navvies hate anyone who snitches to authorities. We'll have to tread careful.'

'What about squeezing him, his money, I mean, cut it off, make it dry up, make him feel even more unwelcome here?' James asked. 'What about talking to the excise officers about illegal drinking, as if we heard a rumour? They're always snooping round; I bet they'd welcome any help to stop his little rackets. And where's the drink coming from? Who brews it? And where? How is it brought in and who takes it to customers? Can't we try to starve him out?'

'Aye. A like the sound o' that, James. Let's be askin' around and settin' others to watch an' ask. We'll not just sit back an' wait for 'im to make a move.'

'Have you ever 'eard of a man called Mr Grantley?' James asked.

Walter shook his head. 'Nay, lad, can't say as I have. Who is he?'

'I met him at the Blue Lamp. Not a navvy or a railway man, o' that a'm sure. More like a shopkeeper or merchant. I had this feelin' that he might deal in grain, or wheat or summat like and perhaps he supplies Bernard.'

Walter looked interested. 'Well, if we can find him, who knows what it might lead to. Let's try a few contacts. A've a cousin who works at Lancaster Docks. A'll write an' ask if he knows of a Grantley in that kind o' business. There's a fair bit o' grain comes in that way. Come on then, laddie, let's get on wi' it an' remember, take special care, there could be problems around the corner. If necessary, well, perhaps ye can gan off to another Midland site for some wider experience. But, in the meantime, ya work wi' me as ma personal assistant for these next few weeks an' stay by my side: agreed?'

James was more than willing to accept. He was cheered by the thought of getting revenge on Bernard: he would do it for Nancy and Grace, risking all to prove his worth. He told Emily, but no one else. She was powerfully stirred to see him so determined to get back at Bernard. She was very ready to focus her own passionate thoughts on the same end, drawing closer to James again, and together they vowed to use whatever means they could to cut this evil out of Batty Green, before it could grow strong once more, feeding on the weak and vulnerable in that unconnected place.

Plan and Counterplan
May 1871

Despite their best intentions, actual progress was slow and disheartening. In the meantime, a letter arrived at the works, simple blunt and unsigned, in which unspecific threats against James and Walter were linked to demands to know where the missing girls were. Bernard was clearly moving against them. The two men told no one, but were uneasy and watchful.

About a week later, in early May, the weather at last settled into a series of fine days with no rain. Winds were suddenly mercifully light at Ribblehead and there was a cheerful whistling of men, instead of the shrill whining of rope, timber and cable that had been more or less constant in the teeth of the persistent storms of the past week. At noon, James felt the unaccustomed pleasure of the sun on his face and he began to climb down from the scaffolding surrounding one of the piers of the viaduct. He reached the ground feeling hungry and then remembered that Hetty had promised him a treat in the lunch that she had packed up for him. He thought that he would get his case from the office, where his lunch was in amongst drawings, ledgers and notebooks, and sit in the sun for a while to eat. He waited for Walter to climb down and became aware that a familiar figure was walking towards him: it was Robert Macintosh. He wore a clay-spattered overall over a dark suit and a dusty top hat shaded his face. James noted the faint residue of bruising around the nose and one eye, but he also noted the warm, open smile with which he approached.

'James, I thought it were you, how are you?' Robert strode forwards energetically and offered his hand.

James was a little surprised at the friendly greeting, where there was usually caution and sometimes thinly veiled hostility, but was glad of any gesture of friendship at this time. He shook the hand warmly and asked how Robert was.

'I'm grand, just now, thank 'ee kindly for askin'. I 'ave bin in a bit o' a scrape, as you have perhaps 'eard, an' it knocked me back a bit, but I've pulled meself together an' a've got plans now an' things to look forward to. But a hear ...' he paused as if conscious that he needed to be careful with his words, 'that you've been through some ... difficulties yerself, like.'

'True, I have.' James was unsure how far to open up to this new friendly Robert and so the brevity of his reply threatened a quick end to their conversation, but Robert swiftly adjusted and did not take offence.

'Well I'm not asking for details or owt,' he offered reassuringly. 'But a just wanted you to know that if you need any help or there's owt a can do, just let me know at the brickworks or at Aidan's Hut.'

James stammered a "thank you", but still seemed at a loss to appreciate how far he could trust the man, who had often been an aggravation and sometimes a rival. Robert seemed to read his thoughts.

'A know that we've not always been the best o' friends an' you probably wonder what a'm up to, behavin' like this, but a met up with Jack and Ethel t'other day, helped them move some stuff in fact, up to their new place, an' they told me a few things that they had kind o' guessed at, you know how folk like to chatter on about other folks' business. But they reckon on how you had some part in them girls escaping from that evil swine Bernard an' the Blue Lamp an' if that's the case, James, then a want to say that a'm proud to say a know you, cos you've done summat as the rest o' us perhaps should 'ave done a while back.' He almost did a little bow towards James, but ended up just nodding forwards, with a touch of embarrassment. 'Don't forget what a said, will you?' And his speech finished, Robert turned and moved away.

James called to him to stop, still unsure how to handle this new relationship, but anxious to make some gesture in return. 'Emily was saying that she wished you would call in some time,' he stated, truthfully enough. 'Why don't you?'

'You still going to Elterbeck at the usual time?' Robert asked. James nodded. 'Shall a walk down wi' you later an' say hello?'

'I would be pleased,' James replied and meant it.

Walter climbed down soon after and within a few more minutes, James was sitting outside their office on a wooden crate, his hat off and his neat, regular face raised to catch the warming beams of the sun. It was by no means a peaceful scene, for there was always the clatter and hiss and commotion of men and their machines, but he was so used to it now he could blot it out, fold it to the back of his mind and make space for his own thoughts.

He was eating chicken and bread supplied by Hetty and was looking forward to the oatcake and milk that she had supplied to follow, when he thought of the patient, loving care that Hetty was giving. He had asked her to give him a few weeks to sort things out and she had kept her word, waiting with stoical fortitude. But she would be distressed if she knew just how completely Nancy engaged most of his waking thoughts and fantasies, and sometimes his dreams, too. He constantly relived their days and nights together and he wove imaginative worlds of glamour and sensuality around a future reunion. He knew that in his present state, if she wrote and asked him to join her, then he would go.

He turned to throw a chicken bone to an old dog that was watching patiently, his grizzled head down on his paws, and as he swung his arm, he just caught the movement of a man's cap as it ducked behind an untidy pile of rails some way to the side of him. He swivelled to watch the spot again. Had he imagined it? Surely not! There was someone there who must have been watching him and did not want to be seen.

Quietly and very slowly, he eased himself down off the packing case. Then he slipped round behind the office and did a quick sprint towards the pile of rails. There was an equally untidy pile of bricks and stones in the way, but if he could get up to the top of it at least he would have a good view. He scrambled up as quickly as he could, knocking stones over that clattered down towards the rails. Gasping for breath, he reached the top, just in time to see a burly fellow in a blue jacket and black cap scurry away towards the brickworks. He caught a glimpse of a dark, drooping moustache and a yellow neckerchief. James did not recognise the man.

He went back to finish his lunch and report this to Walter. Walter also had news. A letter had arrived and the cousin in Lancaster did know of a Mr Grantley, who was a respected merchant in the town who sold flour, but also barley, wheat and other grains, to customers all over the region, including some in Settle, Ingleton and Dent. What was more, it so happened that the constable for Batty Green, Archie Cameron, came into the office just as Walter was reading the letter and so Walter asked him if the name Grantley meant anything. He said he thought he had seen it on a wagon parked outside the Gearstones Inn just the week before.

'So, laddie,' Walter smiled his reassurance, 'we have to watch out for this wee fellow in the blue jacket and yellow neckerchief and we have to pay a visit to the Gearstones and have a word or two up there. And a've been told as th'excise men are coming this way in the next day or so, so we can have a parley wi' them an' all. We may be gettin' somewhere soon.'

James walked slowly back to Elterbeck with Robert, both of them leading their horses, and James found himself once again giving an edited version of the events with Nancy and Grace. They stopped at the Hill Inn, sharing a jug of beer and finding a quiet space to discuss the various possibilities that lay ahead. James felt a pleasant glow of self-congratulation seeping through him. He told his story differently each time now, with a few grace notes of embellishment, and he enjoyed recreating himself anew as the protective hero in a tale of two vulnerable young women. Robert could see that James had risen in stature in his own eyes, as well as in those of others, and he smiled to himself, but was genuinely pleased at the outcome and this binding of a new relationship. There was something to be said, he reflected, for a young man enjoying the pleasures of a beautiful and adventurous young woman and in casting a modest reflection of that pleasure on to his listeners. He was jealous. But he could also see mutual benefits in developing this friendship with James and was honest enough to say so. He was especially eager when he knew that Emily was being kept informed and that she wanted to be involved where she could. It was time for him to make that link again, if the opportunity presented.

'Tha'll need help to see off Bernard, a'm thinkin'. A'll be glad to be of assistance in any way a can. In return, if all works out right, a may ask for some help meself, before too long. A've been asked to go and set up a new brickworks near Glasgow. T'would be a good opening for me and a've a mind to do it. But there's a couple o' bits o' unfinished business that a want to see to afore a go. An' a may need to call on thee for assistance. What do you say? A'll help thee rid thee sen o' Bernard and wi' great pleasure, too. Will you help me later?'

James was very ready to agree and he told Robert of the threatening letters and the young man seen earlier in the day. They earnestly discussed tactics and possible moves. James drew strength from the comradeship that was offered here, as he had elsewhere. The two men moved on, feeling closer and stronger in this new bond. But at Elterbeck they found consternation and a buzz of anguished discussion. Their opponents were again ahead of them.

With unusual sentimentality, Emily had kept an old grey mongrel as a pet; he had come from Selside with her when she first came to the farm, almost her only link with her past. In warmer weather he liked to shelter in the trees behind the farm, where the limestone clints just held enough soil for some scrub oak to survive. As the day had waned, he had been heard whining plaintively from there and was eventually discovered struggling to drag himself down, his back legs bound cruelly together with twine, which was then wrapped round a large stone, and there was a letter tied round his neck The contents were simply stated, in a simple hand: where are the girls? Give them up or others will get hurt. The dog's hip had been dislocated on one side and he had to be put out of his misery. A search revealed no intruder and no one had been seen, but the familiar hillsides seemed ominous now.

There was anger and distress, with guilt and frustration rolled into it. They drew together to discuss the threat, acknowledging that Bernard was certainly behind it and that changes would need to be made around the farm. Robert felt in the way and he did not stay long, but the incident firmed up his resolve to help his old friends, including James, and he told them so. Emily rewarded him with a glowing smile that spread warmly through him like fine ruby wine.

Surprisingly, George was the most deeply affected by the death of the dog, though he was not indulgent of animals and was ruthlessly efficient when the time came to kill or to cull. Besides, the dog was old and was never any practical use to them: he would have been put down sooner or later. But George could not tolerate deliberate cruelty. It depressed him and it became quickly fixed in his mind that this was just the start of more such trouble; all of it emanating from Batty Green. Quite illogically, he also connected the appearance of Robert with the new threats to Hetty and James and Elterbeck. It now seemed to him that every new contact with the place brought a risk and even whilst he consoled Emily and considered how to keep the farm more secure, he chewed the inside of his cheek, with a slow, burning anger, and said sourly, 'In a couple of years, they will be finished an' gone an' t'day can't come soon enough for me.'

He made changes that Emily resented but could not argue against. Morgan and Joshua were to take charge of driving the cart to Batty Green each day and seeing that the women were kept safe. Emily, despite her unease, was amused at the thought of the bubbly Joshua trying his songs and jokes on the damp gloom of the biblical Morgan.

Hetty was only to go with Emily on a Saturday. Emily might go on other days, provided she was accompanied and provided that Ethel would meet her and help with their sales at the camp, but they would no longer walk from hut to hut. They would rent a space and set up a counter and little store and customers would come to them. Taking milk and other goods up to the more distant encampments would now involve only Joshua and Morgan.

Emily saw the reasonableness of all this; yet, she felt stifled and uncomfortable and cut off. It was an old and familiar feeling, as if a tiny cauterising iron had been inserted somewhere inside her and it was beginning, very slowly, to cut off the blood to her heart and her womb. She felt she was shrivelling. She loathed the grim, sour presence of the Welshman, with his Bible tags and bilious outlook, and she quickly began to think of him as her jailer. When she tried to explain this to George, he countered that he had to be sure that she was safe and she had to go accompanied or not at all.

'Oh, he'll keep an eye on me alright,' she said. 'Trouble is that while one eye's on me, t'other is usually watching the top of Whernside; fat lot o' bloody help that is.' George did have the grace to laugh at this description, but he would not shift from his plans. She found it hard even to speak to Morgan. 'God give me strength to be good, patient and kind and not to take an axe to his fat head,' she murmured. She drew closer to Hetty and they suffered the mouse with indifference and the mole with active distaste. Meanwhile, Emily was giving Hetty advice on how to proceed with James. It was the kind of advice that the "chapel twins" would have been scandalised by. Emily enjoyed her role all the more for knowing this.

The more serious skirmishing continued whilst their enquiries went nowhere. A couple of days after the dog had been killed, James and Walter were approaching the scaffolding round one of the viaduct piers, part of their regular rounds, when a wooden spar began to roll off a cross-beam 20 feet above them. James heard the slow rotation of wood on wood, like a clumsily accelerating drum roll, and he looked up just in time to catch the movement. He shouted and they both scrambled to safety as the stout timber crashed heavily into the earth. But if it had not been unusually quiet, if he had been less alert, then they might have been hurt. They found the spar had been held by a slip knot and activated from some distance, but again no one was seen

They could smell the malevolent taint of Bernard in these "accidents", but it was more than this: the very air seemed to be infected. Bernard was reaching out for them, using others and suborning them to his cause. They needed to do something, before he got to them.

Intuition
May 1871

First, they held urgent talks with the excise officer, who knew well of Bernard's reputation, but had never managed to catch him when money had actually passed hands.

'He's very clever with it,' the officer stated, almost with a touch of admiration. 'We've seen bottles and flagons passed over, but he always says that they're just gifts. He must collect his money at some other time or in some other way, cos he keeps himself very clean.'

He was interested in the connection with Mr Grantley and without asking too many questions about their involvement, he agreed to watch the Blue Lamp closely and to renew efforts to put Bernard out of business.

Then, Walter and James paid a visit to the Gearstones Inn, but learned little, other than that the wagon did stop there from time to time, driven by an old fellow known as Willie, or Wet Willie behind his back, on account of his weak bladder and a smell of urine that seemed to follow him everywhere. No one knew quite where Wet Willie's customers were and he refused to say, but he brought a wagon over half-full every couple of weeks and headed off up the dale. Someone thought the cart might have Grantley's name painted on the side, but the road was busy these days and memories weak when ale fuddled the landscape. James and Walter knew they could not just wait for him to return. They felt that they were making small steps forwards, but it was painfully slow and they were anxious for a more significant breakthrough. It was nearly another week when their breakthrough came, from an unexpected source.

Morgan had been given the job of setting up the new shop at Batty Green. They had secured a location between the Railway Inn and the reading room, within view of the end of the light railway. It was no more than a shabby old storage hut, which they had to paint, repair and make safe. Emily insisted on their trademark yellow and a sign saying Elterbeck Dairy and she had to admit that Morgan made a good job of it all, making a stout doorway and creating a hatch that could be pulled up and locked from the inside. There was a large, clean storeroom behind the shop, strewn with straw. They even moved in some old furniture and Morgan fitted up a little stove to keep it warm and to give them the means to boil a billycan or to cook simple food.

'God makes his ways right for the righteous,' he pronounced smugly when he had finished. Emily smiled and nodded her thanks to him, but could not resist a reply.

'If t'heathen try to get in, we'll mek sure they pay first an' that they wipe their feet, don't tha fret.'

He said nothing, but looked sourly away. She sent him back to Elterbeck to collect some shelves, a couch and an old cupboard that they would use in the store, whilst she and Ethel continued to set things out as they wanted them. Then they sat on the step for a while, waiting for him to return, watching the ways of the camp.

Ethel suddenly sat up and pointed. 'Look, there's Mavis and Agnes. A' hear as they're doin' rather well for themselves these days. Let's have a look.' And so saying, she pulled Emily to her feet and the two women sauntered over to intercept the mother, daughter and small child. They certainly seemed better presented than when Emily had last met them, which had been some months before in the hut that Ethel had lived in. Mavis looked cleaner, but still the overall impression was of an unshapely mass of black cloth, topped by the blotchy red face of a regular drinker. Agnes held the child Thomas by the hand and he continued to inhabit his dull satellite position with sullen displeasure, silently attached to one or the other of the two women. Agnes had a new bonnet and gown and with studied practice she lifted her nose slightly as the others approached, ready to extract any advantage that would serve to bolster her need to feel superior. Pleasantries were exchanged and questions given and answered about the children. Politeness soon exhausted, they began to move apart, when Mavis nudged Agnes and pointed up towards the toll road.

'Here's your Arthur back from Ingleton.'

All four women looked up to see a horse and cart turning off the road and beginning to wend its way down the busy track towards them. It was Ethel who, in all innocence, made the necessary observation and asked the key question, without knowing where it would lead.

'Looks like a new horse and cart to me, does that, Agnes. Must be doin' all right, your man. Is he after getten new work?'

Agnes could not help herself. She beamed, 'Oh yes. My Arthur is now working for … someone … else and has a man to help him. We are going to move to our own cottage soon.' Emily was intrigued by the hesitation and the new wealth and she wondered why Agnes should have to be so careful about names and so she watched with particular attention as the cart approached. Ethel was asking questions about their lodger and Emily focused again when she heard Agnes say, 'Come up to t'hut and see what a've made of it. Perhaps you shall see the lodger. Oh there's no need, he's here now. Young Will Hodgson works for Arthur and he's in the cart, see there.'

There was just a hint of too much excitement in the way that Agnes referred to the lodger that again raised suspicions in the mind of Emily. Arthur was driving, looking neat in a dark suit and bowler hat. He was a little man, older than Agnes, with sharp features, clean-shaven and very self-contained. Emily had seen him once before, upright and proprietorial by the side of his wife. She was amused by his trim appearance: it was as if Agnes polished him for effect and then put him away, neatly pressed, in a box at night, taking him out for work in pristine order the next day.

He raised his hat to the women as the cart moved past them and Emily saw Will Hodgson in the back, reclining casually between some sacks of grain, broad-shouldered, with a dark head of hair and a drooping moustache. He stared at them, unflinchingly. He had his jacket tightly buttoned but, with or without the yellow neckerchief, Emily was immediately willing to believe that this was the man who had been threatening them and who had tried to hurt James. She noted that the cart contained large wooden cases, with straw packing just escaping from the sides, as well as perhaps a dozen large sacks, some of coal, some of grain. She could make out the sound of bottles rattling against each other in the cases. She said nothing as the cart moved on and Ethel went off with Agnes, but Emily excused herself, needing time to think.

Later, Black Jack came by with the children. Emily was part way through explaining where Ethel was when she returned. They then began to talk about Agnes, Arthur and Will. Emily was too brimful of her ideas to hesitate. She questioned Black Jack straight and he hesitated at first to answer, shifting uneasily from foot to foot, pulling his hat down lower and lower over his dark brows. He knew that if certain navvies learned that he gave information that led to the illegal whisky supply being shut down, then he would be very unpopular and might take a nasty beating. But he was no match in words or determination for Emily and Ethel. They soon got it out of him and Black Jack slipped quickly away, unsure of what he had done.

It all confirmed Emily's suppositions. A former navvy, an all-round nasty piece of work called Iron Harris, feared and loathed for his easy resort to violence, had left Batty Green suddenly. Then, within the week, Arthur had a new horse and cart to drive and then the young man Will had appeared, saying little, but often moving round the camp at night, knocking on doors and sometimes travelling in the cart with Arthur. Agnes had let it be known far and wide that her prospects were improving and that her young lodger had his eye on her. Black Jack offered his best guess that Arthur might now be the principal agent for Mr Bernard, having taken over from Iron Harris. Emily almost skipped with excitement. It was so easy! All they had to do now was just follow these two and see where they went. She immediately sent out messengers. She was gathering her men around her.

Later that evening, when they were all assembled, there was a flurry of excited planning at Elterbeck, hurriedly managed, and as soon as the light began to fade a wagon left the farm and made its way to Ribblehead. From the wagon, two small groups moved out and split up. At last the hunt was on.

Traps
May 1871

Walter Hirst was five years younger than his brother Charles. He was sharper, more aggressive and had less to lose than his married brother, who had family obligations and responsibilities. Walter now led one group, with James and two young Scottish navvies, half-cousins of Walter, who owed him a good turn. Their target was Will Hodgson: to confirm his part in recent events, find out whom he was working with and frighten him off. Robert led the other group, with Emily, Morgan and a friend of Robert's called Stuart, who worked at the brickworks. They were to find and question Arthur and to try to find out what his part was in all this and hopefully trace it back to Mr Bernard. Hetty was to stay with the wagon.

George had been the only negative factor and for a while his opposition had threatened to stop everything. He refused to be involved personally and had strongly opposed Emily's participation, despite Robert's best efforts to insist that she would be safe and that she would be more likely to get something out of Arthur than they were. He had conceded only when she defied him, in a private but passionate outburst, and threatened to go on her own anyway, and when she had agreed that Morgan would go to act as her guardian. Her flesh recoiled and felt thick and clammy at the thought of the miner being anywhere near her, but she knew she had little real choice. Morgan declared that he would not "follow the horns of Beelzebub into any abyss that they opened". None of them stopped to try to understand what he meant.

Agnes had renamed her hut The Cottage, but Ethel had earlier confirmed that the inside was just as it had been when she lived there. In the chill night air of a spring evening, with a breeze gathering from the south, there were stoves burning at both ends of the hut. Naphtha lamps were also lit, pulling in the early moths, and in the absence of curtains it was a simple matter to establish that Agnes, Mavis and the child Thomas were at one end, with another small family and a baby at the other. Will Hodgson presumably slept in one of the middle rooms, but at the moment there was no sign of him, Arthur or the horse and cart. The two Elterbeck groups, having converged on the hut from different sides, now moved away to wait and watch.

It was easy to blend in to the background here. People were still moving in the area, passing by on their way down to the Welcome Home or the Railway Inn, and a few small groups of men and women were braving the cold to stand outside and smoke their pipes, talking softly, but it was not a night for lingering. A few wagons were still moving around, a light engine was panting and stuttering and several small gangs were on the viaduct, mostly masons and their labourers, working by candlelight on the lower parts of the piers, the sound of hammers on chisels echoing with sharp, rhythmic pulses round the basin. They would stop soon, but the animals would continue their background wall of sound throughout the night: Emily could hear pigs snuffling warmly and she wondered where they were.

Walter and James were watching from the north side of the Batty Green huts, observing the road down from Jericho and the Blue Lamp. Robert and Emily, snug inside the Elterbeck shop and peering through the hatch, were watching the other thoroughfare from the Ingleton Road. What none of them expected was that the two men they were looking for would suddenly appear from behind the hut, coming from the direction of Belgravia, leading the horse and an empty cart on a pathway that they did not know existed. They carried no lamp and the two spoke briefly in front of the hut. Then Will went on with the horse and cart and Arthur stepped inside before anyone had a chance to do anything.

With no more than a nod, Walter, James and the two navvies slipped out of the shadows and followed Will Hodgson at a distance.

'Just follow,' James hissed. 'See where he leads us. There may be a store or something. We'll grab him when he gets there.'

In the confused alleys and byways around the viaduct workings there were huts, sheds, storerooms and compounds of all kinds. The horse knew its way through the network and Will walked casually beside or even behind the cart when they squeezed through one particular gap, a fence on one side, a brick wall on the other. He unlocked double doors in a palisade wall and swung them open; the horse pulled through without prompting. There was the sound of a lamp being lit, the harness being removed and the horse being fed and watered; otherwise, the only sound was a group of masons in the distance, voices rising above the chipping of stones and the rasp of a saw. Walter and James crept forwards with the navvies and they positioned themselves, two on each side, behind the doors.

'Tek him when he comes out,' Walter whispered. In the event, Will made it easy for them, walking through the doorway and pausing to look up at the night sky, yawning loudly and stretching his arms expansively upwards. Before he was half aware of movement, his arms were grabbed and he was hauled backwards into the shed and thrust against the tailgate of the cart. Walter found a rope.

'Tie him tight to the cart, lads, and tek his boots off. Then let's get a light on him, shut the doors and see what we have.' It was soon done.

Will Hodgson did not struggle or speak, maintaining a sullen glare, half standing, half leaning on the cart, his stockinged feet soon wet from the mired floor. James stood in front of him.

'Know me, do you?' There was no response. James unbuttoned the man's jacket and pulled out the yellow neckerchief. 'It's 'im alright.' He paused, gathering the distaste like phlegm in the mouth and focusing on the memories of what this man had done or tried to do. 'We 'ad to kill the dog. Pet animal that 'un, a friend o' mine wor quite upset.' Will lifted his upper lip in the faintest sneer. James stepped back and with all the force he could muster, he brought his fist hard into the man's midriff. He doubled up, coughed and heaved for breath and then he straightened up slowly and smiled weakly. He's younger than me, thought James.

'The dog was just a warning,' Will wheezed chestily. The accent was southern, the timbre quite gentle and educated. 'Next it's the women.' He gasped for breath. 'There's some missing money and some missing persons and they have to be returned.' James was about to reply, when Walter stepped across and gently moved him aside.

'I think you know me as well, laddie. There's the wee matter of a hefty piece o' lumber that could ha' crushed my skull a few days since. Here's my reply.' Walter swivelled and hit Will full in the face. He crumpled against the cart. 'Now, there's plenty more where that came from, do you know what a mean? A've two young cousins here that owe some favours and both o' them are handy lads from the more select areas of Glasgow. They would quite enjoy taking your face apart and that's before we drop yor kecks and ruin your marriage prospects. So be a clever laddie. Whatever Bernard is paying you, it's not worth it for what's goin' to happen to you here. It's Bernard that a want. You just tell us where he meks the moonshine and how he sells it and you can go. A'll even put five pounds in your pocket, tek you to Ingleton and put you on a train: no police, no more beating. You can just disappear. You have ma word. Don't mek this harder for yourself than you need to.' Will Hodgson did not speak, staring and licking at the ends of his moustache instead. 'We'll give you a wee whiles to consider the offer,' Walter added, patting the younger man on the shoulder in an avuncular manner. 'Come on, laddie, see some sense.' James smiled at the phrase. He had heard Walter use it more than once with the younger engineers.

Walter then got them searching the shed. Another lantern was lit and they soon found a smaller door, hidden behind a crude partition of straw bales. The door was robustly constructed and it was locked. Walter returned to their prisoner.

'Where's the key, Will, to t'other room?' There was a pause.

'In the tin box. Under the straw in the manger.'

Walter smiled at him and acknowledged the help with a nod.

'Good. You're seein' some sense. A like that in a young man.'

The room was long and narrow, running most of the length of the shed, lit by a few dingy glass panels high up. There were signs of regular habitation: a truckle bed neatly made up with sheets and blankets, a jug and ewer of water, some toiletries and towels, a small table and some candle ends, even a couple of books. And beyond that a stack of about a dozen wooden cases all containing bottles or jars. Walter opened one and took a swig.

'Grand stuff,' he chortled. 'A could stay here all night.'

They took the bottle back with them and passed it round. James took a pull at it and the familiar hot, peaty texture hit his throat and brought back a welter of memories.

'Untie one of his arms,' Walter instructed one of the navvies. 'But keep the other one well bound behind his back.'

This was done and Walter passed the bottle to Will, who drank greedily and passed it back with a nod of thanks. He stroked his moustache and then spoke defiantly.

'That's all the help I can give right now. You robbed me and beat me up. Could happen to anyone.' He drew himself up and the sullen stare reappeared.

'Och,' Walter grimaced. 'You're a silly boy.' He turned to the others. 'Put him on 'is back. Tie him up tight, arms and legs spread wide. Oh, and tek his kecks off first.'

It was then that three pairs of hands immediately set to work on Will, whilst Walter turned and went back to the inner room. When he returned, the prisoner was spreadeagled in his shirt and thick stockings.

Walter carried a razor and another bottle. He set himself up beside the cart, taking off his jacket and rolling up his sleeves in a businesslike manner. Then he uncorked the bottle and drank greedily.

'Nothing like a wee dram to settle the nerves before a little cutting, eh, Will? Good of you to provide the razor.'

There was no reply, but the young man's pallor was now waxen white and his eyes nervously followed the razor as Walter stepped up close. He flinched.

'Grab his head, Jamie,' Walter ordered.

The young, brawny navvy jumped up onto the cart and braced the man's head from behind. Walter spoke gently to Will.

'Anytime you want to talk, you just start straight in, eh? But don't leave it too long, cos a few more drinks and a'm not so sure that a can be sure how steady ma hand will be, if you can follow the meaning.' Walter drank again, noisily. 'For now, a'll start with some of your face.'

Without further word, he grabbed the waxen moustache with one hand, he tugged the handlebars away from the man's face and cut them with two quick slices and then threw them down. Will let out the breath he had been holding and sweat broke out on his brow. Walter savagely held the man's nose aside and with quick, rasping stokes he began on the rest of the moustache. He had removed half, when the young man whimpered.

'No more. I'll help you.' Walter stopped, but held the razor still aloft and waited. 'I'll tell you it all, Mr Hirst, but you need to help me first.'

'You are not really in what a would describe as a strong bargaining position, but we'll listen,' said Walter.

'I work for Bernard, but not out of choice. My father's a ... member of the board of the Midland Railway, or at least he was before he resigned. He visited Bernard a few times, a year or so back, when he was down south. Something happened there, I think it involved one of the girls, I don't know what exactly and I don't want to. My father wrote some letters, I'm not sure what about, but Bernard has kept them. He's already taken money from my father and I was in debt myself, so when he promised to give the letters to me if I came and worked for a month and did whatever was asked, well, I thought I could do my father a good turn and perhaps make some money, you know, sort a few things out. If I fail, then the letters go to the newspapers or the board, or somewhere. I didn't know what he wanted, really. I still don't know all of it. I just had to collect money from the huts and then frighten Mr Taylor, not hurt him too much; you know, just get him to talk and recover the money and the girls as well if I could, for a big payout. Mr Bernard's determined to get his daughters back. I didn't mean to cause any serious harm to anyone.'

'Keep talking,' said Walter, reaching for the bottle. 'When a've heard a canny bit that's new and useful, we can talk terms and cut you loose.'

Will talked and after a further half-hour he was sitting on the bales with them, one half of his moustache still intact, an empty bottle on the floor, and a new plan was sketched out with Will's help. He seemed relieved to be switching sides. Walter and James felt the warmth of rough whisky and the glow of success.

Meanwhile, Emily, Robert and Stuart, with Morgan in distant attendance, had decided to get Arthur out of the garden room by the simplest approach. They sent Stuart to knock on the door, say that Arthur was needed urgently at the Blue Lamp and then leave. Stuart played his part well, being brisk and non-committal, refusing to answer any of Arthur's questions, fading quickly into the night. A few minutes later, a muffler wrapped round his neck and lantern in hand, Arthur had come out and turned up the causeway in a hurry. Then, 10 yards from his door, Emily stepped out in front of him and told him to stop. Robert and Stuart materialised behind him instantaneously, took one arm each and then spun him round and back to the Elterbeck shop, his feet just skimming the ground and terror in his eyes. He wriggled liked a worm on a hook and gasped like a fish.

Emily took a strong dislike to the man. They tied him to a chair, which at least kept him upright. Up close, the neat exterior was a cover for a yellowish skin, poor teeth, palpitations and an inclination to sweat. He put up not the slightest resistance. No force was needed, or any threats, except the threat to tell Agnes exactly the nature of the business he was in, then hand him over to the police and the excise officers. Robert turned the screws on him.

'Eh, Arthur, lad. It's lookin' bad, tha knows. Quite a list of offences to bring out in court. Prostitution, illegal sale of alcohol, extortion of money, blackmail, threats and intimidation. Dost thou think Agnes will come to see thy finest hour in court, Arthur? Will she bring Thomas? And dost think tha'll be alright in prison? And will she wait ten year for thy release? Or 'as she already lined up summat a bit younger and more socially acceptable? And what about Mavis? How will she cope without 'er regular supply o' drink? A assume it's Bernard's moonshine that she has a bit o' a likin' for, am a reet? A wouldn't fancy yor chances at home when news o' this breaks out. Them two women will flatten thee, stamp the livin' daylights out o' thee and then turn thee o'er to polis next mornin'. It's lookin' bad, ain't it.'

Arthur looked sickly and just stated, at regular intervals, that he only drove the horse and cart. Having asserted that fact a few times, he then seemed to lapse into a dazed panic that left him capable of little more than nervous nods and blank smiles, mostly directed at the roof of the adjacent hut. His interrogators withdrew to consult.

'Guilt's written all over him so large that we 'ardly need ask any more,' said Robert, almost with regret. 'It's like trying to discuss the future wi' one o' these religious types as thinks t'end o' the world has just 'appened. We're gettin' nowt but the grinnin' o' a sheep wi' wind. Meks me want to bray 'im just to get 'im to act like some sort of a man.'

'What we want is information that we can use to lock away this Bernard man or to destroy 'is business,' Emily added. 'Yon weasel is terrified of summat. It may be Bernard himself or his own missis, or us, or mebbe he thinks the Welsh dragon over there is going to eat his liver for breakfast, or the whole lot put together, but a wonder if he'd give more willingly if we offered protection, not the law.'

'You can't let the worm escape,' stuttered Robert. 'He may have driven the horse and cart, but 'e knew what 'e wor carryin' an' what methods were used to get money an' keep clients. He can smell evil like the rest of us, I reckon. He's not innocent, even if he's weak as watter.'

'No,' Emily smiled at Robert's indignation. 'A don't mean as how 'e gets away wi' the lot; but it's not mainly 'is skin we want, is it? Let's just try a softer approach and concentrate on Bernard and closing 'im down.'

In the end, Robert agreed and Emily sent the others to sit outside. Then she untied Arthur, made him some tea and promised him that if he told her all he knew, then she would do her best to keep him out of prison. He was soon in full flow, relieved to have the burden lifted from him, and he was home within the hour, pledged to silence. Emily felt that she could trust him, weasel though he was, and she was also confident that she had all the information that was needed. Robert went along with her decisions, a reluctant putty, but soft in her hands.

So it was that the two Elterbeck groups and Will put their stories together at midnight in the farm kitchen and found that the details matched. They had a clear picture, but little evidence, though Will was willing to testify and Arthur had promised the same, but no one trusted him. Nevertheless, they planned ahead eagerly, drank moonshine and celebrated noisily until the early hours, including a ceremonial shaving of the remaining part of Will's moustache. Morgan and Ruth showed their disapproval of the noise by banging on the wall and George went out and did not return. James went off to the cottage, Robert opted to sleep in a chair in the kitchen and the rest, including Will, slept in the barn. Emily crept down from her bed when all was quiet and stood in the kitchen doorway, watching Robert as he slept. A few minutes later, she turned and went back to bed, thoughtfully and with some regret. Self-sacrifice was hard for her.

Bernards

May 1871

It was Robert who put it bluntly to them all the next day, between mouthfuls of breakfast, just before six in the morning.

'Celebration's grand, but Bernard is still out thir and we mun strike against 'im 'ard, before he gets to know what we've done to disrupt 'is work. If we can't go t'law yet, then we shall 'ave t'find this distillery of 'is an' smash it up an' we mun do it today.'

They all agreed that they had to move before Arthur's resolve weakened or news leaked out in some other way that might warn Bernard. They now knew pretty well where the moonshine was made. They also knew that Bernard had the liquor distributed by his "clerk", apparently free of charge, but to known customers only, who had to negotiate with him personally to get supplies. The same "clerk" collected payment later, always after dark and in private. Iron Harris had efficiently carried out this job with a dour relish. He was an intimidating, glowering ex-navvy, very unsubtle, who had a liking for bare-fist fighting, kicking in doors and breaking furniture. He had once had a bare-fist fight with Policeman Jack that had started in the evening and had reached a stalemate after some murderous hitting, after which they had agreed to resume at six the next morning. He had worked for Bernard for several years. During the day he fetched and carried. Each evening he took a list, collected cash and threatened to break the bones of any defaulters or troublemakers. He kept a shilling in every pound for himself. Apparently, the only records to prove any of this were in a notebook that never left Bernard's pocket.

It was now clear that when Nancy and Grace had escaped the demented Bernard, in outrage and fury, had turned on everyone near him, including Iron Harris, who had refused to be bullied and had threatened to "settle it" with Bernard there and then. In the ensuing confrontation, Bernard had sliced Harris' arm with his swordstick. It was a slice too far. Harris had knocked Bernard down and only spared him when the women had intervened. Then, within hours, Harris had left, taking the horse and cart, well loaded with liquor and the few pounds that he had just collected. In a rage and also in a dilemma, Bernard had hastily turned to Arthur, who had been an occasional client and was easily blackmailed. He recruited Arthur to drive and deliver, but wanting more muscle he had blackmailed Will's father to send the young man to work for him for a month. Will had had a reputation, as a law student, for drunken riots and fist fighting that left him without hope of a career and with some pressing debts. Now, he was on his way to catch a train, hoping for his father's sake that Bernard was quickly and permanently broken.

Walter and James decided to go for the distillery first, taking just the two Scottish navvies Jamie and Harold with them, and if possible Constable Cameron, and an excise officer if they could find one at short notice. They were going into bleak terrain, which could be inhospitable, even in the spring. For two and a half miles beyond the Gearstones Inn the road to Hawes climbs steadily, the rough limestone upland becoming bleaker and more barren all the while. Here, wind, rain and ice have scoured the slopes for centuries, stunting the trees and sending all but the hardiest life forms scuttling for shelter. Part way up the road a number of becks run down the dreary western flanks of Great Wold; one in particular plunges into a little ravine, choked by boulders and filled with the buffets of wind and falling water, a harsh place and one of menace, not of fascination.

This is Far Mares Gill: a rough track leading up to it appearing to end in little more than a pile of stones. Yet, tucked within this ravine is a primitive hut, used by shepherds for many generations, leaning against a sturdy out-barn that stores provender and hay through the worst of the winter. They had learned that this was the site of the distillery. The present shepherd, an unpleasant character of unpredictable disposition, was called Albert and was rarely seen, except on Friday nights, when he turned up at the Gearstones, collected any messages that were left for him and then took up a corner seat of the parlour and drank steadily for two or three hours.

Albert was the gatekeeper for Far Mare's Gill: supplies of barley grain, oatmeal and meal seed were dropped off regularly by Wet Willie at the end of the track, together with coal and certain foodstuffs. They had heard that the shepherd himself did the fetching and carrying and that he watched the area for strangers. The water supply was plentiful and of good quality from the Gill and not a soul came near such a remote spot for months. It was therefore a well-chosen spot for illegal brewing and it produced a fiery whisky that might lack subtlety but made up for it with kick. Neither Arthur nor Will knew who operated the distillery itself. Orders were sent to the Gearstones and when they collected the hooch, they only saw Albert, who rarely spoke.

It was early, just after eight, as five men left Ribblehead and rode steadily up the Hawes road in a covered cart, a fine drizzle seeping into them on a steady breeze. The constable, a popular and friendly sort called Archie Cameron, was with them, but the excise officers were out of the area and it was hoped that messages sent would bring them back by the afternoon. Archie showed himself eager for action. He had swapped his jacket and helmet for an old coat and hat, to keep the element of surprise as much as possible. They moved briskly, doing their best to watch out for any movement in the area, peering through the wet haze that was the air and sky, but there was no sign of life, apart from sheep and crows.

Once they left the road and crossed the open fell, their approach would be on foot and obvious to anyone who was watching, so they agreed to take it as quickly as they could and then, if necessary, to break their way in, without any concessions or discussions with whomever they met. The track was rough and the gritstone was slippery with the rain. Sloughs of peat lay between the outcrops, trapping boots and sucking limbs downwards. They pushed on, sometimes quickly but occasionally moving cautiously beside the stream bed, where there was a little cover. But there was no sign of any observer and when the end of the track came into view, they gathered under a spiky hawthorn bush.

They had all brought cudgels and now armed themselves and scurried forwards to the pile of stones at the end of the track, where they peered over, down into the ravine. A few alders dripped desolately over the footpath that curved down to where the beck gurgled and spattered over stones in a rough ford, but then the path turned away from the spur, climbing jaggedly up the opposite bank, well strewn with boulders, heading up to the ridge, to drop down again on the other side.

At the top, they could just make out the tip of a chimney, giving out a blue smoke that slid out of sight northwards, and then a portion of a rough slate roof that must be part of the out-barn, tucked behind the ridge. The noise of the beck and the soughing of the breeze through the alders drowned out all other sound. There was no movement.

'The dogs will be the problem,' whispered Archie. 'Albert always has at least two with him and they'll set up a right din when they hear us. Luckily, we're downwind. Try to be as silent as you can and avoid the path, cos there's too many loose stones. Spread out a bit on t'hillside and tek it slowly and then when I say the word, we'll rush the door. With any luck, they'll still be abed. Now mind, no broken heads ... unless it's really necessary.' They all grinned and then one by one they slipped off down the path behind him and through the ford, gritting their teeth as the cold water swept over their boots. The far hillside was pitted with loose stones of various sizes, but there were also limestone outcrops and hollows, where peaty puddles gathered, whilst patches of young bracken crunched underfoot. They wound their way upwards in slow zigzags, placing their feet carefully. A dog barked ahead of them, just once, and they all froze, then all was quiet again.

Reaching the top, they peered over and saw the lean-to shepherd's hut, with just one door, which was slightly ajar. Smoke meandered from the chimney and slipped away. They now saw that the barn had a central door, though from their angle they could not see if it was open. They knew it would have at least one window, possibly boarded up. A couple of slates had come off the roof, or been pulled off, and smoke was filtering out of this makeshift chimney. Outside, the ground was heavily trodden, dirty and littered with debris. The dogs must be inside keeping warm. A muddy path led down the steep slope on the other side of the ridge to a pool held within boulders, with a waterfall spluttering half-heartedly into it on the far side. Small barrels and pails lay around the edge: obviously, they had to carry their water up the hillside.

In whispers conveyed in cupped hands, the constable organised them. He and Walter would go for the hut. James and Jamie would cover the door into the barn and Harold was to watch the windows for any attempt to escape. They cautiously eased their way down the slope. A stone skittered away from someone's boot and a dog barked. They held their breath. The dog barked again and they heard a low mumbling voice and then a shadow fell across the hut doorway as someone moved.

Archie waited no longer. He gave the nod and began to run down the rocky path, jumping from stone to stone, and they all followed, the blood bruising through their veins as they flew recklessly downwards.

Dogs were suddenly barking wildly, voices were raised within the hut and there was a sound of something smashing and the hiss of water on hot coals. Walter took a dangerous cut across the steepest part of the slope and jumped heavily down into the doorway. He barged through it as two dogs flew at him, barking fiercely, and he knocked one aside brutally and kicked out at the other as a human form came slowly forwards, something held menacingly towards him. Walter squinted and stared through the smoky gloom, but a glint of metal suggested that it might be a pitchfork. He was a clear target against the light of the door, so he jumped quickly to the side, kicking over some cooking pots, and then swung his cudgel hard at the weapon, managing to knock it aside. Behind him, Archie came crashing in and shouted, 'Stop. Police.'

Walter could now see more clearly that their opponent was a stocky man in late middle age, in filthy clothes, one dog beside him barking and snapping, the other whining. He guessed it was Albert and he could see that it was an old pitchfork that he had snatched up and which he now pointed at the policeman's throat. Walter bent down and grabbed the metal pot that he had kicked over. It still held some hot liquid. In one sweeping movement, he threw it at the shepherd and man and dog ducked and howled, almost in unison, as the liquid hit them. He followed it up by striding quickly forwards and grabbing the old man from behind, just as Archie closed in from the other side. It was all over then, but the noise from the barn told them that there was a lot still going on in there.

James had reached the double doors of the barn just ahead of Jamie as Harold ran past them and up the side. He could hear hurried movements and the sound of glass and pottery being smashed inside. There seemed to be two voices, one darkly masculine, the other a kind of mumbling, but lighter. He pushed at the doors, one side and then the other, but they were heavily barred from the inside. James swore and hesitated. Then there was the sound of wood splintering and Harold shouted to them for help. They dashed round the side to find him slumped backwards on the ground, holding his face. A wooden board had been torn from the window and from inside, a wooden mattock was smashing out the other boards, a burly arm shooting into view as another of them gave way. 'Bastard hit me wi' the hammer,' Harold moaned. 'It just came out o' the dark when I peered in. A'll be alright in a minute or two.'

Jamie said nothing, but with a thunderous look, he grabbed a rock bigger than his fist and, standing to one side, he waited until another board gave way and then threw it through the gap with all his might. There was a roar of pain from inside and a torrent of curses. Then came more words, threateningly hissed, but too low for them to hear.

'Get the rest o' these boards out o' way,' he yelled and he and James threw more rocks at the boards and then leapt forwards in a frenzy, pulling at the shattered pieces that were left, watching and listening all the time for any response from the person inside.

There was silence, just the hiss of steam escaping from something and the crunch of logs falling, tumbling into ash. Then they heard the muttering again and the faintest rasp of one piece of metal being drawn across another, whilst a narrow shaft of sunlight began to penetrate the gloom. 'Front door,' yelled Jamie and they both raced back round the barn just as one of the doors was being carefully pulled inwards. Jamie did not break stride but threw himself, feet first at the door, thumping into it so hard that whoever was behind it was bound to be smacked backwards. He followed through and grabbed at the bundle of clothing spread on the floor, bringing his knee down hard. But he knew at once that there was something wrong. This was a scrawny being, an old woman or child, and looking up through the gloom he saw the silhouette of the window and a large figure climbing out. Already, one leg and shoulder was over the sill and the man was hauling himself through. They had fallen for the simplest trick! Jamie cried out as if in pain himself and was about to jump up, when a wooden board came smashing down on the side of the man's head and he slumped and fell back clumsily into the room. 'Well done, Harold, laddie,' shouted Jamie.

'Was me, actually,' said Constable Cameron, poking his head through and smiling. 'I thought we'd likely have at least one broken head today. Now we seem to have two.'

Their heavier assailant was barely conscious and was now easily rolled over and so his hands and feet were tied securely. He was then dragged out into the daylight and propped unceremoniously against the outer wall. Walter then appeared with Albert, similarly trussed, and he was left alongside his accomplice. The old woman, for that was what was inside the bundle of rags, seemed none the worse for her ordeal and was set to rebuild the fire in the lean-to and brew them all some tea, which she did quite cheerfully, nodding and dribbling a little. Harold, meanwhile, had pulled out a broken tooth and was groggy and in pain, but nothing else seemed to be broken, though a heavy bruise would soon show across the right side of his face. He sat thoughtfully whilst the others got the barn doors open and surveyed the scene.

The barn was squalid and filthy. The big man they had captured must have panicked when he had heard their approach and had tried to destroy the evidence of his craft. A variety of pails, barrels and jars had been pushed over or smashed, so the air was heady with fumes of fermentation. Yet, weaving through the cloud were the sinuous odours of paraffin and other strong spirits, whilst a peaty smog hugged the ground where the fire had been kicked over, so that they wondered that the whole place did not explode.

At the heart of the scene was the still, fixed to a wooden platform; the worm and condenser had been partly smashed, spigots thrown to the side, and everywhere liquids still dripped slowly, to mingle with the sodden earth. All kinds of utensils were heaped around and barrels of fermenting malt and jugs of hop juice stood ready for use. Further towards the walls of the barn was a filthy mess of waste products and human excrement, with rats moving only languidly away, as if unused to any challenge in their dominion.

If anything, the shepherd's hut was worse and they searched it for evidence in grim silence, turning over filthy bedding, piles of old rags and decayed food; even the remains of a dead animal lay in the furthest corner. It was a dispiriting exercise and produced little except a bundle of money and a few yellowing papers that had rows of figures on them.

'Och, this is terrible. Having seen the state of this place,' Walter grimly concluded, 'a may never touch a drop o' spirits again. The smell will bring back some severe memories. Let's leave the rest to the excise men to record what was made here. We need to get to Mr Bernard, before he hears o' this.'

'Which Bernard do you mean?' James asked, with a wry smile. Walter and Archie both looked confused. 'Just tek a look at big man out there,'

James went on. 'Imagine 'im without the dirt, with his hair cut and his beard a trim black, and see who you think we have. I've a feelin' it may be Bernard's older brother or his uncle. I think he's also a Bernard.'

They went out at once to look at the man and found him just coming round, groaning and slowly turning his head from side to side to shift the pain. Albert was slumped over, as if asleep. Archie nodded his agreement to James and smothering his habitual smile, he began his formal proceedings. James was amused to observe the cloak of authority being pulled so assiduously into place by the young constable.

'Well, Mr Bernard,' he began, with a very straight face. 'I think you should know that I am Constable Archie Cameron and I am putting you under arrest for the production of illegal liquor. We can probably add resisting arrest and violent conduct towards my friend Harold, an attack with a hammer won't sound good in court. You will be taken in charge until you can be presented to a magistrate. We are now going after the others involved in providing you with the means to make this alcohol and those who are selling it. Any information you can give us would help your case when the magistrate deals with you. Do you have any thing to say?'

'Aye,' the man raised bloodshot eyes and swept back his thick, matted hair. 'Go to the bleedin' devil, the lot on ya.'

'Very well,' said Archie, a genuine look of distaste now clouding his face. 'I think we can leave you in the charge of Jamie and Harold, who can escort you back to Ribblehead. It's a tidy walk and Harold in particular will be keen to see you keep moving at an uncomfortable pace. If you change your mind, Mr Bernard, please speak up and we will listen.'

Albert suddenly raised his head. It was immediately obvious that he had been awake and listening all the time. He started to whine, watching them for a response. 'A'm an awd man. A can't tek no lock up. It'll be t'end o' me. An' who'll tend t'dogs, eh? A can't be parted from beasts 'ere, a'm t'only one as knows whir they are an' how to fetch 'em in. Is thir onny way as you can gi' me a chance, young Archie?'

'Just tell us all about how things worked here,' said Archie. 'Who came, when they came, how it were all set up and paid for. And be ready to tell the story in front of magistrate. Then you may keep out o' jail. It's your only chance.'

'Damn you, if you blather,' Bernard suddenly snarled, straining to move towards Albert. 'I'll tek you limb from limb if you do an' you know someone else who will do more than that.' Archie cracked him across the side of the head with his cudgel and for a while all was quiet.

It was just before noon when the constable, bright and assertive in his full uniform, led his team up to the Blue Lamp Hut. This time, they walked straight up to the door, zealous and confident, only to be immediately deflated, when they found the door hanging open and the hut empty of its inhabitants, but with clothing, bedding, food, books and papers strewn everywhere; all the evidence of a hasty departure. Bernard must have known that the trap was closing around him: but how?

The fact that he had fled was some sort of victory, but a hollow one for James and Walter and sadly lacking the crowning glory of a final confrontation or even much hard evidence. The notebook was certainly not left behind. Meanwhile, Emily blamed herself when it soon became clear that Arthur had gone with Bernard, deserting Mavis and Agnes and the child Thomas. Nearby huts reported that Arthur had helped the Bernards load the cart in the early hours and they had crept quietly away, well before dawn. They were later seen boarding a train at Ingleton, heading south, the horse and cart abandoned in a field near Langber House. It had to be left, therefore, to the agencies of time and police enquiry to try to locate the Bernards or Arthur. There was still no news of Nancy and Grace.

So it was that a brief euphoria came and went at Elterbeck Farm and in the ensuing pause there was reflection and redirection of energies. Relationships had realigned into a new pattern: James and Hetty drew closer; George talked and occasionally prayed with Morgan and Ruth, but did not know how to speak to his wife. Emily fell into a grey silence at home and came alive in her trading at the camp, sometimes taking refuge in her old childhood habit of pouring out her frustration to any tree or bush that would listen.

Yet, she could not remain passive for long; stasis chafed her and her nerve endings tingled. Soberly, she watched the advancing spring for some sign of a breakthrough in her personal quest for fulfilment, determined that she would somehow be part of all this action and reaction. But, as before, events threatened to baulk her.

Realignments
May 1871

George suddenly fell ill with a fever and took to his bed. He ached, he writhed in distaste and he glistened with sweats and was plagued with restiveness. The doctor was called and he pronounced cautiously that he did not know what the cause was, but that the cure would almost certainly lie in rest, quiet, comforting drinks and a mild infusion to calm the nerves. Emily nursed and soothed diligently, but it was Ruth that seemed more settling and skilful and Emily withdrew: after all, the farm needed her. She made up a bed downstairs and shared the night duty with Ruth – days of uncertainty passed.

Then news spread across the whole area, confirming the rumours that had been around for days: smallpox had definitely broken out at Batty Green and an inky anxiety shrouded the thoughts of every inhabitant in the valley and on the moor. The doctor was called hurriedly back to Elterbeck and he examined the patient again and then told them to be enduring and sensible. As far as anyone knew, George had not been near Batty Green in recent weeks; the fever was probably nothing more than a cruel coincidence: however, if George began to develop headaches, backaches or any kind of lesions, then they should really start to worry and call him at once. In the meantime, they must pray, stay calm and continue the treatment. 'Calm, calm, calm: A spend my blessed life being calm,' thought Emily. 'What a want is to scream.' A couple of days later she almost got her wish.

It was late afternoon, the sun had dipped behind Whernside and the shadows were cooling quickly. The cows were in and being milked. Emily had done her share and so she left Ruth and Hetty to finish off the last half-dozen. Crossing the yard, unwrapping her pinafore as she went, she noticed that the hens were scuttling in nervous zigzags towards her and just then, the dogs chained at the far end of the yard began to bark. She looked up. The lane was partly in the shadow of some alders just beyond their gate. The dogs were soon jumping at their chains, snarling excitedly, their heads all pointing that way. Something or someone was there. After the incident with her own dog, Emily was cautious. She picked up a large fork that they used for mucking out and walked slowly forwards, shushing the dogs. It might be a fox skulking under the trees, but she would not take any risks. As she opened the gate and stepped through, she detected another note, another deep animal growl, a larger dog perhaps. Before she had time to react, a tall woman, with flowing grey hair, stepped forwards from under the trees, a large dog with her. The pair were instantly recognisable.

'It's only me, Emily,' came the low voice, vaguely transatlantic. 'It's Bella.' Something coalesced in Emily and she felt her venom rise.

'A know who thou art,' Emily snapped. 'Question is: what dost thou want?'

There was a hesitation and the speech was strangely halting. 'I heard a rumour that your husband had the smallpox. I wanted to know if I could help. I have nursed other smallpox victims. I am immune. I had the cowpox as a girl. Can I help you at all?'

A silence developed and the air between them seemed to tremble. Emily felt her breath coming and going in shallow shunts as she struggled to fight down her suspicions and anxieties, not knowing what to trust or how to react. Tears sprang to her eyes, but somehow her vision seemed to clear in that instant. She spoke bluntly, leaning hard on her Yorkshire vowels.

'As long as a'm alive, thou'll not set foot on this farm,' she said coldly.

'Why do you say that, Emily?'

There was a trembling note of unease now in the tone of the older woman. It was that very faltering and the hint of appeal in the voice that emboldened Emily to follow her hunch. Her heart and intuition drove her reply, waiting for denial with bated breath.

'Because … a've reason to believe thou knows this place very well. A believe that tha knows George or at least tha did. A believe … th'art his mother, but tha left 'im when he wor six and tha thinks tha can come wheedling thy way in again now and offer us a service. Go to hell an' may tha boil there forever.'

The dog growled, picking up the hostility. The two women stared at each other, until Bella finally turned her gaze aside.

'At least tell me how he is,' she pleaded.

A surge of triumph flooded through Emily. Her guess had been right! She stemmed her heave of conviction and concentrated all her energies on getting rid of this woman.

'He'll live,' she said brusquely, beginning to turn away. 'An' 'e don't need the likes o' thou anywhere near 'im.'

'I know I have done wrong and I don't deserve another chance ...' Bella began, but stuttered to a halt, with a touch of sourness, as if her earlier misdemeanours were haunting her unfairly.

Emily turned back to face Bella again and spat out her words, loathing mounting within her now, jarring her ribs, expelling the air as if struck by hammers. 'Tha deserves nowt but contempt. He wor just a bairn an' tha went off following thy fancy. Tha didn't just rob 'is father an' this farm, tha robbed George of a normal upbringing. A'd rather die than see thee 'ave another chance o' hurtin' 'im.' She felt ablaze with the will to defend her husband from any more pain and humiliation from this woman.

'Won't you at least come and talk to me? Listen to my side of the story? You, better than anyone, will understand the situation I was in.'

Emily knew that this appeal to fellowship was a threat. She now hated that she had talked so freely to this woman about her marriage and her longings. She wanted her a thousand miles away. 'The only person a shall speak to if a ever see thy face 'ere again will be t'magistrate. Now get off our land.'

With an imperious gesture, she pointed the way back up the lane and Bella and Bane turned and began to walk. Emily watched with a rising pride and certainty. But after a few paces, Bella turned again, took a step back and looked with pointed intensity at Emily. Something new was coming. Emily held her breath. The voice, when it came, was now level, husky, low and penetrating.

'Does your husband know that you mix with the whores on pay day?'

Emily held herself rigid, but could find neither voice nor words to reply. Bella smiled and with an appearance of casual ease, she dropped to one knee beside the dog, stroking his head, so that now two long faces, framed with unkempt hair, stared out.

'I watched you that day. I was there, too, but not working. I'm a bit beyond that these days. But I know some of the girls. What were you doing there, Emily? What were you doing before I got there, eh? My son made an interesting choice of wife. I like you, Emily; we have a lot in common, I think. Will you please just come and talk to me, in my hut, just one more time?'

Emily felt more exposed than ever and with nowhere to turn. She nodded hastily, promised that she would call and speak to Bella and went back to the farm, her thoughts churning like water sucked into a shifting pool of pebbles. She sent Ruth away with a peremptory gesture, wanting space for herself and George.

She sat for a long time that evening in an upright chair near to George's bed, whilst her husband dozed restlessly. At nine o'clock, she woke him, washed him and changed his nightshirt, fed him some soup and then read to him from the Lancaster Guardian as he settled again. His fever seemed to be abating and she was hopeful that the worst was over.

When she pulled herself stiffly from the chair in the morning he was awake and watching her. She was pleased to see him smile weakly at her.

'A've had some strange dreams, lass,' he said wryly. 'In one a wor a lad again an' mi mother wor cryin'.' Emily felt herself weaken at the knees and could only smile nervously at him. 'An' then a train seemed to come through a tunnel an' into farmyard and went tanglin' off across meadows.' She could not bring herself to comment and so she turned the talk to news of the farm stock. She kissed him as she left. She knew that if he were on the mend, then she would be better able to deal with Bella and would need to do so quickly.

With some tentative hope in her heart, Emily went to Batty Green that day and opened her shop as usual. The news was that the smallpox seemed to be mainly contained within Sebastopol and Jericho, but nevertheless there was nervous apprehension everywhere: groups did not loiter to gossip or pass the time of day, everyone seemed watchful for signs and whilst they wanted news and reassurance, they were loath to wait where it might be found. Her customers were quick to buy and quick to leave.

Ethel was tearful and seemed very much on the edge of collapse herself when she arrived. In the hut next to theirs was a family called the Fassams and the smallpox had struck down the whole family, including all four of the children, the same children that Georgie and Laura played with sometimes. That morning, young Harriet Fassam, aged 2, had died.

Emily sent Ethel back to her family after calming her down, but the fear itself was sticky and it clung to Emily's thoughts. She hurried home and rejoiced to find George out of his fever and although very weak, he did feel well enough to sit in an armchair at the kitchen door and enjoy the warmth of the sun. The smallpox gave a focus to their thoughts and their hearts, which made it easy to talk. Neither of them was one to hide from hazards when others were in need. They talked about inviting Ethel and the children to stay at the farm, but could not be sure of the risk they would be taking. Emily said that she would find out.

Later the same evening, just after George had gone back to bed, James came back late from work to tell Emily that he had heard that his friend Ann Hargreaves had the smallpox. She was to be moved the next day into a new isolation hospital that the Midland Company had hastily established to stem the outbreak and protect their workforce. He explained that a dozen carpenters had been pulled off their normal work, two large huts had been emptied and whitewashed and were now being refurbished. They would then be connected by a covered way. An oven was being set up alongside the huts to bake the clothes of the infected patients; a male nurse and two superintendents had arrived to supervise the work and to settle in the first patients, some of whom were in a desperate condition. The huts that they had lived in were all being limewashed. Poor Ann had recently taken sewing back to various clients, including a shawl to Mrs Fassam, where she had taken tea and read to the children: she now shared their fate. James, who had not visited Ann since the escape with Nancy, simply stated that he intended to visit the hospital and that if they were worried that this might spread the infection to the farm, then he would stay at Batty Green for a while.

Emily's heart went out to him in his serious, gentle vulnerability, always wanting to please and worried about giving offence. Yet, she could not give him a clear answer.

'Do what you think is right, Mr Taylor,' was all she could say. 'A'm not so sure that they'll let you near any patients, but go and find out an' come an' tell us what's goin' on.'

She paused and looked at him. He had changed so much in the last few months. He had filled out a little. The sun and the wind had coarsened his skin, giving him a more rugged look, but there were still shades of the nervous, solitary young man glimpsed from time to time in a shrug, a fractional disengagement, a flicker of a smile that came to nothing, as if he did not trust it. Today, he looked burdened and anxious. She stepped close to him and wrapped her arms around him, hugged him and then gently pulled herself away.

'Tek care, James. We're all fond o' tha, my lad.' He smiled and turned away. 'An' mek sure this time that tha tells Hetty what tha're up to,' she called after him.

The next day was cool and damp. James took some time off after lunch and made his way through the network of lanes and tracks that gouged ever-dirtier channels across the landscape over the whole basin at Batty Green. On slightly rising ground, the new hospital stood out starkly in its coat of new white paint, the huts almost at right angles to each other; one was quiet and curtained, the other was the site of fervid activity by carpenters and painters, working in unusual silence. Metal bed frames were lined up on the grass as if waiting for orders, whilst sacks of bedding and other supplies stood shapeless and forlorn nearby. A group of men was building the covered walkway, others were putting together a large oven beneath a canopy, and he could see a group that was clearing the perimeters and putting up a fence.

James read the signs on the door of the porch to the quiet hut, pulled the bell handle and waited. A middle-aged man in a black suit and waistcoat, but with neither hat nor tie, came to the door. He looked hot and flustered. As the door swung open, James could make out the crying of a child and the murmuring of adult voices and he was suddenly conscious of smells; smells of paint and something sulphurous and again a sweet, sickly aroma that he did not like. He was unprepared for this and almost stepped back. The man's voice broke through to him.

'I'm Charles Halifax, the superintendent here. What can I do for you?'

James almost stuttered. 'James Taylor at your service. I am acquainted with a lady called Ann Hargreaves. I was told that she was here. Can I speak to her?'

'Out of the question, young man, unless you happen to have been vaccinated, but I find that few in these parts have ever heard of it, let alone taken heed of it.' Mr Halifax was brisk in his speech, but not unkindly in his smile as he stood buttoning a cuff and watching James.

'How is she?' James asked.

'She is in the early stages. She has the fever and a light rash has begun to appear today. She is in some pain, but is brave and undemanding. It will get worse in the next few days and we must all pray for her. We are doing all we can to preserve life, but this is not a forgiving disease once it takes hold. Mrs Fassam died this morning and the other children are all infected. Things are likely to get worse before they get better.' He waited for James to reply, the air of urgency subsiding as he gazed around and savoured the damp summer air.

'Will you tell her that Mr Taylor called and sent his best wishes?'

'Of course.'

'Is there owt I can do?' James appealed, almost pleaded.

'Look in on the mother. She was very distressed. Make sure that the young lady's things have been thoroughly washed or burned. Make sure the hut is scrubbed and repainted. Watch the mother for symptoms.'

The two men looked at each other. Mr Halifax noted the drawn look on the younger man's face, the shallow breathing and beads of sweat on his brow. 'Takes courage to come here. Thank you, Mr Taylor.'

James nodded an acknowledgement and gave his word to help Mrs Hargreaves. After work, he went straight there. When he got there he found her to be ashen and fragile, but determined to think the best. There was little for him to do. He was introduced to a tall woman in her sixties, who was brisk and cheerful and who had already sorted and cleaned Ann's possessions. She had also scrubbed the hut and was waiting now for the painter to come with the limewash. She had volunteered to help with the smallpox victims and she explained to James that she had lived through a smallpox outbreak before.

'Where was that?' he found himself asking.

'Oh, in America,' came the reply, with a salty, transatlantic drawl.

She introduced herself as Bella Roberts and a few questions from her quickly established who he was and where he lived. 'I'm a friend of Emily's,' Bella told him. 'Give her my best wishes when you go back to Elterbeck.' He promised to do just that and set off for the farm, relieved to be so easily dismissed. Yet, being still in a state of heightened anxiety, he had forgotten a more immediate promise that should have kept him at Batty Green.

The strata of his emotional life were like layers of fine sediment, easy to read in quiet times, but times of turmoil threw him into cloudy confusion. To his utter consternation, recent events had left him thoroughly and nervously unsettled, so much so that he was beginning to believe that he would never experience the certainty of a love invincible to change.

He had newly reconciled himself to the sweet vulnerability of Hetty, when the illness of Ann had suddenly turned his head towards the thought of her needs and how his patient, selfless devotion could serve her. This extreme of adversity made her more attractive to him and he was puzzled by it. And then, that very morning, a brief, unsigned note had finally been delivered, which he knew to be from Nancy, and the very shape of the handwriting had suffused his entire being with battalions of blood. The note had given away little, except that she was "doing well" and that Grace was "completing her education". James was intrigued by the studied ambiguities. Nancy had revealed that she would wait, each Sunday for the next six weeks, at the Queen's Gate entrance to Hyde Park at three o'clock.

James knew that this was his chance; that he was bidden to join her; but he also knew that most probably he would have to take that chance along with others, who would also be paying homage. He felt the burning pull of her sensual being, memories crowding his consciousness and setting his pulse simmering and his taste buds yearning for the salty reality of her, and all other thoughts were briefly eclipsed. Yet, the colder part of him said that he had little to offer Nancy in the way of prospects or establishment and he would most likely remain a pleasant and loyal plaything. He found his timidity dispiriting and so lost in these thoughts was he that he forgot that he had promised to call on Robert Macintosh that evening.

The Winding Gear
May 1871

It has to be said that Robert's disappointment at James' failure to meet him on this particular day was brief and not profoundly felt. Robert had a suspicion that James would not have relished what he had planned and Robert felt an easing, a release, in the prospect of working alone.

It was early evening. A moist morning had declined into a dull and murky drizzle in the afternoon. Brief openings had brought hot sun to set the steam rising from the cobbles and flagstones, but the becks were filling and the dark would come early and cling.

Robert strode powerfully up the tramway line, looking neither left nor right, his coat tightly buttoned and a soft cap pulled low over his brow. He was heading for Blea Moor. Some shifts would change later, others would end, and he wanted to be in place well before then and out of sight. He had fashioned a deep pocket in the lining of his coat and hidden there was a heavy bludgeon of weathered oak, a knife and a few short coils of rope: they swung heavily against his thigh. They were not his only chosen tools. He had reconnoitred the ground on a moonlit evening two days ago and in a narrow defile running down off Blea Moor, he had hidden a lantern and a ragged collection of clothes, topped by an old felt hat: the whole assemblage, seen from a distance in the twilight, would pass for a man sitting. Halfway down the defile, there were a couple of stunted hawthorns that the rough peaty path looped around. Now, he went back there, lit the lamp, arranged the dummy figure and stretched taut one of his coils of thin rope, ankle high, between the trees. In the damp and gathering gloom, it would be nearly invisible. He made sure that he knew exactly where the trip rope was.

His target was Tar Brush. The physical damage inflicted by the beating was now almost healed, but if he twisted sharply to the side he still sometimes felt one rib jar against another and that pulse of pain kept his memory sharp. Time had certainly not healed the wound to his pride and self-respect. It still glowed and smouldered, dark red. He had promoted Tar Brush to ganger, trusted him and paid him well. But the man had always been merely mechanically compliant, whilst at the same time managing to convey an underlying insolence, through tone and gesture, especially to the older men. The arrival of Marty had made matters worse, even before the accident. With Marty as audience, Tar Brush had lifted his quiet disrespect a further notch and had taken even less care to hide it. The memories still chafed. Tar Brush had leached away Robert's self-esteem and he now planned a cold revenge and would have it now, before either he or Tar Brush left Ribblehead.

Blea Moor Tunnel was being built on a curve and on an incline that would lead to and from a summit level of 1,151 feet. It would slide through the darkly impacted rock over 300 feet below the ground and would stretch for over a mile and a half. Work was well under way at each end but, in addition, there were three permanent shafts and four temporary shafts, each one dug down 300 feet from the top of the moor to the foundation level, so that sixteen face gangs could work at once.

At each of these headings, teams of miners, masons, bricklayers and labourers worked round the clock, hacking, blasting, clearing, shoring and lining out the tunnel with arches in brick or stone; all by candlelight, in fetid air, with water seeping into their joints and a misty powder of tobacco smoke, dynamite and rock dust sinking into their lungs. Pumps ran noisily, removing hundreds of gallons of water every hour; steam engines lifted tons of rock and waste and lowered tons of bricks and mortar; men and materials were in constant movement, creating noise to and from each face and up and down each shaft in skeps or large buckets. It was crawling with life, with nearly 200 men at work at once, and room for far more; yet, the darkness of the silent earth and the slow erosion of peaty water was never far from them. They made just a brief intrusion.

They were now using thousands of bricks every day, so that Robert had made full use of his supervisory role to make visits, and he knew that Tar Brush was currently leading a small team that was finishing the number one shaft, pointing it out and building the housing at the top.

Since the first few face teams had broken through underground, this shaft was no longer in regular use for heavy materials during the day and neither was it in use at all at night. Robert had seen his chance and moved quickly.

He guessed that when they were brought up at the end of their shift, Tar Brush and his small team would fasten up the winches, release the pressure on the 12-inch winding engine and set it to idle to a halt. Robert was relying on Tar Brush himself seeing to the engine. He was the ganger here, but he was also well known for having a fascination with all kinds of machinery and could not leave them alone. Other men would soon be passing, as shifts ended along the tunnel length: Robert knew he would have to act promptly and convincingly to get Tar Brush away on his own.

He crouched down in a hollow just behind a spoil heap nearest to the shaft, where debris from below ground had been haphazardly thrown. In the dark that was spreading around him he could see little and could hear nothing from the shaft, except the shuffling clatter and the chesty breathing of the little engine, like a small dragon tethered to the spot in it's shed. An old man was on duty and when he suddenly pulled himself upright and groaned as he moved forwards to manage the winch, Robert knew that they were coming up. He crouched on one knee and craned forwards for a better look. It was difficult to make out, as things happened quickly, and very few words were wasted as the heads and shoulders of the navvies appeared, urging the old man to look lively in their haste to get home. The bucket cage being secured, Robert noted that only three men climbed out, but one was unmistakably Tar Brush: perhaps the other workers had gone more directly home along the tunnel bottom. Some words of farewell were grunted and two of the men, and then the old man, turned away quickly, moving downhill towards the tunnel huts, complaining of the rain and the muddy track as they went. It was as Robert had hoped: Tar Brush was closing things down.

Robert took a deep breath and swung round the back of the spoil heap, hurrying forwards, snorting heavily, pretending to be out of breath from hurrying. He called ahead.

'Is that you, Tar Brush?'

The man swung round at the voice and stared fixedly through the dusk and haze at the shapes around him.

'Macintosh? Is that you?' he shouted suspiciously. His fists bunched instinctively and he stood tall, balanced, leaning forwards slightly, ready to defend himself. He had been half expecting a meeting like this. His eyes quickly scanned the ground, looking for a weapon.

'Aye, it's me,' called Robert, still moving forwards and still heaving breath into his lungs dramatically. He now added a note of irritation. 'A've come on an errand o' mercy kind o 'thing, though seein' as it's you, a'd rather see thee sittin' bare-arsed on hot coals, drinkin' piss wi' devil.'

'What dost mean wi' talk o' mercy errands?' Tar Brush shouted across. 'An' come no closer, dost tha hear, a don't trust thee.' The two men could just about see each other now with the aid of a lantern at the shaft head – a bubble of light in a miasma of mist.

'Fine by me,' Robert called, pulling up noisily a few yards from the shaft and pretending to be struggling to get his breath back. Bent double as if winded, he was enjoying a moment's excitement. He felt a rush of anticipation sweep through him. It was on! He knew it would not be easy to take Tar Brush, but the battle was on and he would see it through and be damned if he wouldn't win. He needed to clear this out of the way. It was like lancing a boil; it would hurt for a while, but not for long. Yet, he did not underestimate his foe. He knew he had to be crafty and keep the element of surprise. He pulled himself up and launched into his pitch.

'A met thy nephew Marty. Lad's in a reet state. He's getten some news from home for thee. He wouldn't say what, but a recken thir's a death in it somewir or summat serious. He began to blubber a bit an' wanted you urgent. He's bin on t'road wi'out food or water's far as a can mek out, so a'd to help 'im, a owed 'im that much. A've gi'en 'im a sup or two o' brandy and some bread and cold beef, but he's still shaky. He didn't want to be seen by t'other men, so a've brung 'im up so far and then left 'im down yonder wi' a lantern. A'll show thee where and then a'm out o' 'ere. You can go 'ang for all a care, but the lad's in a bad way an' 'e seems to need you: no other bugger does, but thir tha goes.' The bait was laid.

Tar Brush seemed to hunch and consider. When he spoke, there was conflict in his voice and in his manner. He sensed a trap, but the news of Marty, who had disappeared weeks ago, was as powerful with him – as Robert had hoped.

'Show me where 'e is.' There was a fine layer of pleading wrapped in the demand, 'but keep your distance, ten paces at least.'

Robert smiled. He's hooked, he thought to himself. Now to reel him in. So saying, he turned on his heel and set off, cutting north, away from the main path and down the hill towards the headwaters of his old foe, Little Beck.

It was dark now, the moon occasionally sailing out from behind heavy clouds and then being smothered again, and rain was always threatening, moistening the edge of a cold wind and then spattering against their faces. He paused after a while and shouted over his shoulder. 'Come on, man, a've not got all night for your bloody business.'

Without lanterns, progress was difficult and instinctively the two men drew closer as darkness invaded the landscape, near and far. The dark slash of the defile could just be made out ahead, cutting sharply down the slope to the meagre tree line, and Robert could distinguish the dim glow of the lantern and what looked like a hunched figure sat on the ground beside it. He was pleased with his handiwork. He stopped, stood aside from the path and pointed downwards. 'He's there an' this is far enough for me.'

Tar Brush squinted malevolently and waved Robert aside. 'Back off, Macintosh, a don't trust thee an inch.'

'Thir's gratitude,' sneered Robert, stepping back a yard or two. 'A could be at 'ome by fire, but a'm up here in pissin' rain an' all you can do is show your usual spite an' ill temper.'

'Call 'im,' Tar Brush ordered, pointing to the figure he could just make out in the hollow below them.

'Call 'im thi sen,' Robert spat back at him. ''E's yor bleedin' nephew. A'm out o' here.'

He wanted Tar Brush to go ahead, hastening down the dark path to trip and fall heavily, so that he could overpower him and teach him a lesson, but he had not anticipated so much hostility and suspicion. 'Not so fast,' Tar Brush shouted.

Tar Brush moved quickly towards him, until he was just a few paces away, and Robert now saw that the man carried a short iron bar, no doubt picked up at the mouth of the shaft. Robert's mouth went dry and he cowered a little. He did not want this, a clumsy struggle here amongst the wiry clumps of heather and peaty sheep runs, where one slip and a fall would lend an easy advantage to an armed opponent. Moreover, his own coat was still buttoned and he noted, with some alarm, how agile and rangy Tar Brush could be when necessary. He felt constrained and short-winded by comparison. He had to play for time. He shouted, wanting to make Tar Brush stay back for now.

'Tek it easy. Th'art a merciless animal at times, always wantin' to be top dog. More balls than brains. Just think! It's Marty as should be your concern, not me. Thir's not much sign o' life down thir.' He gestured over his shoulder. He had to shift Tar Brush's attention and so took the risk of turning his back and pretending to call down the hillside. 'Marty, a'm back and a've got thy uncle wi' me. Are you alright, lad?'

It worked. He glanced over and saw Tar Brush peering into the basin of dark trees and black sedge, eyes riveted on the weak glow of the lantern, craning forwards and cupping his right ear. Then, Robert remembered that the man was deaf on one side from a mining accident.

'A can hear nowt,' the ganger mumbled.

'Well a can,' Robert almost jeered. 'A think 'e's blubberin' and whimperin' as if 'e's in pain. Can't tha hear that! The lad's not reet tha knows and neither are you.'

'You go ahead,' snarled Tar Brush, raising the iron bar threateningly.

Robert cursed him and stood still as if to defy him. Then he raised a hand and sighed, as if in submission, and set off. He had to go with it and avoid the fight here. Going first could still work if he was careful: provided he could get over the trip rope safely, then he would be well placed to pounce, but he had to get well ahead.

In near total darkness, he threw himself as fast as he dared down the path, every faculty, nerve and muscle focused on placing his feet and keeping his balance, not daring to look up or back, sensing the trees approaching as black shapes within the darkness. The path flattened and widened briefly and he skipped from side to side and then suddenly found himself almost running into the first tree, his chest heaving and eyes goggling into the dark. He listened and knew that he had made some distance ahead of Tar Brush, who was blundering down behind him and cursing. Robert now felt his way forwards, bent double, hands outstretched, and found the rope. He stepped over it gingerly and then crunched down the steepest part of the path and snatched up the lantern. He waved it excitedly and shouted upwards.

'Hurry, man, a think the lad's nearly gone.'

He put the lamp down and, keeping low, scurried back part way up the slope, undid his coat and prepared for the last part of this drama. He heard the old ganger muttering and crashing forwards; saw a shape loom up that fumbled and then clutched at the tree; then the figure swung round sharply down the slope; then there was a stifled yell, a scuffle of stones and the sound of the wind being knocked out of a heavy object as it hit the ground heavily. Then silence. Robert waited.

The silence began to stretch. It extended and thickened, until Robert could touch it. Was he now in a trap set by Tar Brush?

He took out the oak bludgeon and on hands and knees, with his coat dragging in the dirt and the stones cutting his knees, he crawled slowly upwards. He found Tar Brush lying quite lifeless, thrown onto his back, his head downhill and blood seeping stickily into the dark. His breathing was shallow and erratic. He had obviously struck one of the rocks on the side of the slope in his fall. Robert felt round the head, his fingers sinking into a bloody gash where his ear should be: the ear seemed to be hanging off. Robert cursed bitterly.

'This is not what a wanted,' he said simply.

A further clumsy examination brought a weak groan from Tar Brush and confirmed that he was, in fact, alive. Robert could feel no obviously broken bones, so he dragged the man round and into a partially upright position. Then he scurried down for the lantern, came back up to untie the trip rope and used it to tie Tar Brush's hands together in front of him. He then squatted down and held the lantern close to the head of the ganger to look at the wounds.

Robert felt little concern for the suffering of the hulk in front of him, but jolted back swiftly when the eyes suddenly opened and the older man stared oddly at him. A moment's observation confirmed that there was no recognition in the stare and the eyes began to close again, slowly, as if a wick was being turned down by imperceptible degrees. Robert sat back, across the path, put the lantern between them and felt defeated.

'Can tha hear me? Tha's an evil, uncircumcised piece of shit, cheatin' me o' revenge. Thir's no pleasure in this. A wanted to see thee squirm and feel the pain each time a hit thee. But it seems as how tha's escaped again. A rue the day a iver set eyes on thee. An' look at this mess! Tha's just a bleedin' nuisance, a lump o' sick flesh that's hardly worth the savin'. Shall a leave thee here to rot?' He left the question hanging in the air between him and the inanimate Tar Brush and pondered for a few minutes, silent in the invasive dark.

But, somehow, the hatred had cooled as soon as the contest had ended. He had to admit that the rage and shame of a few weeks ago had also faded, like the bruises themselves. Now, he just wanted to be clear of the whole business and he knew that he would be forced to get Tar Brush to somewhere safer. He pulled off the ganger's greasy neckerchief and used it to bind his head and ear as tightly as he dared.

The bleeding began to seep through again, but he guessed it would soon stop. He pulled Tar Brush to his feet and held his loose limbs in an embrace that was too close for comfort. Then he worked one arm free and shouted at Tar Brush, slapping his face.

'Come on, man, you stink and a canna cope wi' this much contact, tha's got to 'elp. Tek tha weight an' get movin', ox-head, or we'll both be 'ere all bloody night.'

Tar Brush stirred clumsily and Robert realised that he would have to untie the hands to have any chance of dragging or pulling him along and he would have to leave the lantern behind. He swore with vehemence. So, with a combination of encouragement, abuse and rough handling, Robert half dragged, half carried the stumbling figure back up the steep path and then laboriously began to cross the open moor towards the spoil heaps and the shaft opening. Rain came in cold spasms on a fresh wind from the north, bringing shivers to Tar Brush and cooling the sweat on Robert's face and arms, whilst it ran in rivulets down his back as he struggled onwards. The path was narrow in places, winding between tough heathers, so that Robert had to turn and stagger backwards, arms round Tar Brush's chest as the ganger lolled back groggily, his head rolling, feet trailing and snagging from time to time. Robert grunted a stream of abuse.

'Tha stinks worse than rotten horse flesh; even the sheep would run scared from such as thee. A can't even leave thee for rats; they have some standards tha knows.'

What would he do with Tar Brush? He almost laughed when he realised that he had no real plan. Leave him overnight for the early shift to find? In this rain and cold? He might not survive and if he died, would Robert escape a murder hunt? Raise the alarm himself or contrive for others to search? But how to keep himself out of it? Nothing seemed foolproof, but something had to be done.

Weak from his efforts and beset by uncertainties, he finally dragged the older man to the shaft head and propped him against the half-finished wall, covering him as best he could. Then, he wearily retraced his steps, collected the lamp, rope and bundle of clothes and trudged back, exhausted. Tar Brush was breathing in shallow gasps, but was clammy and cold to the touch. Robert hung the lamp and looked around. The boiler house was filthy and crowded. He could fashion a shelter of sorts, but the cold and damp would still seek him out. He looked at the ganger again: he seemed to be shrinking, the black beard making a ghoulish contrast against the waxen skin.

'Blast and blast and blast you.' He was tired of the whole damn business and was thoroughly miserable.

Then, the wind dropping momentarily, Robert realised that he could smell smoke and hear oddly echoing, distant voices and the rumble of machines. The shaft! Of course! A hundred yards below him gangs of men were working, horses were pulling wagons, fires and candles were smouldering. Help wasn't over a mile away; it was a two minute ride in a bucket! He sprang to work revitalised. It would take time to stoke the little steam engine and build the pressure up again, but he did not need that, for he knew the winch could be operated manually. Could he hold it steady enough on his own to lower Tar Brush safely down the shaft? He thought he probably could, having managed loads of bricks in the past on many a site.

He double-checked that the bucket was securely chained at the rim of the shaft and went back to Tar Brush. Again, he had to drag and wrestle the dead weight and then slide him into the bucket, feet first, cradling his head to rest it gently against the metal side. He did not dare to get in himself, not trusting the brake, but seeing one leg become clumsily curled under the torso, he had to lie on his stomach and lean over to try to free the limb, manhandling Tar Brush like some fiendish marionette that had to be refolded. Tar Brush began to moan and stir as Robert tugged at the leg.

'For the love of God don't wake now, dung head.'

But Tar Brush was coming round and in the gloom, with half his body hanging over the edge of the shaft, Robert was unaware of the man attempting to focus his eyes on Robert and slowly turn his head.

The first that Robert knew was when a cold, scaly hand suddenly grabbed his shoulder. Robert yelled an oath in horror and almost slid into the bucket in fear and shock, his heart thundering in his ears.

'What's happening?' Tar Brush slurred. Robert tried to struggle upright, but he was pinned and the grip was steely.

Robert had to shout into the bucket, blood rushing to his head. 'Tha had a bang on t'head, an accident like, lost thy footin' on t'path. A'm just going to winch thee down to the main trackway. Plenty o' folk thir t'elp thee. Just shout for 'elp when tha touches bottom.'

The grip relaxed and Robert was able to pull himself up to sit on the edge of the shaft and gain control of his breathing again. He looked at his old foe, slumped but still fighting.

'An' no mention o' ma name, Tar Brush, or a'll see to it that tha never walks again. A think that we're abowt even na. What dost say?'

The eyes narrowed and a familiar look of appraisal and scrutiny swept over the ganger's face. It was the silent calculation that Robert had seen so many times before. Then the eyes narrowed as he began to think it through.

'And what about Marty?' So he did remember! It was a struggle for Tar Brush to speak, but cunning and determination marked him for their own.

'Not 'ere; seen no sight o' 'im. That wor just a story to get you out on your own.' Tar Brush nodded slowly as if he approved of the plan.

'Now, shift thi sen over t'middle o' bucket if you can an' stay still.'

Tar Brush stirred clumsily and a bolt of pain drove through his skull. He put a hand instinctively to the side of his head and felt the mess of kerchief and flesh there. 'Did you carry me up t'shaft?' he asked.

'Aye. Wa'nt too keen on you dying out thir,' Robert replied truthfully, with a grim laugh.

The bucket lurched sideways as Tar Brush shifted again and then shot his hand out towards Robert.

'Then a reckon you're right: we're about even.' Robert froze for a few seconds, then took the hand and shook it, feeling a surge of emotion that surprised him.

'Now, sit still you old bugger an' keep her steady.' He stood up and found a lantern for Tar Brush. Then he placed himself square, balanced himself at the winch handle, released the chain and brake and with back and shoulders solidly braced, he began to turn the ganger down through all the layers of Blea Moor.

Bella's Story
Summer 1871

That summer would never be forgotten by George and Emily or any of the adults living in and around Batty Green at the time. Smallpox continued its sporadic and frightening incursions into the consciousness of all and it wrought its excruciating havoc in particular cases. By the end of May, the Fassam family had lost its mother and all four children, the eldest only 6 years old.

Ethel was drawn, throughout this time, to walk near the hospital, hoping for a glimpse of one of the family or news of a reprieve. Her vigils achieved nothing, except that she could frame her thoughts around their suffering. She said that she could sometimes hear the children crying helplessly as if all possible comfort had fled. Despite her anxieties for her own children, she could not be brought to leave for the farm and so lived in restless fear.

After a brief lull that raised some hopes, the outbreaks began again in June, leading to a number of deaths in apparently isolated centres, and six more patients left the hospital for the graveyard at Chapel le Dale, now filling rapidly. Some thirty new graves had been dug; grim reminders that death was a regular acquaintance to those who journeyed to and from Batty Green. Moreover, these deaths became a source of morbid dread and tales of the sinister lesions peeling off in hardened sheets of "black pox" were whispered abroad, out of the hearing of children. Survivors were often cruelly scarred or blind, or both.

Ann Hargreaves survived, but with considerable afflictions, and her mother took her away as soon as they could travel to live a more secluded life with a distant cousin. James continued to attend to their needs whenever he could and he admired the dignity of their forbearance, but was never alone with Ann, who kept to a darkened cot.

Bella Roberts nursed and supported with calm efficiency and kindness and she refused to take any payment. That summer she gained the confidence and respect of many and her name often reached the ears of Emily, but the two women did not meet again until early in July, when Bella came to the shop one day. They spoke briefly on practical matters and without awkwardness; the presence of other customers preventing any unease. Emily refused to take payment from Bella, thanking her for the support to the Hargreaves women. Bella looked at her searchingly. 'I would still like us to talk,' she said, with simplicity and some resignation, as if she was expecting rebuttal.

Emily was aware that age was affecting and changing Bella, and herself also. As she returned Bella's gaze, she felt something relax inside her, where some pride or possessiveness had kept her defiantly puffed up. It was as if air held in constriction had been suddenly released and she knew at once that her resentment had spent itself, and that she did now want to speak to this woman, who seemed to need her help and had proved herself a stalwart in helping others. To refuse would be petty and uncharitable. She agreed to call the next day in the afternoon.

It was a visit that was to remain sharp in her memory for the rest of her life. Emily had few women friends, her closest confidant was probably Hetty, and things were kept back there, on both sides. Her own mother had been a dull, well-meaning woman, but one who lacked drive or conviction and the ability to articulate her thoughts. Moreover, she seemed to be in awe of her own daughter; the daughter, therefore, turned elsewhere for guidance and direction. She had a friend Mary from those days, now living in Kingsdale, but had seen her only a few times since the navvy camps had been set up. For a while, Ethel had been a blessing and a comfort, but was now too ridden with her own anxieties over the future of her three children. So Emily sat now with Bella, the dog Bane again stretched out on the hearthrug, even though there was no fire in the stove, and they drank tea laced with brandy and they once again talked easily. To begin with, it was all Bella, in her husky, smoky voice and her strangely blended accent.

'I'm a-going to tell you something of my life story, so that you can maybe see why I've a feelin' for being reunited wi' my son. It's a fair long story and some o' it mighty strange, but I'll try to be brief and clear, though some o' these things are never really clear to those involved, if you know what a mean.

'I married Harold when I'd just turned 17 year old. I think Harold must ha' thought he had gotten himself a docile little wife to warm his bed and wash his pots. Me, I wor just glad to get out o' ma home and get some proper food and a decent bed, and a roof that didn't leak.

That first year I was mostly quite happy. I had George when I wor eighteen and the trouble started then, or just a mite before that time maybe, and I left the farm when I wor twenty-four. I'm not proud o' leavin' and what I did and the way I behaved, but I wor beaten down, boxed in and confused, and too young to see any ways round it.

'You see, Harold and I ran the farm on our own, there was no hired help, 'cept an old shepherd, who was closer to his sheep than any human being and seemed to have lost the power o' speech. So Elterbeck wor no paradise for a young lass with a bit o' spirit: it wor hard and lonely work and as soon as I began to question and challenge, then Harold showed himself a sour and mean partner, who had to have things his way or not at all. I frightened him. He was old before his time, hard on his knees o' Sunday and hard on his wife the rest o' the week. Butter wouldn't melt in 'is mouth in public, but in private he'd treat me like an animal sometimes. He had no understanding of women or children and more than once, when the bairn was crying, he lost his temper and wouldn't have either of us in the house; we had to sleep in the barn with the animals. Yet, when I asked to go to Ingleton or to take George to see the travelling fair, he would kick up a fuss and refuse to gi' me any money. So I started to steal from him and somehow it made me feel better. I learned to get ma own back, you might say.

'I did my best for George and loved him dear, but I had a temper, too, and when I wor really riled, I used to hit back at the old man: hit him with a pan once, when ma blood wor up, knocked him out cold. I think it wor the biggest shock o' his entire life. He wor gett'n ready to beat me for that, next night, when I stood up to him again. Harold went wild. George started to cry, so he grabbed a plate off table and threw it at the child. It bounced off table and smashed and a piece cut his brow, it did; I shall never forget the blood running down his little face: he didn't know what it was.

'It wor hell after that for a while, a kind o' war, and I began to see that either I let him bully me and George or I stood up to him and he might try and get 'is own back on the littl'un, or in the end we would have to leave. None o' it seemed right and I think a wor in danger o' going mad at that time, almost imprisoned in that farmhouse. Some weeks went by and I never saw another soul. I blamed meself for mishandling Harold and I did find meself thinkin' o' ways to kill meself or kill him.

'I could see no way out, but in calmer moments I came to believe that Harold wouldn't really hurt George if I wasn't there to provoke him. I wor the problem, not the child. Harold wor mean and hopeless, but not a monster. It wor me he couldn't handle. If I'd been one o' his cows he would ha' managed, brutality would ha' won. So I talked to the vicar's wife, when she came one time, and I wor near desperate, so I asked her, straight out, what would happen to George if I left or died. She said that she would make sure that George was properly looked after. I made her promise, on a Bible: a think a half scared the woman to death.

'About that time, ma father died and I went to t'funeral and then stopped wi' mother a day or two. Met a soldier there, an army sergeant. What can I say? He wor kind and funny and he made me feel alive and special. It were like coming out from under a thunderstorm into clear, free light. We came to an understanding and a month later, I got a letter from him, through mother, and that night I left Elterbeck, taking as much of Harold's money as I could find. I called at the vicarage on the way, bold as you like, and told the vicar that his wife had made a promise about George and would he kindly remind her.

'Sounds heartless, I know, Emily, but I had kind o' convinced maself that the only way to help ma little boy was to leave Harold, leave Elterbeck for good. I had met ma soldier, 'cept he wasn't a soldier any more, and we bought passage on a ship straightaway and sailed to New York. Then, two days out from England, I allowed meself to think about George and I started to cry and I think I cried for the rest of the crossing, but there wor no way I could go back. A've thought o' George every day o' my life since.

'I can't begin to tell you about ma life for the next fifteen years wi' ma soldier, cos a always called him that, though truly he wor Thomas Roberts. We lived as man and wife round New York and then moved, bit by bit, right up to the St Lawrence and got work where we could: well, mostly it wor me that wor working and him that got us into trouble or debt, mostly through gambling. But I loved him dearly, he wor full o' fun and we had a little boy. I called him George, but he died before he wor 1 year old. Then, in forty-eight, by chance we had a few dollars after some good runs with the cards and just as we wor about to move on, we heard about the gold found in California. Next thing a knows, Thomas has spent the money on train tickets to St Joseph, Missouri, which a'd never heard of, and before too long we're there and gettin' equipped wi' a wagon, two oxen, two mules and a mass of pots and pans. And the love o' my life says, "Cheer up, princess, only 2,000 miles to go."'

Bella talked on and told a good story. Emily listened, carried away with tales she only half understood of wagon trains, salt licks, bison, Red Indians, Rocky Mountains, unexpected deserts and the dreaded Humboldt River. It was here that Thomas died and Bella learned hard lessons in survival. She laughed about it grimly.

'I think, when I pass on from here, I would be foolish to expect much mercy from them as keep t'heavenly gates, St Peter and his self-righteous lot. If I go straight to t'other place, I expect it will look like a 300 mile trail beside the Humboldt River and I'll be forced to follow it again to what I know is at the end.

'At first, you know, damn river ripples and flows like the Ribble and trees and shrubs protect you from the blazing heat. But slow and sure, and you don't notice where it starts, it turns a bit fuzzy, tints of yella and ochre begin to filter through the water, and at first you think it's kind o' quaint and mysterious. Then, the grass starts to turn to cat's claw, mesquite replaces trees and the cattle drink the water and get sick and slowly die. And the humans boil it, get sick and mostly live and can't go back, cos the nightmare leads you on, but it's a burning nightmare, gaudy and unreal. Ya follow the river and you don't trust it an' the water now begins to go a milky green, foamy and thick, and there's no shade.

And the sun dries the sap in your flesh and chars your bones, until you can't believe it, an' the river just breaks up into a filthy swamp, right in front o' your eyes. And then it sinks and bubbles away and you're left looking at scum, nothing but scum. Ahead, is bone-bright desert, four or five days trek, and no water for man nor beast.

'Death and sickness creep alongside you, kind o' becomes familiar, like one o' the party, and folks and animals die. Bodies o' loved ones are just left where they fall, no time for ceremony, no hope tears. We wor all close to the end and ma Thomas tries to keep our spirits up and he's a singin' a bit an' playin' his ole mouth organ and then one day, hot as hell and we have to stop, not a patch o' shade for 50 mile, he gets a little dice game going, back o' wagon, just for pennies. Next I know, he's got a knife stuck in his neck by another man, who says that Thomas was a-cheatin'. It's happened and a'm all weak with lack o' water and food. Wagons start to roll and there's Thomas, thrown on the hard sand, dead, meat for flies, and me just lookin' at him: I still wake at night thinkin' about it. I think a went a little crazy for a while and don't know how a got out o' there, a truly don't, Emily. All a know is that later that night I caught up wi' t'others and nothin' was said about Thomas. He wor just another death in the Humboldt Desert.'

There was a pause as Bella filled her pipe and Emily poured more brandy. Bella was just forty when she reached California. The land of dreams that had been the spur for thousands turned into a land of turmoil for many. Bella worked in saloons, making a living as best she could, until a violent act, only hinted at to Emily, saw her flee south, working the paddle steamers and bars, to end up in New Orleans. Here, at last, she found a role that shaped her future, when she took a sick companion to a dissolute and drunken French doctor and had to sober him up before he could do anything. She stayed to become his assistant, keeping him and others from death, whilst learning and changing herself.

'I worked for more than five years with that doctor, and then with other healers, and finally in the hospital in New Orleans. More and more I thought o' the ways in which us women are treated wrong and bear a deal o' the sufferin' in the world. So, whenever I could, I chose to work wi' women, in childbearing and in other problems. And then, one day, thinkin' of Elterbeck and my lad George, I realised I'd missed another goddam birthday, so I thought it wor time to come back and try to make amends if I could, cos my conscience was always a bit sore for leavin' him like that.'

But returning home after twenty years was never going to be a simple matter of walking in to take the empty chair waiting beside the hearth at Elterbeck. She knew that genuine penitence does not guarantee a warm welcome, even among so-called Christians. No word of her husband and son had ever reached Bella and she did not know how to proceed. She had some savings, so she found rooms in London for a while, but felt out of place, so moved north and settled herself in Lancashire for a while as she looked about her for news, for hope and for direction. She kept the name Bella Roberts, though never formally married, and after several years she finally bought a cottage near

Clitheroe: its main attraction being the long, narrow garden that led down to the river.

'I'd love to show you my cottage, Emily. I made it so homely. An' I was soon busy again, too, doing some healin' and helpin', so I needed fruit and flowers and herbs an' so I growed 'em. A had a few bitty hens and a couple o' dogs, strays mostly, 'cept for Bane, who was a gift from a travellin' man, when I helped his wife, who was a-dyin'. A lived within sight o' Pendle Hill and I know for sure that some o' the locals thought I was a bit o' a witch. But best of all was the riverbank and I went there most days and watched the water come smoothly by, wondering when rain fell at Ribblehead how long it was gonna tek comin' down the valley to me. A would dip ma fingers in it and fancy that perhaps George had done the same.' She paused ruefully and Emily could see that the years and the loneliness had taken their toll.

'I don't suppose I would ever have plucked up the courage to follow that riverbank right back up here. Anyway, I was well settled by then and comfortable, and who would ha' wanted me back? I knows country folk and they have long memories and little sympathy for women as leaves their children. But then a heard o' the railway and the camp. And I saw men on the march from Liverpool and Preston and from further south, coming right past ma door and stopping sometimes for a chat. So, when a friend offered to look after ma cottage for a year, I thought, why not, girl, it may be one o' the last journeys you make.

'So I set off to walk. A let ma hair grow a bit wild, a changed ma clothes and a kept up wi' this funny accent an' a came up here. Wi' thousands on the move, who was going to take any notice o' one old biddy? By then, I had heard o' ma husband's miserable end and ma son marryin', but a only saw you once, by chance, and a were wonderin' how a could take the next step, when you walk right on in here, kind o' edgy, but with some real grit, too. I admired you that day, but I could find no way to help you, though I wanted to. I thought at the time, how could I ever make amends to George, if the first thing I did was to encourage his young wife to look around for someone else to father her child? I have a different view now, by the way.

'So I kept myself to myself and I wor puzzled what to do, so I avoided you, the markets, the country around Elterbeck and any o' the farming families. Then the terrible news o' smallpox started and amongst the tittle-tattle a hear tell that the doctor's called to the farm, cos the farmer's taken down with it; fair riddled with it is the story, you know what folks are like. An' I just felt a terrible dread and so I walked straight there, a-grievin' and upset and desperate to see ma son. And damn it, if you don't turn me away! How did you know, all of a sudden, who I was? Who told you? Who else knows?' The question was put lightly, almost with relief. Perhaps she had wanted to be recognised after all.

Emily was sensitive to the mood; reassured by it. 'No one else knows,' she responded brightly. 'When a wor here last, a kept thinking that tha wor familiar in some way, that we must ha' met some time before, but a couldn't fashion any connection. Then, as a wor leavin', tha said summat and rubbed thy hand across brow and it wor just the same action and voice as George. It wor a shock, a can tell thee. So a think a just stared and then saw t'same nose and eyes and a kind o' guessed. But a never told a soul. A couldn't see any use in tellin' anyone.' She beamed, pleased beyond measure.

They talked of Emily's family and then of George and the farm. It was languorous and uncomplicated and when Bella rose stiffly to go and relieve herself, Emily sank back comfortably and once again was intrigued to know how Bella managed to put her so much at her ease. This was more like the mother she should have had.

When Bella returned, she drew her chair much closer to Emily's and reached over and took both of her hands into her own. 'Thank you for coming today, Emily, and for listening awhile to me. I hope we can be friends always. I sure would like that. You know what I want. I'm getting old and I would wish to be reconciled to ma son, somehow, and you can help me there, I know that you can. But a want to help you in return and I think I can, but only if we trust each other, really trust each other.'

She looked straight at Emily, holding her gaze, the pale blue eyes probing, sifting, as if reading a distant language through gauze.

'I remember very well what we talked of when you came here before. But I have this powerful feeling that there is something that you are not telling me, Emily. I thought so then and now I'm even more convinced. Am I right?'

Emily dropped her gaze and felt the floor shift and a doorway open, but the hands held her steady. Words would not come. At last, she lowered her head further and a tear came, unbidden, to trickle slowly down one cheek.

Her voice was damp and low. She spoke slowly. 'No babies come to George and me and a grieve for that. It makes me bitter and ... agitated, sometimes. I have evil thoughts and ideas and sometimes a'm right angry an' at other times a'm horrible. An' sometimes ma thoughts go to other men. A dream about an Irishman a once met. Such dreams as mek me blush.'

She sank lower into herself, her hands were hot, her voice almost a whisper. 'What is worse ... is that the longer it goes on, the less regard I have for ... ma husband ... thy son ... cos a know that ... I can have babies.'

Emily stopped, almost defiantly, and holding her breath she looked up at the older woman, her dark eyes lustrous with tears. Something passed between them. Emily felt it register and she saw Bella's eyes widen fractionally.

Bella released one hand and brought it gently to the side of Emily's face and stroked her cheek. Emily reached up and held the hand to her face. She saw the kindness and the sadness in Bella; she smelled the tobacco, brandy and herbs on her skin and it made her smile. But Bella was serious. 'You've had a child,' Bella stated.

Emily nodded but could not speak.

'How old were you?'

'Fifteen,' Emily croaked, tears now spilling from her eyes. Bella waited, her eyes almost closed, her whole being focused on the girl and trying to ease this buried grief.

'It wor a village lad an' we wor both daft and ... tha knows ... it happens. Ma father beat me and said he couldn't live with the shame, which wor quite a statement coming from him as hadn't done an honest day's work for two year. An' then he left us for good, so Mother blamed me for that an' all. She took me to her sister's in Horton. It wor a little boy and a called him Jack. But he only lived a few days. So, after a while, we came back to Selside. It's funny, a've not really thought about it for a long time, but now that I mention little Jack a can picture his little face, all pinched and shrivelled. A was supposed to love him, but I didn't, I just cried.' Sobs broke from her again and she fell forwards into Bella's arms and was comforted.

Sometime later, in the cool, early evening air, she found herself walking home beside the cart. She was in a daze: the horse knew the way and the road was quiet. She could not remember leaving. What she did recall was that no definite promises had been made or plans secured;

yet, despite this, she felt released and strengthened, if not a little drunk. In companionship, there was hope. In love and in the absence of censure, there was hope. In sharing stories and drawing horizons closer, there was hope.

She mused on these thoughts as she walked, feeling more optimistic than she had for some time. There was little traffic on the road, but her attention was caught at last by the sight of a pony and trap coming towards her at a steady trot, with what looked like two or three other horses tied at the back. The driver was sitting back with careless ease, the reins held loosely in one hand and a long whip held up in the other, as if it were a flag. He was a young man, neat, relaxed and comfortable with himself. He wore no hat, had an open shirt beneath his long black coat and had long dark hair, which was flowing backwards over his shoulders. She knew at once who it was, stopped her horse in the middle of the road and waited, with as much composure and gravity as she could muster. Yet, she wanted to laugh, in pleasured excitement.

Was she dreaming this? Had the rich brandy fumes pulled him from her past to taunt her and rouse her again? Yet, the clatter of hooves and restless shifting of her own horse seemed to tell her that it was real, as did the damp sweat down her side.

He stopped just 6 feet from her, stepped down and walked slowly towards her, the long whip still in his hand, a quizzical smile enlivening his weather-beaten face. His horse stamped and shook its harness. He clicked his tongue and the horse was still. She did not speak, still reluctant to confront reality or even put it to the test, lest he suddenly disappeared. However, he was less abashed. He bowed, giving a fanciful flourish with his free hand, a mocking tribute, but all done with an ingratiating look at her that made her feel as if a bright light was suddenly shining. She tried to stare at him coldly, but could not help herself from smiling at his strange charm and his cheek. He smiled back, the blue-grey of his eyes seeming to lick round her face. But she would not let him have it all his own way. She put on a severe expression and gave him the briefest of curtsies, half mocking him in return. 'Mr O'Reardon. Hast tha come back to rob us again and attack George a second time?' She blushed. 'That's ma husband, by the way.'

He shook his head and put on a mock solemnity, but the eyes still held her mischievously. 'Mrs Wright, the unkindness is not worthy of youse. I swear on my mother's grave and on the Bible of Holy Mother

Church that I was not after knowing that my brother had followed you. And when I found he was gone, I went there as fast as my poor legs could carry me. But then, as far as I could see, your husband was a-going to run the lad through with a very large metal implement, which might ha' been a bit inconvenient for all concerned. Now, I am not saying that Brendan didn't deserve that fate, but I had little will at the time to be attending yet more wakes, having just been to one, and I was all for avoiding any talk wi' the polis, so I did my best to put an end to unnecessary bloodshed. Was your man hurted?' He ended by tilting his face downwards seriously and frowning, as if greatly concerned.

She laughed again at what she thought must be his play-acting. 'Aye. But 'e got over it.' There was a pause as both looked questioningly at the other. She tried again to preserve a cool, level approach, looking as calmly as she could into his eyes, but still found she could not judge him harshly.

At last, she asked, 'Where are't tha going now then, Mr O'Reardon?'

It seemed so unreal. She was full of wonder that he was actually there, but beginning to feel already the pressure of time, wondering if he would be snatched away, as in a fairy tale or a dream, and the moment might evaporate.

'A bit o' business away at Hawes tomorrow,' he said. 'Just a few horses I'm in the way o' selling and some other things unfinished at Dent that are calling me back, as well as the thought o' seeing you, Mrs Wright. We might have become the best of friends, I'm thinking, if my brother had been more amenable to sense and direction.'

He stepped towards her and reached out now to stroke the nose of her horse. She watched with a kind of envy and fascination as his hands ruffled the horse's ears. She was bereft of words and her mouth was dry.

He seemed to realise that she was passive and that he must make a move and so he stepped up again, now running his hands down the flanks of the horse, which nuzzled him affectionately. She was lost. He stood before her and took her hand. His was warm and damp from the heat of the horse. 'Sad to say now, Mrs Wright, I can't be delaying on this road, a sore temptation though that is, as I have to reach Hawes before dark. No rest for the wicked, eh? But I shall be this way again before long and I shall make a special point of renewing our friendship then.'

He raised her hand to his lips and she stared as he kissed her knuckles. She saw how his boots were dirty and cracked and his coat threadbare. She wanted him, but she feared him.

'Tha must be on thy way then, Mr O'Reardon,' she croaked. 'A shall watch out for thee. But a'll mek sure that the silver plate is locked away, just in case.'

'That is the most unkind o' thoughts, Mrs Wright. It's a beautiful woman like yourself that I crave, not your family treasure, though I could probably give you a good price for that and all.' He laughed and turned away.

She smiled, but was no wiser about him. She pulled the horse and cart to one side and he swung briskly around her, blew her a kiss and flashed his broad smile, before moving away at a brisk trot.

She continued her walk home, once more deep in thought; thankful for the surprises and the blessings the day had brought her. That night, she urged George into the most passionate love-making that they had known in months. He asked no questions of her, but watched her with interest.

Joy and Anxiety
Late Summer 1871

James finally proposed to Hetty on the first of July, on her sixteenth birthday, and they announced that they would be married exactly one year later. He took her off on a week's holiday trip to stay first with his aunt in Skipton and then with his family at Pateley Bridge. It was the longest and most exciting journey she had ever undertaken.

Emily bought her some new clothes and boots for the occasion and went to Ingleton to see the couple off on the train. Hetty took the arm of her fiancé and walked the platform with an impatient twirl of skirts and parasol, as if she caught a train every day of her life and was bored with waiting. Emily was moved to see how nervously happy the girl was, despite her best attempt to look a little bored; her fair hair, washed and combed out, caught the sun as it escaped at the sides of her bonnet and she stopped at least twice to look down at her elegant new boots. Emily noted that the girl's slender frame was beginning to fill out and her blue eyes sparkled as if they knew that all would be as wonderful as this for evermore.

Perhaps it will, thought Emily.

She was pleased for James. 'She will mek thee a loving an' a lively wife, in time, a know she will,' she had said to him when they were alone one day. 'She will have limitations, like we all do, lad, but you can make her more than she is an' you shall just have to settle for the rest.'

He had listened quietly, a half-smile playing on his lips as he had nodded his agreement. He was resolved: he had buried his doubts and scotched his dreams. Emily had reached out her hand and held his arm gently.

'She is not your Nancy, a know that. But Nancy would ha' teken some keepin' up with, tha knows! You will be happier with Hetty in the long run. An' she just worships you.'

Whilst the couple were away, Emily decided to prepare a special tea in their honour for the day of their return and to invite Robert and Ethel, Black Jack and the children to join them. George wanted Morgan and Ruth to be invited, but Emily saw her chance and refused outright, stating bluntly that it would spoil the day for her, declaring that she wanted them out by Christmas.

George immediately saw this as an attack on his friends and values and it put him into a resentful mood. What is more, once he knew of the decision, Morgan made it clear that he and his wife would like a day's holiday away from the farm to consider their future. He did not approve of Emily or James and he resented Hetty's dominant position.

Emily had to work hard to charm George into a celebratory temper, but she succeeded in good time; the sun shone brilliantly and the tea party went ahead with a flourish. Tables were set in the garden with bowls of flowers, and the best cutlery and plates were brought dustily into the daylight. They had ham, eggs, salad and cake and trifle, with tea, beer and lemonade to drink. Hetty was almost overcome with excitement and she chattered endlessly as James beamed with pleasure alongside her and said how proud he was of the way she had charmed his family. Robert did his best to keep in the background, Ethel fussed her children and kept them on their best behaviour, while Black Jack was a dignified observer. Emily kept the table supplied and George kept the jugs of beer filled. Toasts were drunk to the young couple and as the day began to wane and the children and adults began to tire in the unaccustomed heat, George hitched up the wagon and offered the visitors a lift back up to Batty Green.

Emily sent Hetty and James away to "do some courting" and was singing cheerfully, whilst drying the best plates, when she was surprised to hear the dogs barking and the sound of a harness jingling against the steady crunch of wheels on stone, suggesting that a horse-drawn carriage was coming down the lane. The gate had been left open for George and all the doors and windows of the farmhouse were also open, to catch any breeze. Emily was therefore even more surprised to see that it was an old-fashioned black vehicle, a closed carriage, with the curtains pulled. She came to the doorway, a cloth still in her hand, her face red from the sun and the exertions of cleaning and carrying, her black hair straying across her sticky brow, but some instinct told her that her appearance was not likely to be significant here. She leaned her hip against the door jamb, shouted to the dogs to be quiet and waited. The carriage came to a halt and then the curtain moved a fraction and a male voice, quite light and cultured, called to her.

'Mrs Wright. I wonder if you would have a word with me. I am afraid I cannot easily get out of this carriage, so I would appreciate it if you would come closer. I mean you no harm.'

Emily was surprised to find that her breathing had shortened and she was unexpectedly struggling to stay composed. She summoned her defences. What was the matter with her? Why should she feel threatened?

She was drawn forwards, reluctantly, not sure why she moved at all. She stopped a few paces from the carriage, tucked the cloth into her apron and swept the clammy fronds of hair from her brow. Again, the curtain moved slightly, but the sun was in her eyes and she could make out little, except a large black shape, a man, leaning forwards, both hands resting on a silver cane. The voice was oily and insinuating, almost feminine.

'Thank you, Mrs Wright. I apologise for this intrusion and for not getting out of the carriage to introduce myself properly, but I am not well. I fear that once I got out I might struggle to get back in again and for me to be stuck here would never do, would it now? It might prove difficult for both of us when your husband returned.'

Emily was rooted and numb. The voice fascinated her: it seemed to caress her and draw her closer, as if it acted hypnotically. But how did this man know her and why should George be concerned? Her breathing was nervously laboured.

'My name is Bernard. I believe that you once met two of my daughters. Indeed, if my sources are accurate, they once set off in one of your carts from this very yard, with Mr James Taylor, one of your lodgers.'

Emily felt herself go cold with dread and she failed to suppress a shiver. She felt breathless again and flighty and she looked around for some sort of a weapon or just something to lean on: she felt exposed. No sooner had this sensation registered than she felt tears begin to surface and with a wriggle of distaste, she screwed up her face and told herself to stay calm. She was being watched and the voice this time was lower, more intimate.

'You obviously know who I am, but really, you have no need to be anxious, Emily. May I call you Emily?'

She nodded almost instinctively, without thinking.

'You see, to be perfectly candid with you, my dear, I am more than ill, I really do believe that I am dying. I have a large growth in my side and another in my stomach and the doctors say they can do nothing. So, you see, my dangerous days really are over and I am quite alone. The coachman hardly knows me. I just hired him and this old vehicle to come here.'

Emily maintained her silence and fought to calm herself. On this day of all days, she was unprepared to deal first-hand with the devil. She would offer nothing, neither sympathy nor solace, but she would just listen and listen carefully.

'Sadly, I must be brief, Emily. So pleased to meet you at last, by the way. I have heard so much about you, especially from Arthur. It was a shame that he got away from you that time: I expect you were rather annoyed by that, would I be right?'

Again, she stood immobile and mute, though reeling internally.

'My congratulations to Hetty and James. Such a lovely couple. I caught a glimpse of them earlier today. It will be quite a marriage, won't it.'

Emily had now gone from cold to hot, startled by his familiarity and the sinister voice snaking out from the darkness. The pressure was threatening to overwhelm her. She knew that she could no longer remain passive; it was too much to ask. She jerked up her head and shouted.

'What's tha want?' She meant to sound strong, but to her ears it sounded like a childish plea.

'Yes, good girl. Time to talk business. I mustn't be here when George comes back, must I! He doesn't like visitors from Batty Green, is that right?'

'What's tha want?' she repeated, more weakly this time.

'As I told you, Emily, I don't think I have long to live. This is probably my last journey of any consequence. And believe me, I am a reformed character, no more drinking, quite proper and churchgoing in my new home. I gave money to restore the organ loft, which made me almost respectable. But ... my family is split asunder and I do want to bring it together, Emily, just once, before I die. I miss Nancy and Grace, especially Nancy; she was such a treasure, so full of life and beauty. I had such plans for her.'

He dropped his voice a little. 'You don't have children, do you, Emily? Such a shame. Must make you unhappy, I should think.'

She shook her head, part defiance, part confusion, and gritted her teeth, making a barrier to words. Bernard now seemed to becoming breathless, almost gasping.

'So, what I want is to find my daughters. I have looked, as you might imagine, but so far I have failed and I am not used to that. Also, I find travel so difficult now and quite frankly, I think I may be running out of time. The approach of death is sharpening my resolve and so I am taking some liberties whilst I can, hence my visit here at this interesting time, just at the end of your little tea party, eh? I need information, Emily, and my guess is that the only person who can help me is your young man James. Practically a son to you now, isn't he, Emily? You're particularly close, aren't you, eh? Almost the same age, I believe. Could have been you he was marrying.'

She hesitated, hating the way his thoughts seemed to crawl under her skin. She wanted to claw at them as if she had a rash. How did he know so much? Who told him all this? A flash of memory recalled to her how she had driven Bella away from this very yard. Emily remembered her temper then and her instinct to protect her own. Yes, James was one of her own and she would not be bullied.

'The lad knows nothing,' she snarled.

'Oh, I doubt that, Emily. He is not going to tell you everything, is he now? I know for a fact that he got very close to Nancy, he did, did you know this, eh? The three days in a hotel in Lancaster. Only left the room to eat, apparently. And not always then: champagne and oysters ordered up to the room. I spoke to the owner of the hotel: rather scandalised, he was. Oh, after that, I bet your James has some news. Nancy is not easily forgotten, even when you are engaged to Hetty. Don't you agree?'

'Leave 'im alone, you evil … pig.'

'Oh, steady, Emily, steady … I told you, I am no threat to anyone now. I intend to leave James alone. No, it is you that must find out about Nancy and Grace. Use your influence and charms on him.'

Emily was baffled. 'Why should a do anything that you ask?' Her spirits rose and she stepped closer to the coach.

'Because you care about James and you are very close to young Hetty. Such a fragile girl, I think, and so happy today, wasn't she.'

Emily's heart began to sink as the air seemed to turn cold and grey about her. She struggled to frame her thoughts and speech. 'What if a don't help you? What ... what ... wilt tha do?'

'Oh, make trouble, I suppose: anonymous letters to the vicar, giving some saucy details of James and Nancy, that kind of thing. I can dress it up a bit, Emily. I do a good letter. Nice man, your vicar. Been going on about moral weakness in the young recently, hasn't he? Wrote a few letters to the paper, I believe. Will he still agree to marry them in church when I tell him of the scandal at Lancaster? And then there's Hetty's parents: poor but proud is what I hear. Well, I could tell them a tale of Mr Taylor might make them think twice. They might not agree to the marriage. Such a shame for the girl. It's bound to be distressing and, of course, she probably doesn't know the full details of what went on with Nancy, does she. Perhaps I should tell her.'

Emily felt cornered, just as she had with Bella, and out of her depth. How did he know all this? That question began to echo harshly in her head. She stood stock-still. The cry of a curlew wafting its descending ripples into the yard made her look up. She wished life were simpler. The voice began again, more urgently and more directive now.

'You have until Thursday. Put pressure on James. Use your charms on him. I hear it usually works. Write down all that you find out for me. A stranger will come into your little yellow shop and ask you if you have a letter for him. You give him the letter. It won't be me, so don't look for me, I will be many miles away. If you fail, or if I hear that there are police there, or there is any attempt to follow my messenger, then I will take other actions against you and yours that will be far worse for you. I can still pull a few levers up here and believe you me, I will. Now I must leave.'

Then, as if in defiance of his last statement, Bernard opened the carriage and heaved himself forwards to put one foot on the step, so that she could now see him clearly. Their eyes met and she stared. He was fat and jowly, his black suit stretched and stained. The skin on his face was muddied, like dirty water, and heavily beaded with sweaty globules. The beard was streaked with white. His eyes were pale and cold, but fixed in a stony glare, and there were flecks of foam at the corners of his pursed mouth.

'So you can see, Emily,' he wheezed. 'You see I am sick. I just want to see my daughters again before I die. Help me, Emily, help me. I am tired of hurting people. I wouldn't care to hurt you or Hetty. It will all be over soon.'

She stared and could not speak. He shuffled, wheezed sharply, slid backwards, pulled the door to and then banged on the roof. The carriage turned and left. Emily went inside and with a mechanical reflex she continued to dry dishes, but when George returned she was sitting in a chair, shaking. She wanted to pour it all out, but felt she could tell him nothing.

Journeys
Late Summer 1871

Emily lay awake most of the night, uneasy and confused, nervous of silence, yet troubled by the slightest noise. George eventually grumbled himself awake and was finally moved to ask her what the matter was. She sat up in bed, black hair spinning around her, and was unable to respond. What could she say? He had made it more than clear that there would be "no more o' that Bernard business". She wished that she could say the same. George sank back into sleep and at last she fell into a fitful doze, richly laden with fractured dreams. She arose tired and stretched nervously, but with plans and one piece of intuition to put to the test later.

The plans were urgent and she began by intercepting James as he left the cottage and arranging to meet him later in the morning at Batty Green. There, she told him what had happened. It was difficult news for James. He paced restlessly, gnawing at the side of one finger, waves of anxiety and guilt threatening to overwhelm him. He blamed himself for drawing Hetty and Emily into all this and was cold with frustration at the reappearance of Bernard with his threats and manipulation.

'The man's truly evil,' he warned her, 'and is not to be trusted in anything he puts forwards. He will stop at nothing to get even. This business of him dying could be true, but it could also be just another of his scheming tricks to get our sympathy or to put us off our guard.'

'Well, all's a can say to that,' grinned Emily, 'is that 'e completely failed on both o' them. First, if he reappears today, a'll run him through wi' a pitchfork meself. Second, a'm so much on my guard and looking about me a forgot to mek breakfast this morning.' James laughed and it brought a warmth to Emily's heart. This was better than moping.

'What would I do without you, Mrs Wright, eh?'

'Well, firstly, after what we've bin through, tha'll call me Emily when we're alone and secondly, tha doesn't have to contemplate doin' much wi'out me, cos we shall plan this together. Agreed? So tha can stop looking mournful. Tha's not to blame for every ill in t'world.' He nodded sheepishly. 'Right, here's what a reckon we should do. First off, tell him the bare facts of what you know, write it down and a shall pass it on. Least that gets him off our backs and sends him off to where'er this lass is living. On same day as he gets this news, we pass t'same information to police. They are still looking for him on a number o' accounts an' they can follow 'im as well and perhaps act quicker than he can.'

'But that leads him and the police straight to Nancy and Grace! I can't do that,' James protested. 'They will be in danger on both sides.'

'Aye, a thought o' that,' Emily retorted. 'We have a few days start on Bernard. We need to write to Nancy at once and warn her. Then, if she chooses to stay thir and meet her father, well, that's her decision. Leastways, that's how a see it and a do think she has the right to know that he is dying, or that he says he is.'

'There's just one problem,' James added with a wry smile. 'I don't have an address to write to.'

He explained that he had an arrangement to meet at three o'clock at the Queen's Gate into Hyde Park on one of a series of Sundays. There were just two such Sundays left. Then, with an awkward turn, he added, almost reflectively, 'Looks like I shall have to go and tell her myself.' He avoided Emily's eye.

'No,' she barked. He looked at her, surprised. 'You listen to me, young 'un. A can see the drift in your thinkin' straight off an' it's not good enough. You're pledged to Hetty an' a'll not stand by an' see you off after Nancy again, no matter how honourable you pretend your motives are. One crook o' Nancy's little finger an' you'll be trotting off like a soft puppy, wi' your tongue hanging out and all brain power lost between your legs.' He looked pained, embarrassed and then amused by turns.

'Happen you're right,' he said.

'A bloody know a'm right,' she laughed.

They looked at each other and the moment stretched suggestively between them. Neither looked away and a breathy silence developed. He noticed her high colour, a strand of her black hair falling loose on one side from a clip, her dark eyes bright with mischief, her lips red and parted and the rise and fall of her breasts. He wanted to touch her, put the hair straight, caress those lips and crush those breasts. She saw the softening in him as he edged forwards; his calm face was fixed as he centred on her and he brought his tongue between his parted lips. She saw the danger and turned aside, forcing her thoughts back to their problem. She stuttered back into speech.

'But, we can't just leave it thir. A'm sure that a don't want Bernard to get near her, either, or the police, unless she chooses. So, someone has to go to London an' tell 'er. George would never let me ...' There was a pause and this time she looked at the floor, urging herself to stay focused. 'Wait on ... a've got an idea,' she suddenly exclaimed. 'Come to the shop in a couple o' hours an' a may have some news.'

A couple of days later, after hasty planning and some further persuasive work on James, Emily passed a note to a stranger that came into her shop and at almost the same moment, Bella joined the mainline train to London to look for Nancy.

Bella had agreed to help willingly enough, but armed with nothing more than a brief description of the girls and their father, and with sketchy details of where to meet Nancy, she was not convinced that this would work. She had said to James and Emily, with all the weight of her transatlantic background, 'Youse two are fine people an' you sure are full of good intent, but I suspect that you'll be thinking of Skipton on market day. I'm actually goin' to search in London on a summer Sunday in Hyde Park. I've been there. Just think o' the biggest crowd you have ever seen, and multiply by about a thousand, and then add more carriages, horses and riders than you can imagine.'

Nevertheless, she had friends she could call upon in London, and Midland Railway tickets for her travel and hotel, and she wanted to help, so she agreed to go. They were full of speculation. No one knew what action Bernard would take, or the police, but the local officers had seemed unimpressed with the idea of mounting a trap in London on such thin evidence as they had been given.

When Bella left her carriage at St Pancras, she did so with a familiar sense of energising anticipation. Now, as before, arriving in a big city could set her senses stirring in ways that pastoral scenes rarely could. It seemed as if the steam and smoke charged her with energy and she absorbed it greedily. This great station was a cauldron of noise: a stuttering engine jostled and banged its way backwards on the neighbouring platform, matched by another on a different line; guards shouted; hammers chipped and rattled; a hubbub of voices, bubbling and frothing, filled the lower air and elsewhere, an unseen whistle cut sharply through her consciousness. She stood, relaxed and waiting for the air and the crowd to clear, so that she could look up to the fine new roof above her. The elegant curve of shining glass, carried so smoothly on clean metal girders, cheered her even further. The effortless span seemed to be a token of the age.

Yet, as she moved forwards, she was soon aware of confusion at ground level and the bustle and detritus of work unfinished. The grand frontage of the new station was still half complete, its outside facades a complex mass of walkways, scaffolding and cranes, obscuring the detail and thwarting the eye as it tried to trace the emerging shapes. But everything was alive with clamour and movement and its vigour was palpable. Stepping aside to avoid a porter uncertainly urging a laden barrow through the crowd, feeling others beginning to press towards her from behind, she caught sight of a beggar, a barefoot woman with a small boy, also trying to make her way through the crowd. The woman was hunched, ragged and unsteady and she held on hard to the poor waif by the hand; he snivelled and whined. City life. It always generated energy and bustle; it promised profit and opportunity; and yet she knew it also sustained another life, characterised by squalor, unhappiness and crime. More soberly, she joined the crowd funnelling through a series of arches and was sucked out into the busy street, dense with noise and dust and an agitation of movement.

By contrast, Hyde Park on a warm, sultry Sunday afternoon offered a very different prospect. Here, the rich and fashionable, the eligible and the hopeful, mingled in a public display of status, wealth and aspiration that brought crowds out just to watch the show. Carriages of all kinds – phaetons, traps, broughams, gigs and all manner of other elaborate equipages – along with scores of individual riders, lined up to enter the park. Some were open, conveying elegant ladies shaded by parasols, attended by men in boaters and white jackets. Others were offering shadowy glimpses of less fashionable wealth, identifiable by coat of arms or the dress of the footmen. As the carriages moved cautiously into Rotten Row, it required burly policemen, sweating under their helmets, to hold back the curious and envious, amid a babble of comment and an occasional catcall. Throughout the park, sounds of distant bands mingled with those of children and adults shouting, horses snorting and dogs barking, costermongers calling from the distance and vehicles on the edges of the park hooting mournfully or sounding tiny bells, which seemed to filter mysteriously though the trees. Wrapped round it all was the murmur of a warm breeze, rattling the dry leaves of the trees after a succession of sticky days with brassy sunshine. There was a mood of holiday laughter in the glare and cool release in the shade.

Bella had taken the omnibus along the Strand and then alighted to join the crowds strolling along Pall Mall and through Green Park to Hyde Park at its famous Knightsbridge corner. Then she walked slowly down to Queen's Gate, where Nancy was expected to be waiting. The day was becoming more humid and Bella, sensing that a storm could erupt, looked nervously at her flimsy umbrella and felt the sweat begin to trickle down her back and hang damp about her haunches.

She sought some shade near the row of coffee stands just inside the gate as the time approached three o'clock and watched the rising human tide, released from the relentless burden of work or daily routine. Crowds surged into the park and flowed around the variety of objects that stood in their way: stalls, hucksters, benevolent bobbies, stranded old people or ungainly perambulators with attendant nurses. In spite of the threatening ferment in the heavy air, there was a touch of festival in the sunshine. The stream of humanity broke into knots and groups and Bella scanned them all as they passed the coffee stands or struck across the park towards the Serpentine. She was alert for a tall, elegant young lady, possibly caring for a teenage girl. It was a combination that presented itself several times and each time Bella craned forwards vigilantly. Once, she made a move towards such a pair, her heart in her mouth lest she lost them, only to find that their speech suggested that they were certainly foreign: she doubted that Nancy would be trying that form of disguise.

Surrounded by such a sea of humanity, three o'clock came and went and Bella was beginning to lose heart. A few drops of heavy rain fell and the wind lifted a little, occasional gusts pushing the damp, sticky atmosphere to one side and then to another. All around her anxious glances swept skywards to see where the approaching storm might be.

Then, in a gap between vehicles, Bella saw, on the other side of the carriageway, an oddly matched man and a woman standing together, but not speaking; in fact, they were facing in almost opposite directions, scanning the crowds as she had done. The tension in their posture and the urgency of their stares attracted her attention. He was tall and heavily built, with greying hair, a neat beard with a white streak in it, and even in this heat he was wearing a formal suit and carrying a silver cane.

But for all of his polished presentation, he was standing awkwardly and his mouth was open as if he could not catch his breath. The woman looked peevish and nervous. Bella was sure at once that it was Bernard and his wife. A carriage blocked her view and came to a standstill. She edged sideways, but the crowd and a passing horseman again blocked her and when it cleared a little the couple were gone.

She began to feel an unexpected anxiety. They must have moved quickly, which could only mean one thing. She pushed her way forwards and ducked between two riders, startling the horses: a large grey ridden by a portly gentleman pulled up sharply. The man snarled and other shouts pursued her. From somewhere, a whistle blew, but she strode across the track, forcing one carriage to rein in sharply, and with a rush she reached the other side and pushed her way back through the throng. But there was no sign of the couple, Bernard and his wife, if, indeed, that was who it was.

Then she became aware of some disturbance much further back, on the edge of the park; heads were craning round and there was a pulse of agitated noise stemming from a group of people in the near distance, pulled together like a knot. More people and at least one policeman were heading towards the core of this event. She hurried on again, following her intuition, now heading towards Knightsbridge Road, her attention centred on this growing cluster of bodies, which appeared to be concentrated round one of the benches.

Perspiring, determined and almost angry at the situation she was in, she strode on, willing herself to be in time, forcing her way through the bystanders, appealing to them to let her through. When she was a few yards away, she was tall enough to see over crouching heads to where Bernard, if it was him, was stretched out on a bench, very still, his white skin a lifeless parchment in contrast to his grey-black hair and dark clothing. His wife was kneeling beside him, clutching his arm. A tall, graceful young lady with dark hair, in a blue silk coat over a silk dress in ivory and cream, stood to one side, her arm firmly gripped by a young policeman. She looked ice-cold, while the officer looked hot and very uneasy. A girl of about twelve stood quietly alongside the pair, chalky white and frail.

Bella, claiming that she was a nurse, asked the bystanders to move back, knelt beside the wife and quickly examined the man. He was still breathing, but only with difficulty. She could see scratches, but no serious wound, which reassured her. She made him comfortable, removed his neck cloth, loosened his collar, gave the wife some instructions and then went over to the policeman. Gambling on his inexperience, she gave him a full smile and a confident set of instructions.

'Officer, I am a nurse; we need to move the crowd away to give this man some peace and quiet. Then he needs to be taken to hospital, as he may have had a seizure of some sort. He is still breathing, but he needs a doctor. I am sure that you can let this young lady go, as I can assure you she is not dangerous.'

The policeman pulled himself up straight. 'Do you know this young lady, mam?'

'I certainly do. She's my niece and so is this other young lady. I lost them in the crowd and was looking for them. I am sure there must be a simple explanation for what went on here. Isn't that so, Nancy?' Bella kept her gaze firmly fixed on the policeman, waited for a few long seconds and turned at last to look at Nancy, hoping that the ploy would work. The young woman showed not the least surprise at this turn of events and with the merest nod at Bella, she turned to the officer and gave him the full force of her most expressive smile, yet tinged with nervous unease, as if recovering from a nasty shock.

'I don't know the man,' she said, pausing to nibble her lower lip nervously, 'but he seemed to be following me and in the crowd, he tried to … touch me, so I got away and Grace came with me. I'm sorry, Aunt,' she turned to Bella, 'I thought you were behind me. Then we sat here to wait for you and he came up to me again and started to pester me, so I stood up and pushed him away. He seemed to stumble and fall and then he went white and shouted. It all got very confusing.'

She withdrew a handkerchief from her sleeve and with a trembling movement, she placed it gently to her lip as if she needed the touch of it against her, all the time conscious of the constable's eyes fixed upon her. She heaved a heavy sigh and looked as vulnerable as possible. Bella could not resist a little smile at such a performance.

She then looked across at Grace, who seemed fretful and very pale, as if she might be about to faint. Bella was alarmed. What was happening to the younger girl?

Grace was truly in torment. Yet, the day had started well for her. Since their move to London, she specially looked forward to Sunday. It was the highlight of her week. She and Nancy would spend the whole day together, starting with a proper breakfast in their dingy rooms above offices off a little courtyard in Whitechapel. Today, she had sung a new French song to Nancy and they had practised the piano together.

Later, as always, they went to the park. Sometimes, a gentleman friend of Nancy's would take them boating on the lake and once they had even been taken in an elegant carriage and pair all around the perimeter. But always, Nancy insisted, they had to be at Queen's Gate for three o'clock and any gentlemen followers would be coldly dismissed for an hour. Grace always enjoyed the moment of Nancy's imperious command: moreover, she knew that she had Nancy all to herself again.

How she loved Nancy. How dull the hours were when Nancy was away at Mrs North's. Grace had her lessons to go to, her dancing classes and her French conversation. Nancy arranged it all, paid for it and insisted that Grace went. Then, Grace would clean the meagre three rooms and do their shopping and washing, after which she waited for Nancy. Sometimes, if Mrs North's was very quiet, it would come early: the scurry of feet on the stairs, the key in the lock – it would lift Grace's heart. Then, Nancy would quickly change and they would cook and then sit together to eat. Nancy would tell her everything about her gentlemen: who they were, which ones were married, which ones couldn't manage it, what presents they brought her and how often they said they loved her better than any of the other girls. Grace believed it, too. Who would not love her Nancy: so brave, so beautiful and so clever.

But, sometimes, Nancy was very late and tired and occasionally grumpy. One day, she had a bruised and swollen lip, where a boorish, drunken aristocrat had given her a backhander to show her who was in charge. She told Grace the story of how Mrs North had summoned Mr North and how the gentleman had been manhandled down the front steps, his coat and top hat thrown to him in the street. Grace drew a picture of it.

Today, at Queen's Gate, as for many Sundays past, Grace had waited and watched with Nancy at three o'clock. They often talked of James and told and retold the story of their escape from Batty Green. Nancy did not love James. Grace knew this: perhaps, of the two of them, she had a deeper feeling for him. But to both of them he was their diffident, cautious, modest hero, their angel that led them to freedom. He had been so utterly captivated by Nancy and they both knew that he would have walked on coals to the ends of the earth for her. Yet, Nancy knew, at the end, how it had to be and she had sent him back to the life he understood. Gently, kindly, even tearfully, but always with conviction that it was for the best. Once she had cut him loose, she had immediately headed for the anonymity of London, for whatever life she could make for Grace. They now waited, dutifully, as promised, but did not really expect him to come.

They often talked of Batty Green and their mother and sisters. But never their father. Nancy would not even allow his name to be mentioned. Grace could have been more forgiving and sometimes, lonely in her quiet room, she rocked herself to and fro, crying for the loss of her hopes, her family and her younger self or just for loneliness. On such nights, if Nancy was late, she would creep into her sister's bed and curl herself round Nancy's nightgown.

Grace did not thrive and Nancy watched her zealously. With every moment of anxiety, every half-finished meal, every hour of pale lassitude that she witnessed in her sister, Nancy cursed her father anew.

For her own happiness and solicitude she was careless, but Grace was lost and grieving and Nancy thought only of her. So she encouraged her regular gentlemen to bring her little gifts and made them promise not to tell Mrs North. She worked to please these hapless benefactors, quickly learning who liked to laugh, who liked to talk, who liked domination, who liked a game of chance, who liked the riding crop and who liked her to dress, speak and act like the commonest whore. Yet, as she undressed, as she sucked, suckled or cursed, the prize in sight was not her own flush and sweep of ecstasy, or even a new gown, it was another half-guinea or pearl necklace, quickly slipped into the special pocket she had sewn into every one of her petticoats. Mrs North paid the girls, but expected them to share their treats, and for the sake of form, Nancy occasionally dropped a few coins or a cheap brooch into the box, but most gifts were converted to coin and went home to Whitechapel, to a tin box beneath the floorboards. She kept no secrets from Grace and every week they counted their treasure and talked of their dream of going to France to buy a little hotel somewhere on the coast. They would work hard, but Grace made Nancy promise that they would never work on a Sunday. She never dared tell Nancy that she often prayed that the whole family could live together again, in modest gentility.

It was therefore with very different and contrasting feelings on that Sunday afternoon that the girls responded to the sight and sound of their father pushing brutally through the holiday crowds, just yards away from them. Nancy saw him first: black, powerful, grasping, fleshy and hot; pushing and reaching for her. She screamed and flung herself away, knocking others sideways. Grace swung around sharply, fearing that Nancy was being attacked and ready to help, but pulling back in confusion when she saw her father's hand outstretched, covetous, but pushing her out of the way, his claws clutching for the fuller flesh of her sister. He did not even see her!

She screamed in grief and loss and she felt a flame lick through her that in an instant burned and died. But he should not have Nancy: no! She flung herself in front of his heaving mass and again he smote her sideways, unfeeling, unaware. But it was enough. Nancy wriggled free, Bernard crumpled and fell with a roar like a felled animal and Grace was tangled and dragged down, breathless beside him. The crowd scattered and some shouted abuse at the man, whilst others quickly moved away, bubbling and agitated, and then began pressing back in to see what lay there.

And Nancy, desperate to escape, nevertheless heard it all and spun round to see the black mass of her father stagger and spread, falling face first into the earth, and a lighter flurry that was Grace crumpling beside him. She felt the crowd begin to be sucked in towards the bodies and so she pushed firmly through to snatch up Grace, pulling her roughly away from the prostrate fiend, anywhere but there. Then, without any break in her motion, in the same arc, she spun again. First releasing Grace to the safety of the crowd, she pirouetted and flung herself savagely onto his back, fists flailing, beating him, pummelling and scratching at that hated flesh, that depravity, that offence. She was crying and shouting and wielding her fists like a mad woman and did not know it. The crowd was aghast and embarrassed, until at last the officer pulled her firmly away and with slow, fitful encroachments, Sunday in the Park crept back, a little ashamed, and the distant music of the bands began once again to spread calm harmonics through the trees.

Bella stayed for a week and came to know the family well. Bernard was not likely to last long, she knew that, and the doctors confirmed it. She and Grace moved between the rooms in Whitechapel and the house in Camberwell, where the Bernards were, indeed, regarded as a model family. They nursed the dying man, who refused to notice them, and they sustained the family, who came to rely on them. Nancy refused to see her father, even in his slow, final hours, when his hands scrabbled at the bed sheets and his gaze swept sightlessly past those present, scanning the room constantly. He could not speak, but they all knew that he watched for her.

After his death, she came and asked to be left alone with the body. In troubled anxiety and dread, they listened and after a long silence, they heard her sobbing convulsively. Later, she emerged, pale and smiling, and to their great relief she smiled, hugged them all and took over.

She quickly ascertained that the family's assets were considerably more than she expected. Once the funeral was over, she and Grace could travel at once to France and start looking for premises and they could all start again, in the hotel trade. They wanted Bella to go with them. She said that she had unfinished business in the north, but perhaps she might join them later. Gifts were wrapped for Emily and George and for Bella and a wedding gift for James and Hetty. Bella also collected two interesting pieces of information. Bernard's family had revealed that one source of information and his main working partner in many deals was a certain Mr Grantley, the creeping lecher that Grace had said smelled of biscuits. Grace declared that she wanted the man killed, but they eventually found enough documents to prove Grantley's involvement in the illegal brewing enterprise and posted these off to the police in Lancaster. Bernard himself had also let slip that his information about James and the farm had come from a Welsh couple working there. Bella had a feeling that Emily would be able to make good use of this news and she lost no time in putting it into a letter.

Coming and Going
Autumn 1871

The letter confirmed Emily's earlier intuition. She felt a moment's joy in the confirmation, followed by a renewed surge of passionate distaste for her two workers. She would deal with them herself.

She decided to wait a few days, knowing that George was going to a distant cattle fair that would mean him staying away overnight. Then, as soon as the afternoon milking was over, she placed Hetty on a chair just inside the parlour, with instructions to listen carefully, and summoned Ruth and Morgan into the kitchen. She had every intention of starting slowly and unpeeling their layers of deceit in slow stages, but seeing them there in her own kitchen – cold, blotchy and ugly – she found them so offensive that she could do nothing to disguise the contempt and anger that bubbled frothily to her lips. Their very nationality seemed a provocation and she hit at them venomously and without warning, in her broadest vowels and with staccato force.

'Thy friend Bernard's dead. Has t'news reached tha yet?'

They exchanged shifting and uncertain glances, saying nothing, but edging back a little. She pursued them, sneeringly, focusing on Morgan's blunt face.

'Lost thy tongue, eh? None o' your prayers an' bits o' Bible sayings now, eh, Morgan. No holy scraps or well-chewed titbits quite right for this "pertickler sitivation", as me grandad would ha' called it? How did thy God tek to the idea o' you helpin' the likes of an evil dog like Bernard an' no doubt tekin' his brass, that's what a should really like to know, Mr Holy Bones?'

The man looked up, stung and stewing, malice and spite in his ferrety eyes. She lashed into him, punching the air with her words, hammering them down. 'Tha's aware, a'm sure, that he made his livin' out o' brewin' and then sellin' strong drink, illegally. He also forced his wife and daughters to act as whores; two o' them were just bairns, scarce old enough to go to school. Mek tha feel good, Morgan, knowing that Bernard sold his children to t'highest bidders to do wi' as they pleased? Took brass for their bodies, he did, and then 'e blackmailed the men for good measure. Broke up a few good homes an' families, a reckon. Some o' that money came thy way, a should think. Could tha smell the spirits on it or the sweat o' those men that had teken their fill o' little girls? Tha art a miserable heap o' horse shit, wi' thy pious words, standin' ready to condemn others at the drop o' a feather, when thy own hands are black wi' scrabblin' in t'muck for Bernard's money. Tha daren't deny it, a notice.'

Ruth took an unsteady step to one side and sat nervously, as if shocked. Morgan, given more space, became more bull-like, lowering his head and swivelling to glance sideways at her, as if shielding his soul from her corruption. 'I knew nothing of the man. I don't fill my ears with the gossiping of the criminals of Batty Green as some do. He said that you helped to part him from his daughters, who had attacked him and stolen his savings, and that you helped Mr Taylor to escape with his youngest, to debase and debauch her further. He sought God's blessing for his search and we went into the church and prayed together. That's all, look you, and no evil comes of prayer, except when it's in the heart and mouth of the devil's disciple.'

He looked pointedly at her. She shook with frenzy. She knew this was getting out of hand, but her blood raged. She wanted to crush him and that part of Bernard that had infected him. 'No evil comes … tha filthy, mean hypocrite. No, how can more evil come, when tha's already in the hands o' the devil himself. Th'art an ignorant dolt, Morgan. Young James, as is worth twice o' thee any day, risked his life and his whole future t'elp them girls. A saw him cry wi' grief at state they were in and what wor happening to them. But tha … All tha cares about is thy own road to salvation. An' don't reckon as there wor any fine motive in this. A know what thou saw in this, nothing more or less than a chance of mekin' trouble for James and mebbe for me. Tha's been lookin' for a chance like this 'un, just to have a go at me, so tha sold thy soul for a few pieces o' silver.'

She stepped forwards, screeching at him. 'How much wor it worth then, Morgan, to betray those as took thee in and gave thee a roof over thy 'ead, eh? A few shillin' would buy thee most days, am a reet? Specially when thir's a bit o' morality thrown in. Cleanin' up, wor tha? Sold all our little secrets, did tha? Told 'im about who helped them girls and where they went. And about James and Hetty and what the vicar might say or do, eh? Does your God approve o' you mekin' a bit on t'side like this? Too ashamed to tell me, eh?'

She taunted him, pushing herself closer, spraying him with her saliva. He clenched and unclenched his fist and stared back through blackened slits for eyes.

'God nourishes the pure in heart,' he intoned breathlessly, his fists still clenching and unclenching, his ugly head wobbling. 'I know that my redeemer is waiting for me and will reward me in heaven for the work of his that I undertake here. And the abuse I suffer from the … ungodly.'

Emily stood, stock-still, face-to-face with him, and fought and fought to control her limbs and weigh her words. She made herself speak slowly, quietly and personally, though tremors still surged through her words. 'If tha's an example of God's chosen ones, then a'm reet relieved to be one o' the ungodly. An' if heaven's full o' the likes o' thee, Morgan, it's no place for me, cos a'd scratch thy eyes out first time a saw thy smug face. Heaven's well beyond my control today, but a can choose ma own companions here and now. A want thee off this farm before t'end o' t'week wi'out fail.'

She stepped back. She had not intended to go so far, but she would have them out now, whatever the cost, and George could go hang. He seemed to sense a moment of doubt in her and his glowering look softened a little, as if he had seen a means of escape by a side door. Native cunning guided him to the weakness. 'Is George aware of what you are doing?'

But she would not yield on those lines. 'Not yet, Morgan. But let me just tell you both,' and she turned to draw in Ruth, the anger again blazing in her: 'A'm his wife. You may get him on his knees wi' you when he's miserable, but I get him on 'is back when he's full o' life an' that counts for a lot. A shall tell him all this sorry tale an' if he prefers thy saintly company to mine then he can have it. Cos either tha goes or a go.' She paused. 'And a've a feelin' that Hetty may feel t'same.' She turned to call over her shoulder: 'Am a reet, Hetty?'

The girl came slowly from the parlour; lines of tears still wet on her cheeks. Hers was a face of shaken sorrow, not anger, and her words were quiet and low. 'A'd rather spend rest o' my days on top o' Whernside than spend another hour wi' you. A'm with Emily, all the way.'

Ruth raised herself wearily and resting her hand on Morgan's arm, she muttered something to him and then they both turned away and moved to the door. Morgan had his hand on the latch when he turned back, stolid defiance still ablaze in him.

'I curse the pair of you.' He spoke with level, unflinching malice. 'As you reap, so shall you sow. I know what corruption lies in your hearts and how Batty Green has led you deeper into the pit of your iniquity. Your harvest will be a barren and unhappy one. You do not walk with the Lord.'

'A'll walk a pitchfork up thy sainted arse if th'art here much longer,' Emily spat back at him.

The next morning, Ruth and Morgan agreed to leave if they got two week's wages in advance and within the hour they were gone. That evening, when George returned from the cattle fair, he took the news badly, quickly became very angry and refused to listen to the story that Emily had to tell. Any reference to Bernard, Nancy and Grace seemed to inflame him dangerously and hot, bitter words were exchanged. Emily felt bruised, torn by conflicting obligations, but resistant to his absolute demands. He returned to his request that she stay at the farm and not go out to work. She refused. It was too high a price to pay. To cut off all contact with Batty Green now would be like cutting off her arm. She would not be bullied into keeping to the confines of the farm kitchen, its keeper and its domestic symbol, which was what she thought he really wanted.

The argument became confounded with moral issues, as it often did these days in any issue that was discussed with George, and she felt the influence of Morgan in her husband's words, which did not improve her temper. But she lacked the subtlety of argument or the mental discipline to attack his position effectively and he wasn't listening anyway. He had once been the advocate of change. Now, he wanted nothing more than to turn it aside from his door, make an invisible but palpable barrier that would preserve Elterbeck and what he thought of as its traditional values and forms behind a moat. He wanted to keep himself and his own immune from outside influence. Yet, Emily fought him all the way, demanding her right to make, do and live in the murky uncertainties of the camp and its inhabitants. For her, it was the outside world and she would not give it up.

As the fight subsided, he told her that he was weary of it all. Because he could not bend her to his will, his anger settled, by slow degrees, to an acid indifference and the talking stopped. He summed it up quite formally: 'I don't know as I can trust you any more,' he said to her later. 'All this goin' on behind me back and I'm not so sure, even now, that you've told me it all. I fear for the years ahead, for you and me. I don't know who you are sometimes.'

He shuddered and fumed, drawing away from her. He sometimes slept in the parlour, curled up on an old divan. She turned to Bella more and more. Did she know who she was or which part of her was her true self? She also had doubts.

Dark Days
Autumn 1871

Blasts of winter came early to Ribblehead that year. A sequence of storms in late October gave way to arctic sheets of ice as the wind swung round to the north-east, bringing bright, withering days with clear nights that drove the cold in thin shards through anything but the thickest walls. Emily and George were fully stretched. New workers had to be set on quickly to replace Ruth and Morgan and two more local girls, including Hetty's younger sister Rose, now moved into the other side of the farmhouse and had to be fed, clothed and trained. A new farmhand was needed to handle the increase in cattle and horse stock and George busied himself with looking for more land or even another farm.

All was turbulent for a time, a time when the demand for fresh food was growing steadily as Batty Green continued to spread and into its greedy maw there was poured more and more of the lifeblood and produce of the area. Tradesmen now did regular rounds of the huts and their settlements: potters' carts, brewers' drays, butchers, bakers, vendors of meal and flour, drapers and grocers all plied their trade. Yet, the Elterbeck Shop continued to be popular and busy and had to be enlarged and improved. Most of the neighbouring farms sold through Emily and Joshua now had his own yellow cart and a young helper, managing the busy rounds of the area on his own, building up trade steadily with his banter and charm. Everything around them burgeoned. The brickworks was at full production, there was a blacksmith's shop, a saw mill, a carpenter's shed, stabling for over 100 horses and stores for all the materials needed to move the engineering forwards. The school was full, there was a grocer's shop, a hospital and another reading room up on Blea Moor. And where there was such a flux of activity and high wages that there was money to spend.

But for all the provision that the contractor Mr Ashwell made to make life tolerable to the men and their families, there was always the countervailing deterrent of the weather, the isolation and the sheer difficulty of some of the work. Boulder clay lay over much of the terrain. It froze so solid that explosives had to be used to break it up. Yet, when it was wet, a navvy could swing a pickaxe at it, watch it slide in deep and then would struggle to pull it out again, often achieving nothing but tired limbs and a foul temper. If the navvies could load it into a cart, the rain would turn it into a slurry that settled like glue into the wagon and when tipped, it would take the cart over as well, sliding down the embankment, to the frustration of all. One infamous day saw sixteen carts thrown down in this way on one embankment alone and all work halted in confusion for a while.

And all the time the men and their families came and went. In some weeks as many as fifty new hands might be taken on, to replace those who had had enough. As the penetrating cold yielded at last to sleet and snow, Emily also found herself losing old friends. Ethel was with child again and struggling to cope, so she had decided to stop work for a year at least. Then, Robert Macintosh sent a note to say that he was going to manage new brickworks in Glasgow and would leave by Christmas.

Emily felt deflated and threatened by the year in prospect. Hetty and James would marry and perhaps move away, Ethel would have her fourth child and be preoccupied and Robert would have gone altogether. Bella was a comfort, but she was now asking more pointedly when she would meet her son, which made Emily uneasy. Not that she hadn't tried. She had insisted that George listened to her praise for her friend Bella Roberts; her skill with medicines and herbs, her support to the smallpox victims and her dash to London to find Nancy. But George was unimpressed and rolled out his usual grunting reply.

'We'll have no more visitors from Batty Green. A'm absolutely fixed on this, Emily. They bring nowt but a heap o' trouble. See your friend up thir yoursen. Thou spends enough time thir. Why don't thou move in with this Bella if she's that marvellous?'

He glared at her and she felt the meanness in him. Was this how his father had been, she wondered, when Bella left the first time. It was a grim reminder and a warning, as chill as any winter blast. She seemed to have lost the knack of making him laugh or even smile. And they seemed to have so much to do. Sheer tiredness almost threatened to overwhelm her at times and George was grey and lined. Yet, she knew that the long hours and extra demands would have counted for little if they were happier with themselves and with each other. They often bickered.

In a rare moment of calm discussion, they found themselves discussing their childlessness as they neared the end of their ninth year of marriage. George surprised her by suggesting that she went to see a doctor to see if "anything can be done". She could scarcely refuse, without revealing the secret that she had kept hidden from him for so long. So she went dutifully to Kendal, to someone recommended by her own local man. The doctor talked to her, discussed her bleedings, her diet and her health generally and then examined her. He was brisk and clear in his summary. He saw no reason why she should not have a child, but admitted candidly that there were sometimes factors that prevented this. The fertility of her husband might be a factor. It might take longer; certainly, for some people it did, whose fertility was hit and miss. She should not give up hope and should pray to almighty God for the outcome that she craved.

'A've tried the Almighty,' she said. 'A was 'oping for a more earthly kind of assistance.'

George took the news badly and blamed himself. 'You should not 'ave married an older man,' he said. 'Perhaps a'm just past it,' he added with a wistful sadness and self-deprecation that made her want to cry. She rallied him, like in the old days, and teased him into better humour, but it soon evaporated. And in some senses, so did George.

What was happening to him? What were his feelings now? She had to admit that she scarcely knew. She watched him sometimes and felt that he had slipped silently and deliberately into a dour middle age, retreating from life, putting himself at a distance from her and perhaps from their childlessness. He seemed so disillusioned with everything.

He was richer and busier than ever before, but he seemed to have grit in his soul, not hope. He was spending more time at the church and at the Hill Inn, rather than sitting at home with her, either side of the fire, as they used to. 'Let's be fireguards,' he used to say jokingly. 'You get that side, an' a'll tek this an' we'll get toasted and cosy.' In their early days, they had sometimes thrown a pile of blankets on the floor in front of the fire and taken their clothes off, even in the middle of winter.

Now, they went their separate ways, in sorrow, but deep down they both retained some hope and some connection, because they had some of what they wanted and they had been happy once. Meanwhile, the days and weeks drew forwards inexorably and the railway workings grew towards their peak. All was bustle and endeavour through the upper Ribble Valley and across its grim headwaters, with progress hewn from the landscape with the sweat of men's backs and the occasional loss of life or limb.

But there were moments of bright relief, bringing welcome respite from the struggle with harsh terrain and fierce weather. One such diversion was the annual fair in Ingleton, held every November. It was already well known for the amount of ale consumed, but with the swollen population surrounding the village the fair promised to be bigger than ever this year and the indulgence in drink guaranteed to reach new heights. The unusually cold, wintry weather at the beginning of the month had changed again to sleety rain, with grey forbidding barriers of mist, but it did little to keep the crowds away. Emily and Hetty braved the weather to take a morning off and join the throng in the narrow streets; eating roast chestnuts, indulging in some girlish banter and jostling in the crowd, contentedly shuffling from stall to stall, eventually buying some dress fabric and new bonnets. It felt like the short break that they both needed.

They retreated at last to the front room at The Wheatsheaf for a warming drink, before setting off back to Elterbeck. It was usually a quiet place, but today it was crowded and already there were signs that drinking had started in earnest and started early: several figures were slumped over a table, barely holding themselves upright, but nevertheless holding tight to their pint pots and maintaining an occasional mumbled conversation. Others were noisier.

The door opened into the main room and she recognised one figure, who was on his feet but swaying. Tom Borston, their local shepherd, was easy to spot, with his red face and twisted back. She could hear him talking loudly and with a drunken slur, telling someone that gimmer lambs were plentiful this year and grouse were far fewer and how he had personally told Mr Farrer that "days o' grouse were over".

She smiled and turned away to say something to Hetty, when there was a lull in the chatter and quite clearly intruding into that lull she thought she heard part of a reply. Except she registered nothing of the words, but only the soft, lilting timbre of the voice. It was soft Irish: sweet, low and musical. Her heart beat a hasty tattoo. It sounded just like Dermot O'Reardon: the handsome young man who had appeared as if in a vision on her journey home weeks ago; the same young man who had gallantly escorted her from one of her own barns many months before that and had suggestively invited her to return. He was recognisably the shadowy phantom that had come to her in her dreams; a dark, intrusive force, slippery and yet metallic, always heralded by the soft drone of a lilting voice to warm her and to warn her, but like a low song heard distantly.

Without a word, and as if compelled by an unseen force, she rose to her feet and pushed forwards to glance round the door frame. It was him! He appeared to be trapped on the end of a settle, almost against the edge of the inglenook, with the old shepherd now standing over him, talking at him in a loud, persistent drone. Just a glance was enough to sweep confusion through her and send a flush to her temples. He looked up and saw her. She did not flinch. Neither could she help but smile to see him, though she did not know what to make of him in daylight. Had his previous behaviour been sufficiently explained? What power did he retain over her?

He seemed to know her at once and raised his hat to her in a rakish, familiar salute, the twinkling smile shining like a beacon that sank into her. She went back to her seat automatically and with no further thought she sent Hetty to buy some apples that they had looked at earlier and said she would meet her by the church in a little while.

Hetty left and Emily sat in a cocoon of silence, a bubble of her own crowded thoughts insulating her, despite the babble developing all around. She was suddenly and fiercely convinced that the whole of the rest of her life might be changed by whatever passed in the next few minutes. She also knew that she had to act: too often since Batty Green had arisen from the moss she had allowed events to overtake her, block her way. Now, it was up to her. She must seize this moment or regret it forever. Wherever it led her. Dermot was a key, a sign, an opening. She had to go with that. She nodded abstractedly and made her move, her brain stalling and her body doll-like and stiff.

She rose and pushed her way through to the main room, where all the time more people were crowding in. In the confusion, she manoeuvred herself towards the fire and soon caught the eye of Dermot as he scanned the room as far as the bent form of his shepherd friend would allow. She did not speak. She merely nodded towards the door and turned, pushing back again through the farmers, the navvies and their various wives and womenfolk, who were packing ever tighter into that hot, noisy space. She had no idea if he had followed.

The cold air hit her as she stepped out and yet the sight of the busy stalls spread all along the street cheered her and were both relief and reassurance. The one closest to the Wheatsheaf was selling herbs, medicines and remedies. She joined the edge of the crowd that was listening sceptically but in good humour to a frock-coated old gentleman, telling them of the benefits of his tonic. She stood still, her back to the public house, and waited, shaking a little, eyes almost closed. The air on her face was cold, but then she felt the warmth and stir of a body that moved quietly alongside her, brushing very close. She could smell whisky and tobacco and something else, perhaps leather or horses. She did not turn. He was taller than her. She felt a tingle of expectancy as he leaned forwards.

The voice seemed lower and more insinuating than ever. It began its foray towards her, reaching over her shoulder. 'It's so very glad I am to see you again, Mrs Wright. I was hoping that I might renew our acquaintance when I was next in this part o' the world and I am surely pleased to see you looking so well. Have you any tenants in the barn o' yours at this moment in time?'

She glanced at him, though she did not trust herself to turn to face him yet, but a rush of excitement filled her and she spoke unflinchingly.

'Well, a wor wonderin' when tha would appear. Thou art inclined to spring up again from time to time in a most surprising manner. Tha'rt a bit like a Jack-in-the-Box. What are thy intentions this time, Mr O'Reardon?' she asked. 'Is a body safe wi' the likes o' you around?'

Now, she turned more fully and met his gaze with her dark brown eyes, probing his as if the real truth were there, if she only looked long enough.

'I'm on the way over to Dent again.' He looked more serious now. 'When my brother's wife died in childbed last year, we brought away the old man and the younger fellow, as you know, but we left a wee child in the care of a neighbour. I've come to collect him and take him home. But I have had the devil's own luck with one thing and another, too tedious to recount at a time like this, though seeing you here today has given a powerful lift to my dull feelings. I'm thinking that providence is truly merciful to send an angel to bear me assistance. Though I also

270

have to admit to being astonished that an angel can have such beautiful dark eyes.' She sensed a movement of the arm that was closest to her, as if he might bring it around her waist.

Something inside her seemed to rise and fall in hope, but she subdued it with a shudder and stiffened herself. 'Tha's got thyself a reet oily tongue, Mister O'Reardon,' she managed to say with a straight face. 'A'm not some tender-hearted, flighty young thing that thou can worm thy way around wi' a few choice compliments.'

His warm, open face crumpled slightly. 'Now heaven defend me, I only speak the truth, Mrs Wright. Surely I am not to be condemned for telling a woman what I see in her?' He looked down and some of the spirit seemed to fade from him. 'I have walked a goodly way today and have little to live on at the moment, dat's the God's own truth, so I am in need of a friend. If dat's not to be you, Mrs Wright, then I must try elsewhere for some charity now.'

She felt a sudden panic twist her insides. She looked down at his coat and his boots: she could see that they were dusty and well worn. He was probably telling the truth. What could she do with him? She certainly did not want her phantom to disappear again. Her voice dropped to a breathy croak. 'Where will thou lodge tonight, then?'

He looked calmly at her. 'I was after hoping that I might find a bit of a quiet barn, with a good stock o' hay, and perhaps a kind body might bring me a blanket and some food and drink.'

He licked his lips and looked hard at her. Her heart smote her. The church clock struck in the distance as if it recognised its cue. Time was a threat, foreshortened and hungry. She must act. She forced herself to think, but at the same time she was getting flustered. Territory and landmarks were unfamiliar here. Her heart was thundering: she wondered how many people could hear it.

'Barn's locked,' she mumbled. Then something settled coldly inside her. 'Meet me there as soon as it's dark.' She faced him now. 'Can a trust you?' she asked.

'I think we are after knowing each other quite well already and I feel comfortable together,' he said soothingly. 'Isn't it always the way that there cannot be real trust until we have put each other to the test? And you won't know that, until we now take this friendship a stage further. But I would not want to be hurting you, Mrs Wright, so I wouldn't. Why should I? My brother's not here and between you and I, well, he was the problem last time. Me, I'm just trying to do right for my family, but it's not so easy as you might tink.'

She could not tell if this was just a subtle evasion or something deeper, but she had no time to argue and she lacked the willpower. 'Don't let me down, Dermot O'Reardon.' She turned away, but he caught her arm and held her gently.

'Trying to escape already, is it? And I don't even know your first name.'

She swayed a little giddily and told him. Then she pulled free and moved up off the street to join Hetty and get through the afternoon as best she could.

The weather eased. Time limped by. George was surly and grumbled through his meal. Then he went out early, saying he was "off t'Hill for an hour". She knew that that usually meant two or three hours. In a mental fog, not focusing at all on the consequences of her actions, but simply on the planning of them, she got herself ready: blankets, lanterns, food, drink and keys were secured and discreetly bundled into an outhouse.

As the light began to fade, she made an excuse of visiting the next farm and slipped out up the lane, grabbing her bulky load as she went and concealing it as best she could, praying that no one saw her.

At the gate to the field she hesitated. The walk across the barren field would be exposed, even in this dim light, so she dropped her bundles behind the wall and hurried nervously round the side of the field and then scurried across to the barn. Would he be there? Her heart was beating rapidly and she felt shaky and insubstantial: like a dry reed flexed by the wind.

The barn door was slightly recessed, but there, in the murky shadows, was his huddled figure, wrapped in a long black coat and muffler, his hat pulled low; but the smile was as bright as ever. She did not speak, but pulled out the key and hurriedly unlocked the door and stepped inside. He followed. It was gloomy and damp. He stepped towards her and she slipped into his arms. His lips, cold to the initial touch, sought hers and pressed into her softly and subtly, and then more forcefully began to search for her. They drew together in a bulky embrace that nevertheless roused her powerfully, but she broke away and smilingly sent him off for the bundle.

'Let's get us organised, eh?' she said. 'Before we forget summat.' She watched him go.

So this is how it is, she thought. This is how you set aside your husband for another man. She thought of George sitting, morose and dull, in the back room of the Hill Inn. He was like a shadow of a man to her, the man she had once loved and given herself to, but he had slipped past her and gone and he seemed so unaware of her now. Or had she sidestepped him and moved herself away? She tried to examine her feelings further, but could not get beyond her own pulse and fingertips and the trembling of the moment. It was as if she were possessed. She wanted to dance and spin. She felt excitement and need and wanted what she felt she had been denied. Now, she would have it and not hold back. She felt it was her right. It was the gift of the time, the gift of Batty Green. The railway, with disruption and ferment, had sowed the seed of her discontent and now would come the harvest. She would ride the beast of this passion and ride it hard. And so she did.

She stayed with Dermot for an hour. They bedded down in the loft, rolling naked and passionate at last in the scratchy blankets on a thick bed of fragrant hay, with only the rats to witness their coupling; coiling and twisting, unabashed.

Afterwards, almost tentatively, he reminded her that he had to leave the next day. She did not speak for a while and then quietly withdrew and began to get dressed. She would not think of that, not yet. She held herself tight, as if putting on her clothes made her again a responsible woman, and then she stood still and watched him as he eagerly bit into a chunk of cold beef and drank the beer she had carried sloppily in a bottle. She told him how to leave the barn, where to put things and how he must wait for her in an alleyway behind the shop the next day, to which he agreed.

'Aren't we after making a lovely couple,' he said after she had given him his instructions. 'Not only are we surely the most beautiful people in the northern half of England, but we are quite practical, the way we are planning here, in the darkness of the night.'

She watched him as calmly as she could. She did not know him, but he already seemed a shadowy part of her, a hidden part that she had only just discovered. Yet, this might be their last meeting! She might never see him again. He seemed unaware as he chewed busily and swallowed. She noted how hungry and how absorbed in himself he was. Her mouth turned down and now he had stopped eating, he noticed and came striding over to her: naked, with bits of hay in his beard and one piece twined in his pubic hair, like a ribbon. He held her tight. She opened her old coat and drew him in, running her hands wonderingly down his back and cupping his hard buttocks. He murmured in her ear.

'Isn't it long the nights are, to be on your own and missing those you care for. It will be a mean parcel of time till I see you again, Emily. Be brave and maybees the time will slide by, like the foxy litle divil it is, a litle more nimbly.'

She had no idea what he was saying, but she loved the mazy rhythms of his speech and his damp breath in her ear. She went home quietly, not knowing whether to laugh or cry, and could not sleep for several hours. George sank into a whisky sodden sleep beside her and snored monstrously.

The next day, everything close to her seemed a little remote. She followed routine, travelling up to the shop and making a point of not stopping to look wonderingly at the barn, as she wanted to. She smiled and chatted and worked, but not for long. What she mostly wanted was to be on her own. She achieved it at last, lingering aimlessly to brood, to daydream, to soak herself in the memories of his body, his touch, his smell. It was as if she had been drunk. She lived again through a hazy recall of their lovemaking and what she could put together of the words and gestures of the day before and all the time she wanted to chase the clock and urge it to move faster. She could not think or plan beyond their next meeting, if and when it happened.What would she do if he were not there?

At last, the late afternoon sun began to dip and time unhooked its talons from her skin and allowed her to move. She hid the day's takings, locked the door and stepped out nervously. She walked blindly and held her breath.What if …? But there he was, just as instructed! His smile wiped the doubts from her mind and made her tingle. She walked excitedly up to him as he waited just behind her shop, where the horse was tethered. He made to move forwards as if to embrace her, but she quickly frowned and stiffened.

'Not here,' she mumbled. 'Too many people around.'

Indeed, a steady flow of navvies and various women and children were moving around, carts were passing and someone waved and shouted her name, but she could not tell who it was. Was it Bella? She glanced around. It looked like Bella, but she was moving away from them. Emily wondered if Bella would approve and the thought intrigued her, but then she dismissed it. There could only be one focus for her now. She forced herself to stand calmly and ask the question that had been rehearsed a hundred times in her head that day.

'So th'art moving on now, Mr O'Reardon?' She sounded formal and false and she coloured at her clumsiness. But he smiled broadly and warmly at her and her bones threatened to melt. He moved closer.

'Well, Mrs Wright, I've a mind, actually, to stay a wee while more: certainly one more night. That is, if I can persuade my landlady to look kindly upon a poor travelling man, as needs succour and sustenance, and other ... more ... personal attentions. Are you in the way o' tinkin' that the lady might grant me this little favour?'

He raised one eyebrow and tilted his head at her. She wanted to laugh at his ridiculous gestures and then cry. She knew that her brain had gone to water and was aware that her mouth might have sagged open. Then, she jolted upright as she finally took in all of what he had said and her heart soared. Oh yes, she would let him. And she would have him again!

They looked at each other, carving a moment's intensity from the flux of the late afternoon. She was about to set out how and when they would meet, when she became aware that her name was called again, from nearby this time. It was definitely Bella. Emily could pick her out, even among the steady procession of people coming down the path now from Jericho: the tall, distinctive figure, with Bane lolloping along beside her, and there was another woman with her that Emily did not recognise. Dermot followed Emily's gaze and waited for her to speak.

She was never certain why she did it, except that her instinct was to conceal what could never be public, but she quickly thrust the keys of the shop into his hand and told him to wait inside for her. He moved quietly and silently away and she stayed to talk with Bella for five minutes and meet one of Bella's new friends, a rather downtrodden, unhealthy-looking woman, who said nothing. Bella explained that Ruby had been beaten by her husband and that she was "spending some time away from the man, while she gave some consideration to her future". Emily could not focus and so the conversation soon faltered. She found Bella looking closely at her.

'Is everything alright, Emily?' she asked.

'Aye. It's just that a'm a bit worn out, you know, with new folk at t'farm an' t'extra work an' all.'

Bella again fixed her with an attentive eye. 'And who was the dark-haired young man that slipped off when we came along?'

'Oh. Just a customer as owed me some money and says he'll see me right later.' Her brain seemed to be lagging behind her tongue. She realised what she had said and the clumsy, unbidden words made her blush.

Bella just smiled and shook her head gently. 'I always said that you were one of the most interesting people I have ever met. I now realise that you are also quite mysterious at times.'

Getting no further response, except a look of embarrassment, Bella moved on and Emily waited until she was out of sight, before quickly returning to the shop. She closed the door hurriedly behind her. It was already gloomy inside. Then his voice came. 'Lock the door. The key's just in the lock there.'

She locked it and as she did so, he lit a lantern. He was in the back room. Amused and a little uncertain, she lifted the counter flap and went through. He was sitting on her old battered couch, his coat was off and his shirt undone. He stood and held out his arms to her. How she loved his lithe movement, his slender, elegant form and the burning light in his blue-grey eyes, like glinting metal. He almost growled at her.

'Come here. Have I told you today that you are a real sight of joy; you must be the most beautiful woman in Batty Green. I've thought o' nothing but you all the livelong day and I am after tinkin' that I cannot wait another moment till I get my hands on you.'

Somehow, she had glided to him, his hands slid to her hips, pulling her close, and his mouth was on her neck. She threw back her head, closed her eyes and felt how good it was to be alive.

Later, as she dressed, he surprised her by giving her back the key to the barn, saying that he had met some Irish friends and they had offered him a bed for the night in their hut at Sebastopol. 'It's probably as well that I don't hang around the farm too much,' he said.

She bit off some disappointment and they agreed to meet again the following afternoon. He was jaunty and whistled as she dressed. She was disheartened that he should seem to be happy to be parting from her so soon. He was like a subtle animal, she decided as she watched him. Like a dog fox, perhaps, sharp and adaptable and always on the hunt. She began to feel a sense of alarm and foreboding. But he was sweet and loving in his caresses and her doubts slid quickly away, like ice down a waterfall.

'I tink we should look around for a regular bed for our next meeting,' he said, holding her face and sucking softly on one of her ear lobes. 'There's so much of you that I have an urgent desire to explore.' He was mobile and insistent: every contact sending rolls of heat and energy flooding through her as she craved him once more.

In the end, having dressed for a second time, she reluctantly pushed him out of the shop into the darkening lane and slowly tried to put her mind, body and business back into some kind of order. Afterwards, she put out the lantern and sat dreamily on the couch, aware of the smell of him, the taste of him in her mouth, feeling again his lips and tongue slowly circling over her, puckering her nipples, nuzzling through her pubic hair, making patterns on the slopes of her thighs. She felt bruised by passion, altered, her joints dishevelled from his touch and yet so warm and hungry she wanted to call him back and do it all again.

But, after a while, hearing a sudden shout outside and beginning to register the sounds of the camp around her, she shook herself awake and began to move. She relit the lamp and prepared to leave. It was then, in a moment that coldly jarred her whole consciousness, that she found that all her takings for that week had gone; every single coin. She searched and searched again, her temper rising, her nerves jangling now with unease and her bile rising within her as she saw how completely she had been taken in and betrayed.

The money had been tucked away in a canvas bag, inside a biscuit tin at the back of the bottom shelf beneath her counter. He must have done a thorough search to find it and must have done it whilst she was talking to Bella! She pictured it in her head. Having taken her money, he must have brought the lamp to hand ready, removed his coat, loosened his shirt and sat back and waited for her in the dark. He had her money and he would have her body, too! She could just imagine his smug smile and a licking of lips: the foxy devil, indeed. How pleased he must have been to have found such a willing, nay eager and simple victim.

She had given it all to him, without a pause for thought. She sat for a while in humiliation and disbelief and then she hung her head and cried bitter tears. It was night outside now and she was late. Again, she rallied, buttoned herself up, made her way home and told no one, but slept with shame making sour puddles in her heart.

Light and Shade
Winter 1871

The next day, they were late getting to the shop on a cold, featureless morning at Batty Green and she was grateful that her cherub Joshua helped her unload, tether the horse and get set up. Then she sent him and his lad off on their rounds. Without Ethel to help, the first hour was busy every day. Some of her regulars were already waiting and she busied herself dealing with the first group and putting everything tidy.

After a restless night, she had resolved not to brood on Dermot O'Reardon today. She was fortunate that way. She had the capacity to suppress unpleasant thoughts, provided she was busy. She hoped to draw an immediate and heavy curtain over what she had done and what she had become, resolutely locking down the memories and the hurt, at least for now. She did not enjoy being taken for a giddy fool, a silly girl swept away by the young man's good looks and an easy prey to his willing hands. She would face this later, when the ache and the memory had faded a little. Now, she created for herself the image of a box, with a lid, and she carried it hidden inside her. And in the box he went, just for now, and all that they had said and done, as the lid was pushed on tight.

In the throes of these thoughts she was doubly shocked, therefore, when he suddenly walked in, leaned on the counter and smiled his roguish smile. 'I'm after getting on my way this fine day, Mrs Wright, and I wanted to see you. And how is it you are today?' She could not frame a response, but stood and stared, as if at a painted devil. He went on, a little more nervously. 'I wanted to thank you for your very open and obliging assistance these last few days.'

Her anger swept her forwards, her face contorted and confused, and to her immense annoyance there were tears in her eyes. He drew himself upright and raised a placatory hand, hurrying his words. 'Hear me out. now. There's a joy to see you so full of life and spirit. You truly are a very fine and spirited woman, but ...' he raised his hand again and held the counter down tight with the other, as she threatened to lift the flap and throw herself at him, 'you will not see me again, that I promise, and I can understand you being a little disappointed with me, just at the end there, though I am sure you'll be agreeing wi' me that you were willing enough up to that point, at least to my way o' tinkin'. In fact, I'd go so far as to say that you were after me like an old weasel tracing a rat.'

Again she fought to get at him, but he held on hard to the counter flap. 'But I admit the loss of the money may have been a hard blow. Try to understand that I need it for the wee lad that I am to fetch, as the little man needs a doctor and some special care, or so I am told. And there's me old da, back in County Mayo, as is a trial and a burden and is away wi' the fairies the livelong day. And me brother is locked up again for poaching rabbits, would you believe. So it's none so easy for me to take the more regular kind o' work. I am not truly made for toiling, moiling, digging from the dawn till dusk, with never the sight of a pretty woman or a fine bit o' horse flesh to cheer me.'

She hesitated, cooling a little, breathing heavily. What was he after now? He went on, more coldly, more hurriedly, staring intently at her.

'And so I am after asking you to find me, well, shall we say, just another five pounds, before two o'clock this day, just for the laddie, you know. And if you don't have it ready, well, then I shall just have to get someone to call down at the farm later and have a word wi' your good man George about it. Tell him that you truly promised it to me when you were in the way o' undressin' me last evening and begging for me to pull your clothes off. I can't quite recall whether that may have been the first time that we did it, or was it the second, when we were on the floor, or perhaps the night before, in the barn? Well, George will be able to sort out the order o' things, I've no doubt.'

He paused and stared at her. She hated him now, with his cruel, mercenary appetites, and knowing this she could stand more calmly, waiting for him to finish. He sensed her hardening. 'I hope that you are understanding me, Mrs Wright. You and I need to help each other still. I can't have you walking the world telling out your story now, can I? I'll have to get my version out there first and I will, by the elements and stars of night. And I'll shame you if I have to.'

'Get out,' she said, shocked and seething.

'I will be back at two o'clock, Mrs Wright. Oh, and no excuses for not paying: no lies, no blather. I have no doubt that you can lay your hands on a few pounds when you need to. And no tricks, no traps, please. I will have a couple o' my friends from County Mayo just outside, in case o' any bother. Either you pay up or you and your husband get hurt and you'll get the reputation of a very immoderate woman of noted misbehaviour, with a liking for a bit o' rough wi' a travellin' tinker, if you get my meaning. Don't let me down now.' And with a tilt to his hat and another bright flash of his teeth, he was gone.

Emily slumped over the counter, put her head in her hands and began to heave breath back into her lungs. She wanted to cry or scream. But a mother and small child came bustling in just then and she had to quickly turn away and set herself straight. The door opening brought the sound of a steam whistle and the shouts of a ganger to his men. There was a clatter of iron against stone. Wheels kept turning and the work went on.

She sold eggs and butter to her customers, almost without speaking, and somehow found herself alone again. She shut the shop and retreated, sitting disconsolate on the couch in the storeroom. She felt ill. The floor was slipping and sliding. She was losing her balance and she could not focus. The box had failed; the demon had escaped and was going to hurt her.

She thought of George and how he would react. He would be humiliated and ashamed of her. But he would be wounded, too, and she did not want that. In black self-pity, she could also imagine what heavy moral judgements he would make. But what would he do? She hung her head and tears dripped from her nose and made dark splashes in the sawdust at her feet. She had to stop Dermot. She would have to find the money and hope that it would be enough for now. But he might return and ask for more and more. For now, she could think of nothing better. She had to act quickly and plan later and she could not act alone. That thought stirred her. She remembered the anger that had saved her before. She had to find it again, fix it on Dermot and harden herself to her shame.

Soon, she was on her feet. She unlocked the door, looked around outside and found a couple of lads playing nearby. She called them over, wrote quick notes and sent the boys on errands to find Ethel and

Robert and ask them to meet her at Bella's hut. She then went to Bella. She found her at home and after a gush of heavy tears, she began to tell her what had happened. Her luck continued to hold. Ethel arrived and agreed to look after the shop, until Emily returned just before two o'clock. Emily sent her off and within minutes, Robert arrived, in his work clothes, but bright and eager to help. Her hopes soared.

Years later, she would always recall that hour at Bella's as a turning point. After some initial embarrassment, she found it possible to tell them both what she had done and they seemed to understand. And if they judged her in the wrong, they did not say so. Robert and Bella seemed to quickly settle to liking and trusting each other and Emily lapsed into the warm arms of their care. They even found room to laugh amid their pondering. Bella loaned her the five pounds and would return with her to the shop, sending Ethel away early. Robert would go to get changed and arrange some time off. Then he would return and hide in the back room. Later, he would follow Dermot and make sure that he did not return. Emily thanked them both and almost without thinking added, 'I owe you both so much. How can I ever repay you?'

There was a pause as the three looked at each other.

'Well, my dear gal,' Bella smiled. 'You know what I want from you. The time is come for you to get me down to Elterbeck Farm.'

'I will,' Emily promised.

Robert, unaware of the background to this, simply smiled. 'A'm leaving in a few weeks,' he reminded her, and her heart lurched to see the shadow that came over him as he said it. Then he added, with rather a lewd and knowing look, 'I can think o' summat you could do for me before you leave.' Something moved inside her. They both coloured, but not awkwardly. It was a natural request and she did not resent it. It had always been there between them.

'You could both do worse,' said Bella, at which they all laughed conspiratorially and a little nervously.

Dermot arrived after two o'clock, pushing the door open cautiously, peering in, crouched and suspicious. He had his black coat unbuttoned, with a white scarf tied round his neck and his familiar soft black hat angled over his handsome face. Emily was standing behind the counter, Bella was sitting in a corner just behind her and Robert was within hearing inside the storeroom. Emily drew herself up, pushed out her chest and challenged him brazenly. He would not see her cowed again!

'So tha's come creeping back in, like a bad smell. Well, stand up, man, what ails thee? Lost tha nerve?'

'Nay. I was just after checking that all was well. I see you've a friend there with you.' He nodded towards Bella, who remained impassive. 'I've got a couple o' my lads here, too.' He stepped back and turned to call behind him. 'Michael, will you be coming to hold the door now, please.'

They heard boots clatter on the steps and a squat, heavily bearded man in breeks, a short blue jacket and a tall hat took the door without a word and wedged himself in the doorway. 'That feels better, now we're both in the way o' havin' a friend with us,' said Dermot, moving towards the counter. 'I'm hopeful that you have found that wee sum o' money that we talked about for the little lad, cos then I can be on me way, so to speak, without any further disturbance o' your time, Mrs Wright.'

He raised his hat a fraction and again inclined his head in the briefest of bows. He had a neat, square frame, with long legs. He turned slightly, opening his chest and setting his legs astride, as if reminding her of what she had enjoyed. The smile flashed at her, but she remained stony. Yet, a small part of her still liked to see the contours of his body and found his attentions flattering. She found her anger beginning to melt and stopped herself at once.

She spoke coldly and stared him in the eye. 'Thou art a common thief and a cheat, with no more conscience than this bit o' bench,' she said, bringing her fist down on the counter top hard enough to make him flinch. 'If it were not for the feelings of others and that they might get hurt, a would gladly see thee put in Wakefield Prison. And how many other poor women have you tret like me an' then robbed them when they were looking t'other way?'

A smile of collusion crossed his face, but was chased away by a sour grimace, as if in that moment he decided that she was no longer worth the effort. With this, she began to see that his charms could be switched on and off at will. Now, he no longer kept up any pretence, but cut bluntly to the point.

'I'm hardly thinking that I need to take any lessons in morality or proper behaviour from the likes o' you, Mrs Wright. You were quicker and easier out o' your clothes than many a dirty whore I've been with.' Emily recoiled and felt Bella's sharp intake of breath behind her. He went on briskly. 'Now, the money, if you please, and this unpleasant conversation can come to an end. Do you happen to have it or don't you?'

'Aye,' she replied, feeling more in control now. 'A've your brass, tha filthy Irish worm. But tha's needing to give me some reason to believe that tha won't be back for more o' the same'

'I give you my word,' he said with a smile and leaned forwards, much closer towards her, unable to let the moment pass without reminding her of what had existed between them. 'I may have stolen from you,' he said, 'but I have never lied, especially when I told you how desirable you were. Neither will I ever forget.'

She replied, with a cold, glimmering smile. 'A'd sooner stick thistles in my eyes than ever see the likes o' a heathen like you again. A may have lost my senses for a while, but a'm no fool, so save your greasy words for others, before a tek ma fingernails to your face.' He stood up and they stared with mutual hostility. 'Now,' she went on, pulling a Bible from beneath the counter, 'in front of these two witnesses, swear on this Bible, in the name of the holy church and the blessed Virgin Mary, that tha will niver return here again.'

He took the Bible from her, kissed it and placed it between both hands. 'I swear,' he said, smiling all the time, and then held out his hand. She passed him a bag of coins from beneath the counter. He dropped the Bible, turned on his heels and suddenly he and his friend were gone.

Even before his footsteps had died way, Robert came bustling out and positioned himself at the side of the door, wanting a glimpse of Dermot. 'Is that him? Slim, with a long coat and white scarf, walks wi' a bit of a dainty strut?' He pointed and Emily came forwards and followed his line of sight.

'Aye,' she said, observing Dermot hurrying away, with his squat companion. 'He said the other man wor called Michael. A see he only has one supporter. Look, 'appen they're arguing.'

Bella came forwards also and they all watched, as well as they could. Luckily, other bodies were moving busily along the pathway and this meant that Dermot and Michael were forced to stand a little way out of the flow of people, in clearer view. It did, indeed, look as if a disagreement was taking place. Then, Dermot handed over some coins from Emily's bag and the two men split up, Dermot heading away towards the turnpike road to Hawes.

'This suits me fine,' said Robert. 'A'll be away.' Emily put out her hand and held his arm tightly.

'Don't get hurt,' she said. 'A can repay the brass. A just don't want him coming back.'

Robert nodded and moved away in the weak afternoon light. He bustled along the busy pathway, making the best speed he could, but got to the clearing beside the reading room and could see no sign of Dermot in any direction. He reckoned that the young man would probably have to collect a few belongings before setting out, but was unlikely to stay at Batty Green, at least not with Emily in such a volatile mood. Robert circled the area for a while, checking the paths and tracks, specially alert for any carts or wagons going towards Dent, but there was no sign of the young man. A mist was drawing in as the light faded further. Whernside and Ingleborough had long disappeared from sight, but now, looking up, Robert could not even see the top of the scaffolding on the first few piers of the viaduct, where carpenters were beginning to form the frames for the arches. If he did not find Dermot soon, then he would lose any chance of following him. He had to choose, just as Dermot did. Assuming his story to Emily had some truth in it, would he go to Dent via Blea Moor or would he take the longer journey by road? In these conditions, and perhaps hoping to get a lift, surely he would take the road? Robert pulled his coat, hat and scarf tightly in place and set off across to the turnpike. If necessary, he would walk to Dent and find him there.

Gearstones
Winter 1871

A few people were moving along the turnpike road, heads down in the cool, damp air, and a few heavy carts were lumbering along. Nothing suggested itself as a likely hiding place for the tall, slim Irishman. Of course, Robert could have missed him; he might be some way ahead. He hurried, striding briskly along, scanning the road and the countryside in the fading light. Then, suddenly, he saw a figure emerge across country from his left, from the east, perhaps cutting over from Belgravia. It was him alright and still on his own, a bag slung over his shoulder.

He joined the road a few hundred yards ahead of Robert and turned north, towards Hawes and the junction with the road to Dent. Robert walked faster, wanting to close the gap a little, but not to come alongside him, until they were in quieter country. He settled to his new pace, thought of Emily and how this might all work out and grinned to himself comfortably, but suddenly Dermot dipped down off the road and disappeared into the Gearstones Inn. Robert cursed. This would slow him up.

Gearstones was a popular inn. For generations, its passing trade had been the monks, merchants, farmers, traders and itinerants passing from the valleys of the Ribble and the Lune to the valleys of the Swale or the Ure, continuing on by various routes across to the Great North Road or the Yorkshire coast. Moreover, every year there was a big cattle fair on the adjoining fell, with drovers bringing herds from Scotland and all over the north. So Gearstones was built to survive bustle and to accommodate workingmen and travellers, meeting their needs. Now, it was always busy, with the new migrant workers – the navvies or others connected to the railway workings in one way or another – and so the ale continued to flow, the fires burned and food could be had at any hour. Robert knew the place well. There was one large main room, with trestle tables, benches and a large fireplace. Beyond that was a large kitchen, where the ale was drawn and food served, but also a favoured drinking haunt in its own right. Apart from the front door, the only exit was through the back kitchen, which was usually the sole domain of an irritable woman known as Doll, fat and greasy and with a foul tongue.

Robert knew at once that Dermot would have to come out the way he went in. He followed him in and saw that there were about fifteen men sat round in the main room and no sign of Dermot. Robert went on into the large flagged kitchen beyond, where another group were sat near the large, open stove, and here he saw the young Irishman already ensconced in a corner, a bottle of whisky and a pipe on the table in front of him, pulling tobacco from a twist and obviously settled for a while. He paid no attention to Robert, who guessed that the young man felt safe here from any pursuit. Robert ordered some ale and retreated to sit near the front door.

All was quiet for a while. Robert found himself drawn into conversation with a shabby young navvy, with badly blistered feet, who was stretched out on one of the benches nearby. He introduced himself as John Butcher, a navvy who was making his way north to Carlisle to find work and to look for a "wench that he wor fond of". It was a navvy tradition to help anyone that was "on the tramp", so Robert bought him a quart of ale and gave him a shilling for food. John dragged his boots on and was about to go into the large kitchen to order something, when a confused shouting broke out from inside. Both men paused and listened. There was the noise of men moving clumsily, knocking into furniture and a shout to someone called Cheshire. There was some laughter and then a slurred voice saying, 'Gi' us some o' t'whisky or I'll blow the bloody house down.'

Then there came the voice of Alice Yates, the landlord's daughter, telling someone to, 'Shut up and sit down, ya drunken fool.'

Robert and John moved over to the doorway to peer in. He could just see Dermot, still in his corner seat, a nervous smile on his face. The table in front of him was empty. Standing in front of the fire grate was a bulky navvy, unsteady on his feet, his shirt all undone and a red cravat tied haphazardly round his throat. He had a twist of tobacco in his hand. He must have snatched it from Dermot and another man, half slumped in the opposite corner, was clutching a bottle of whisky that looked to be empty. Others had pushed away from the fire, either to get out of the way or to just to watch the fun, and several were clearly the worse for drink.

The man in the middle swayed again and turned to the one in the corner and again shouted, 'Gi' us some o' t'whisky, Cheshire.'

Cheshire Cat, to give him his full navvy title, waved the bottle back. 'S'empty, George, s'empty, me old pal. Ask nice Paddy for another one.'

It was obvious that Dermot, who was probably celebrating his recent winnings, had been generously passing round the strong drink. He now rose to his feet and announced that he would be, 'Moving on, gentlemen, having a ways to go tonight,' whereupon he thanked them for their company.

Robert was about to step back out of sight, when George, in the centre, grabbed Dermot's arm and said, almost formally, and with slow, deliberate elocution, 'Have you hever had the pleasure of using dynamite?'

Dermot laughed aloud and shook his head. Others grinned and stamped their feet and there was much nodding and nudging. Nobody had any idea what the man intended, but it was likely to bring a laugh.

'Stand there,' said the drunken George, pushing Dermot into the space near the door, within a foot of Robert, and blocking most of his view. 'Watch now!' he shouted, almost militarily.

Then, the drunkard pulled a tin out of his pocket and took from it two cigar-shaped cylinders, deftly wrapped them in tobacco paper and with an almost whimsical sway and flourish, as if conducting an orchestra, he threw them into the fire.

Robert had seen enough to know the danger. In one swift reflex, he instinctively grabbed Dermot by the scruff of his neck and pulled him backwards, ducking behind the wall separating the two rooms. The blast hit them, throwing them to the floor, rocking the whole house and sending shards from the metal grate flying in all directions. Dust and debris rolled around and billowed out of windows, whose glass had now been shattered. There were loud cries, groans, coughing and spluttering and a dog that had been asleep near the fire howled and whined. Robert had fallen with Dermot half on top of him and he quickly pulled himself free and dragged the young man to a seated position.

Dermot's face was blackened and he had minor cuts but appeared unhurt otherwise. Robert felt that the air had changed rapidly in his lungs to a gritty soup and his eyebrows and tufts of grey hair had been singed: his fingers wandered curiously over the short, crisp textures, but he was not aware of any other damage. Inside the shattered kitchen came moans of injured men and a distant crying, but there was movement, too, the crunching of glass and cinders underfoot as people began to pull themselves up and others pushed in to help. He heard Alice Yates asking men how they were: she was obviously unhurt. Robert looked behind him. The young navvy was sitting on a bench, none the worse for the blast but looking confused. Robert called him over. 'John. It wor a drunk called George that caused that. Mek sure that he don't get away. He's a big lad, wi' a red scarf round his neck. Have a look in there and see how he is.' John pushed through and in a few moments came back dragging George, bleeding but still alive and groaning. 'Get landlord to tie 'im up till police arrive,' Robert ordered. 'Then see who else needs help.'

Robert looked again at the young Irishman, who seemed to be in a complete daze. Robert was bitter. He looked around at the mess in the Gearstones, thought of the injuries that some would have, then added the misery heaped upon Emily and felt a surge of pure hatred. Trouble seemed to follow this Irish dandy. Robert had possibly just saved his life, or at least saved him from serious injury, and he now wondered why. He grabbed Dermot, pulled him suddenly to his feet and leaned in very close.

'Tha's one or two bits of behaviour to answer for. We'll have a wee chat outside.' Then, raising his voice more publicly, he went on, 'Let's get you out into the fresh air, young man,' he said. And without more ado, but without relaxing the firm grip on Dermot's upper arm, he pushed the dazed young man outside, where others were also gulping in the cold clear air or talking in confused groups. He kept walking, his captive blundering along beside him, and slipped away into the night.

Within an hour, Robert was returning cheerfully to Batty Green, most of Emily's money recovered and jingling in his coat pocket. Dermot O'Reardon had been left beside the road about a mile from the Gearstones. He was nursing broken ribs and swollen testicles and he had lost a couple of front teeth. The message he had received and understood very clearly was that his name and description would be widely circulated at Batty Green as a common thief, a trickster who preyed on women, led them on with lies and then took whatever he could get from them. If he ever returned, he would be beaten on sight and without mercy.

Robert whistled as he walked. He was hoping for a warm welcome back from Emily, despite his crisp eyebrows and sooty face. He was going to make the most of his last few weeks at Batty Green.

Oatcakes

Early 1872

The New Year came in wet and stormy. Emily felt that she needed to keep to herself for a while and she now gave Hetty more responsibility, sending her out most days to run the shop.

'A new year, a new life,' Emily murmured to herself.

She felt that the centre of her universe had shifted. The turbulent times of the early winter, characterised in their different ways by Dermot and by Robert, still absorbed her, her body still felt shaped by their touch and her womanhood was confirmed and strong. She regretted nothing. She told herself that she had not acted out of selfish need or wanton lust, but to assuage, to pacify her restless spirit once and for all, to smooth away the jagged peaks of her personality and to remake herself in a more homely form. Now, she could be a better wife and help fulfil the lives of others as well as her own. So she devoted more attention to George, urged him to stay in with her, urged him to bed with her and was patient, winsome and comfortable.

Then, in the middle of the month, she returned to Bella and they planned, prepared and calculated. The pregnancy was still in its early stages and they agreed that a few weeks more would be time enough to break the news to George. Emily wanted to do this herself, in her own time. What they planned was for Emily to insist that in due time, Bella deliver the child at Elterbeck. They hoped that George would be so delighted by the news that he would agree to any demands that Emily made. Once Bella was accepted at Elterbeck, she would make her own decision about how and when to reveal her true identity to George.

George was half conscious that he was being manipulated. He knew Emily well enough to know that she rarely acted without some calculation. He had always loved her vitality. As a young man, he thought of himself, with stubborn pride, as something of a bystander, an interested observer of life's heady currents, but one who would take great care before entering the water. Had he not met Emily, he would almost certainly have remained a quiet and isolated dales farmer, rugged, stoical and unadventurous. But Emily had swept him along, compelled and cajoled him into looking over and beyond his own drystone walls, and then the building of the railway had altered more than his landscape. It had exposed him to ideas, behaviour, attitudes and opportunities that challenged him and had threatened to defeat him. But he had seen it through. And he was different now. He was negotiating to buy a second farm. He might become church warden. He had plans for a new farmhouse. He was looking outwards more, going his own way, and Emily had for so long seemed intent on pursuing her own path that he had only recently decided to fight her no longer. Yet now, just as he saw a road of his own, she seemed to be pulling back suddenly, wrapping herself around him, asking him questions, returning to church with him, taking back her kitchen and some control of the farm. Yet, he loved her still and so he cautiously lapsed into the warmth of the new cocoon she was spinning. There was peace. There was solace. But he was watchful all the same.

Pondering over all this, there came a day when he asked for oatcakes. Emily had always disliked them, but in the early days of their marriage she had made them in the traditional way just to please him. At that time, he said it reminded him of being a boy and the young wife was sufficiently amused by the novelty to humour her husband.

Sometimes, in those early days, alone in the isolated farmhouse in their first harsh winter, they even made oatcakes together, snatching kisses and wrapping arms round each other as they prepared the ingredients. She would spread the oatmeal on a riddle board and together they would mix the batter, often getting floury fingers entwined in hair or clothing. They had giggled and panted as they'd stirred, then they had poured it onto a linen cloth and had taken turns in throwing pieces onto a hot back-stone or at each other. Then, flushed with heat, they would retreat to the old rocking chair and she would sit on his lap, whereupon the chair would groan and grind on the flagstones, as they had writhed in each other's arms, the fire would smoke and the oatcakes would sometimes burn.

So that now, one cold evening in late January, when George banked up the fire, smiled at her in something like the old way and demanded oatcakes, she laughed at his coy grimace and seized the moment. They were rarely quite so spontaneously amorous now, but she made sure that she rekindled some of that earlier sense of fun, flicking oatmeal at him and rubbing against him as he joined her to stir the batter.

'Mek a wish,' she said as she covered his hands with hers on the old wooden thibble as they stirred. She kissed his rough gingery cheek. 'Tell me what tha's wished,' she demanded when the oatcakes were smoking on the back-stone.

'Nay. A'll niver tell thee.' He retreated to the rocking chair and spoke with a forced solemnity, belied by a turning down of the corners of his mouth that she knew meant he wanted it teasing out of him.

'Well then, a'll just stay well out o' yor way until tha reconsiders,' she replied, with an arch look and a sway of the hips as she turned to sit at the table and pretended to be studying an old newspaper there.

He drummed his fingers on the arm of the chair for a few moments and then relented. 'A'll tell thee half if tha'll sit on mi lap and t'other half if a'm gettin' a proper kiss,' he said. She skipped over to him and wriggled herself with blatant heaviness onto him. He groaned. 'Tha's getten a bit more weight than tha used to 'ave,' he said, wrapping his arms around her waist.

Her heart skipped, she felt her cheeks glow and for a moment she was lost for words. She played for time. 'Complaining, Mr Wright?' she responded, putting on a false and rather severe upper-class accent to cover the agitation that had startled her. 'Now, I do believe we have a deal. Your wish, please.'

He looked at her thoughtfully, a little taken aback by her sudden flush and the change of mood. He wanted to work her back to her previous warmth and flippancy and brought his hand up to her face and gently pinched her cheek. 'Ah wished that you and I might be always happy together and mek oatcakes reg'lar, like.'

She felt herself becoming fidgety and on edge, but fought down the nervous tremors that were rippling through her. Her voice died as she looked down into his eyes. She croaked, 'Just you and me?'

His eyes widened and she felt his breathing shorten, his arms go rigid, as he stared at her. 'Who else did tha think o' includin'?' he asked.

'Oh, no one tha knows.' She shifted herself to be better balanced, held his face in both hands and whispered. 'Just the child that a'm carryin'.'

She felt his whole body go rigid and dare not look at him, feeling guilt sweep over her more powerfully than ever. She kissed him eagerly, but he was passive and she felt a surge of dread. She pulled away, but saw neither anger nor disgust, just silent tears running down his cheeks. He could not speak.

'Nay,' she almost pleaded. 'Thir's no need for tears.'

'Oh, but thir is,' he finally declared. 'A think t'oatcakes are burning.'

She tried to jump up, but George, now laughing and crying, sobbing and gulping air, grabbed her arm and would not let her go. He pulled himself up clumsily and wrapped her in his arms, holding her close as he got himself under control, murmuring as he trembled, 'Dost thou think that a really care about oatcakes at a time like this?'

She waited for his next move, comforted by his embrace, grateful that there were no questions, a little nervous at the emotion unleashed. Things were developing almost as she had expected, but she was troubled as well as relieved. She had thought she had it all under control and planned out.

But then George surprised her again by wanting to give thanks in prayer. The tears still wet on his cheek, he quietly asked her to kneel with him, there in the kitchen, and she did so, a little ruefully, wondering exactly which part of her recent history could be claimed as God's work.

After a brief silence, George spoke and her confidence again wavered. There was a questioning tone in his words, hesitation and some doubt, that she felt might be directed towards her, not to his God. Making herself focus on what he was saying, she kept her head down, trying to feel for what he was feeling, see the landscape as he did. His voice was shaken with emotion.

'A pray for guidance and for summat that will sustain us this next year. Difficulties and surprises are part o' life an' we have known some that have nearly foxed us, but the news o' this baby has fair stirred me up. We give thanks, now and shall in days to come, to God for this unexpected gift of a new life. It comes timely and it's a thing that we have waited for, sometimes raising us eyes to heaven; but it's not for us to ask how God works or what his intentions might be. All new life is a miracle and a blessing that we should take in humility and share together.'

He raised his head and looked at her, but she kept a firm, devotional stance. 'A am well aware, that a've not always given the love a man should've given and in ma mind, at times, a've doubted and questioned this marriage of ours an' its ways an' drifts. But a've prayed that it would turn out reet an' a hope that now it shall an' that we can go on to create a family as we can be proud of, wi'out further ado or cause to fret. I thank thee, God.'

'Amen,' she mumbled, uncomfortably aware that she underestimated George when it suited her. She scrambled to her feet and busied herself with the oatcakes, snatching a moment to compose herself as he, too, pulled himself up and stretched, looking round as if the farmhouse itself must have changed. But finding it hadn't, he went to the old oak cupboard in the corner and pulled out a bottle of whisky and two of their best glasses.

An hour later, he was on his fifth glass and they had raced through plans, names and changes that would need to be made. He had agreed to Bella's involvement in the delivery and said she must come down soon to meet him: Emily felt another surge of satisfaction at finally winning this point and then duly gave way to him on other decisions. He was fiery and talkative one moment and almost morose the next and eventually, he had fallen silent.

She had brushed out her black hair until it spun and sparked in the firelight. She sat in an old armchair with her bare feet on the fender and opposite her he rocked slowly, hypnotically, lulled by the heat and the whisky, and studied her through half-closed lids, hooded and dark. There was something new there which he could not see, something about the half smile that seemed to brighten her eyes, the comfortable way she leaned back as if a job was done and done well. What troubled him was that it had been there for some weeks now, since Christmas at least. He felt a burning desire for her, an impatient swelling of joy in this child, but he also nurtured spasmodic unease, like a great landowner looking across his park with pride by day, made restless when the dogs barked at night by the thought of a poacher moving stealthily towards his deer.

A few weeks later, the promised visit of Bella was arranged for a Sunday afternoon. Emily had a new pony and trap, a present from her attentive husband, and she drove up to meet Bella at the old contractor's hut, which still plumed smoke skywards through its little funnel of a chimney. The day was grey, almost dark, even at noon. The wind was spasmodically dragging bursts of rain up the valley and there was an unusual quiet around Batty Green, where most people were clustered round their fires or were drinking at one of the pubs.

Everything dripped, the air was tainted by wood and peat-smoke and rotting vegetation and the cold shrivelled the marrow of older bones. A lifeless, dull light was absorbed before its time, casting dark, damp shadows behind the huts and beneath the massive timbers of the scaffolding on the piers of the viaduct, the line of them now clear across the wet basin at Ribblehead.

Bella was standing patiently beside the road, her old black umbrella tilted against the wind, Bane sitting almost on her feet. Emily drew up and watched as Bella pulled herself slowly up to the driving board, wincing with discomfort as she lifted her left leg into place, and sank back with a weary sigh. 'These winters will be the death of me,' she complained and Emily, noting the marks of ageing more clearly than ever, once again vowed to do more for this woman, to whom she owed so much. They turned and made their way back down the turnpike road, weaving around the deep ruts and potholes that the incessant movement of men, machines and animals had gouged out of the roadway, whist the wolfhound loped casually along beside them, with seeming indifference to his surroundings.

But George was no longer at home when they got to the farm. He had promised to wait in, but Hetty reported that their new shepherd had sent a message that some ewes were lambing in a distant croft and he needed some assistance, so George had gone. Nevertheless, the women settled cheerfully into the farm kitchen, taking off shawls, oilskins and wet boots, banking up the fire and making a big pan of tea to wash down thick slices of parkin spread with butter. Bane lay stretched out, one eye on the fire, the other watching the farm dogs that had uneasily given way to the visitor, but had protested with low, guttural growls and stifled whining. Bella asked about Hetty's wedding plans and then sat in the rocker, taking little further part in the conversation, but nodding and smiling, looking around attentively and glancing frequently at the door. Emily was well aware that Bella was not her usual forceful self and she could sense the difficulty that faced a neglectful mother returning home after so many years.

Hetty had just left to take some tea to James at the cottage, when George came in, wet and rather surly after standing out in a field for nearly an hour. He brought a newborn lamb whose mother had died and without a word, he handed it straight to Emily. She bustled about brightly, drying the struggling lamb on an old piece of sacking, whilst handing George a cup of tea and trying to cut him a slice of cake at the same time. He nodded at Bella when she was introduced, but seemed in no mood to stay and talk. Bella said nothing, but seeing Emily's difficulty, she reached out and took the lamb onto her lap, quickly rolled it up in the sacking and began to rock in the chair, humming to the creature as if it was a child. George looked at her and smiled, grabbed the cake from Emily and crammed it into his mouth. 'I mun get littl'un back to one of t'other ewes straight away,' he said.

'I know that's important, Mr Wright,' Bella replied, 'but finish your tea first; five minutes won't make much difference.' They looked at each other and George nodded thoughtfully. He glanced at Emily, who was watching the exchange with interest, and then he looked back at Bella again, more closely this time. There was expectation in the air: he could sense it, but not understand it. The women talked a little. A silence developed. Then a frown passed over George's face and he shook his head as if chasing away unbidden thoughts. He put down the cup, fastened his coat and pulled on his broad black hat, reached over and took the lamb tenderly into his rough, strong hands and with another nod he moved quickly out into the dark wet of the early twilight. He did not return until later in the evening, when Bella had already gone.

Emily was worried that he might have taken against the woman that was so close to him and yet so unknown, but he was cheerful over a cold supper with her later and he agreed that Sunday visits from Bella would be a good idea, especially as Emily got closer to her time. Emily went to bed early and George drew close to the fire, poured himself a whisky and sat reflectively staring at the embers. Something was not quite in place for him. He wondered if perhaps there was something that he had forgotten to do, but no matter how he shuffled his thoughts, dipping into his memories and lists of tasks, he could not satisfy his curiosity.

'A'm snagged here,' he said to himself and sitting back in the old armchair, he closed his eyes and waited. Into his head came a tune, something from childhood, he thought. He hummed a few bars, finished his drink and went to bed.

Water and Wakening
Early 1872

The cold, wet weather persisted, the downpours becoming heavier, interspersed with a light sleety rain that was relentless for a week. It sluiced off the fells, every brook and gill teeming white water, surging in full spate over boulders and through gullies, with new waterfalls glinting on hillsides that were normally grey backdrops. Every living thing seemed to sulk and cower, sinking downwards into the earth that was itself more water than anything. All the larger farm animals were under cover and the pregnant ewes brought into shelter where it could be found or made. George refused to let Emily travel to Batty Green and Joshua and Hetty took turns to run the shop, while Joshua's lad did the rounds of the huts nearby on foot, and they employed a new man to go further up the line to the tunnel huts. James was forced to sleep at Batty Green, though work on the viaduct was slow as the men were regularly ordered off the greasy scaffolding as conditions worsened.

Only below ground, in the noisy, teeming darkness of Blea Moor, was progress satisfactory as the tunnel was driven forwards from both ends and from faces between, in guttering candlelight, in damp, dirty air.

Then sleet turned to heavy snow for three days and snow turned to ice. Eventually, a slow thaw began, almost imperceptibly, and the dripping resumed; all the time, water ran steadily beneath the crust of snow, falling off the fells into the swollen becks. Lambing had begun sporadically and George worked long, anxious hours assisting the shepherd where he could. But his spirits remained high and Emily, basking in a relieved state of security and welfare, blossoming as she filled out, encouraged him to go to the Hill Inn occasionally and enjoy some well-earned relaxation.

One evening in late February, a full moon sailing out over Ingleborough and the air crisp and laced with spite, he left the Hill Inn with more ale and whisky inside him than usual and set off towards Elterbeck. Dirty snow had thawed and then refrozen and was once again beginning to soften and crumble. The moonlight glinted off hidden crystals and picked out looming silhouettes that took shape as you approached and then slipped away behind you. George rolled unsteadily along the track, chuckling sometimes as his feet slipped and mumbling sociably to himself as if he were a horse. 'Whoa, laddie, whoa. Tha's nearly slipped thir, tha knows.'

The alcohol seemed to sweep him sideways as he lurched and rebalanced and he giggled darkly as the road slid away in front of him.

'Tha's properly o'erdone it this time, laddie, now steady up or tha'll be sleepin' in stables.' He paused whilst he thought over this statement and then laughed aloud. 'But that is whir horses sleeps tha numbskull. Is tha a horse or isn't tha?' He could scarcely decide.

There now seemed to be a roaring in his ears and he shook his head absent-mindedly, but the shaking just made the fields roll dangerously into each other and made his pulse beat ever more loudly in his head.

He forced himself to stop still and focus, but now his stomach seemed to be moving uneasily. 'Oh bloody bugger, bloody bugger,' he moaned. The roaring was still there. It wasn't inside him, he decided, after a long pause, standing stock-still in the middle of the track, his head hanging down, his arms trailing by his side, swaying gently. No, the noise was up ahead. 'That's all reet then,' he concluded loudly and staggered on.

He came to the little bridge and the cause of the roar was obvious, the beck was in full spate, lapping the edges of the track and funnelling with turbulent force beneath the broad slabs of stone that made up the bridge proper. He was properly drunk now, standing with difficulty, hardly conscious of anything other than the dark swirling water, which seemed to be connected to him in a way that surprised him, as if its weighty driving rhythms were arising in his head and he could control it if he only tried. He leaned over to tell the beck to stop bubbling and dipped forwards, almost onto his knees, but then pulled back, jerking his head sharply backwards. A dull pain registered itself and his nausea belched a warning. He told himself he had had enough and he would "sort out t'beck tomorrow".

He was turning slowly and cautiously towards home, when his eye caught something white bobbing in the water, just below the bridge, where the beck broadened a little and had swept over the bank and beneath some alder trees It was a sheep in the beck, alive or dead, he could not tell in the poor light.

'A shall have to see t'poor beast,' he said to himself and moved off the bridge, clambered onto the little abutment and with no further thought, fell onto the field bank with a clumsy rolling sway. He had been expecting deep snow, but beneath the frosty white crust that had reflected the moonlight was now the frothy grey water of the beck as it seeped outwards and George found himself standing in cold running water that he could neither see nor understand.

'What the bloody hell's happening here?' he asked himself and tried to reach for the wall, but suddenly and unstoppably, his foot slid down the hidden bank, lurching into deeper water, and he spun awkwardly, his coat caught by the stream tugging him away from the bridge. He shouted and scrabbled back, floundering and shocked by the cold, but his brain was still fuddled and he could find no purchase and began to drift in a dazed wonder. And then he laughed, relaxing for a moment, enjoying the slow turning and sinking, lapsing, yielding, warm inside and frozen outside. His head felt on fire and his legs seemed to have died and now his arms were going, too.

At last, panic arose in him and he fought and splashed and struck out for the bank, yet he floundered and failed. But the slow movement of water was giving way to another rush as the beck narrowed again and now he felt himself bumping into hidden boulders and branches arched overhead in the gloom. He tried to grab them, but his arms were slow to act and his hands were numb and could not grip. He was nearly up to his neck now and getting heavier all the time. Turning again in the water, he could see a boulder coming close on his left and he kicked off it with his numb feet as best he could as he swept past, helping him move more towards the edge of the current. He knew he had to fight and not give in. His head slid under, icy water seizing his face and throat, and he fought and grappled his way back up. He glanced ahead.

The water was beginning to boil. It was getting shallower and faster. He could not think where he was, but he knew there was a waterfall somewhere ahead. His feet were dragging along the bottom, but he could not make them work.

He saw that there was a bulky white mass, like a huge snowball, stuck against a boulder ahead. He pushed towards it. It was the dead sheep, its horns somehow snagged between two boulders, its neck twisting under the swollen fleece and its bloated body bobbing bizarrely in the water as if alive. He threw himself at it and clung to its greasy back, wrapping his arms clumsily around it, as his frozen fingers could gain no purchase. He pushed his feet down. Yes, he could reach the floor, and he pummelled his legs downwards, trying to drive them into life and feeling. He felt himself swing back out of the main flow as the sheep swung round with him. But the dead sheep would not follow and he at last let it go as he staggered back, scrambled up the bank and fell onto the frozen ground, more dead than alive.

More than anything else, he needed to sleep now, just there, curled in a ball. But his head hurt too much and his heart was beating dramatically, but it was somewhere a long way off. Then his stomach heaved its caustic mass upwards and he rolled clumsily and was sick, but it caught in his beard and down his front and he desperately craved water to clear his throat. The very thought amused him and seemed to save him, because he drove himself up onto numb feet and swayed clumsily. He had to look down to be sure that his feet were in contact with the ground, because he could feel nothing. Then he hobbled off as if on stumps, tottered a few yards and fell again.

He never knew how he got home or how lifeless and bruised he was when they found him. But he did get home and his dogs licking his face clean were the first sensations that he registered. They got him in, stripped him, dried and warmed him. The doctor said it was a miracle that he was alive at all and that he had not lost the use of some fingers or toes, but complications could still arise. He also said that the next few days would be critical. George was feverish, fragile and occasionally delirious and he needed constant attention. Once again, Emily nursed anxiously and prayed intermittently. She sent for Bella and the two women tended to him.

Late on the second day, with the light in the bedroom fading fast, George shifted restlessly, sweating and dreaming, murmuring incoherently. Bella leaned over him, wiped his brow and tried to soothe him. She crooned a lullaby that she used to use in the New Orleans Hospital, learned from the Creole women there: a low, sweet sound, words hardly distinguishable. She had little idea what it meant. It seemed to calm her patient, as if it had broken through his dream, and he suddenly opened his eyes.

'Rest now, George,' she murmured, taking his hand and stroking it, watching the eyes close again.

On the following night, Emily was curled up on a little cot that they had brought up beside George's bed. In the dead of night, she was suddenly awoken by her husband's voice. He asked for water. The voice was harsh, rasping, as if his throat was inflamed. She turned up the lamp, pulled him up in bed and helped him to drink. He seemed calmer, but her arm encircling his back noted how thin and bony he seemed. She settled him back against his pillows.

'A'm pleased to see thee a little better,' she said. He told her that he had been awake for a while and was feeling much better. She smiled, perched herself on the edge of the bed and took his hand. But he failed to respond, looked at her quizzically and then drew his hand away. She felt immediately chilled.

'A reckon a could eat summat light, perhaps a bit o' bead and milk slops,' he said. He was breathy and very serious. She began to feel even more alarmed. He went on, 'What dost think? A've been laying here considerin' o' what a should tek. An' if a wor poorly when a wor a little lad, well, a recalls as how mother used to gi' me bread and milk slops. An' she would sit by me an' stroke mi hand, a remember that clearly.'

He peered forwards, looked her in the eye and she was shocked to see a grim, steely glare in the gaunt, whiskery face. The grating voice became louder and he maintained his harsh, level look. 'An' then a woke an' she worn't 'ere and a wor expectin' 'er to be 'ere. And then, somehow, a worked it out, kind of. It wor no dream. It wor mother, or should a call her Bella?' He paused and gathered his strength into a tight ball of ill-feeling that he almost spat at her. 'So, a'll have bread and slops, but a don't want ma mother t'mek it this time, I want you t'mek it.' Emily held her breath. He went on with a trembling voice, choked with temper, or emotion, she could not tell. 'An' while you're about it, thou can mek it clear to mother that a want her out o' this house before dawn and she'll not set foot in it again, a shall see to that. Now, get out o' this room an' leave me be for a while. You and I shall talk later.'

He slumped back, his chest heaving, a new sweat breaking out on his brow and a moistness around the eyes that made her want to cry, but she dared not approach him. She did not know what to say. She crept quietly away and woke Bella with the news.

Labouring for Love
June 1872

There followed a difficult period of estrangement and tension at Elterbeck Farm, which persisted for weeks. Bella left with a resigned dignity, saying she should have known it would not work, forgiveness being easier to preach than to practice. George recovered slowly, but felt cheated and conspired against: he now bitterly condemned Emily for not warning him about his mother's return and for taking her side and not his. Emily retreated, took broody comfort from her pregnancy and resented the sour grievance of her husband, which made him preachy and unkind. She mourned for the homely, safe and intimate relationship they had briefly rekindled and she strove to win him back to her, but every time she felt some progress was being made there was a setback; two incidents made matters worse.

The first was the sudden death of Walter Hirst. Walter had become a regular visitor to her shop and a great favourite of Emily's and he was almost a father figure to James. His leadership and knowledge was much cherished at Batty Green and little progress was made on the viaduct without his personal stamp of authority and initiative. He was respected and yet approachable; a good combination in his position.

Moreover, his experiences at the Blue Lamp had not diminished his taste for strong drink and this provided another link with the men, which he liked to maintain. His death came at a difficult moment.

After a cold and difficult spring, the weather had improved and this mended the mood of the men and increased the speed of work. Also, as May opened, a landmark was achieved with the turning of the first arches on the viaduct. Already, six piers were completed: the black marble dug from the watercourse of Little Dale Beck was dressed and neatly trimmed into place, tapering up to the point of springing, where the 45-foot span was built out on a wooden scaffolding and trellis.

Walter Hirst insisted on being present when the wooden centres were knocked out and the arches stood unsupported. Each one dropped only a quarter of an inch as it settled. Each one was a personal triumph for Walter and his team, including his assistant James Taylor.

But whilst the first group of arches was being turned, at the rate of one each week, the masons went on strike. They were earning six shillings and sixpence a day, but Walter wanted to make up time lost during poor winter weather. He had pushed them to agree to a ten-hour day, whilst the chance was there. They complained about the extra pay that was on offer and their sudden refusal to work took Walter by surprise. He was all the more shocked because he had been drinking with some of the gangers the night before and not a word had been said. He fumed and bickered for a while, but then gave in. He drank alone and disappointed that night, no one knew where, and was found dead in the morning, curled up in one of the engine sheds, his drawings and notebooks still in his pocket.

The shock to James and the sense of loss was considerable. It was natural, therefore, that when there was spontaneous talk of a subscription for a memorial stone in Chapel le Dale Churchyard, that it was James who took the idea forwards and went round seeking support. He spoke to Emily and George one evening just as the meal was being served and asked them if they wished to subscribe. Emily looked at George and waited. He did not speak, but shifted uneasily in his chair, picked up a fork and fixed his gaze stubbornly upon it.

Emily sensed trouble. She looked from George to James: the contrast disturbed her. George was scowling. His hair was thin now and was swept back in straight lines, his face lined and ruddy, his cheeks pinched and flecked with rusty skin tones. The eyes were evasive and dark. His work-scarred and thickened hands looked crude and dirty to her. He had remained petulant and distant since his near drowning and he now had the look of an ageing, persecuted man. James, however, was open-faced and almost rosy-cheeked, neat and self-possessed. He was compact, well groomed and yet always there was a hesitancy, a withholding. He was flushed now with embarrassment as the silence extended, glancing at Hetty, who also looked anxiously around her. Emily felt her anger rising and knew that George might be calculating on this, but could not hold back.

'We'll give a guinea,' she said with deliberate slow emphasis, smiling at James, encouraging him.

'Damned if we will,' muttered George. 'Man meant nowt to me. Niver clapped eyes on 'im. An' a'll thank you all if we can 'appen have a meal for once without talk o' railway works.' He looked at Emily coldly as if testing her.

The meal was served and eaten in a raw silence. Emily ate little, pushing food around her plate just as she pushed her thoughts and emotions around inside her, in small morsels, scarcely trusting herself to analyse them. As James began to prepare to leave the table she rose quickly and asked him to wait. She hurried out and in the tense atmosphere of the parlour her footsteps could be heard moving around upstairs. She returned and beamed at James.

'George doesn't want to give a guinea, so we won't.' She handed James some coins. 'We'll give two guineas.' There was a stirring from George and a threatening pause, which Emily quickly moved to fill. 'It's ma own money, Mr Taylor, don't be concerned. A was savin' for ... something else, something special, but Mr Hirst was like a kind o' lovely uncle to me an' this is more important to me at t'moment than t'other thing a was planning. Now,' and she almost waved James and Hetty to their feet, 'a've a few things to say to George, if tha wouldn't mind.'

When they were alone, George looked up at her with almost a forlorn expression; all the colour had drained from his face, but there was also a cruel set to his mouth. He did not want this, but neither would he back down. His words were staccato and they almost bruised her.

'A shall be master in ma own home.'

'Then you may have a home without me in it,' she snapped back. 'Remember what happened to thy own father. The pattern o' his marriage may be about to repeat itself if tha's not careful.' She turned and walked. She had a lot she could say, but held back. It was not the first time that both had struck hard against the will of the other, like flint against steel.

They pulled back from the brink, but the atmosphere was volatile. In the meantime, Emily put down some markers of her independence. Without consulting her husband, and despite her advancing pregnancy, she resumed her visits to Bella and to the shop at Batty Green. She even spent time with Ethel, who had just given birth to a child that she named Nancy. She accompanied James and Hetty to the funeral for

Walter Hirst and once again set about rearranging things at the farm to give herself back more of the freedom that she had forfeited for the sake of George. A period of relative calm settled once more and lasted for a few weeks. But then matters were brought to a second and uglier crisis over the wedding plans.

It had been arranged that Hetty would be married from the family home at Cold Cotes, but that the wedding would be at Chapel le Dale, and George and Emily had long ago offered to have the wedding meal and festivities at Elterbeck. Recently, George had taken no part at all in the planning, offering only an occasional surly comment.

Then, late one evening, James and Hetty came into the kitchen, with unusual nervous caution, and said that they wanted to invite Bella to the wedding, after all the help she had given in London and elsewhere, and would that be alright? There was a short, strangled silence. Then George snorted, shot up from his place at the table, knocking over his chair and a jug of water, and declared with venom that Bella would never come onto his land and if she tried, he would meet her with a gun, wedding or no wedding. He looked at them all with a wild look in his eyes. 'For two pins a'd cancel whole thing. Tha can all go to hell an' stay there. Marriage is nowt but a coil o' trouble anyway. Th'art better off wi'out it.' He stormed out of the house.

Emily said nothing immediately. She sat still and thought of the child and how her dreams of the future were scotched by her husband's venomous outbursts. It was not so much the selfishness of his attitude that made her sick at heart, but the weight of malicious nastiness that he managed to convey in the few words he used. She felt her life was in danger of becoming poisoned and she thought of the child growing up in this atmosphere. She went upstairs and calmly packed a bag. They were a month away from the wedding.

She called James and Hetty back into the kitchen and told them that she was leaving, but that they were not to worry, because she would be back, and if George asked for her she was at his mother's hut. Hetty cried and the two women embraced and comforted each other. James said nothing, but took Hetty away, giving Emily a poignant smile as he reached the door.

Emily went out to the shed, where her horse was stabled, lit a lantern and began to prepare the harness and fit the bridle. Whilst she was busy there were footsteps on the cobbles outside and she looked up to see

George standing there in the half-light. He looked ill at ease: bent at an awkward angle, tense and unpleasant. His face was in shadow. She turned up the lamp and looked at him coldly.

'Tha'll not leave,' he said, low and menacing.

'A'll not stay,' she replied, trying to be calm and yet clear.

'Thy place is wi' me: thou and t'child when it comes.'

'Dost think tha can keep me prisoner, George?'

She almost wanted to laugh, but managed to hold it back. Instead, she looked him in the eye, her dark eyes bright and questioning, and her head held proudly, whilst she watched him shift uneasily where he stood. She watched his fists clenching and unclenching; one of his dogs, sensing tension, came sniffing close. He aimed a kick and a curse at it and it spun away. Doves flew noisily away from the barn roof. The horse shuffled noisily and she soothed it gently. They all knew a critical moment had come.

'Tha'll not leave,' he said again, taking a step forwards and pulling himself up tall.

'A'll not stay,' she replied again. 'Not until tha learns to value what tha's got. You need to learn to tret me and others wi' more respect and actually care for anything more than gettin' thy own way.' She began to raise her voice, pouring out her frustration in a liquid torrent. 'A'll not be bullied, downtrodden or locked away. God knows a've tried to love you an' win you over, but now a've had me fill o' thy mean and selfish ways. A want to be me own self, not just part o' thy shadow or one o' the farm trappings, like a piece o' prime beef. Tha'll treat me as an equal or not treat me at all. Mek some choices, George. If tha really wants me, and this child, then you need to start showing it. It's over to you now. A'm going where a know a'll be welcome an' be looked after.'

She turned from him and with shaking hands she finished fitting the bridle. She heard footsteps. The light wavered as he picked up the lantern and suddenly he loomed up on the other side of the horse, holding the bridle with one hand and the lantern with the other. He stared at her over the horse's neck, his teeth clenched, his breathing shallow.

'Tha'll not leave,' he repeated. 'A'll not let thee.'

'If not today, then tomorrow,' she replied. She saw the battle going on in him, but she did not care now.

'Dost think ma mother left like this?' he suddenly asked, in a softer tone, a tremor now visible in one eye.

She would not yield to that trick and replied coldly, 'Why didn't tha ask her that when she wor here? She tried to win your love as well. She stayed by your bed for hours: wouldn't move. Said as she was goin' to mek thee get better by sheer bloody persistence. She would ha' been a comfort to both o' us, but thy mawngy ticks turned her away as well. Like father, like son. What will tha have left, George?'

He closed his eyes and forced down the tears that were threatening him. His hands shook. She was poised on tiptoe, watching closely, sensing his frustration, confusion and distress, fearing that he might turn nastier. Suddenly, he made a grab for her hand, but she was ready and she pulled back quickly, screamed and slapped the horse on the rump, stepping sharply away as the animal pulled forwards, found itself checked by the harness and swung round towards George. By the time he had calmed the horse and righted himself she was gone. He heard the gate banging, unfastened. He had not the heart to follow.

Emily was agitated and uncertain. She moved away as quickly as she could, always glancing over her shoulder. The spring night was mild and dry, but she knew that the clear skies would mean a drop in temperature later. She had been compelled to abandon her bag and had only a thin shawl to wrap around herself and no lantern. Having scurried up the road some way she paused and looked back. Seeing no sign of pursuit, she stood in the roadway for a minute, regaining her breath. Now that she had escaped him she felt a chill of loneliness. She summoned her strength, ran her hands over her swollen belly and murmured, 'It's partly for you that a'm doing this.'

Then she turned away and began the slow walk towards the turnpike road. A rustle and patter behind her made her look back. It was one of their dogs, following her, a few paces back. She recognised it. It was not a working dog, but a stray mastiff that had followed them home one day: a big, shaggy grey thing that they had kept for no particular reason that anyone could think of. She called it to her and it trotted up to be petted. 'Come on then,' she said. 'You can come with me. A'll call thee "Faithful".' And so they moved off slowly into the twilight.

Walking was not easy for her, she felt weighed down and lumpy, and she soon tired. Her legs ached and she struggled to get her breath. She paused and leaned sadly on the parapet of the bridge, where George had gone into the water four months before. Now, there was little water in the beck and an owl swept over the meadows where George had floundered along, half frozen to death. It was near to the spot where she had first seen Dermot O'Reardon. The child shifted heavily inside her, as if sensing her unhappiness, and the dog looked up at her quizzically. She moved on.

A pain started, low in her gut, and for the first time she felt some anxiety, but stifled it straightaway. She began counting her paces, telling herself that she would rest again after fifty steps. But the weariness was increasing and she wondered at herself: this was not like her at all. She wanted to stretch out, support her belly somehow and sleep. It was getting so dark and greyish cloud was now drifting across the moon. In the distance, she heard the rasping bark of a fox. She made herself walk and reached fifty steps. She still was not at the turnpike.

Voices, male voices, reached her through the still air. Perhaps there were men leaving the Hill Inn. Would they help her? Why should they? They were not likely to know her. She had no money. They might pester and trouble her. She stood for a long time, hands on hips, scarcely thinking. The pain in her stomach was getting worse. Her face and chest were getting hotter, but sweat was drying on her back. Her neck and head were cold. She shivered, shook and groaned. She reached down for the dog and stroked his head, glad of the warmth and comfort that spread though her fingers. 'We're not going back, Faithful. Come on. Another fifty.'

She gritted her teeth and began to walk again, but now she staggered a little and lost her count. She started again, but felt worse. She had to sit down. The track rose slightly towards the road, she could feel it sloping beneath her feet, but could see less and less ahead as more cloud slid over Ingleborough and cast her into shadow. She would not give in, but bent her back in defiance of the pain and shuffled on. She would rest at the road.

When she finally crested the slope and felt the rough stone of the turnpike beneath her feet she could not help herself. She staggered to the edge, leaned down clumsily, took her weight on one of her outstretched hands and then lowered herself to the ground, her breath heaving into her lungs. The dog seemed to know this was not a good spot, moved away up the road, turned to look at her, whined complainingly and then returned and sat against her. She leaned on him and gave silent thanks for at least some company.

Almost at once she dozed and then woke with a start as the clatter of hobnail boots and the swinging arc of a lantern indicated that a group of men were coming towards her, going south and west, towards Ingleton.

She was not sure that she could get up, her legs still felt so weak. She realised that she was very cold and that the pain was still there. The child inside her twisted and she gave a whimper. She hunched over, pulled her shawl over her head and hoped to go unnoticed. The men passed in a blur in the darkness and although they saw her, they avoided her.

She knew that it was less than a mile to Batty Green. She addressed the dog quite formally, as if he was holding her back. 'Thir's nowt to be gained by sitting here, old Faithful. We mun "mek some headway" as mi old gramma used to say.'

She shuffled, straightened her back with difficulty and with a deep grunt she got to her feet. She began her lumbering walk, scurried inelegantly past the Hill Inn and resolved not to stop until she was at the Railway Inn. The low, dull pain was worse, more insistent.

'Yes. A know th'art there,' she spat at it, trying to ignore it, refusing to think about it.

She drove herself on, making a broken rhythm for her tired legs by repeating odd phrases in her head, pushing herself forwards with every pulse. 'Come on. Walk, tha bugger. Come on. Walk tha bugger. Th'art strong. Th'art a Welsh cob. Th'art a dragon. Come on. Nearly there. Stop laykin' around. Thou's done this journey hundreds o' times. Come on. Walk tha bugger. For t'bairn.' Time seemed to drift on its own tide and she forced herself on in these broken rhythms until her legs nearly buckled.

The air was colder now; a wind had risen, ferreting insistently at her damp back, circling her neck and bare, clammy arms. Now, she heard more voices ahead, coming down from Batty Green. It was another group of men. There were shouts and laughter. She shuffled to a halt and tried to gauge where she was. She had an awful dread of being seen like this and even worse, being the sport of some drunken crowd. She had to hide. She tried to focus on the stone walls that she could just make out on each side. She knew this road so well; surely, she could tell where she was? With a groan, she made herself move on slowly, one hand now balanced on the dog for support, scanning around, her whole attention now fixed on getting out of the way. And all the time the voices were getting closer. Then, at last, she recognised one particular large, irregular stone going through the wall.

They were the key elements in building such a wall and this stone had a sprinkling of shiny quartz, which she had seen glinting in the sun on many a fine day. She was close to Batty Green. Just ahead, she knew, was a track running down from an old quarry on Close Fell. She could hide there.

With new spirit she drove on her heavy limbs, fought down the rising pain in her stomach and so stumbled breathlessly into the quarry road, where she sank back against the wall and slid downwards with a bump that sent a pain shooting through her. Tears sprang to her eyes. She pulled the dog in close to her and told him to be quiet. The group of men were not far off, but they had no lantern. She relaxed a little, waited and listened hard. The game of hide-and-seek had become totally absorbing to her, blotting out all other thoughts.

Yet, as the approaching voices got louder, she suddenly realised that they were local accents, two or three different voices, young men probably. And then, with joy, she recognised one as the voice of Joshua, her cheerful, fat milk delivery lad. Joshua, the smiling cherub on his two porky legs. Here was hope!

They were already passing the end of the track, so she tried to pull herself up and call his name at the same time. It came out as a shapeless gasp. She cursed herself, fell back and shouted "Joshua" as loud as she could. And then called again. She was desperate and she listened intently at the sounds echoing faintly back off the high fells and stone walls. She thought she heard boots scraping round and a mumble of voices. Then, with almost a convulsion of relief, she made out his familiar voice, though rather slurred: "O'd on a bit, lads, 'o'd on: tha's no ghost. A think a know that voice, it's a beautiful woman, but a'm damned if a can recall who 'tis.'

Emily felt tears brimming in her eyes. He was such an angel! She called again, as calmly as she could. 'Joshua. It's me. It's Emily … its Mrs Wright. A need tha help, lad. Come here, up quarry track, a beg thee.'

There was silence and mumbling. There was an owl hooting and then the scraping of boots on stone. Then there was just pain, a blistering pain tearing at her for a few moments as if pulling her apart.

From the moment that Joshua's moon face loomed out of the dark and smiled at her it all became something of a blur to Emily. She managed to put together a story of being taken ill on the way to visit Bella Roberts and then, fading fast and holding in the pain, she let the three young men take over. Joshua and his friends had been drinking, but the crisis soon sobered them. They quickly fetched a wagon from the Railway Inn and then took her with great gallantry and care to Bella's hut, even looking after the mangy old dog. Then, Joshua went on alone to take a message to Elterbeck, waking up George to tell him that Emily was not well and where she had been found and where she had asked to be taken.

George met him at first with suspicion, but Joshua was so sincere, not to say eloquent and descriptive in his storytelling that even George's mean doubts evaporated and the doctor was sent for. But George, riven with doubts and bitter demons as he was, feared to face what he might find if he went himself. He said he would stay at the farm and wait for news. It was two hours, two bleak and empty hours, in which prayer seemed a forlorn ritual and hope a distant gleam on another planet, before the doctor returned.

Dr Milnthorp was new to the area. He was a young man, brisk and serious, with a booming voice. His report was short and to the point. 'Mrs Wright is recovering. She must rest and not be disturbed. She must not be moved, under any circumstances. She is exhausted, but otherwise unhurt. The child is not in danger now, but labour could start again at any time and she must have constant attention.'

The young doctor then made his way out into the dark yard and prepared to mount his horse. He looked at the middle-aged farmer and went on in a more admonitory tone. 'She should never have been out walking alone in her condition at that time of night. Both mother and child could have been lost if help had not come along when it did.'

George could not find the words to reply at first. Then he asked, weakly, 'Dr Milnthorp. Would tha say that she wor in a safe, clean kind o' place now and is she being cared for proper?'

The doctor was blunt. 'You must go and judge that for yourself, Mr Wright. My own view is that the place she is in is clean; she is very well cared for by a woman who has a lot of experience of assisting with childbirth. I have not been in this job long, but I have already worked with Mrs Roberts in a number of situations at Batty Green. In every case she has given wise counsel and taken the correct action. I would go so far as to say that if she were a younger woman, I would be asking her to take on more cases and help me on a regular basis. I would say at the moment that Mrs Wright is in the best place she could possibly be. You are a very lucky man, considering how and where she was found.'

He gave George a look that made the older man feel guilty and defeated. The young doctor then left, saying that he would call at Batty Green again as soon as he could. George, desolate and relieved, returned to the fireside and riddled the coals, lost in gloomy thought.

George and Hetty
Summer 1872

George did not sleep and was out early to help with the milking. As they assembled in the soft morning light, Hetty and the girls looked at him curiously, but he could not bring himself to speak about Emily's absence. He knew that Joshua would have Emily's story told and retold a dozen times before breakfast and he had no heart for talking about it until he had to and no intention of justifying himself. He knew he would inevitably appear to be in the wrong. The doctor's words were still echoing painfully in his head, as they had for hours. Who could possibly understand his point of view? He was loath to stand accused; the focus of gossip and market-place pronouncements. He hated judgement: not because he was arrogant, but because he knew he was weak and got things wrong.

The milking done, he retreated to the farmhouse and waited. He heard Joshua arriving and Hetty's voice and sat at the table, his head in his hands, and tried to blot out the sound and movement, the memories and his guilty conscience. He knew he had to make some choices, but did not know how to go about it. He clamped his eyes shut, until they hurt and stars burst across them. He relented after a while, but kept his eyes closed and tried to judge himself more calmly.

An image came to him: it seemed to float up on the back of his eye. It was as if he was looking down the dark drop of a mossy well, getting narrower and narrower as it went. Water was dripping. Tiny ferns grew out of wet fissures in the sides. Somewhere at the bottom, in the pale glimmering light, he could see his face dimly reflected. It moved and shimmered and then lost its shape as a rat or a vole swam snakily across the surface, before slowly reforming. Weed was a dark green slime round the sides, his pale face framed centrally in an eerie light. That was how he thought of himself sometimes: a shadowy fragment of a person. What would he be without the farm and the church? If those props were taken away, what would be left to define him? He needed Emily to hold him steady, his buttress against disintegration. The blank, dank tunnel might now be a vision of what was to come, his life without Emily, without his child. His future was narrowing and thinning to a thin sliver of light.

He remembered, as a boy, looking through the wrong end of a telescope once, at Mr Farrer's house in Clapham. It had frightened him. But he also remembered, and he flashed his eyes open at the thought, that the kindly old landowner had shown him how to turn the telescope round. The thought gave him comfort. He could open out his life, surely, just as easily as he had closed it down: win back his wife, his child, even his mother? He remembered Emily's words: she had told him to "learn to value what tha's got". At the moment, he had virtually nothing. He had to start to rebuild.

As if reading his thoughts, Hetty came into the kitchen and gave him a tentative smile. Here was some hope. He looked at her and tried to smile back. She was shocked to see his bleak, haggard and unshaven face. The sickly smile made her shiver. She faltered, did not speak and began to make breakfast. George watched her.

Hetty had always been a favourite of his. The frail, gangly child that had come to work for them was now a strong and confident young woman. She would be married within a few weeks. George felt a pang of jealousy. How good it would be to start all over again. But would he have wanted anything else or anyone other than Emily? He could not easily answer the question. If only she had been more contented, more placid, he thought. But then she would not have been Emily, came the answer from another part of his brain and it soothed him a little.

He sat up. In that instant, the first decision seemed to have made itself; the rest would follow, like the days, like the seasons.

'I s'll go and get washed and changed, Hetty,' he called over to her as she worked at the stove, her back to him. She gave him a nervous glance over her shoulder and nodded. 'Then I s'll go to Batty Green wi' thee an' the milk. Will tha tell Joshua to wait for us?' She turned and nodded again, smiling gently, obviously approving.

'Emily would ha' made bread today, Mr Wright,' she said. 'Shall I start it?'

'Aye, if tha's the time.' He pulled himself up. 'Will tha come wi' me, at Batty Green? A'm not sure where Bella ... where ma mother lives.'

She noticed how his voice shook and his hands, too. She could see how hard it was for him. 'Of course a will,' she said. 'What iver a can do to help. Joshua shall mind the shop.' She hesitated. 'Shall a tell James, about Emily and all?
He would want to know.'

George nodded.

'I s'll run down and feed goslings and then tell James. I s'll be back to serve thy breakfast and start the bread.' She turned and bustled out with a clatter of clogs and a swirl of skirt and hair.

'Well, that's a start,' he thought.

Hetty grabbed some corn and ran as quickly as she could down to the bottom of the field, near the beck, where the early morning mist was drifting silently, swaying through the trees, making ghostly shapes. She felt brimful of energy and almost shaky with excitement. She was shocked by Emily's departure and Josh's tale of where he had found her and the state she was in. She knew already about the doctor's words, which had been overheard by her sister. Now there was George looking like a picture of death and all these words and images flowed through her in a heady mixture.

She also loved that she was trusted, but more than that, she was relied upon. She was important to their plans. She would show them how grown up she could be and show James how she could run the farm and more. She reached the end of the field and slowed down. The geese were her little venture, to be fattened for Christmas. She and James had built little goose hulls: shelters with penthouse roofs of stone and turf. Now, inside, were little silky golden goslings that she loved to count and touch. Today though, she scattered the corn quickly and scurried back.

They were soon on their way. George had never been very far into the navvy camp at Batty Green. His early enthusiasm for the idea of a railway had soon dissipated when he was confronted with the noise, the raw energy and the occasional riotous living, drunkenness and fighting. He recoiled from it in confusion. Like many others, when he did not know how to respond to the new and challenging, he thought it safer to avoid it. Some early outbreaks of poaching and stealing had further disheartened him and had set him on the road to moral censure and evasion; a journey that was sustained when he learned of the Blue Lamp, the illegal liquor and the selling of children. Apart from Black Jack, he rarely met any of the workers. Though navvies came to the Hill Inn, George and the local farmers kept mostly to themselves in a back room, reinforcing their own ignorance by repeated and sometimes lurid tales of mischief and godlessness.

Now, he rode to Batty Green on the back of the milk cart with James, whilst Joshua and Hetty rode up front and gossiped with eager intensity. Skylarks sang blithely above them, while churns and pails rattled a reply. Ahead of them a low, heavy cart, laden with coal and timber, was creaking and groaning through the ruts, pulled by four heavy horses.

George made himself reconsider the picture that he carried in his head of the whole of his valley. He thought of it as he sometimes saw it from the top of Whernside, where the curve of the viaduct, seen from above, was a neat and elegant arc amidst a chaos of workings, mud, water and white boxes that were the huts. Yet, to draw the eye away was to see vast spaces of dappled greens, greys and browns, water glinting brightly and then steep slopes, with wedges of scree, and the sharp profiles of hills swelling from the vast, uneven expanse of the valley floors. He understood afresh just how much of the haunts of men he had chosen to ignore, leaving it to Emily and to others, whilst he took the proceeds and smugly condemned the people, preferring his own mental landscape of what he saw as his birthright. He had been cowardly, he told himself, and he needed to change. He scrambled to the front of the cart and looked ahead. The emerging viaduct, latticed with scaffolding, dominated the distant scene, but the eye was also drawn to the rows of huts, the brickworks with their tall chimneys, the spider's web of tramway lines, the cranes poised like gibbets, the fussy engines and all the lumber and spoil heaps, with men, machines and animals moving around in random directions and smoke rising from fifty fires. He called over to James.

'One time there were nobbut sheep and grouse up here for mile after mile. My father 'ad a word for a place like this. He'd say it wor a "dawley" spot and no one in right mind would go thir. How many folk dost think live here now?'

'There's about 100 working on viaduct. Another 100 or so on tunnel and probably same again on t'embankments, bridges and track. Add in all the others that feed and supply 'em in various ways and their families and that. Happen thir'll be 700 or more livin' here or roundabout, more up on top and more over on Dent side.'

George fell into a brooding silence as they got closer and finally stood back, mute and tense, when they worked their way down off the road to the shop, where they unloaded. James went off to work, Joshua opened up and before long, George and Hetty were ready to leave for Bella's hut.

After the milking that morning, and conscious that he was likely to be visiting his mother's home, George had put on an old dark suit and waistcoat, a clean shirt and cravat and a round hat with a stiff rim. He looked and felt both out of sorts and uncomfortable. So, when he offered his arm to Hetty in a rather clumsy, self-conscious way, he was relieved when she took it gladly, giving him a sweet smile of encouragement, and it was Hetty who talked as they went, pointing out various people and features as they passed. They made their way through the commotion of people, transport and animals to Sebastopol, a cluster of huts now dominated by the viaduct's mighty piers that towered over the area. George looked up at the newly turned arches and shook his head in amazement.

Hetty said, tentatively, 'James could arrange to take you on a proper look round some time, if tha'd like to, Mr Wright.'

George nodded seriously, but did not speak. Hetty realised that his thoughts were actually elsewhere and that in reality, he was nervous and hesitant. She guided him gently to Bella's hut, where the dog Bane was stretched out in the porch. Bane raised his head and sniffed at them as they stepped up out of the mud, recognised them both and sank down again, unperturbed. George again seemed reluctant to proceed, so Hetty took charge and knocked on the left-hand door. Halting footsteps could be heard approaching and Bella opened the door part way, her grey hair tumbling across her face and her body canted to the side as she leaned heavily on a stick. The doorway was narrow and her mobility was impaired as she fumbled with the stick and the door handle. She turned slowly to see who it was, a grimace unexpectedly clouding her features as a spasm of pain troubled her, but when she recognised her visitors her look turned to one of real pleasure and with a broad, beaming smile she immediately urged them to come in.

'I am so pleased to see you both here. Come in, come in and sit. Mrs Wright has just woken up. Follow me, please, but be patient, I am a little slower than usual, as I have a bit of a problem today.'

Hetty went in first, following Bella, and she moved straight to the big bed on the far wall and began to speak quietly to Emily, who was sitting up, her face white against the black frame of her hair that had been combed out and was now spread across the pillow. George stood, irresolutely, near the door, holding his hat as if it were a rare orchid. He was deeply uncomfortable, baffled by uncertainty and irresolution. He screwed up his courage, as if tightening a rope round a spar, and held himself ready. He had no clear idea what emotion possessed him, or what he would say or do. He would have liked more time to think. He was certain of only of one thing: he could not cut and run, much as he wanted to.

He looked round the one large room that Bella used, trying to take in the detail, like a surveyor. There was a table near the door, with plants and herbs, and he stepped forwards and fingered them absent-mindedly. Bella was filling the kettle and settling it on the stove. She turned, took in her son's disquiet at a glance and moved at once to help him.

'George, come over and pull up a chair beside your wife.' He flinched and looked at her shyly. She gestured to one of the upright chairs beside the stove and began to move it for him, but her mobility was limited. He had to help. He shuffled across and took it from her, still silent and only acknowledging her by the slightest of nods. She was grateful for any recognition.

'Hetty, dear. Will you help an old lady down to your shop for some milk and eggs? I'm plumb out of food and we can leave Mr Wright to look after Emily a while, I'm sure. Mr Wright, will you make some tea while we are out?'

He maintained his silence and again gave only a brief nod. Shawls were fetched and Hetty promised to return soon and then they were gone. George drew his chair up beside the bed and sat hunched over, fiddling with the hat that was held loosely between his knees. There was silence. Somewhere beneath the floor a rat was scratching. He glanced up and found that she was watching him fixedly. Their eyes met.

It was a moment that stretched and bulged, the whole hut seeming to take a deep breath and hold it against its ribs. Her eyes were dark and her skin pale and puffy. He had never seen her look so fragile. Grief and guilt possessed him. She saw his misery and loneliness and the tired lines down his cheeks and around his mouth. She had never wanted him to be like this. She brought a hand from beneath the bedclothes and held it out to him. A shy smile warmed his face and he took the hand, bent over and kissed it tenderly. Tears came to his eyes and he let them fall on her hand and he stayed there, bent clumsily, unable to speak, easing his suffering and shame. She was patient with him and frail and was close to tears herself.

At last, he gave a shuddering sigh, shook himself upright and passed his hand roughly over his face. She smiled and shook her head at him.

'Th'art a puzzle at times, George Wright. Thir's a cloth and some water there. Go an' wash thy face an' mek us some tea. An' see if thir's owt to eat: a'm fair clemmed.'

They talked and drank black tea and she ate some dry bread and cheese. There was contrition on both sides, regret and tenderness, and so the mending was easy and this raised their hopes and spirits. They had not got far in their talk, however, when a knocking at the door disturbed them. It was the young doctor and he had barely entered the room, when Bella and Hetty followed: Hetty supporting Bella, who looked exhausted herself. They gathered round Emily, as if staring at an exhibit.

'A can't cope wi' all o' you staring at me,' she said with a smile. George said he would get some air for a few moments and stepped out onto the porch. Hetty followed and stood beside him.

George looked at her. 'I am grateful for your help, lass, this morning.'

'It wor nothing,' she said. She could see that he was more relaxed now and that he had regained a more natural posture and colour. She could not recall many times when she had been alone with George like this, adult to adult. She thought of her own father. Had she ever been alone with him? She knew so little really. She felt that she ought to say something: it was what adults did. She turned to George.

'I'm reet glad that Emily's looking better and that you are ...' she paused, struggling for words, wishing she had not started, feeling that the moment might quickly become uncomfortable. 'A mean that you are together now an' sortin' things out, like.'

'Aye. It needed sortin',' he replied, smiling at her. 'You're a good lass, Hetty. Tha mustn't concern yourself about this. A was in danger o' forgettin' some important things, but I've got it straight now, as sometimes we have to do, you know, straighten out our thoughts and get priorities right. For next few months I s'll mek sure that first and foremost is Emily and the baby, followed very closely by t'arrangements for t'wedding o' James and you. Everything else can wait.'

He asked her about some of their plans and she chatted happily for a while as he listened contentedly. 'You're a good lass, Hetty,' he repeated after a while.

She smiled and looked at him. She wanted the talk to go on. She floundered into it, 'A'm glad to hear … that all that, you know, with Emily, is better now,' she said. He nodded his agreement. And emboldened by the flow of good feelings, and judging that this might be the best time to ask, she went on. 'Mr Wright, will tha let Bella come to wedding? Cos she has been so good to James and me and t'Emily.'

She held her breath, remembering his previous outburst, and glanced across to see if she had gone too far.

'A've bin flummoxed by Bella, a have to admit. It's not easy when your mother suddenly appears at my age. A've bin thinkin' o' this quite a lot. Most o' ma life a blamed her, hated her, in fact, but a can see now as how that wor not a person that a hated, it wor a figure in a story that ma father told me. An' when a wor a young man, whenever anything went wrong or I felt sorry for meself, a could always put responsibility on her somehow an' hate her a bit more. A used to say to mesen, well, if a'd 'ad a proper mother and a proper childhood, things would ha' been different, a would ha' been different. Now, she turns up and is everyone's friend, except mine! She helps you, she nurses me when a'm near dead an' now she's saved Emily, when I drive her out o' her own home. A can't get owt right an' she can't do owt wrong. It's a devil is this one right enough. A'm outfoxed at ivery turn.'

He laughed, rather grimly, and Hetty wanted to laugh, too, and hug him, but did not dare do either. She waited, but he seemed to be lost in his own thoughts.

'So, can she come then?' she asked at last.

'Aye, she can come. I s'll be overrun and ordered around by regiments of women, a can see that. Let's 'ope that child is a lad. Then there's two on us as can be mawngy together from time to time, as men like to be tha knows.'

George might have gone on in this new expansive mode, released, responding jauntily to the interest and sympathy drawn seductively from Hetty, but just then the door opened and Doctor Milnthorp asked them to come in. When they were all assembled, he apologised for keeping them waiting and then in his brisk, portentous manner and booming voice, he gave them his views, whilst he pulled on his frock coat and hat.

'Mrs Wright is doing well and all the signs of an early labour have receded. We must make sure that they do not come back. She must have rest and quiet and no agitation. This child needs a few more weeks yet or there may be problems. I think you agree, don't you, Bella?'

Bella nodded thoughtfully but said nothing. She was sitting heavily in an armchair, her body slightly twisted, the dog standing tall beside her, watchful and poised.

'The question then arises as to whether Mrs Wright stays here or goes back to the farm.'

George began to realise, from the doctor's pauses and from the glances exchanged between Emily and Bella, that there was a complication to contend with. He began to feel anxious. 'I have to say that I am concerned about Bella,' said the doctor. 'She is not well, but will not let me help her in any way, as she says she is managing her own treatment.' He looked at her meaningfully and gave a brief shake of his head. She smiled and shook her head back at him in an amiable mimicry.

He went on in his heavy manner. 'I am not convinced that she is well enough to cope with the task of caring for Mrs Wright, though I have no doubt, even after my very brief acquaintance with her, that she has the knowledge and experience necessary for the job.'

There was a pause and the doctor looked a little out of sorts and he began to fidget with his hat, as if he did not quite know how to continue. George began to see, behind the old-fashioned clothes, the waxed moustache and the penetrating voice, that here was a young man with knowledge but not much experience. Then, out of the blue, the doctor suddenly turned to him and spoke directly.

'Now, Mr Wright: I have just been informed that Bella, that Mrs Roberts here, is in fact your mother, is that so?'

George nodded and shifted uneasily on the spot, not sure where this was going. 'So a'm told,' he said.

'Well, to be blunt,' Doctor Milnthorp continued, 'in my view, the best solution then would be to move both Mrs Wright and Bella, with great care, you understand, down to the farm and bring in someone to nurse them both. That way, we can keep an eye on them under one roof. What do you say, sir?'

They all looked at George. He felt the blood drain from his face and looked down at the floor. He moved his tongue around in his mouth as if he were chasing a forgotten morsel of food. Then he realised, quite suddenly, that he had reached the end of a journey and he was glad.

The first thing he did was to look around for Hetty and smile at her. Would she ever know that an important final step on that journey had been the conversation they had just had outside? He doubted it and it amused him. They all waited.

He looked across at his wife, his voice coming out a little huskily: 'I want nothing more than to get Emily home and see that she is cared for.' He turned his head slowly and with careful, halting dignity and a touch of the doctor's pompous style, he addressed Bella. 'An' I hope that you ... Mother ... will make it your home, too.'

He moved beside her and put his hand lightly on her shoulder. The dog growled and the tension in the room was dissolved in laughter.

Endings
May 1876

The arrival of hundreds of navvies, their families and those who supplied and supported them brought unexpected changes to Ribblehead. Death and burial had become commonplace, where once they had been infrequent visitations. Within a year of Batty Green becoming established, the little mossy churchyard at Chapel le Dale needed to be extended and the roads around it rebuilt and repaired. There were 210 burials conducted at the little church in the years between 1871 and 1876, almost as many as had been interred there in the whole of the preceding hundred years.

On a warm Friday in late May 1876, a yellow wagon, draped in black cloth, carried Bella Roberts from Elterbeck to that churchyard, almost four years to the day after a similar wagon, going with equal care, had carried Bella and Emily home from Batty Green. Those years had been kind to Bella, who managed to combine serenity with humour and always had time for others, even when she was in pain. Her presence at the farm brought peace and comfort to George in a way that he had never expected. It also released Emily, who blossomed into motherhood, but could still find space and time for her restless spirit to seek its outlets. The years also saw the numbers living at Batty Green reach their peak and then begin a steady decline as one by one the works were completed. The Wrights were prosperous and settled, when Bella suddenly died.

Bella Roberts' funeral brought about one of the largest gatherings that the church had seen for some time as a large and varied congregation of mourners gathered to pay their respects. Even the neighbouring farmers and their wives had shown forgiveness and compassion in Bella's last years. George and Emily Wright, with their children Robert and Elizabeth, followed her coffin in the pale summer sunshine. Also present were Hetty and James Taylor, with their child Grace. Ethel and Black Jack were there with all their children, along with many women from Batty Green, women who had continued to seek out Bella at Elterbeck, right up until her last days.

The farm was busy with visitors all day and into the Saturday that followed. Emily bustled around as brightly as she could, anxiety settling into her heart about George, who seemed the most hurt and bewildered of them all. After the funeral on the Friday he got drunk, in an almost silent, determined manner, sitting in the kitchen, despite the fine weather, and waving away all approaches from friends or family, but sharing his whisky bottle with another dour, wordless farmer from the other side of the valley. Emily tried to wheedle him out, but her energies were needed elsewhere. On the Saturday, George woke late in a grisly temper and began drinking again before the morning was out. They all tiptoed round him, the strain beginning to show.

Emily was becoming impatient. She feared that this gloom would settle on her husband for weeks, as it had in earlier times. Did she any longer have the will to tease him out of it or to fight him if he became nasty? She also had other concerns. Death, being no respecter of railway timetables, brought her an immediate dilemma. The very first passenger express was due through Ribblehead that afternoon and weeks before, Emily had promised Robert and Elizabeth that they could be there to see the event. She was resolved to disappoint the children and stay at home, but the sight of the unshaven, bilious George changed her mind. She felt it would be good to get herself and the children away from the farm for a few hours. In her black mourning dress and with the children in their best clothes, she set off in the pony and trap, feeling a spring breeze soft on her face as if it were gently cleansing her skin and peeling away at least one thin layer of her grief and disappointment.

There was a crowd of people and vehicles at the new Batty Green Station, so she was forced to leave her trap at the Railway Inn and walk the last part, carrying Elizabeth most of the way and watching her son very carefully. Robert was a sturdy, dark-haired boy, spirited and sometimes challenging. She told him for the third time in as many minutes not to kick at stones in his new black boots.

'Me father don't fuss about boots,' the child retorted.

'No, and your father don't clean 'em, either, or have to tek you to buy a new pair,' she said. 'A've to do that. So, whilst a'm here, you'll tek care o' boots, young man, or a'll tek care to clip your ear.'

Robert thought for a while. 'If a don't kick stones, can a have sweets if thir's owt for sale?'

'Well,' she replied, seeing a familiar earnest and calculating look on his face. 'I think they will have flags to wave. Should thou like a flag?'

'Aye,' he replied seriously and then he put on a sweet smile for her. 'So long as a can 'ave sweets as well.'

'Th'art nobbut a rogue and a prince charming at the same time. A don't know where thou gets it from.' She paused to shift Elizabeth to the other hip and thought to herself: no doubt he gets it from his father, whichever one it was.

She later thought to herself, in an idle, amused kind of way, that perhaps thinking about a person can sometimes conjure them up, because it was only a little while later – sweets, flags and children organised – as she moved away from the thickest crowds and headed further down the new platform that she saw him. With a rush of blood to the heart, she recognised a figure standing on the very end of the platform, turned away from her, looking out over the viaduct and towards Blea Moor. It was Robert Macintosh.

He was smartly dressed in a dark grey suit and top hat, but she would know that short, powerful body anywhere, the grey wisps of hair just showing at the sides of his head, the musing pose, the air of self-sufficiency.

She put Elizabeth down to totter along with her, straightened her own dress and took her daughter's hand and then her son's stickier one. They made a slow, wavering progress forwards, until they were within a few feet of the older Robert. They stood there in silence for a few seconds. The children looked at her, expectantly. Emily felt stirred with excitement. She stared at her old friend's back, wanting to run her hands down it, but did not dare. At last, Elizabeth sneezed, which brought Robert round to face them: Emily jumped and a flush hurried through her like a wave of rising heat.

Nevertheless, she was quick to master herself. 'Good afternoon, Mr Macintosh. I hope you are well.'

He smiled broadly, raised his hat and bowed deferentially. 'A'm very well, Mrs Wright. All the better for seeing you here and the children. I wor reet hopin' to see you all.'

There was no mistaking the pleasure in his voice and manner. He raised his hat again to her and she felt the blush deepen and roll through her limbs. Then he looked down, dropped quickly to his haunches and smiled at the children. The boy Robert was amused, but Elizabeth tried to hide behind her mother's legs.

'Now then, ma lad, thou were about 2 year old when I saw thee last. So, I reckon thou will be nearly 5 year old now. But a'm blessed if a can recall thy name. Could thou tell me clearly who thou'rt and your little sister, too.' He put on an exaggerated look of puzzlement, took off his hat and scratched his head.

Young Robert removed his stick of barley sugar, but only a fraction of an inch from his mouth, and spoke very formally, but with a belligerent stare. 'I am George Robert Wright, but everyone calls me Robert. I am 4 years old. My sister is Elizabeth and she is 2 years old.' He looked cautiously at his questioner. 'Do you like barley sugar?' He immediately jammed the stick back into his mouth as if exposing it to the stranger might be risky.

'Happen a do,' the man replied. 'A think anyone wi' the name of Robert has probably got a sweet tooth.'

He winked and the child looked at him with mock suspicion, paused in his sucking motion and was about to speak, when a distant blast of steam whistle and a ragged cheer from the crowd indicated that the train must be in sight. Robert stood up promptly and offered his arm with a grand, slightly mocking gesture to Emily. She swept up Elizabeth and gladly took the arm on offer. They turned clumsily, with some laughter, and moved up to the edge of the crowd without further words.

The newly painted engine, in its dark green livery and shining pipework, had pulled lustily up from Horton and through Selside, plumes of smoke pouring upwards and then drifting silently away in neat bubbles, the whistle blasting sharply in the still air and rebounding from the fells, the very ground seeming to tremble. The small crowd craned necks, waved flags and gave a few scattered cheers as the engine slid into distant view, a tiny dart of colour and life that came on with noisy drama as it approached them and then eased back, its brakes beginning to grind and scrape as it levelled out and slowed.

There was more excitement when it coasted noisily alongside the platform, whereupon the passengers waved or rose and came to the window to speak to them. The locals were soon of the view that the luxurious green and maroon Pullman cars – one named Juno and the other Britannia – with their curtains, their upholstered armchairs, their side tables strewn with papers and cups, were the finest they had ever seen.

No one left or joined the crowded train and more cheers erupted when the whistle was blown again. The first full passenger service shuffled and shovelled its way forwards, gathering just a little speed to cross the Ribblehead Viaduct sedately and then pull heavily on towards the portal to Blea Moor Tunnel, leaning hard on the shiny ribbons of steel that bore down into the black of the earth. The crowd watched with pride and pleasure, cheering until the train was out of sight. Years of toil, much expense and many unplanned deaths had brought this to fruition.

As the crowd began to break up, Robert explained that he was expected at the brickworks, which was about to close down. He asked the Wrights if they would like to go with him and share the tea that was being provided.

'Will there be cake?' asked the young Robert.

'Th'art as sharp as Sheffield, young man,' laughed the older Robert. 'I expect there will be some cake and other things for your sticky fingers.'

Emily was happy to extend the pleasures of the afternoon, not relishing an early return to the farm and George, with his drunken depression. They meandered through the crowds, talking of this and that, of George and the farm, but not of themselves. At last, they found themselves standing just off the turnpike road, each holding a child. They put the children down to sit on the grass for a moment, Robert making the barley sugar ever thinner and more fragile; Elizabeth surveying the few yards of turf with regal equanimity.

The adults looked out further, over the wide basin of Batty Green. The huge viaduct gleamed in the sunlight, its powerful curve tempting the eye, but the foreground was now stripped and quiet. Even as they watched, a hut was being demolished and everywhere there were piles of timber and stone awaiting removal. Here and there, piles of rubbish were burning, desultory smoke slowly rising as if from funeral pyres.

She remembered her first Saturday market day on that very spot – how different the atmosphere had been and how much had happened since. The reminiscence pleased her.

'A've had some memorable times here, Robert.' She looked at him and he nodded reflectively.

'I see the shop's gone, then.' He was gazing out over the central area, where the mission hut, the reading room and the few shops, even the Welcome Home Inn, had now all gone. She did not reply, preferring still to cling to the glow of the past.

'A remember your last visit well enough,' she said with a smirk and a coy squeeze of his arm.

'Aye. The shop wor still here then and well used, as I remember, specially that back room.' He grinned, words being unnecessary as they shared memories that seemed to weave them closer than ever.

A silence moved between them, becoming colder as it grew. Then her mood was quickly deflated, when her old friend said quietly, and in almost a formal tone, that everything was changing and that this would be his last visit to Batty Green. She held her breath and felt at once that fate was about to deal her a blow. He seemed embarrassed and as she said nothing, he was forced to continue.

'It's all closing down, lass, as tha can see. Huts on moor are gone already. Jericho and Belgravia's closed down and thir's only enough huts here for the last couple o' dozen workers. Most o' work is now not on railway at all, its mekin' a road up from Selside and finishing cottages and the like. Brickworks is finished and will be pulled down next week. Soon, thir'll be nowt but grouse and sheep, just like it were before.'

She felt her spirits lift a little. He was only telling her what she already knew.

'A know that,' she said. 'We send our milk down to Settle on train now an' butter goes all way to Manchester, can you imagine! We'll be quiet enough, come next spring. But surely you can come and see us, can't tha?'

'Only if you've room for two,' he said with a sheepish grin, quickly overwhelmed by a look of disquiet. 'A'm to be married next month: a widow woman from Glasgow as has her own house an' a business making gates and railings and the like. Seems a'm to be her factory manager as well as her husband.'

Emily felt a barrier descend, as if the sun was eclipsed. But she made herself rally and was gracious in her congratulations. They moved on, rather soberly, to take tea in his old office at the brickworks, with the handful of workers who were left. But she did not stay long and in truth, the children were tiring, so she got ready to part from Robert at the

Railway Inn, whilst her horse was re-harnessed. It was a difficult moment and neither of them seemed inclined to speak. Feeling very ill at ease, she took her place on the driving seat of the trap, one child on each side of her, and Robert took the bridle and led the horse up to the road. However, he did not seem to want to let go and he began to walk along with them towards Elterbeck. At last, he broke his silence with a question that made her blush again.

'A hope you never were bothered again by that Irish fellow, Dermot something?' He was surprised to see her looking flustered.

'Well, it wor a strange thing, but George bought a horse off some Irish lads in Ingleton about three year since. They brought the horse up t'farm for 'im; one o' them wor Dermot. He wor very charming, as usual. George let him stay in one of our barns for a few nights.'

She took off her bonnet and shook her hair free, feeling more like her normal self immediately. Constriction did not suit her. But neither did her lies. The truth was that Dermot had returned, wormed his way into George's confidence, and behind his back had turned brutal and violent, wanting to extract a cold, personal revenge from her. She had finally placated him, but only at a price: a price she paid for the sake of George and the young Robert. It was a tale that she had shared with no one, except Bella. And now there was no Bella to tell, or to dry her tears or tend her bruises. Robert walked on, head down slightly, pondering, as if he sensed her distress. She did not want it to end like this.

'Will tha write to me an' tell me about life with thy widow woman an' being manager and that. And of how fat and prosperous tha's become?' she asked, with more of her old bantering tone. He looked up and smiled roguishly. She always knew how to stir him up!

'Aye. Of course. An' thou will tell me about Robert and Elizabeth, a hope. An' George, of course. Dost think he'll come round an' get over his loss?'

'Aye. He's teken it badly, losing his mother again. None of us likes to lose people, do we. It will be a week or two more, a dare say, then a shall have words an' threaten to leave him. Then he'll wake up and start to be human again, most likely. If not, a shall get on a train, with children, an' come to Glasgow. Or a might go to London or somewhere grand. A've a fancy for seein' more o' t'world than these few acres. Nowt frightens me now.'

Saying this, she brought the horse to a halt and looked at him. They laughed together, pleased with this irresolute ending.

'A shall be off then, Mrs Wright.' He let go of the horse and gave her a bow. 'Maybe I will come and see you again some day, wife or no wife.'

'A hope so, Mr Macintosh, a surely do.' She nodded to him, shook the reins and told the horse to walk on. Robert stood and watched them go, little Elizabeth leaning heavily against her mother, the young Robert turning now and then to give him a wave. He waved back until they were out of sight.

Emily let the horse amble homewards. The road had been repaired and she no longer had cause to steer round ruts and loose stones. She saw that the May blossom was just beginning to show on some of the sparse trees that dotted the edges of her field. Spring was always late in her valley. She felt that another turning point was about to be reached, but was not sure what it was. Spring always made her restless.

'A've not finished,' she said, half to herself, half to the drystone wall that she was passing. Young Robert looked at her quizzically, but was too sleepy to comment. She smiled at him. 'One thing's for sure. A've done with Batty Green, ma lad,' she told him. 'Wir shall we turn next, eh? Shall we go and visit Hetty and James in Derby? They say that's a grand place. Or London, perhaps. I hear Nancy's moved back thir.'

She paused, lost in half dreams of remote and unknown places. Slowly, the present realities filtered through her consciousness.

'But first t'would be a kindness to see how thy father's doin, eh?'

She looked down at Robert, but he was asleep. She shook the reins, clicked her tongue and the horse moved forwards into a trot. In the distance somewhere a steam train whistled.